WHITE SLAVE

RICHARD OWEN

PIATKUS

This is a work of fiction. Any resemblance to persons living or dead is purely coincidental.

To Jeffrey, Jimmy, Jon and Kathy Fox

This edition first published in
Great Britain in 1988 by
Judy Piatkus (Publishers) Ltd of
5 Windmill Street, London W1
by arrangement with
William Morrow and Company, Inc., N.Y. 10016.

British Library Cataloguing in Publication Data

Owen, Richard, 1942
  White slave.
  I. Title
  813'.54[F]   PS3565.W56

  ISBN 0-86188-712-3

Printed and bound in Great Britain by
Billing and Sons Ltd., Worcester

WHITE
SLAVE

1

"LITTLE girl is famous," the man sitting behind Tom Mitchell on the school baseball field bleachers said. "Gets her picture in the hometown paper."

Mitchell didn't pay attention to the man. He was watching the action on the ball field. It was one of those perfect days in late spring when the sky was as blue and the grass as green as sky or grass would ever be. The old green-painted bleachers were full of students and parents and they were all watching the girl on the pitcher's mound.

In her baseball uniform the girl had the look of a pretty tomboy on the verge of womanhood. She looked like any other normal thirteen-year-old girl from a small Connecticut town. But she was the only girl on the field and Mitchell watched her with the happy knowledge that he was watching his own daughter, Kim, on one of the great days of her life.

Mitchell got a kick out of seeing these young kids play. They had all picked up little habits and gestures from their major league heroes and it was fun to see them out there acting like baseball superstars, cheeks bulging with bubble gum instead of chewing tobacco. They took their baseball seriously.

It was the top of the ninth and the visiting school was at bat. Kim hadn't given them much to hit in the early innings. But then a big blond kid with number 11 on his jersey had got a triple off her and the score had evened up. The home school still had a one-run lead; if Kim could just get them out of this inning without giving up a run, they would have the undefeated season that had been all his daughter had been able to talk about for the last few weeks.

The man behind Mitchell kept talking.

"I got stuck at some motel down the road. It was a real dump. The vacancy sign out front was broke. The TV didn't work. I went out and tried to find a bar. . . . Nothing. So then I come back and in the wastebasket there's this sports page, like the management put in to keep the basket clean, one lousy page, and I say, 'Hey, look at this, little girl plays baseball.' "

Mitchell glanced behind him. He saw two knees in the sort of baggy white pants that house painters wear and a pair of brand-new jogging shoes with orange tongues and orange stripes. Nobody was listening to the guy.

Horse's ass must be talking to himself, Mitchell thought. He scowled to give the man a hint before turning back to the game.

One thing you could say about his daughter, as a pitcher she had plenty of showmanship. She was treating the skinny adolescent boy in the batter's box now as if he didn't exist. With her head down and her chin on her chest she seemed to study a speck of dirt on one shoe. Then she was into her windup. Bam! The boy's bat swung on empty air and he walked away shaking his head.

The parents and kids shouted and clapped. "Go get 'em, Kim! Two more to go!"

Kim had been a hot topic all spring. Now you had old farts spouting nonsense about her future in the majors and predicting that the New York Yankees were going to sign her up any day. The plain truth, Mitchell knew, was that she was just a great kid having the time of her life.

But the jerk behind him was too dumb to get the point, obsessed by some silly story he had read and built all out of proportion on a lonely night in a seedy motel room.

"It caused a big stink. People don't like these women getting on TV and talking about their rights all the time. Who needs to hear about rights? Not from some little girl."

Mitchell wanted to turn around and say, "She happened to be the best pitcher the coach could come up with and the coach was no damn fool." But there was a burst of applause as the second batter went down swinging, and he forgot about the jerk.

"Atta girl, Kim!" He pounded his big hands together.

As the catcher tossed the ball back to Kim she raised her glove and nabbed it in a casual gesture. The coach was on his feet, cupping his mouth and hollering, "C'mon, fire it around, c'mon!" The ball completed an energetic circuit of the infield and came back to Kim, who received it with the same casual gesture.

The third batter had stepped to the plate. He held his bat high off his shoulder as if to hammer the ball into the ground. Kim was unimpressed. She had a pretty face with high flat cheekbones and slanted cat's eyes. Her wavy brown hair was shoulder length and cut in long bangs across her forehead. The team's canary-yellow uniform with a green border at the neck and the school's name in large green script slanting across the chest suited her down-to-earth good looks. But the gaze in her eyes was steely. Mitchell was familiar with it, as he had urged her to work on it along with her fastball. "Can't smile at 'em, honey," he would say, whenever they tossed a ball in the backyard. "You gotta look mean." And Kim would scowl at him comically and zing one across so hard it would sting his hand.

Mitchell knew every stage of her windup. It began with the steely gaze. Then her head would go down for the prolonged examination of her shoe and the equation would be made: The boy she had condescended to notice a second ago was no more significant than the dirt at her feet. She would lean forward, crooking her arm behind her back and holding it there as she gazed at the round leather circle of the catcher's mitt. The hand clutching the ball at her back would achieve a distinct sculptural effect. Then her leg would come up and she would raise her arms over her head, as she was doing now. . . .

Just then a black dog trotted onto the field between Kim and the boy at the plate.

There were amused remarks and laughter from the bleachers. The coach, however, was upset. He didn't want some unforeseen interruption to destroy his pitcher's concentration. "Get that dog out of there!" he shouted. The dog trotted up the first base path, eluded the first baseman, spotted the second baseman trying to shoo it off the field, and headed between the two basemen into the outfield. From somewhere in the woods at the edge of the outfield the dog's owner was calling. The owner's voice rose in a far-off cry, drawing out the name of the dog into two long syllables. "Shadow! Shaaaa-doooow!" This occasioned more amusement from the spectators and there were echoes of the cry. "Shaaaa-doooow! Shaaaa-doooow!" At last the black dog trotted off the field and disappeared into the woods in the direction of the call.

Behind Mitchell the man in the new jogging shoes mimicked a line from an old radio show. "Who knows what evil lurks in the hearts of men? The Shadow knows."

The game resumed. But the coach's anxiety proved prophetic. The boy at the plate took Kim's first pitch and slammed it in a high drive that had the boy in left field scrambling to catch up to the ball as it landed in the grass beyond him.

A good throw kept the runner from going to second. But Mitchell didn't like it. It was the damn dog's fault, he thought. The visitors had the beginnings of a rally now. The tying run was on first. The next batter was stepping to the plate.

It was the big blond kid, number 11, who had got the triple. He was bigger than the other boys. Mitchell wondered if he was older and had stayed back a grade. He swung his bat a few times and cocked it. Kim's steely gaze didn't seem to faze him. The pitch came and he let it go. Ball one.

"Good eye, babe, good eye!" his own coach called.

Kim caught him on the next pitch with a sinking ball. The boy swung so hard that his plastic batting helmet fell off. The home plate umpire, conscious of the drama of the situation, cried out like a Shakespearian ham actor. "Striiii-yike!"

The next two pitches were balls, then the boy hit a foul. It was three and two. Mitchell became aware that he was holding his breath. For God's sake, he told himself, it's not the World Series. But it's Kim up there, he thought. Let her win.

Kim went into the spaced and stately stages of her windup. The runner on first was crouched and ready to head for second. Mitchell prepared for the worst, an insurmountable lead.

He would try to console his daughter by saying, "You would have had them, hon, if it hadn't been for Shadow."

When the pitch came the big blond kid hit a line drive right at Kim's head. Her hand shot up and nabbed the ball in the tip of her glove. Then it escaped and Kim bobbled it like a clumsy juggler and lost it. She snatched the ball off the grass and made the throw to first just in time for the out. Mitchell jumped to his feet and let out a shout. Everyone around him was cheering happily. When he sat back down he glanced over his shoulder as if to say, "How do you like them apples?"

But the man in the new jogging shoes had departed.

Mitchell liked to think of himself as a supremely unambitious man. It was his way of poking fun at himself for giving up his job as New York regional counsel in the criminal division of the Justice Department and moving to the sticks, where his most onerous duties were drawing up wills and drafting real estate contracts.

How many more drug dealers did you have to put away? There would be no end to drug dealers, nor any diminishment in the supply of sharp young men and women hot to prosecute them.

It wasn't really that he was unambitious. He had been a holy terror, in fact, known for the ball-busting zeal with which he drove his staff to win convictions, a publicity hog, infamous for his ability to stroke the media. His wife had died of cancer when Kim was nine, and as a widower Mitchell had found it even easier to lose himself in his work. Then abruptly he had chucked it all. Kim was sprouting up and he realized he wouldn't have many more years to enjoy being the father of a growing girl. A year ago when he moved with his daughter to Foxhaven, Connecticut, he went through six months of withdrawal symptoms, missing the excitement and pressures of the job, the ego satisfaction of seeing himself on *Live at Five* or *Eyewitness News*. After that he no longer regretted it; and now, watching the boys on the team converge about Kim, clapping her on the back and shouting victoriously, Tom Mitchell felt that this was what life was all about.

The moms and dads sitting nearby stopped to compliment him on his daughter's performance. The bleachers cleared off and he was left, a rumpled, round-faced man in his late forties with his sleeves rolled up, his necktie loosened about his neck, and his jacket over one arm in the warm late afternoon. There was a ritual postgame gathering of both teams to drink lemonade and eat potato chips provided by some of the moms.

Mitchell rose and felt the sag of each board of the bleachers under his burly body as he climbed down. He crossed the hard dirt of the base paths, and his daughter grinned and gave a jaunty thumbs-up sign.

"One for the record books, Dad," she said.

"It sure was, honey," Mitchell said, putting an arm around her shoulders. "Congratulations."

"Did you see the way she made that putout, Mr. Mitchell?" one of the boys said.

"That was some play, wasn't it, Tommy?"

"Oh yes," one of the others said, "as a pitcher she makes a great juggler."

He imitated Kim's bobbling of the ball and they laughed.

"I'm taking you boys out for that hamburger I promised you," Mitchell said, "so don't eat too many potato chips."

"What do you mean 'boys'? Don't I count?"

"Well, I suppose we'll have to make an exception."

After a while the visiting team departed and the home team headed for the showers. Mitchell stayed talking with the coach about the game, the team's undefeated season, and Kim.

"You've got quite a youngster there, Tom," the coach said. "She knows what she wants and she goes after it."

At the end of the field a single figure broke away from the boys and disappeared alone into the girls' gym.

"Well, I better get on home," the coach said.

It was a lovely early evening, getting on toward suppertime. Mitchell started for town, taking a shortcut through the woods. As he came out into a neighbor's backyard, the black dog that had interrupted the game approached him. He patted it on the head. "Hello, Shadow, old boy, how are you?"

Mitchell had quit after the biggest success of his career. The way it had happened had been almost accidental, like pulling on a tiny thread. But he had recognized the thread for what it was and pulled it until the whole blanket unraveled. He was preparing to prosecute a big drug dealer in his district, when the dealer began to talk, and it became clear that he wasn't so big after all; he was just another lieutenant in an operation that had taken in most of the United States. At the head of this operation was one of those glamorous figures whose success seems a testament to the advantages and rewards of the free-enterprise system. It was a surprise to discover that his wealth and power were based on unlimited drug money. By the time the indictment was handed down he had got wind of it and fled to an island in the West Indies. But his entire network was in shambles. Mitchell had emerged as the man most responsible for rolling up the largest cocaine-distribution ring in the country. After that he supposed he could have run for governor, but he truly believed he wouldn't have had a chance. He was glad he had quit while he was ahead.

He loved Foxhaven, with its old restored houses and village green. His office, where he carried on a small practice, was upstairs over a hardware store overlooking the green. In the winter the hills outside of town were like a great white ocean, with the wet black trunks of bare-limbed trees marking the shoreline. In the fall bees lighted on the windfalls of apples in the orchards and there was a cidery overripe smell in the air. The town wasn't backward or narrow-minded. A number of artists and writers lived there. But both the native and the transplanted inhabitants showed a healthy skepticism for the false, the overstated, and the shoddy, among other excesses of the electronic age. The real plus, for Mitchell, was that his daughter was in her element.

Kim had always been a lively, adventurous girl. She never liked to be told there were things little girls couldn't do that boys could. Last spring, when they had first moved to Foxhaven, she had come home complaining that the boys at school refused to play catch with her.

"Why?" Mitchell said.

"They say I'm not good enough because I'm a girl."

"Well, to heck with them. Let's you and me go out to the backyard. We'll show those boys who's good enough."

Mitchell hadn't known what he was letting himself in for. Kim's interest in baseball wasn't a passing phase, and the nightly practice sessions became a ritual. The end result came a year later in early spring, when the coach posted a notice for tryouts. Kim showed up. The boys greeted her with jeers and disgusted faces. The dialogue, Mitchell gathered, went something like this:

Derisive Boy: "You're not gonna let Mitchell pitch, are you? She couldn't strike out a flea."

Kim: "I can strike *you* out!"

"Oh yeah? How much you wanna bet?"

"As much as you like, big mouth!"

The coach was a crusty sort. Kim's proposal to try out for the team offended his conservative nature. But he also didn't care much for the know-it-all taunts of the boys. He was interested to see if this young lady could make these pipsqueaks shut up. He let her pitch to the Derisive Boy. The Derisive Boy struck out. "Just luck," he grumbled. One after another Kim went through the whole lineup, yielding little or nothing. When it was the Derisive Boy's turn again, he struck out again. This time when he walked away, however, he was heard to admit in a squeaky voice, "Say, she's pretty good."

Kim made the team.

Mitchell wasn't the kind of father to push his daughter to constantly achieve. She was a bright, happy girl, not simple-minded by any means. She would do well, whatever she did. Right now she was talking about becoming a lawyer, like her old man. But that could change. She might decide to go to med school. Or she might fall in love and get married and have a family and write gothic romances in her spare time. He had complete faith in his daughter's ability to get the most out of life. It was Friday. He was planning to take Kim fishing on the weekend.

In town Mitchell stopped at the newspaper store and bought an evening paper. The headline said: BRITONS GIVE CARTER FINE WELCOME AS HE SIGHT-SEES PRIOR TO SUMMIT.

The winning number drawn Thursday night in the weekly Connecticut lottery was 42-Orange-267.

The drugstore had the quaint hometown look that Mitchell associated with old movies of the thirties and forties in which boys aspired to become soda jerks, as opposed to an earlier era when they had dreamed perhaps of becoming riverboat captains, and a later one when they all seemed to want to become rock stars. In the summer kids in bare feet would come in to browse through the comic books or buy fish bait, which Al the proprietor sold in addition to making hamburgers and filling drug prescriptions.

"How'd she do today?" Al asked.

"She murdered 'em," Mitchell said. "Four-three. Gave up only four hits."

"That girl is amazing. Where does she get it from?"

"Beats me. The only thing I was ever good at throwing was the bull."

Gradually the boys began to drift in, hair wet and slicked down, and they got to work on Al's hamburgers, sliding ketchup bottles back and forth, loading on the onions and relish, and talking with their mouths full.

"Where's Kim?" Mitchell wondered.

"She must still be in the shower," Tommy said. "You know these girls, always taking their time."

"I'll go see what's keeping her. Al, feed these hungry savages until they can't take it any longer."

Mitchell felt no sense of urgency. He was a man who constantly rehearsed pleasant exchanges with his daughter in his head.

"Where you been, hon? Your teammates are already on their seconds. We better hurry."

He would put his arm around her and they would proceed to the drugstore with a feeling of affectionate companionship.

The last orange edge of the setting sun was visible in the spaces between the shops as he went down the street. He didn't take the shortcut through the woods. The girls' gym was by the main road and Kim would come that way instead of cutting back across the ball field.

He stopped at his own house on the edge of town to see if she was there. Upstairs her room was empty. Mitchell stood in the doorway, gazing at the familiar disorder of his teenage daughter's room. The school yearbook for the class of '77 was open on her desk. Her bed had been made hastily, her drawers had been rummaged through—signs of a girl late for school. A pair of ballet slippers for dancing class lay on the floor beneath a black leotard dangling from a bedpost. From a colored poster over her bed Tom Seaver eyed the mess with a sublime lack of concern.

Kim must have gone the other way after all. She might have wanted to go back to the baseball diamond for one more look at home plate. Mitchell picked up the telephone on her night table and heard the off-key notes of the number he dialed. A voice answered, "Drugstore."

"Al, this is Tom. Has Kim shown up?" He could hear the boys gabbing in the background as Al glanced out the window to see if she was coming.

"No sign of her yet."

"Well, I'm sure she'll be along. Tell her I walked up to the school to look for her."

Mitchell went out and up the road to the school. There were several athletic fields occupying one long, wide field. At the far end was the baseball diamond, but he couldn't see anyone crossing it. He cut across a corner of the football field, climbed a short, steep embankment behind the goalpost, and came onto a dusty path worn away by countless feet in front of the girls' gym.

The gym was in an old converted barn of brown splintery clapboards. The front door was near one end.

Mitchell pushed open the door and called inside, "Kim!"

There was no answer and he entered. He felt no hesitancy about entering the girls' locker room. His daughter would be the only girl there.

The heavy door with a self-closing mechanism at the top wheezed shut behind him. Mitchell stepped past the end of a row of lockers on his left and glanced into a basketball court on his right. A single basketball looked lonely and out of place in the middle of the court.

There was another row of lockers, and turning away from the basketball court, he gazed down between the two rows along the length of what had once been the cavernous hallway of a barn. All the lockers were shut, and there were no clothes lying about on the benches. It occurred to Mitchell that nothing was messier than a locker room when it was being used, and nothing was less messy than the unvarying faces of gray metal doors when the room was not in use.

The only flaw was a field-hockey stick lying about half-way down. It seemed as out of place as the lone basketball, the one surrounded by the empty space of the court, the other by the empty faces of the lockers. It suggested the presence of a phantom athlete, leaving a telltale trail of strewn athletic equipment.

"Kim!" His voice was deadened by the metal doors and concrete floor.

The light from the basketball court was at his back. It was getting dark at the other end of the locker room. He was suddenly, uncharacteristically worried. Where the hell was Kim? His theory that she had taken the main road to town now seemed doubtful. But he hadn't seen her crossing the baseball field either. She might have already entered the woods, of course. It was silly to worry. Mitchell shook himself out of it.

He went down between the lockers. He didn't know which one was his daughter's.

"Kim! You there?"

He picked up the field-hockey stick absently and went on to the end of the row. As he stepped around to the other side he came upon an open locker. On the bench was his daughter's baseball glove; her cleated shoes lay in a pile with the canary-yellow pants and jersey of her uniform on the floor. He heard water running in the shower room nearby.

She's going to shrivel up if she stays in there much longer, he thought.

"Hey, Kim!" he called. "What you trying to do? Drown?"

There was no answer.

"It's your old man. We're all waiting for you."

Mitchell guessed she couldn't hear him because of the water. He tried once more loudly.

"Get out of there! You're wasting water!"

This time he knew she would have heard him. But she didn't holler back. My God, Mitchell thought, something has happened to her.

He could see the middle of the shower room, where water was swirling down a drain. But he couldn't see the shower itself. Kim had fallen and hurt herself. Or maybe she had been attacked and was lying stabbed and bleeding.

Mitchell stepped to the entrance of the shower room, annoyed at his unreasonable alarm. There was an instant of relief. Look, no dead body. You're getting jumpy in your old age. But even as he tried to joke he felt cold fear about his heart.

"Kim, for crissake, where are you!"

His voice was swallowed up by the hollowness of the old converted barn. The water ran in a steady stream from the rusted nozzle. The shower room was empty.

He was the only thing moving along the path that had been made through the deep snow on the sidewalks. He was the only presence in the cold dark night. He was something but he wasn't sure what, something that had retained the habit of putting one foot in front of the other, long after he had forgotten why. He was moving past the high banks of snow that had been shoveled and piled up away from the shop doors. In the dark the snowbanks glowed phosphorescently. But he himself was a dark figure, like the black trees with ridges of snow crawling out along bare black branches. The branches creaked and swayed in a cold wind. He guessed he was a man. But he felt more like a ghost condemned to linger after the man has died, moving darkly through an eerie white landscape, haunting this town on a cold bitter night when only ghosts would be out of doors.

In the windows of the houses outside of town were Christmas trees strung with lights. But the house he stopped before now was dark and there were no cheery blue and green and red and yellow lights of Christmas.

Tom Mitchell looked for his house key a little stupidly. He had been to the bar in town. He had stayed late, sitting alone with his drink while three young men played the shuffle bowling game and the bartender, discouraged in his attempts at conversation, stood staring into space, waiting for close-up time. Mitchell found the key.

The path to his front door was crusted and precarious with frozen snow. He had done a halfhearted job of clearing it. He went up the porch steps. As he was putting the key in the door, a gust of wind rose, freezing his fingers, getting under his overcoat collar, biting his ears and nose. He got the key in and turned it and entered.

The door closed behind him with a dead final sound and

he stood in a pitch-black hall. On this night, after the first big snowfall of winter, the house seemed darker and emptier than ever.

Upstairs Mitchell got ready for bed, putting on his pajamas, brushing his teeth. He had to pass his daughter's room twice on his way to and from the bathroom down the hall. He resisted looking at her closed door. In his bedroom he turned on the television. An unnatural glow filled the room, the slogan of a commercial blaring in the silence. Mitchell lowered the sound. He was old enough to have once satirically denounced the age of television as an abomination. But after Kim's disappearance he had moved the set into his bedroom. It was a substitute for company. The blather of TV personalities, together with normal human weariness and a few drinks, kept him from thinking and helped put him to sleep. Now, though, with the night outside emphasizing the emptiness in the house, his mind seemed to get away from him and go straight to the source of his pain.

Kim had been gone for seven months, and he knew she was gone forever, no matter how often he went back to the night of her disappearance and tried to stop it from happening.

On that night Mitchell had left the girls' gym and hurried to the police station in a panic. "She's probably with the others at the drugstore," the desk sergeant said. He placed a call, but Kim wasn't at the drugstore. Then he radioed a patrol car to go to the school and check out the gym.

"She's not in the gym," Mitchell said. "I was just there."

He felt the common frustration of a frightened man at the mercy of methodical police procedure. The procedure was geared to handle the majority of cases. It quickly became clear that the police assumed Kim was a runaway.

The youth officer was called away from home. When he got to the station he spoke breezily to the desk sergeant, as if to reassure Mitchell that there was nothing to worry about.

"A popular summertime fruit," he said.

"I give up," the desk sergeant said.

"Watermelon. It was worth fifty points on *Family Feud*."

The youth officer's wavy black hair exuded a smalltown vanity. He was out of uniform and wore white shoes with tiny air-hole punctures. Politely he asked Mitchell to come into his office and sit down. At his desk he began to fill out a form.

"Your daughter's name?"

"Kimberly Mitchell."

"Age?"

"Thirteen."

"Tough age," the youth officer said, clicking his ball-point pen sympathetically.

The questions went on. Height, weight, hair, eyes. When had he last seen his daughter? Had Kimberly recently had an argument with him? Was she having trouble in school? Did she take drugs? To Mitchell each question represented precious time being wasted.

"Look," he said, "we can both save a lot of time if you'll take my word for one thing. My daughter did not run away. She just won a big game. She was going to join me and the boys on the team for a victory celebration. It's plain as hell something terrible has happened to her."

"You'd be surprised at the number of parents I hear say the same thing," the youth officer said, "and their sons or daughters always show up a short time later. The majority of missing persons, especially your daughter's age, don't stay missing very long. As you say, she just won a big game. She might have decided to go off and celebrate in her own way."

Mitchell leaned across the desk calmly, almost paternally. He was aware that every cop in town knew who he was and what he had once been, and it was time to use his muscle.

"This is what you're going to do," he said—an order. "You're going to notify the state police that my daughter has been abducted. I want the highways watched for suspicious vehicles. Then you're going to pull some men away from the boob tube and start looking. Right now."

Mitchell saw the same hangdog look as when he used to bawl out inept assistants. The youth officer left the room, presumably to do as he was told. He returned full of obliging humility.

"Did your daughter have any boyfriends, Mr. Mitchell?"

"Tommy Ryan takes her to the movies. He's a good kid. He was with the boys at the drugstore tonight."

"She ever get any crank calls? Like when she was trying out for the ball team?"

"I suppose there were some Archie Bunkers who thought she was part of a feminist conspiracy. But none of them ever went so far as to call her."

"Do you know of anyone who might have wanted to hurt Kimberly in order to get back at you for anything you might have done . . . as a prosecutor, say?"

"I doubt it. I've been out of it more than a year. People have forgotten who I am." Mitchell rose to leave; he was anxious to help look for Kim. "There was a man sitting behind me at the ball game today. He had read about Kim in our local paper. It had gotten to him in some weird way. I didn't get a look at him, but he was wearing new jogging shoes with orange stripes. You should mention that to the state police."

"I'll do that, sir."

At home Mitchell found a police car out front; one policeman was checking with the neighbors to see if any had seen Kim, another asked Mitchell for permission to search the house. They went through the house together, opening closet doors, going down to the basement and up to the attic. After the cop left, Mitchell stood in the dark, staring out his bedroom window. The two cops were below, searching the woods behind the house with a flashlight. Far off through the trees was the flashing red light of a police car parked outside the girls' gym. The eeriness of the scene coincided with his feeling that he was in the middle of a nightmare.

Mitchell could not sleep—would not let himself sleep—on this night that was the worst of his life. He got a flashlight from the linen closet and joined the policemen outside and spent most of the night prowling the woods. But in the end there was only the dog Shadow, nosing lugubriously in the underbrush and lifting his leg on a tree.

After that his hope was gone. He pretended to have it but he knew he was fooling himself. It was easier to pretend as long as you could contain it—in a girls' locker room or a small town or even the precise circle designating the three-mile search area that had been drawn by a state trooper on a map spread out on the hood of his car in front of the gym the next day. They had brought a bloodhound and let it sniff some of Kim's clothes, but it hadn't picked up a trail. Outside the circle hope dribbled away, imperfectly sustained by the various required steps of standard procedure. Kim's yearbook picture and a description of her were printed in the newspapers. The papers kept the story going for weeks in hopes of generating leads. Even the flimsiest leads were followed up, including interviewing every little old lady who had ever said anything mildly critical about Kim playing baseball. Kim's locker and those around it were dusted for fingerprints, and known sex offenders were paid a visit.

Mitchell supplied the names of some of the people he had prosecuted over the years. The police questioned any that might have been in the New York or New England area on that night. It wasn't a completely pointless exercise. He remembered the time he had taken Kim to Central Park, while they were still living in the city. There, sitting on a park bench, he had glanced up from his Sunday *Times* and seen his daughter talking with a man whom he recognized at a distance as a man he had once sent to prison. He had stared, frozen an instant, expecting the man to pull a gun or a knife. But the only thing the ex-con had pulled, finally, were some samples of the poetry he had written in jail.

Now the names he had given seemed just another old bone tossed to a hope that was already gone. Mitchell forced himself to acknowledge once again that his daughter was dead, regardless of by whose hand.

In his bedroom he got up and turned off the television. The eerie glow vanished and he went back to bed and lay in the cold darkness. Outside the wind blew and the shadows of the bare branches moved on the new white snow.

When Kim Mitchell had gone to the showers after the game she had found the girls' gym empty. On most days, after practice, it would be filled with the members of the softball team, Kim's classmates, and there would be the normal bedlam of young girls showering and getting ready to go home. But on days when she pitched a game Kim was used to no one being there, the game having usually outlasted the school day.

She entered and went down between the two rows of lockers, her cleats clicking on the concrete floor. Her own locker was around the other side, at the end of the row nearest the showers.

Kim undressed, sitting on the bench to untie and let drop

each cleated shoe, then standing to pull the jersey of her uniform over her head and slip out of her baseball pants. She left her underclothes on the floor with her pitcher's glove, got a towel from the canvas bin, and padded to the shower room. There were a dozen showers around the wall and Kim turned one on and tossed her towel where she could grab it when she got out.

She felt the stream of water to judge its temperature and was about to step under when she realized the gym wasn't empty after all. She heard the sound of a bouncing basketball.

Huh, Kim thought, one of the girls must have stayed late and was out on the court. She listened to the steady thump, thump, thump of the ball, followed by a second of silence as the toss was made and then by another thump as the ball fell through the net and hit the floor. I wonder who it is.

She put the towel around her and left the shower running and walked back down between the rows of lockers. She couldn't see either end of the basketball court or the girl who was apparently there, shooting at one of the baskets. There was a loud bang as the ball missed the net and hit the clanky backboard.

Kim was expecting to see one of her girlfriends and was about to say hello. She came out to the edge of the court. It was filled with late-afternoon sunlight through the windows around it. Over by the basket on the left was a man.

She took a step backward, surprised. The man was getting ready for a shot. Kim started to turn away and the man saw her.

He was medium height with a muscular build, a bland face and a crew cut of white-blond hair. He wore eyeglasses, a T-shirt and baggy white pants, a necktie around his bare neck, and a pair of thin white gloves.

"Hi!" he called cheerfully.

With his crew cut and young face he might have been a pimply adolescent counterboy at McDonald's, all set to take an order for one Big Mac, french fries, and a Coke. "That to go or to stay?" he would ask.

He bounced the ball, one, two, three, and fired. The ball wormed through the sinuous mesh of the basket. He caught it and got ready for another shot, as if it were perfectly natural for a young girl to be standing there, undressed, holding a towel about herself.

Kim was angry. She didn't want to turn her back on the man. She intended to see him on his way out.

"What are you doing here?" she said.

"I don't know," the man said. "I thought I was playing basketball."

"You're not supposed to be here," Kim said. "This is the girls' gym."

"What!" the man exclaimed. He stopped bouncing the ball. He sounded upset. "I didn't know that. I guess I should beat it, huh?"

He came over to her with the ball. Standing, holding it under one arm, he took off his glasses and examined them. Up close, with his glasses off, he didn't look so young. The flesh around his eyes was puffy and worn. He hadn't shaved and the black stubble of his whiskers didn't go with his bleached blond hair. On the front of his T-shirt was the face of Judy Garland with the words OVER THE RAINBOW. Kim saw he was wearing new jogging shoes with orange tongues and orange stripes.

The man licked one lens of his glasses with his tongue and began to rub it with the folded end of his necktie. "There's no sign on the door. How was I to know? But I can see you're a girl, so this must be the girls' gym all right."

"You better go," Kim said.

"Right away," the man said. He started on the other lens, cleaning it conscientiously, as if to wear the lens away by the smoothing action of his thumb.

"Do you always wear a necktie with no shirt collar?" Kim said sarcastically: a hint that he should clean his glasses outside.

The man grunted. "Actually it's not really a necktie. I mean, it's a necktie but I don't wear it to dress up. I wear it because you never know when a necktie might come in handy. Know what I mean?"

"No, I don't."

"It's that a necktie is good for things, like tying up packages and stuff like that. I carry it around my neck because that's the usual place for it."

"Please get out," Kim said. "I've got to take a shower. The boys will be waiting for me."

"Boys? What boys?"

The man squinted dimly at the floor. Then he put his glasses on and looked up at her. His face brightened.

"Say, you're the girl on the baseball team, right? I thought I recognized you. That was quite a game you pitched today. There's not many girls could throw a baseball like that. I was never much good at it myself. Now basketball . . ." He began to bounce the ball again. "That's more my sport. The thing is, you don't need a team. You can play it by yourself. I have a net and a backboard where I live. I can go two, three hours tossing a ball. It makes the time pass. You ever play basketball?"

"Get out," Kim said levelly. "If you don't get out right now I'm going to call the boys."

"I bet you'd be good at it," the man said. He bounced the ball several times, as if he hadn't heard her. Then, without warning, he tossed it at her and shouted, "Catch!"

The ball came at Kim so fast she didn't have time to think. She flung up her hands to catch it. The towel she was holding fell to the floor. For a second she stood naked, clutching the ball with a look of surprise on her face. Then she threw it at him angrily. "Get out!" She grabbed up her towel and fled back down and around the corner to her locker.

Kim grabbed her panties from among her clothes. She wasn't embarrassed that the man had seen her naked and she wasn't exactly frightened. She thought he was the sort of creep who got his thrills by exposing himself harmlessly to women. He looked like a wimp. He hadn't gone after her when she dropped the towel. He had just stood staring with his bland expressionless face. Kim figured the man had already left, now that he had got a look at her. She wanted to run to the boys' gym to see if they could catch him before he got away. She struggled into her panties and snatched a shirt, and just then the man spoke.

His voice was right on the other side of her locker. It was so close that she knew he had moved with sudden speed, out from the basketball court, lightly and quickly in his new jogging shoes. The idea of speed scared her more than the voice itself.

"I'm sorry," the man said. "I didn't mean to embarrass you like that. I was just kidding around. I didn't even get a good look."

Kim dropped her shirt and grabbed a field-hockey stick from her locker. She whirled and raised the stick to strike the man as he came around the corner. But the man didn't appear. He kept talking out of sight on the other side.

"If I really wanted to see you without your clothes on I'd just come around and take a look. But instead I'm respecting your privacy. I'm standing right here."

Kim, frozen with the field-hockey stick upraised, saw her chance of escape. While the man was on the other side she could run down along the row in her bare feet and dart out from behind the end and make a dash for the door, leaving him still talking up at this end.

"You promise not to come around," she shouted in a shaking voice.

"Of course I promise. Believe me, I won't budge."

Kim didn't even put the stick down. She whirled and ran. As she reached the end and came out from behind, she saw the man. He had moved with the same scary quickness as before, and was standing in front of the door, blocking her way.

"You sneaky little bitch!" he said.

Kim swung at him with the stick but the man ducked. He grabbed the stick and wrenched it away and flung it clattering to the floor.

Suddenly the necktie was around Kim's throat, and she was struggling for breath. She felt her panties being pulled down. She felt a needle stab her in the butt. Then the tie seemed to loosen and she was free to escape.

But she wasn't struggling anymore. She was taking a long fall into darkness.

Seven Years Later . . .

2

THE messages on the answering machine, for the first two days, had been short. "Hello. Where you been? What you doing? Hey, call me, man. Is important." They didn't leave a number to call. Often they didn't leave a name, and if they did, it was only a first name, like there could only be one Frank or George or Mike operating in the drug trade in all of South Florida.

Then on the third day Joaquín saw his partner, Rhodes, pick up the earphones when the tape began to wind. But this time, instead of just holding one to his ear, he put both earphones on and listened.

Joaquín watched him listen.

Rhodes always wore a jacket and necktie on a stakeout, out of a sort of poor farm boy's earnest regard for the conventions of proper attire; on moving surveillance he always hung up his jacket in the back of the car to keep it from getting wrinkled. His red hair, fair complexion, and Southern drawl added to the impression of an unsophisticated rube. But Joaquín knew it was the look in his blue eyes—a cold, hawklike gaze—that was the true Rhodes.

After three minutes the reels on the tape recorder stopped. The caller had hung up. Rhodes removed the earphones.

"What you got?" Joaquín asked.

He was at the window, where he had turned away from a pair of binoculars on a stand. The window was in a storage room on the ninth floor of an apartment building that was an exact twin of the one he had been watching on the other side of the Intracoastal Waterway.

"Boy likes to talk," Rhodes said.

"Say anything?" Reuben asked indifferently.

Reuben was lying on one of the two cots that had been moved into the storage room. The cots were for Joaquín and Rhodes. Reuben went home each night and showed up in the morning with a bag of doughnuts, two take-out coffees, a copy of the *Sun-Sentinel,* and a tout sheet for Gulfstream Park. He was with the Fort Lauderdale office and had been assigned to help out when Joaquín and Rhodes had come up from Miami to conduct the surveillance. Reuben was a fat, slovenly, bald-headed man with a fringe of gray hair. He had been a street agent all his life and his favorite phrase for the work was "shoveling sand against the tide."

"That's all we're doing," he would say. "Shoveling sand against the tide. It don't matter how much we shovel. The tide keeps coming in."

It was a motto that seemed to justify the amount of time he spent lying on the cot during the day.

"Did he say when or where?" Reuben said.

"No, but I'm pretty sure he said what."

Rhodes reversed the tape and played it back. There was the beep of the answering machine. The voice that followed didn't rattle off a message and hang up. It was super casual and vastly amused at its own sound, and it gave itself a name.

Numma One. Even more useless than Frank, George, or Mike.

"Numma One here. Roger, Numma One. Go ahead. Got a little problem, amigo. I'm up to my ass in dead grunts. I need somebody to take 'em off my hands . . ."

Joaquín glanced at Rhodes and raised his eyebrows. Reuben was scratching the inside of his right nostril with his thumb.

"I been bouncing a basketball all morning," the voice said. "So I figure, what the hell, I might as well come inside, crack a beer, and draw a few lines, talk about whatever you want to talk about. Like, whatever happened to the Carib Indians and why should anyone give a fuck?"

The answering machine, Joaquín could see, brought out the comedian in Numma One.

"For instance, I bet you never knew that the word *cannibal* comes from *Carib*. See, when Columbus was sailing the ocean blue he ran into two kinds of Indians down here.

The good guys were Arawaks. The bad guys were Caribs. Don't ask me why, the Caribs were real shits. They sort of wandered up from South America, going from one island to another, doing a number on the poor old Arawaks. Kill and eat the men. Take the women as slaves, do what they want with them. . . . Remind me of a guy I know got exactly the same mentality. Just like a real Carib."

A pause. In the silence Joaquín became aware of the cramped, sunny storage room that was barely large enough for the two cots and the table on which the wiretap receiver and tape recorder sat. They had moved out a lot of stuff with the help of the security guard who was letting them use the room. But there were still bottles of window cleaner, a pail, a mop. Joaquín watched the reels of the tape recorder winding voicelessly; he could almost see the owner of the voice chopping and thinning two lines with a razor blade. He listened. Heard the prolonged inhalation of two nostrils, one at a time. Boom. Boom.

"Hey," the voice resumed, "give 'em their due. They were gourmets. Cooked the babies. Smoked the arms and legs of the men. Like you smoke salmon, you know? Rather eat a Frenchman than a Spaniard, shows you something right there. The Caribs are just about kaput now. But this stinking little island is named after them, and the worst part is, I'm stuck on it with ten dead white boys that are gonna turn brown and shitty if I don't get help fast. Enough said? Okay," the voice seemed about to hang up. Then, "Oh by the way—" and for a second Joaquín had the eerie feeling he was being addressed directly "—any fuckface who shouldn't be listening, this is for you." The sound of a beer can being crumpled next to the phone was followed by a resonant belch. "Roger and out, sucka."

The voice was gone.

"Were those your ancestors he was talking about?" Rhodes said.

"My old man used to eat smoked arms and legs for breakfast," Joaquín said.

"Well, we know what his name is anyway."

"Yeah, and where he's bouncing a basketball."

Joaquín thought of the chain of islands like a crooked finger above the South American continent and of the tiny

island at the southern end of the chain. And as always, like
a knee-jerk reflex, he thought, Kane. As if he could never
think of one without the other. Carib. Kane.

"That little island, right?" Reuben said. "What is it I'm
trying to think of? Something to do with Carib."

"I don't know," Joaquín said with a straight face.

"Sure you do! It's right on the tip of my tongue."

"Guy's sitting there with ten dead white boys," Rhodes
said.

"Big deal. So he's got some flake to sell. If we had a tap
on every fucking phone in town, half the callers would be
saying the same thing. You think the stuff is gonna come
into Miami? Probably be Dallas."

Reuben had been with the Dallas office before being
transferred to Fort Lauderdale.

"They probably already got a guy waiting for it at the
Ramada Inn next to Love Field. But even if we knew, would
we tell Dallas? Hell no, why should we let those bums get
the credit?"

"Good point, Reuben. It's all shoveling sand against the
tide anyway."

Joaquín was glad they had gotten off the subject of Carib.
He bent back to the binoculars. No sign of Jerry.

"You really an Indian?" Reuben asked. "You look like
an Indian. Hard to tell, though, name like O'Keefe. Sure as
hell don't sound Indian."

"O'Keefe is my stepfather. I'm half Indian."

"No kidding. Like where from?"

"Venezuela."

"You were born in the jungle?"

"That's right."

"Huh," Reuben said. "What was it like?"

"There were a lot of trees."

"I mean being born there."

"I was raised by a monkey and we lived in a tree."

"That's what I figured."

"You want me to tell you about the last time I saw my
father?" Joaquín asked.

"Christ," Reuben said, "I'm stuck with a Florida redneck and a Venezuelan Indian. I heard you guys were hot
shots."

"I didn't know it had got around," Rhodes said.

"Oh yeah, all you guys from Miami are hot shots. What was it about some undercover job you pulled off? I sort of remember. Some big wheel in the government of some country I forget the name of. Wanted to be paid in blue jeans. A thousand blue jeans, something like that. Figure, where he comes from, that's a hundred dollars a pair, eight hundred thou, not bad, and you're the guys who are gonna get it for him 'cause you supposedly got this big warehouse full of hijacked blue jeans, right? Am I right so far?"

"So far."

"Only the guy surprises you. Comes up before you're ready for him and asks to see what he's gonna get. So you gotta run around pulling blue jeans off the racks of every store in town."

"We had to hit every store all the way up to Palm Beach."

"So okay," Reuben said, "the big wheel falls for it. A few days later he flies up with some general in the army of whatever country it is, and you bust 'em with the goods. Only the general pulls a gun and shoots one of you."

"Nobody got shot."

"You sure of that? I thought one of you spent some time in the hospital with tubes up your nose."

"That was another time."

"Which one of you was it?"

"Me," Joaquín said.

"How'd it happen?"

"I walked through a guy's front door without taking adequate precautions. It was a dumb move."

"So I got the stories mixed up. But it's the same point. You guys are hot shots."

"Thanks, Reuben."

"Yeah sure, only even hot shots are human. Like that other story, how you lost some big informer. I mean, it's nothing to be ashamed of, happens all the time. Only I guess this guy was sort of special. Took you three years to nail him with something big enough to scare the shit out of him about all the time he was gonna do if he didn't talk. Next day he's gone, and what is it, two weeks, some kid is walking along Miami Beach and he sees a plastic garbage bag washed up in all the seaweed and shit, and he opens it up and there's the guy's head staring at him with his tongue cut out. So it makes you sort of wonder what the real reason is for you guys coming up here to put a tap on some young punk who's only been in town a couple of months. I mean, just 'cause he's the nephew of the guy who put a contract on your informer's head, don't necessarily mean you're grasping at straws."

"We got the tap," Rhodes said.

"Oh sure, nobody ever said you couldn't find federal judges stupid enough to believe anything. Piss load of good it's done except for one call from Carib . . . island nobody ever heard of except for whatever it is I can't remember . . ."

Reuben lay scratching his nostril reflectively. "Carib. Carib. Hey that's it! It was what's-his-name . . . Kane."

Bingo, Joaquín thought. He felt like a green kid again, like he had just wet his pants.

"The big dope dealer," Reuben said. "Guy so big he didn't bother to buy local protection; he bought national protection. When the shit hit the fan he skipped the country and went to Carib. And nobody can touch him there . . . 'cause the president of Carib is a red and only takes orders from Uncle Fidel."

"You got a great memory," Joaquín said.

He wished Reuben would drop the subject now. But Reuben, having made the connection, was eager to follow it up.

"I knew it would come to me. It seems a long time ago. About seven years."

"Eight."

"There was something funny about it. The way Kane managed to get out of the country without being caught. It was this kid who was supposed to keep an eye on him, only Kane pulled a fast one. He found a double, guy who looked just like him, dressed like him; you couldn't tell 'em apart. So this kid, straight out of agent school, tails him to a Cuban restaurant and waits for him to finish lunch. Finally Kane comes out. Only it's not Kane. It's the double. But the kid don't know it. He goes merrily along tailing the double. Tailed him, Christ how far?"

"All the way to Key West," Joaquín said. "About three hours."

"That was it. And you know all about it 'cause you were the kid. Right?"

"That's right, Reuben."

"It was a classic fuckup. I was in Dallas at the time but it even got around out there. So lying here I'm beginning to develop a theory about why you're such a hot shot. If I was a kid that fucked up like that . . ."

"Reuben . . ."

"I guess I'd spend the rest of my life trying to be a—"

"Reuben . . ."

"—hot shot. . . . What?"

Joaquín had come away from the window, and he stood looking down at the fat bald-headed man on the cot. The story was that Reuben had been transferred from Dallas because he had supposedly dipped into the drug buy fund in order to pay his racetrack debts. But Joaquín didn't feel like being nasty. He just stood over Reuben long enough to let a certain hesitation seep into Reuben's gaze.

"What's your problem?" Reuben asked.

"You sure you don't want me to tell you about the last time I saw my father?"

"Don't bother."

"Okay, I won't tell you."

Joaquín went back to the window.

The story was this. Joaquín was five. He was running through the jungle with the other boys of the village. They were carrying stick spears to attack an ant hill, little boys in the jungle being no different from little boys anywhere. Running, when all at once they stopped and looked up. High in a tree was a human skeleton, polished clean. The eyeless sockets stared down, and Joaquín stared up and he knew it was his father, who had recently died. In the village it was considered an abomination to bury people in the ground; a human skeleton in a tree was as normal as a gravestone in other parts of the world. So, as Joaquín told the story, he simply stopped and looked up with a five-year-old boy's fatalistic recognition of his father's nearly ultimate remains. "And then," he always concluded, "we ran off and speared the shit out of those ants."

He used to tell the story to the girls he dated in college

and law school to impress them with his primitive background. The truth was, the priest at the mission station had
long before introduced Christian burial to the village; his
father's burial had been no more primitive than any rural
small-town burial—a circle of mourners in a quiet glade, the
priest saying a few words. But now, watching the high-rise
across the Intracoastal, waiting for a sign of Jerry, the nephew
of the guy who had put the head in the garbage bag, Joaquín
thought of the story and of the man about whom he had made
it up, whose bare buttocks he had often followed with complete trust through the woods on a hunt.

Joaquín felt no sense of dislocation between his two lives.
His father had died. His mother had arranged with the priest
to have him flown out of the jungle. The only remnant of his
early life was the bowllike cut of his hair, which his mother
had preserved while clapping on him his stepfather's sur-
name of O'Keefe.

Then he had just been another spoiled rich kid growing
up in Palm Beach, big, friendly, outgoing, good at sports,
and smart enough to get by in school without having to ap-
ply himself. At Columbia law school he had grown used to
incessant allusions to the Banango Oil Company, pigged out
at Mama Joy's Deli, and wasted three hours a day playing
hearts in the lounge; he had married the girl he was sleeping with, Susan. Girl who seemed the perfect match, right
down to her rather superficial outlook. Then, surprising them
both, he had decided after graduation to become a narcotics
agent instead of joining her daddy's law firm.

There was no overly idealistic commitment to law en-
forcement in the decision. It had seemed like something exciting to do for a while; he wasn't blind, either, to the benefit
that might be derived from such a career, if he should ever
decide to go into politics.

Eight years later he was still a narcotics agent, still on
the street, and his marriage had foundered on his wife's
growing discontent with the fact. It was easy to see her point.
All those hours sitting in cars waiting for nothing to happen.
Or talking to informants who were the scum of the earth,
guys who did everything, snorted coke, dealt it, the sort of
cold-blooded shits who carried a gun as special insurance
against their easily wounded vanity, but who were allowed

to remain free because they had perfected the game of playing both sides of the street. There was also the "shoveling
sand against the tide" factor. Typically it went this way. You
busted the little guys and scared them into turning informer
against the big guys. If you were lucky you kept them alive
until the trial and they got up and said exactly what they
had agreed to. Then the jury went out and came back with
a verdict. Not guilty. Because who the hell would believe
those scumbags you had for witnesses?

Toward the end his wife had even thrown Kane at him.
That was the real reason he couldn't leave. Kane had made
a fool of him when he was starting out and now he was stuck
trying to get even or to prove it had never happened. "But
it did happen," she said. "And you can't get even. So you
might as well forget Kane."

At certain moments Joaquín was ready to concede all this.
About the only argument Susan couldn't really use was the
poor pay, since his old lady was one of those wealthy Palm
Beach matrons whose name appeared regularly in the society page. But by then he had also come to a clear understanding of the sort of safe, predictable life his wife aspired
to. What it came down to, Susan was a snob. She didn't want
to be married to a wild half-breed who didn't have the sense
to work in a civilized profession.

His old lady, now, hadn't been a snob. On one of her
solo flights she had experienced mechanical difficulties over
the Venezuelan jungle. She had been forced to land her small
plane on a pitiful mandioca field that hadn't been quite long
enough to keep her from banging into the trees at the other
end. The man who was the headman of the village had come
running over to her and leaned into the cabin, big, handsome, muscular, brown-skinned. Also witty. When he saw
she was all right he smiled and remarked in mission-taught
French, "*Ça pourrait être dangereux*," which Joaquín's
mother had translated loosely as "Don't you think that was
going a bit too far?"

That was the man who had become his father.

"Got me a twenty-five-foot Mako. Hundred and fifty
horsepower Evinrude, does about thirty knots. Two outriggers, two rod holders, a live bait well . . . pretty little thing."

Rhodes was telling Reuben about the love of his life.

A girl in a bikini was sunning herself on the bow of a yacht coming down the Intracoastal. Marvelous tummy, very kissable belly button. She sat up and put on sunglasses and stared straight at Joaquín as if she could actually see him crouched behind his binoculars on the ninth floor.

"She sure is," he said.

Rhodes slouched over, cigarette dangling. His hand jerked up and mussed his hair before he bent to the binoculars. He stayed with the binoculars intently.

"Mighty nice set of outriggers," he said at last.

It was hard to tell if he meant the girl or the yacht. He slouched back to his chair.

"Took her out to the Stream the other day, before we started this job. I'm trolling live bait over about eight hundred feet of water, and it is hot, lemme tell you. The bait is dragging in the water like wet toilet paper. So I said, hell, might as well put on a couple of yaps, at least that way I'll get me a breeze."

"What are yaps?" Reuben said morosely.

"Big red plastic lures; you use 'em for speed trolling," Rhodes said. "Only this time I don't even get a chance to speed up. I let one out about a hundred and fifty feet and as I'm letting the other out I turn and there's the rod bending slowly and I see this big head going back and forth, bill the size of a baseball bat, son of a bitch musta gone three hundred pounds."

"Did you boat it?"

"Nah, it spit out the yaps."

"It don't count just to have it on," Reuben said. "You gotta boat it."

Reuben was full of maxims.

"We should get out there, Wok," Rhodes said. Wok, as in Wok-een. "The blue marlin are moving through."

"I been thinking of going home for a couple of weeks," Joaquín said. "I mean Venezuela. Why don't you come?"

"What's the fishing like?"

"You catch dorados. They're good fighters. You can have a lot of fun with them on a fly rod." He saw Rhodes was interested and he began to push the idea. "I mean it. . . . We'll fly down in my plane. You'll have a great time. You can hunt, fish, take it easy. The marlin will be gone by the time we're done with this anyway."

"You're right."

"So what d'you say?"

"I dunno, let's see what happens."

Rhodes seemed gloomy at the thought of all those blue marlin escaping north. They had been partners for three years. Rhodes was the son of a poor Florida Panhandle farmer. The way he told it was that one night he had found himself in a drunk tank with a bunch of boys his own age, all bragging about how short their lives were going to be. It was a dumb redneck thing to be proud of, and it had come to Rhodes that a long happy life was what he truly wanted. So he had graduated from high school and gotten a degree in accounting from the University of Florida. Then, instead of becoming an accountant, as planned, he had done a little backsliding and joined the agency.

"Me being an accountant wouldn't have meant much to my daddy," Rhodes said. "But when I told him I was gonna be a cop it really perked the old boy up."

His father had been in the hospital dying of lung cancer at the time.

Joaquín thought of all the times he had been hunting and fishing with his partner. Up to a town that wasn't much more than a post office and a general store, had a funny name. Rhodes a good old boy come home, able to swap stories and talk politics with the other good old boys, sitting on the front porches. Find out where the game was, how the fish were biting. The good old boys would eye Joaquín with polite suspicion—an outsider; worse, a South Floridian—their basic hostility temporarily suspended, on account of he was a friend of Ernie's.

"Listen, Rhodes, damn you," Joaquín said, "I've let you drag me up to cracker country more times than you can count. This time you're going to my hometown."

Rhodes laughed.

Reuben said, "What the hell you wanna go to the jungle for when you can stay here and go to Gulfstream Park?"

A white Chevy pulled out of the parking garage of the high-rise and Joaquín recognized the chubby young Cuban male in a *guayabera* shirt at the wheel. The car turned left onto the boulevard, heading away from the drawbridge over the Intracoastal.

"There goes Jerry," he said. "What d'you think? Two cars?"

"The fuck for?" Reuben said. With an effort he pushed himself off the cot. "I could tail him on a tricycle."

"I might as well stick around," Rhodes said, "just in case he comes back without you boys."

In the hall Joaquín held the elevator door as Reuben came shambling after him.

"I forgot these." Reuben had his newspaper and race-track tout sheet.

The door closed and they started down.

"Dick's Picks," Reuben said. "Son of a bitch Dick is losing me money. Costs me a buck fifty for his lousy sheet and he never gave me a winner yet."

"Why do you use him?"

"I'm a sucker for advertising. See what it says?" He pointed to the headline at the top of the sheet. " 'Guaranteed to pick you a winner.' "

They emerged into a Klaxon-like wail filling the overheated air of early summer. Barriers with blinking lights were coming down and the drawbridge was opening. Joaquín waited in the line of traffic that had been stopped to let a sailboat through, Reuben beside him in the front seat. The bridge closed and they crossed it. Jerry was out of sight.

"What's your hurry?" Reuben said. "He's gonna make a few phone calls and pick up his girl. Then you and me get to go to Gulfstream and sit around watching him pick winners and pat his girl's fanny every time she gets up to place a bet."

Joaquín drove along the Strip. Ocean on the right. Blocks of bars on the left. The bars looked seedy and deserted in the bright sun. They would be crowded with sailors at night and the hookers would be cruising up and down. Spring break was over and the boys and girls wouldn't be back until the next annual orgy. It would be like a riot zone then, with a dubious sense of structure supplied by such organized events as beer enemas and wet T-shirt contests.

The white Chevy was parked on a side street. Joaquín

drew up to the curb several blocks past. He got out and walked back along the blocks, glancing indifferently into the bars. Jerry was at a pay phone in the dark at the rear of one of the joints. Joaquín had a beer at the bar, watching him make his calls. Jerry was the sort of flamboyant personality who liked to shout when he talked, gesturing emphatically with a bare forearm. But he turned his back in his colorful shirt and lowered his voice whenever necessary. Returning all those calls to Frank, George, and Mike. He avoided using his own phone. He took the messages from his answering machine and called back on public phones.

Uncle Kiki would be proud of him.

It was hard to touch a big dealer like Kiki Soldano. Kiki never came near the stuff, never even saw his money until it was washed. He hid behind half a dozen legal businesses, including a small chain of drugstores, which helped keep him in benzocaine and procaine. He had an eye for good public relations, supporting anti-Castro groups and driving around town in a succession of luxury vehicles bearing the license plate WHO DAT, a celebrated trademark in Little Havana. When public relations wouldn't suffice there was always the bribe that only a saint could refuse. And if that didn't work, you put somebody's head in a garbage bag.

Eight calls later Jerry came away from the phone and stepped up next to Joaquín, drumming the bar top with his fingers and clicking two quarters together impatiently.

"Hey, how you doing?" he said to the bartender. "If nothing's happening, man, you gotta make it happen. Know what I mean?"

"Rum and Coke?" the bartender said.

"You got a good memory, my fren."

Standing next to him, Joaquín got a closer look: black hair, oiled and combed in a flashy pompadour, jaw still visible in the beginnings of a double chin, eyes too close together, and on the pinky finger of one hand a diamond ring, like a badge of his profession. Jerry downed his drink, pulled out a big roll of bills, dropped a five, and said, "See you, amigo." A moment later the white Chevy squealed backward around the corner into the face of oncoming traffic and took off down the Strip.

Back at the car Reuben was going through his *Sun-Sen-*

tinel. He laughed. "They got this political cartoonist Chan Lowe does a funny Ronald Reagan." He folded the paper as they caught up with Jerry making a turn onto Las Olas.

"What I tell you?" he said. "Jerry's picking up his girl. It's Saturday. She don't work on Saturdays."

The girl lived on Isle of Venice, one of the striplike islands that extended into a lake in the Intracoastal. She was waiting outside her apartment complex; she had evidently been on the other end of one of Jerry's eight calls. She sauntered to the car, late teens, rich wavy black hair, Latin complexion, nipples showing through a crimson tank top, and white skirt swaying to her walk. The dope dealer's girlfriend. Mm mama, Joaquín thought. Lucky Jerry.

There was a quick run back along the Strip and over the drawbridge to the Galleria, where Joaquín got a lesson in the advantages of being a dope dealer's girlfriend. Inside the luxury shopping mall old people were walking up and down for exercise; they came to enjoy the free air conditioning and would stay all day.

He watched Jerry and his girl hitting the stores. Saw Jerry pulling out his roll of bills. He watched, and he thought of a boy walking along the beach in his bare feet, the surf boiling up about his ankles. The salt air. The hazy sun. In the glare the boy hadn't seen the garbage bag until he was almost up to it and then it had been there, lying in a clump of seaweed decorated with the tiny deflated blue balloons of Portuguese men-of-war. Opening it he had met the unpromising gaze of Jerry's predecessor.

Joaquín tried to think objectively about the caller they had heard that morning on Jerry's answering machine. Guy who called himself Numma One. Sitting on ten dead white boys. Gabbing about the Carib Indians, about bouncing a basketball in the hot Carib sun.

Carib, he thought. Carib, Kane.

And it seemed then that nothing would ever happen that didn't finally bring him back to another boy, older than the one who had discovered the head, but a boy all the same. A green kid just out of agent school, thinking he was hot stuff. Sitting in a car outside a Cuban restaurant. Waiting for a man in a white tropical suit and dark glasses to come out and climb into a white Cadillac and drive away.

It couldn't have been more obvious if he had been wearing a clown suit. But that's all you saw, the white suit, the dark glasses, the white Cadillac; you didn't see Kane. You were hot stuff with your Columbia law degree and your stepfather, the admiral, whose pull in Washington got you posted to Miami, where the action was.

Reuben was right. Kane hadn't bothered with local protection; that was for his lieutenants spread out across the country who kept the whole thing going, took whatever Kane gave them, hustled product, and got rich—rich enough to stay in business, if they didn't get careless. One got careless. Big wholesaler New York area, thought he was Captain Marvel. Wouldn't shut up on the telephone. Jumped red lights for the fun of it. The usual symptoms of too much money and toot. Eventually found himself trying to make a deal with a stubborn federal prosecutor who didn't let up until he heard the magic word: Kane.

It had been a big surprise to most people, who saw Kane as a glamorous corporate raider picking off legitimate businesses like a sharpshooter—except that the businesses, as it turned out, were just to launder his drug money and keep the IRS off his back.

Kane had been one of the few national czars, and of those few he had been the biggest. He knew how to make friends in high places and how to court the media; he had even been mentioned as a possible secretary of commerce. Kane had possessed a ruthless understanding of just how far immense illegal wealth could take one in America.

And you were the one they picked to keep an eye on him, Joaquín thought.

Merrily, as Reuben said, he had tailed the white Caddy all the way down U.S. 1. The two-lane highway made it easy to keep the car in sight from far back. Key Largo . . . Seven Mile Bridge . . . Stock Island . . . right into Key West. It was night. The man in the Caddy stopped at a joint called the Half Moon. Joaquín followed him inside and had a drink at the bar while the man used the telephone; and as the man finished his call and stepped up to the bar, a terrible sinking feeling had come over Joaquín as he saw for the first time past the costume of white suit and dark glasses to the superficial resemblance that the man bore to Kane.

He had made a frantic phone call to Miami, but it was too late. Kane was already in Carib.

Then Newton Bishop had gone after his ass. He was Joaquín's supervisor and he had been made to look bad. The grand jury had been secret; there was only a discreet informing of Washington, which passed the word quietly to the Miami office. At a press conference Bishop declined to rule out the possibility that the young agent assigned to keep Kane under surveillance had been bribed to take the scenic route to Key West. Rhodes, dirt poor, would have been canned. Nobody could believe that Joaquín needed the money. So his ass had been saved, and Bishop had since moved on to Washington, where he was in line to become the next director.

Another reason why you should get out.

In the mall now, Joaquín caught himself wondering if Jerry's flaky caller from Carib might be connected to Kane. But he cut the speculation off. That was falling into an old trap. His ex-wife had been right. For eight years, in one way or another, Joaquín had seen Kane in everything.

Jerry's girl came out of a store, tilting her lovely head, one way, then the other, to attach a pair of earrings to her lovely earlobes. Her name was Nellie Ochoa. They had run a check on her. Eighteen years old. Hairdresser. No criminal record, and no way she could afford the rent in her funky, Art Deco apartment complex on a hairdresser's salary. Jerry gave her rump a proprietary squeeze as he helped her into the white Chevy outside.

"Any hot tips?" Joaquín asked Reuben as they followed the Chevy west on Sunrise.

"Whiz Bang in the fourth," Reuben said.

"What does Dick say?"

"He says, 'Can do.' You know what that means? He'll do squat."

"You gonna bet him?"

"I might put a couple bucks on him."

Jerry bore south onto Federal Highway. He obviously derived a lot of satisfaction from being able to display that big roll of bills. But there were even more tangible rewards for his generosity. Nellie Ochoa ducked out of sight in the front seat and didn't come up for most of the drive to Gulf-

stream Park. Toward the end a truck driver drew alongside
the car and looked down from his cab appreciatively. When
Nellie raised her head with a sheepish look the truck driver
honked his horn and blasted away.

Imperturbable behind a pair of shades that he had extracted from his sun visor, Jerry saluted him, man to man,
with an upraised finger.

Nellie Ochoa was looking at the mess on her kitchen table and thinking, Shit, this is worse than working in a beauty
parlor.

Bowl of coke in front of her and she's trying to work up
some enthusiasm about starting to cut it. But she had been
on her feet all day and she had to get up early for work
tomorrow. It would be another day of bending over other
women's heads. Getting a rash on her hands from henna
rinse. Breaking her fingernails because they were soft and
mushy from being in water. All Nellie wanted now was to go
to bed.

Jerry would want to celebrate after making the sale tonight, like he always did. That meant he would probably
expect her to do what she had done three days ago in the
front seat of his car, while they were driving to the track.

Nellie was still pissed off about that. All the time her
head was down, Jerry saying, "Oh that feels so good, baby,
keep it up, don't stop," some truck driver was watching her,
and she didn't even know it until she looked up and saw
him afterward. She had sulked the rest of the way. "Get away!
Don't touch me!"

"Ah c'mon, baby, that guy wishes he had a girl just like
you," Jerry said, and finally he had given her a hundred-
dollar bill to bet on the first race and she cooled off.

Jerry was putting the final touches on two more kilos now.
She watched him sprinkling the mix with the solid little
lumps that he had saved out. Show his customers they were
getting good stuff. He had taken off his gun and put it by
the bread box on the counter. He always wore the gun
whenever he picked up a shipment because you never knew,
he said, when some scumbag might try to rip you off. He
was spreading the lumps around, talking, telling her as usual
how easy it had been.

Saying, "These brownshirts make me laugh. Up where I come from you see some blue it scares the shit out of you. But down here the cops wear brown. Like a bunch of Boy Scouts. So I pull up in front of Air Bahamas and this sheriff's deputy comes over, giving me a hard time about how I'm not supposed to be there. I hand him a five and he walks off. You wanna know the kind of guys they got doing airport traffic duty? Either young guys that just joined the force who ain't got a choice, or guys who get stuck with it 'cause they fucked up. They're out there working for the tips."

Jerry poured the mix into two kilo bags and sealed them. "All the passengers are coming through and the mule comes out. I open my trunk, he puts the suitcases in, I close the trunk. The mule don't even smile. He's like a zombie, walking away . . . Hey, what the fuck you doing," Jerry said, looking up and seeing how Nellie was staring at the bowl in front of her. "We gotta finish this shit. Lucho is gonna be here any minute."

"I'm tired, Jerry. I gotta go to work tomorrow."

"I told you to quit that job. What're you working in a beauty parlor for? You got me."

"I gotta maintain my independence. I don't want to be a kept woman."

"Who says you're a kept woman," Jerry said. He put his hand on her ass; she was wearing tight white slacks, and he patted her like he owned her. "C'mon, let's get this over with so we can have some fun."

Nellie emptied a kilo of lactose into the bowl and began to turn the mix over with two plastic paddles. She didn't mind being a kept woman. She was a knockout and she deserved to be kept. But she could see how Jerry was always looking at other pretty girls, and she wanted something to fall back on in case he dumped her. She figured maybe if she was real nice to him he might buy her a beauty parlor of her own. Then she could be the boss and run the place.

Part of being nice to him was letting him cut his stuff in her apartment. Jerry paid the rent, so she couldn't squawk too much. Still it made her jumpy, him keeping all his tools there; strainers, measuring spoons, paddles, bowls—the cops couldn't make much of that, but what would they say about the gram scale, the cans of lactose, the bag sealer, and all

those plastic bags? Jerry told her to stay cool; he had never
been popped yet. But it always scared her when he showed
up at her apartment with a suitcase.

There had been two suitcases tonight. Ten kilo bags. The
stuff was always pure, so Jerry knew he could hit it one-on-
one and turn the ten bags into twenty. Dump out a bag of
coke, then an equal bag of lactose, and go to work on it,
mixing it over and over until your arms were sore. There
had to be an easier way of doing this, Nellie said. Why didn't
you just put it all in one big bag and shake it up? It wasn't
professional, Jerry said. You did it right or you didn't do it;
that's how his uncle had got where he was and that's how
Jerry was going to get where he wanted. Pick out the big
lumps, give each new bag a nice dusting of pure.

They were almost up to twenty bags now.

The door buzzer sounded and Jerry, working on the last
bag, turning and mixing it with his two paddles, said, "That's
Lucho. Give him a drink and tell him I'll be right with him.
Make sure he's got the money, and close the door!" he
shouted after her. He didn't want to be seen doing anything
undignified.

Nellie let the kitchen door swing shut behind her and
walked across the soft carpet of her living room and into the
little alcove to her front door. Without thinking she reached
for the security chain, because she was tired and Jerry had
said it was Lucho, the guy who was coming to buy the twenty
bags.

Nellie opened the door a crack and saw Lucho, a skinny
little guy, curly black hair, black mustache; she had never
liked him much. He had a big grin on his face but his teeth
were clenched together and his eyes were rolling around
nervously. Nellie thought he must be stoned. Another guy
was with him and he had his arm around Lucho like they
were bosom buddies. Big, handsome, a real Indian with black
black hair and high cheekbones, sort of guy you might see
at the beach windsurfing or playing volley ball, having a good
time. Nellie thought, What's this, there wasn't supposed to
be two, and her fingers hesitated on the chain. Then the big
guy smiled, the nicest smile she had ever seen, all for her,
and Nellie fell in love. Where they been keeping this hunk,
she thought. She lifted the chain and unhooked it, and wham,

suddenly the smile was gone and the big guy was pushing
Lucho through the door at her and she saw he was holding
a gun and that Lucho's arms were handcuffed behind his
back.

Another man came around the corner, not as big, but big
enough. A white man, pale skin, red hair. He swung Lucho
around and slammed him up against the wall and tried to
grab her. But Nellie was already going after the big guy,
trying to warn Jerry he was coming. She was angry at the
way he had tricked her with his smile. That was what really
pissed her off, deep down.

Nellie got to the living room just as the guy was going
through the kitchen door. He hit the kitchen door like a truck
going through a guard rail. In the bright light, with all the
stuff spread out on the kitchen table like in one of those TV
shows where they teach you how to cook, she saw Jerry dive
for his gun. But the big guy hit Jerry the same way he hit
the door. He picked him up and threw him down and got on
his back and stuck the gun in his face, and that was when
Nellie caught up with him. She flung herself on his back
and began to beat him with her fists. Because the only time
Jerry ever smiled at her like that was when he won big at
the track. In the second that the big guy had smiled at her
Nellie had been ready to do anything for him. The guy had
jilted her and he didn't even see it. He didn't even notice
her now. Trying to hit him. Screaming. Crying. Her heart
broken.

"You bastard! You bastard!"

3

As the passenger jet descended through wispy clouds, there was the sea, dark blue with here and there the striking green scimitars of sudden shallows. Then a coastline, distinguished by a curling line of surf and a shabby two-lane highway. Beyond, the countryside stretched away, scorched and barren under a glaring Caribbean sun.

On the movie screen appeared an image of the pilot and co-pilot. This was an innovation meant to give passengers a bird's-eye view of the landing. But to John Mulcahy the two heads silhouetted against a wedge of approaching runway were murky and unenlightening. It was preferable to look out the window for a plain old side view of the runway itself, bordered by dirt and clumps of weeds, colorless in the glare. The plane touched down with a bump and Mulcahy's portly body sagged forward as the jet engines roared in reverse, then the plane was taxiing leisurely toward the terminal.

Mulcahy unfastened his seat belt and rose. He was the only passenger in first class. The small island nation of Carib, off the Guyana-Venezuela coast, didn't attract big tourist dollars. The passengers were mostly natives, black men and black women, shabbily dressed, jabbering in a sing-song patois, and carrying odd bundles in their laps.

Mulcahy was informally elegant in a tailored suit. He had a plump face and a forelock of gray hair that invariably managed to droop photogenically over one eyebrow whenever Washington press photographers were near.

"I hope you enjoy your stay, Senator," the stewardess said as he disembarked.

"Thank you, it was a marvelous flight," Mulcahy said.

He dispensed the word "marvelous" with a sure sense of the favorable impact it would have, coming from a senior member of the United States Senate.

A hot breath of air hit him as he stepped down the ramp. It was salty and touched with odors of ripeness and decay.

The tiny terminal had a look of seedy tropical neglect. Inside, a big black man in a seersucker jacket, khaki pants, a white shirt, and no necktie approached Mulcahy.

"Senator? Mr. Kane send me to collect you. Do you have your passport?"

The immigration official stamped the passport automatically as the man led Mulcahy through.

"You wants, you can wait in the limousine out front," the man said. "I'll get your baggage."

"I only have one small piece," Mulcahy said. "I'll be able to spot it quicker."

The baggage claim area was crowded and noisy with the natives off the plane. The air was muggy and there was a smell of body odor. With an abrupt groan the conveyor belt began to move and the first bags appeared through a curtain of dangling rubber strips. Then just as abruptly the power went dead, leaving most of the baggage outside. At the same instant, as if the two events were somehow connected, a pipe burst upstairs and water poured through the loosened tiles of the ceiling at one end of the room. It splattered down, washing dead cockroaches, cigarette butts, and black grime across the floor.

"You be in Carib now," the black man remarked philosophically. "I might have to go out and get your bag myself."

But the power came on and the belt moved again. The man waited, a little embarrassed and stiff in the senator's presence. He was an enormous man with a big, ugly, yellowish brown face, scarred and pockmarked, and a big bald head sparsely covered with frizzes of hair. The lower part of his body seemed small in comparison with his huge chest and shoulders, but when he put his hands in his pants pockets his jacket hiked up over a vast rear end. He greeted some of the natives amiably, though not by name. Mulcahy got the idea they were simply familiar faces to him. Once he grabbed a slender young man and they both laughed and clapped each other on the back like long-parted friends, the young man's grin strained by the pressure of a tremendous bear hug. But he didn't seem to know this man's name either. Under the seersucker jacket the big man was wearing a gun in a holster.

He took Mulcahy's suitcase and walked out through Customs. The Customs inspector let him go without glancing up. Outside the man shooed away the taxi drivers and bootblacks who descended noisily on Mulcahy. In the limousine, as they were pulling out of the airport, Mulcahy asked him his name.

"Herbert Jones," he said. "But most peoples just call me Jones. That's a habit they fell into."

"Is it far to the estate?"

"Hour and a half. Mr. Kane lives way out, other end of the island. It's more peaceful out that way. Not so many people as in the capital."

"How long have you worked for Mr. Kane?" Mulcahy asked.

"Oh, I been with him since he first come down . . . five, six years ago at least."

"Closer to eight."

"Could be. Time goes."

The highway left the airport and went along the coast. The ceaseless action of the sea had drilled holes upward into the porous rock cliffs over the ocean. When the waves came in, spray would shoot up through these holes, rising and misting away in the glare, like a whale's spout. They passed a shanty town of shacks, crossed an elegant old sandstone bridge over a big river with a harbor at the mouth, were caught up in a rush of tiny honking cars around a traffic circle, in the middle of which stood a statue of the president of Carib who, years after Independence—and in spite of his disdain for free elections—was still referred to as the Liberator. Instead of joining the main flow of traffic into the capital the limousine continued on around the circle and came back onto the highway, and Mulcahy settled back for the long drive "way out."

"What do you do for Mr. Kane?" he asked.

"I do everything," Jones shouted happily. "Let's put it this way . . . Mr. Kane ask me to do something, I do it. He's a tough man. You know exactly where you stand with Mr. Kane. Never any confusion on that point."

"How well I know."

Jones laughed. He had a deep, gravelly, infectious laugh that went especially well with his big crooked teeth.

"Basically I'm what you would call a bodyguard," he said.

"I see. That would explain the blunderbuss you're wearing."

The black man's weak smile in the rearview mirror suggested he was unsure of the term.

"Your gun," Mulcahy said. "Do you ever have any call to use it?"

"This? Oh no, very seldom." Jones looked troubled. "What was that word you said?"

"*Blunderbuss.* It's an old kind of gun."

"I thought I knew every word for a gun. But that one I never heard before. Down here you got people call it a piece or a pipe. But *blunderbust* . . ."

"*Buss,*" Mulcahy said.

"Hmph," Jones grunted in puzzlement. "I thought maybe you blunder into it and it bust you one."

"Do you need a permit to carry it?"

"Oh yes. . . . But that's no problem. I know everybody on the island. I don't just mean in the capital. You ask in the countryside. They all know Herbert Jones. I was born and grew up right here on the streets. I been making friends a long time. The ones I don't know from being on the *right* side of the law I know from being on the *wrong* side of the law."

He laughed again, as if with great abiding affection for the criminals and honest citizens who were united in their agreement that it was all right for Jones to carry a gun.

Mulcahy stared out at the poor sun-scorched land and thought of its sad little history: the squabbling over it by one Old World empire or another, the decimation of the native Indians, the bringing over of black slaves in the holds of sailing ships to work the wealthy plantations. The slaves had been emancipated and there had been a period of benign, or at least constitutional, oppression under British colonial rule. This had been followed by oppression of a more ruthless sort under an ex-army colonel named Livingstone Coote, the Liberator. Of particular concern to Mulcahy's colleagues on the Senate Foreign Relations Committee were the Liberator's warm relations with Cuba, underscored by regularly photographed hugs from Fidel and regular shipments of Cuban arms and Cuban workers. The United States had broken off relations with Carib years ago.

Which was fine with Wilson Kane, Mulcahy thought.

Officially Mulcahy was in Carib to meet with officials of the government, who were eager to court an influential Democrat opposed to the current administration's hostile policies. But the real, unofficial, and secret reason for his visit was to see Kane.

The countryside went on without change, poor black men working at the roadside, green sugarcane fields colorless in the afternoon glare, here and there little hamlets that the limousine was in and out of before any sign of life could be discerned. The big event of the journey was a dead mule in the middle of the road, its swollen belly looking ready to burst.

There was a town then. The limousine slowed to make its way through a cramped maze of brightly colored shacks. The wood boards were warped and peeling, the pastel hues faded by weather and sun, and the sides abundantly plastered with the image of Livingstone Coote. They came out into a square consisting of a little park with idle men sitting on benches under palm trees, surrounded by old municipal buildings, a glimpse of ocean in the distance: the other end of the island.

"This be Raleigh," Jones announced. "The town where Mr. Kane lives just outside of."

After several more blocks they escaped the blue, green, and pink shacks of the maze and were on a desolate country road. A high stone wall topped with broken bottles appeared, and they drew up in front of a gate. A short, stocky Indian stepped out of a guardhouse. With no expression he swung open the gate, and the limousine wound up a driveway lined with palm trees. Through these Mulcahy glimpsed landscaped grounds with rolling lawns and bright-red flowers.

Mulcahy hadn't seen Kane for eight years, since Kane had fled the United States to avoid arrest. They were old acquaintances. Their relationship went back to when Mulcahy had been a young congressman.

Kane was waiting for him on the front steps of a large old plantation house. He hadn't changed, a husky man with powerful shoulders, casually dressed in sport shirt and slacks. His mustache was thin and black, like a gigolo's. But there was nothing effete about his face. It was hard and direct. It had the intimidating effect of a hatchet. His handshake was strong and masculine.

"A visiting senator," he remarked.

"Wilson," Mulcahy said. "Good to see you."

"You're in the guest cottage. You'll have more privacy there. I'll give you a ride around the place. Then we'll come back and you can freshen up for dinner."

"Splendid."

"Jones will put your bag in your room."

Mulcahy watched the big black man lumber off down a cobblestone path toward the guest cottage. The two men were silent in the peaceful surroundings.

Abruptly Kane said, "How is Newton Bishop these days?"

"He's done quite well for himself," Mulcahy said, "as you know."

"You bet I know. I've been in this shit hole eight years. When do I get to go home?"

Mulcahy didn't let the bullying tone ruffle his urbane composure.

"You couldn't go home as long as the government's star witness was the happy beneficiary of the federal protection program. You had to allow some time in any case for public opinion to achieve a neutral disposition. Eight years is the traditional American time span for memory lapse. It's about what it takes to forget who ran for vice-president and lost."

"Four years."

"But it took eight for the man who was going to testify against you to die of colon cancer. The government hasn't much of a case now. I gather there's a strong possibility the charges will be dropped."

"How much is it going to cost?"

Mulcahy was annoyed; he couldn't allow Kane to talk to him like this. He pretended to admire the grounds.

"You really have a lovely place. It almost makes one wish he were an international fugitive from justice."

Kane studied him, his eyes almost invisible behind the dark lenses of his sunglasses. After a moment he gave a snort of amusement. "Maybe we can arrange it."

Mulcahy burst out laughing. The sound of his laughter relieved his tension, and as he and Kane went down the steps together he was gregarious again.

"It's really good to see you, Wilson. And by the way, I want to thank you for your generous contribution. . . ."

Mulcahy much preferred the limousine to the jeep he spent the rest of the afternoon bouncing along in. But Kane's estate was a marvel.

"My God, it's huge," he said. "It must be one fifth the size of the country."

"It's only a few thousand acres," Kane said. "Mostly jungle."

Near the house were a swimming pool and a tennis court. Then a riding stable with horses in the paddock out back. The stable marked the outer limits of the landscaped part of the estate. The paved road ended and became a dirt track.

At the edge of the jungle a movable barrier blocked the road. There were two men, short stocky Indians like the guard at the main gate. One wore a safari jacket and shiny black shoes. His black hair was sleekly combed and his face had a bloated, well-fed look. He had got out of his car and was giving instructions to the other Indian. When the jeep drew up he came over, wearing a gun in a holster on his belt.

"This is Senator Mulcahy," Kane told him. "He's staying in the guest cottage. I want you there personally, in case he needs anything."

The Indian nodded, squinting one eye against a curl of smoke from his cigarette. The other Indian swung the barrier aside and Kane drove on.

"I notice you have quite a few Indians working for you."

"There aren't many left on the island. That one I just spoke to is named Dog."

"Dog?"

"Joseph Dog. He's in charge of security on the estate. When he came to work for me the word went out and all his relatives trooped down out of the hills, looking for jobs. He used to be with the president's secret police."

"And you're not afraid to have him lurking about?"

"He's good. Nobody gets on this estate that he or his boys don't know about. The one thing you can say about the secret police is, they keep politicians in their place."

They had entered the jungle. The jeep snaked this way and that along the ungraded dirt road, with leafy vegetation whipping past on both sides. Mulcahy was reminded of some dreadful amusement-park ride he had been bullied into taking when he was a plump bookworm of a schoolboy. He had the feeling they were rushing headlong toward the edge of a steep cliff. Then suddenly the road opened into a clearing and they stopped.

In a compound overgrown with weeds and surrounded by barbed-wire fence was a large old factory of peeling paintless boards and grimy windows. It was in shadow this late in the day, except for patches of orange sunlight filtering through the drooping palm fronds. At the gate stood another short, stocky, solemn-faced descendant of the original inhabitants. There was a peaceful whistling of birds.

"It's the old refinery," Kane said, turning the car around. "The estate used to be a sugar-cane plantation."

They made two more stops. The first was at an airstrip with a tarmac runway and a two-story hangar. Then the road came to a dead end. They were at a beach. There was a boathouse beside a dock. Mulcahy was struck by the picturesque solitude, a line of immaculate white sand curving away, peaceful waves, the sun setting far out to sea.

"This is perfectly delightful," he said. "You could do anything you wanted and no one would know the difference."

Kane said nothing. There was no reason to acknowledge the obvious.

The Indian named Dog was outside the guest cottage, and Mulcahy joined Kane on his veranda after freshening up. He was standing with a gin and tonic in his hand, gazing across green lawns and jungle forest to the sea, about to mention Newton Bishop again, when a lovely young woman came out through the French doors of the dining room.

Mulcahy was surprised. Kane hadn't mentioned they would be joined for dinner.

"This is Nicole," Kane introduced her.

"It's a pleasure to meet you, Senator," Nicole said, smiling warmly and giving Mulcahy's hand a slight squeeze, as if to arrest his attention.

But there was no need for that. The woman was too attractive not to deserve Mulcahy's full attention. She had the long leggy look of a fashion model. But she was healthier-looking than most models, who were all skin and bones nowadays. She had beautiful wavy brown hair and a striking face with high, slightly flattened cheekbones. She was tastefully dressed in a white silk evening dress and wore a minimum of jewelry, a thin gold necklace, white pearl earrings. Kane had always had a reputation as a ladies' man, but the women he had escorted when he was living in Miami had been a harder, more professional type than this young lady seemed to be.

Mulcahy held on to Nicole's hand in response to the pressure of her fingers.

"Wilson, I was just saying to myself that you would never be able to match the beautiful view . . ."

Nicole laughed. Kane remained unsmiling.

"You're just in time to tell us about the recent Democratic bloodbath," Nicole teased. "We've been reading all about the primaries."

"I would say that the word 'bloodbath' very accurately describes what has been going on in the Democratic party in the last few months."

Mulcahy sat beside her on the colorful cushion of the veranda sofa, while Kane watched and listened, seated on a white wrought-iron chair.

"The time has come to close ranks. Because, mind you, Mr. Reagan is not going to be easy to beat. He's at the economic-summit meeting in London now, being seen in the role of a statesman, and meanwhile the Democrats are still squabbling."

The servant brought a glass of white wine for Nicole and then passed a silver tray with a cakelike hors d'oeuvre.

"This is delicious," Mulcahy said, examining the layers of the slice he took. "What is it?"

"That's caviar on top, of course," Nicole said. "Then avocado, sour cream, and chopped egg."

"Have another," Kane said.

Mulcahy helped himself, holding a napkin under his chin to keep from spilling chopped egg on the flagstones.

"Now where was I . . . Oh, yes, in my opinion Mr. Hart should withdraw from the race. As a matter of fact, that's exactly what I urged him to do in a private meeting before coming down."

"What did he say?" Nicole asked.

"It wasn't exactly printable. Let's just say that Gary and I have never been the closest of associates."

The servant announced dinner. They went inside and ate by candlelight. Mulcahy sat across from Nicole, Kane at the head of the table between them.

The appetizer was gazpacho, the main course red snapper with shallots, capers, lemon, and butter. Mulcahy, the gourmand, approved. He didn't object either to the two bottles of Sancerre '82 that he and Kane consumed. Nicole drank sparingly while Mulcahy's replies to her questions became increasingly verbose. He was curious about her. How long had she known Kane? Did she live in Carib or was she down on a visit? But every time he tried to turn the subject toward her she evaded him pleasantly. The conversation remained impersonal, and Mulcahy began to feel he was being questioned by a bright, pretty television reporter. Once he noticed a dazed faraway look in her eyes, and he apologized.

"I'm sorry, I've really been going on."

"No, it's fascinating," Nicole said, and he saw her gaze come back.

Abruptly Kane said, "What do you make of this economic summit that Reagan is attending?"

"Well, it might not turn out to be the big public-relations success the President is hoping for. The Europeans are extremely disturbed by U.S. budget deficits, as well they should be. Any gains the developing countries have achieved have been wiped out by high interest rates. Reagan met with leaders yesterday to reassure them. But I seriously doubt they were convinced."

They were having flan for dessert, and espresso.

"I get the feeling it's going to be a bland affair," Mulcahy said.

The big bodyguard, Jones, appeared at the far end of the dining room. He was still wearing his seersucker jacket, precariously held together across his huge belly by a single button, and bulged on one side by the gun in his shoulder holster. Kane's back was to him, but he saw Mulcahy and Nicole glance up, and he turned.

"There's that call you wanted me to tell you about," Jones said.

Kane rose without explanation.

"We'll be here when you get back," Mulcahy said, "but I might finish your dessert."

His laughter, relaxed and convivial from good food and wine, caused a slight tremor in the flames of the candles.

The dining room had a floor of red tiles. At the other end two short steps led out of it. The girl watched Kane departing. In the candlelight the side of her face was turned to Mulcahy and he admired again her beautiful shoulder-length hair and lovely bare shoulders.

"You know, I love that old forties way of doing your hair. Of course, I'm dating myself terribly. It's the way so many of the glamorous movie stars did their hair when I was a young man."

The girl ignored his compliment.

"There was a period when short hair was in. It was attractive enough in its own way. Then came the sixties and we were back to long hair. But my God, there was no style to it. It looked more like somebody had stuck their finger in a light socket. That's the way my daughter looked, anyway, trying to be a hippie. But the forties . . ." Mulcahy strove for the kind of pronouncement he was famous for in the Senate. "In my estimation they epitomized everything that was elegant and sophisticated in American society after the War, and we will not long see—"

Kane reached the two steps, went up them, and disappeared down the hallway toward the other end of the house. The girl turned, and Mulcahy was surprised. She wasn't smiling. She hadn't been listening. She didn't even bother to hide the fact. The look on her face had nothing to do with anything that had gone before.

"You've got to help me," she said.

"What?" Mulcahy stared at her, startled. "I don't understand . . ."

"You must understand. Kane will be coming back from his study any minute and I won't be able to talk."

"Nicole, my dear, I haven't the faintest idea what you mean."

"My name isn't Nicole. That's the name he gave me. He even keeps a fake passport in his safe to humor the police chief in Raleigh or anybody else who asks. My real name is Kim Mitchell. My father was Tom Mitchell."

She was talking rapidly. There wasn't the hint of a smile on her face and Mulcahy felt annoyed, uncomfortable—and frightened.

"Is this Wilson's idea of a joke or have I had too much wine?" he said, sipping his espresso to hide his discomfort. "Whatever it is, I don't think it's very funny."

"Did you ever know Kane to play a joke? Please, listen to me. Kane is holding me prisoner. I can't get away. He kidnapped me. Years ago. He did it to get back at my father. . . ."

Mulcahy was confused and intimidated. He remembered Tom Mitchell as the prosecutor who had run the grand jury that had indicted Kane; his politician's memory fastened specifically on the one day of publicity generated by Mitchell's announced intention not to run for governor, after which he had dropped out of public life. But Mulcahy couldn't believe what the girl was telling him now.

"You don't seem like a prisoner to me," he said testily. "I've had a wonderful dinner and cocktails. You seemed perfectly at ease."

"If I had tried anything Kane would have had Jones bring me upstairs and claimed I was hysterical. It wouldn't be the first time. I'm his crazy wife or niece or whatever he cares to describe me as. It was seven years ago. I was only thirteen. There must have been something in the papers about me being missing."

She leaned across the table urgently and insistently. Mulcahy thought of the faces of missing children that you saw everywhere nowadays, on milk cartons and shopping bags and supermarket posters. They all looked alike—they were the faces of children who were gone forever.

"My dear," he fumbled, "there are thousands of missing persons reported a year in America. I can't keep up with the cases in my own state."

"I'm from Connecticut. It's where my father moved when he retired. I once tried to call him long-distance. Jones came back into the study and caught me. He saved my life. If I had gotten through and my father had gone to the authorities, the word would have got back to Kane and he would have killed me and denied knowing anything about me."

"You've been held prisoner for seven years and you've never tried to get away?" Mulcahy said in disbelief.

"Of course I tried! I'm never allowed off the estate. Jones goes with me wherever I go. You've seen all the guards. It's impossible to get out. Even if I did, what good would it do me? I once did escape. The police chief brought me back. I should have known better but I was young. The whole country is in Kane's pay, even the president."

She glanced toward the other end of the room and turned back anxiously.

"I could disappear tomorrow and nobody would care."

"I know Wilson isn't a saint," Mulcahy said, "but I can't—"

"Kane is a crook. He had to run away to keep from being sent to prison. Did he show you the sugarcane plant? It's not for sugarcane," she said bitterly. "I get to use the swimming pool or go to the beach. He buys me expensive clothes and lets me read the books in his study. He even treats me well, as long as I don't try to run away or tell anyone. But he does what he wants with me. I'm his slave. Don't you see?"

Mulcahy stared at her. He had never tried to fool himself about Kane. In politics one couldn't afford to be overly pious about some of the people one dealt with. The dope business was big business in America. Mulcahy had the same grudging admiration for Kane that he would have for any successful capitalist. He knew there were unsavory aspects of the business, but these he avoided thinking about.

The girl had undergone a change before his eyes. She

was no longer the sophisticated beauty who had charmed
and flattered him by pretending to be interested in his political blather. She was a young girl whose face was only
seven years older than the faces on the milk cartons and
shopping bags.

Mulcahy realized he had never really known Wilson Kane
except as a force that had been exerted, often ruthlessly, on
his own career. He had no trouble imagining that Kane was
capable of doing what the girl said.

"A man with Kane's money doesn't need to kidnap
women," he said without conviction.

"I know it's hard for you to believe, else you wouldn't
be down here—but that's the kind of man Kane is." She was
trying earnestly to persuade him. Then she broke off and
Mulcahy saw something new: contempt.

"You don't believe me," she said.

"I do believe you," he said sternly.

The girl didn't lose her composure. But her eyes grew
moist, as if she had been steeling herself against not being
believed.

"Which isn't to say that I'm not completely shocked and
incredulous." The instinct for oratory took hold. Mulcahy
heard himself mouthing words that had no relation to his
distress. "The irony is that I came down to Carib to tell Kane
that there's a good chance the charges against him will be
dropped. But after what you've told me, I don't think Kane
could return to the United States without risking a lynch
mob."

"Please," the girl said, "you've got to help me."

"I intend to talk to him at once."

"He won't listen."

"He'll have to listen," Mulcahy insisted.

"Kane can't afford to let me go. You said yourself; he
would never be able to go back to America. You'll have to
force him."

The idea of forcing Kane showed Mulcahy how ludi-
crous his show of indignation was. He shook his head,
frowning.

"You're a United States senator," the girl said.

"I doubt there's a man in existence to whom that title
means less. The United States has no diplomatic relations

with Carib. If I storm out of here threatening to take action, what will happen to you?"

On the girl's face was a helpless admission. She had no official identity beyond the passport she claimed Kane kept in his safe. Everything she had said about Kane's immunity on Marxist Carib argued against her.

The servant had entered so silently from the kitchen that Mulcahy was afraid they had been overheard. But the old man's lusterless brown face with kinky gray puffs of hair at the temples was empty of everything except a harried weariness. He was so thin and wiry that his white serving jacket looked like it was hung on a hanger instead of a pair of shoulders. As he took the girl's dessert plate, extending one arm warily from a distance as if to swipe it from before her face, he appeared to balance on tiptoe. At Kane's place he hesitated.

"Will Mr. Kane be wanting to finish his dessert?"

"You can leave it," the girl said tensely.

The man came around to Mulcahy and took his plate. Then, seeing that Mulcahy had finished his espresso, he said, "Can I get you some more coffee?"

Mulcahy declined with a polite gesture. He was worried now that Kane would return and find them talking about him. He didn't want a scene. He had detected a tremor in the girl's voice and he was afraid she was going to break down. She had been under a terrific strain and it crossed his mind that maybe she was crazy and had concocted the whole bizarre story. She looked younger than he had first believed. Seven years ago she had been thirteen. She was only twenty. It was terrible and Kane was a brute—if the girl was telling the truth. But the last thing Mulcahy wanted was an angry confrontation with his host. He had come down on a private visit and he wanted to keep it private.

The servant disappeared into the kitchen. It was time for Mulcahy to do the convincing.

"Kim," he said gently and firmly to reassure her, "the worst thing I could do would be to try to take you away against Kane's will. It would only endanger your life and it might well endanger mine, not that the latter is a serious consideration as far as I'm concerned. But the point is, neither your death nor mine will serve our main purpose, which is to get you out of here as promptly and safely as we can."

The girl smiled gratefully at his last words. She dried her eyes with her napkin. The light from the three candles in the silver holder between them wavered on her face as she gave him her direct, sober attention.

"There's an Indian with a gun standing outside the guest cottage now, and after what you tell me, I'm beginning to not like the idea of that very much," he said, as if to underline his point.

"His name is Dog. He's in charge of guarding the estate."

"I guess that makes me part of the estate, at least until I'm off it."

This raised another smile and Mulcahy saw the girl was going to be all right.

"What I propose to do is to pretend for Mr. Kane's benefit that you and I haven't had this conversation. I'm leaving tomorrow and flying back to Washington. Once there, the appropriate steps will be taken, again with your safety uppermost in mind. Does that make sense?"

"Yes," the girl said quietly. She looked down. Then she faced him again. "Call my father, please. He lives in Foxhaven, Connecticut . . . if he's still alive. Tell him I'm all right."

"You have my word," Mulcahy said.

Kane was coming back. They both turned to see him enter the room from the hallway. The girl, Nicole, or was it Kim Mitchell from Foxhaven, Connecticut, picked up her demitasse and sipped her coffee. Mulcahy felt his cheeks bunch under a strained smile as he watched Kane coming toward them.

Kane wasn't smiling. He came up to the table and there was something in his hand. His eyes were on Mulcahy and he said flatly, "You know, there are certain benefits to living in a commie dictatorship like Carib, certain things you can get. . . ." He thrust out his hand as if holding a gun. In the candlelight it took Mulcahy a moment to see that he was being offered an after-dinner cigar.

"Castro's finest," Kane said.

4

KIM Mitchell's bedroom had a king-size bed with bedsheets that were changed regularly by the maid. It had an antique armoire with a full-length mirror and inside, clothes for horseback riding, swimming, and tennis. Kane allowed her to enjoy these sports in the ever-present company of Jones. Jones was too clumsy to be a good tennis player. It didn't help that he always wore a gun under his left armpit. Kim would tell him to take off the gun. But Jones would grunt contemptuously at the suggestion. He played tennis with the gun and rode horseback with the gun. He couldn't very well go swimming wearing a gun. But he would drive her to the beach along the narrow dirt road through the jungle, coming out on the lonely stretch of beach with its soft sand and crystal-clear water and gentle waves, and he would wait, his huge body sweating in the shade under a palm tree while Kim swam.

In the clothes closet were expensive shoes and dresses, picked out for her by Kane. In the bathroom a bidet and a Jacuzzi. The bedroom walls were painted white and they had no windows. There were paintings, however—island scenes of black men cutting sugarcane and women carrying bundles on their heads. When Kim had first been brought there she had imagined herself escaping through those paintings, into the sugarcane fields or down the country lane where the women walked. But she had long ceased to indulge such fantasies.

Kim came into her bedroom now and closed the door.

She had remained talking downstairs for a while, trying to cover any signs of discomposure that Kane might detect in his houseguest. Senator Mulcahy's plump face flushed perceptibly when Kane came back, and he was unable to make any kind of convincing small talk. But Kane didn't seem to notice, and gradually the senator recovered his gift of gab. Kim excused herself, saying she was tired.

"I quite understand, my dear." Mulcahy had stood, gracious and debonaire with his drooping forelock of hair, and the pressure of his puffy fingers as he clasped her hand offered a special reassurance. "Dinner was marvelous and you look lovely. I hope we'll be seeing more of each other."

As she left the room, Kim glanced back and saw the two men standing with their cognacs and cigars. She had begun to be afraid that her own nervousness was showing, and felt she better retire before Kane got suspicious.

In the bedroom now she made an effort to remain composed. Inside she was shaking. Kane had finally made a mistake. He had left her alone with the wrong man. But she had to be careful. She tried to think calmly of the sequence of events. Mulcahy would get back to Washington. He would be cautious because he wouldn't want to endanger her. But the right people would be contacted and something would be done. Only she couldn't let Kane find out; he would kill her.

Kim sat at her dressing table to take off her earrings. Her arms were trembling. She lowered them to the table and let the trembling take over. It went all through her body, and the bottles of nail polish and perfume and moisturizing cream began to click quietly on the glass tabletop. Oh God, she thought, oh God.

At last the trembling subsided. When she was completely calm she raised her hands to one of her earrings, looking up and seeing in her mirror a young beautiful face, whose expression of composure she had perfected after seven years of knowing there was absolutely nothing she could do about her situation except to pretend and wait.

In the beginning she had fought. Kane raped her. She was locked in her room. When food was brought to her she stole a fork and tried to stab Kane. But Kane was strong and the fork only enraged him, and he hit her with his fists. In an extreme moment, seeing she was a prisoner, not knowing how long it would go on, and gripped with despair at the thought of her father's anguish, Kim seemed to grasp the essence of insanity, a state that had always puzzled her. Insanity was an imaginary flight from terror.

But Kim wasn't the type to take this form of escape. She had a real flight in mind.

She stopped putting up a fight. She didn't steal any forks or knives or even a spoon. She began to shower every morning and wash and brush her hair, and to do calisthenics and stretching exercises to keep in shape. She asked for something to read, and Jones, apparently taking the first book that came to hand, brought her *Gods, Graves, and Scholars* by C. W. Ceram, and she learned all about the birth of archaeology. The library in Kane's study eventually became her school. It even had a schoolteacher, Archibald Rice, the British manager of the former sugarcane plantation, who imposed his sturdy catholic system of knowledge on her as surely as if he were a real presence standing before her in a classroom instead of just a signature scrawled in all the books he had collected over the years. There were at least a hundred books and she read almost all of them, works of history and philosophy and science, the plays of William Shakespeare, novels by Swift, Tolstoy, Kipling. Books that seemed dull or obvious or difficult when she was fourteen became meaningful when she tried them again a year or two later. The only person she had loved and trusted in seven years was Archie Rice.

When Kane let her out of the room it was a major victory. You couldn't escape from a room with four walls and two paintings. The grounds of the estate and the jungle around it were no illusion. They existed in a real space and not just on canvas.

She began to observe this space, especially with regard to the entrances and exits. There was the main gate, always guarded. There was an airstrip. At the farthest edge was a beach and the sea. All around, front and back, was jungle. With Jones constantly watching her, the estate might as well have been an oil painting. Kim had to keep telling herself it wasn't. You could move through it, if you could somehow slip away or grab a gun.

Jones and Dog always wore guns. Jolly, who kept an arsonal of weapons at the airplane hangar, wore a gun only when he made his trips to Peru. In any case she didn't see much of Jolly.

Jolly was the man who had kidnapped her. The last real contact she had had with him was when she regained consciousness and found herself handcuffed in the back of a small single-engine plane, and the first thing she saw was the back of Jolly's head, his sunburned scalp visible under his blond crew cut, the necktie around his bare neck. He was flying the plane.

"Where are we going?" Kim said.

"Oh you're awake!" Jolly said. He turned in his seat and offered her a candy bar from which he had taken a bite.

"Have some," he said.

She turned her face away. The idea of sharing a candy bar with him was disgusting. She felt nauseous from the shot he had given her.

"You must have given me something to knock me out."

"Just a little something. How about an apple?"

She took the apple. Holding it between her handcuffed hands, she ate it.

"Where are you taking me?"

"The big leagues," Jolly said. "You're going to pitch in the majors now."

That, and the apple, which had put her back to sleep, had been the most she ever got from Jolly.

After that, Jolly was like a sort of phantom that she would glimpse from time to time around the estate. Sometimes, driving past the airstrip with Jones on the way to the beach, she would see him outside the hangar, bouncing a basketball and tossing it at a net.

Dog's surliness discouraged proximity. Of the gun wearers Jones was the most approachable. One day, when she had just gotten out of the water and was talking with him on the beach, Kim made a grab for his gun. She was still young, fifteen or sixteen; she wasn't thinking. She got hold of the gun but Jones snatched it away with one swipe. He slapped her hard in the face several times.

"You ever try something like that again I'll tell on you and you be in big trouble. You hear?"

It had been a stupid move. She had acted out of desperation. There were other stupid moves, such as the time she tried to use the phone, when she should have known that the country's primitive switchboard would never get her call through before Jones came back into the room; or the time she blabbed to one of Kane's dinner guests, a seedy local politician who stood in awe of Kane. Jones had kept silent about the phone incident, as it reflected badly on his watchfulness. But Kane had witnessed the attempt with the politician, and Kim paid for it. She realized she would have to do better if she was going to stand a chance.

She was eighteen when she escaped. Jones was out by the swimming pool. She had gone into the cabana to put on a bathing suit. Over the toilet was a shutter that hung partly open and backward on two short chains. She had had her eye on it for some time. Usually Jones waited outside the door for her. But today he was hot and lazy and had collapsed onto a pool lounge. Kim climbed up over the shutter and dropped to the ground in back of the cabana. She walked across a hundred yards of lawn and entered the jungle. Then she ran.

Around nightfall, after running and hiding for hours, she ventured onto the road that led to town. She thought of hitching a ride. But Jones and Dog would be driving up and down, and she kept ducking back into the jungle whenever she saw a car coming. In this way she made it to town and the police station.

The police chief's frown was held in place by two deep creases in the tired brown flesh of his cheeks. When he opened his mouth to speak, his pink gums were startling.

"He has been keeping you against your very own will, miss?" He had the British accent of the islanders. "I'm afraid that is not what I've been given to understand."

Jones appeared at the door and the chief looked up with relief.

"Ah, there you are. The young lady is here. She's quite all right . . . a bit upset is all."

"She's been taking medication, chief. I'll bring her home."

"Yes, yes." The chief made an impatient gesture. "We are not in the business of intruding in domestic squabbles."

And that had been the end of her escape.

Kim had paid for that, too. But she had learned something as well. It wasn't impossible. She could get away. Sooner or later she would have another chance.

Kane came into her bedroom as she was taking off her other earring. In her dressing-table mirror Kim saw the door open. The door couldn't be locked from inside and there was no way of preventing Kane from coming in. She had been hoping he wouldn't, that he and Mulcahy would stay up late drinking and talking.

Kane closed the door and stood looking at her. She glanced away, outwardly calm, removing the earring.

"How did your talk go?" she asked.

"What talk?" Kane said.

"About whatever Mulcahy came down to talk about . . . your problem in the United States."

"I haven't got a problem. It's Mulcahy's problem and he better do something about it."

Kane watched her as she took off her necklace. The thin chain of the necklace collapsed into a tiny heap of gold links in her palm. Kim looked up in her mirror and saw at the door across the room a face that she hated. It had once been the face of a stranger. And then it had become familiar to her, so that she hardly noticed the separate features. But the basic expression of cold contempt hadn't changed since that day seven years ago when she had been brought before it, a young girl asking angry questions: "Who are you? What am I doing here? Where is my father?"

The face had only answered, "Your father will never see you again."

She couldn't afford to show her anger now. She spoke as Nicole, a willing mistress, the way she had learned to.

"Will you help me with my dress?"

Kane moved from the door, his face passing out of sight until all she saw in her mirror, as he came up and stood behind her, was the large rectangle of his belt buckle with its inlaid design of turquoise stones. She felt his strong fingers at her back, undoing the top button.

Kane took his time, breathing audibly, as if from exertion. He came to the last button and undid it. Then put his hands on her bare shoulders.

"Tell me what you said to Mulcahy."

Kim froze. She managed a shrug.

"At least he's more interesting than the local politicians."

"You don't like our little band of amateur pickpockets?"

"I guess you have to do business with them."

"They have to do business with *me*," Kane said.

"Whatever."

Kane moved the shoulders of her dress outward to her arms. Her bodice slipped down, exposing the upper part of her breasts.

"Carib politicians aren't good enough for you? Is it because they don't move in Washington society? Or is it that they always have their paws out, looking for a gratuity?"

Kim was frightened. Whenever Kane talked like this he was dangerous. The slightest thing could touch him off and his rages were insane.

"You prefer the company of real pros like Mulcahy. Right?" He pressed his thumbs into her back. "Am I right?"

She said nothing.

"The funny thing is, the locals don't think much of you either," Kane said. His hands pushed the shoulders of her dress down her arms. With a slight tug the silk fabric fell from her breasts. "You're just my crazy white bitch. They still talk about the night you showed up at the police station. Half the people are out of work and they're lucky to have a few scraps of pork to put in their rice and Kane's crazy white bitch shows up complaining about life at the country club."

He put his hands under her breasts and lifted them in his palms. He was standing close against her back.

"What were you and the senator talking about?"

"You were there. Weren't you listening?"

"I mean when I left the room."

"I don't know . . . one thing or another."

"One thing or another."

"He talks a lot. I guess that's what senators do."

"That's true. I notice they've all become very good lately at getting a little lump in their throats when they're on the podium, showing tears of compassion. They're great compassion pushers."

Kane's hands left her breasts and he gripped his fingers in the hair at the back of her head.

"And what did you say?" he said.

"What do you mean?"

"I mean what did you say to the senator when he did all this talking?"

"Nothing. I listened. It was hard to get a word in edgewise."

He tightened his grip in her hair. "Is that all? You must have said something."

"You're hurting me," Kim said.

With sudden force Kane jerked her head back. "Nothing? Is that what put that shit-eating grin on his face when I came back?"

"I don't know what you're talking about."

"You've come up in the world. . . . Not like the tantrums you used to throw in front of guests. But you're still the same deceitful bitch."

Kim tried to look confused. She felt her life, and maybe even Mulcahy's, depended on not letting Kane know what had happened.

"Nothing was going on," she said.

"Tell me." Kane twisted his hand in her hair.

"I'm telling the truth."

"I was gone for ten minutes. Somebody must have said something."

"I told you. He talked."

"About what?" Kane twisted again. "One thing or another?"

Kim answered painfully. "The economic summit . . . high interest rates."

"That was before I left. What did he say after?"

"I can't remember. It was politics. Please, you're hurting me."

Kane jerked her around and slapped her hard in the face. "You lying bitch!"

Kim let out a cry. She spun away and fell off the upholstered stool and he let go. She scrambled up and Kane came after her. He swung his fist hard into her face. The slap had triggered something inside him and he had gone wild. He knocked her down and began to kick her. Kim curled up and felt the toe of his shoe kicking her over and over in the small of her back, her buttocks, her side. She told herself it would end. Whatever Kane did she couldn't admit she had talked to Mulcahy. Just let him get away, she thought, let him get away.

The kicking stopped. Kim lay in her nylon-stockinged feet, the upper part of her body naked, the top of her white silk evening dress down around her waist. When Kane spoke he was out of breath but his voice showed no emotion.

"Mulcahy told me all about it, as soon as you went upstairs," he said.

He was standing in front of her now and Kim stared at his elegant black loafers.

"Did you think, after all the shit you've pulled over the years, that I would leave you alone with somebody I can't trust? You put a crimp in the senator's evening. He seemed to think you want him to go home and send in the U.S. Marines. But after I talked to him he realized that that wouldn't be so practical, especially for him."

Kane stood over her, black curls of hair visible in the open neck of his sport shirt, and gazed down at her with cold indifference.

"Mulcahy is going home to Washington tomorrow," he said, "and he's not going to do a thing to help you."

Kim felt a yawning despair. All her ability to deceive, to wait, to plan, left her. She wanted only to kill him. She jumped up and ran to her dressing table and grabbed her hair dryer. A startled look came into Kane's face as she sprang, making a vicious chop. The front of the hair dryer caught him squarely on the forehead, and suddenly there was blood, streaming bright red. Kim managed to catch him once more, smashing the hair dryer down, before he grabbed her arm.

"You bitch! You slut!"

She struggled to hit him but Kane was too much for her. He had his hands around her throat and she was being forced backward onto the bed. Kim tried to fight but her breath was cut off and she felt the full fury of his strong arms. He's going to kill me, she thought. I'm going to die. She saw blackness and knew it was over.

Then the hands relaxed and she could breathe.

She didn't fight now. She lay in a daze of anguish as Kane tore her dress off. With a furious motion he used it to wipe the blood from his face and flung it aside. Then his hands were on her again, jerking violently at her panties.

But Kim didn't fight. She didn't want to be choked again.

Kane climbed on top of her and forced her legs apart. With his hand he groped down around the mound of hair between her legs. She felt his fingers probing, then with no other preliminaries he shoved into her. She winced but made no sound. Kane settled himself deep inside her and began to move.

"Bitch," he said.

Kim stared at the white ceiling. She was beyond tears. Tears were for the young girl who had been raped by Kane and left on the floor of his swimming pool cabana the first time she had met him. It was the only time she had cried that she could remember. Maybe she had cried other times but she had forgotten—the times when she was a young girl out by the swimming pool, where Kane had made her wear only a shift and nothing underneath, so he could reach his hand up under it and feel her, and then tell her to go into the cabana and wait for him with the shift off until he finished his beer. She had learned to retreat to someplace inside her where she could cling to an image of who she really was, the girl with the fastball, her father's stubborn, determined daughter, who one day would get away.

But all she saw in the whiteness of the ceiling now was her certainty that she had lost her chance and that Kane would kill her before she ever got another.

Kane's thrusts became quicker. She felt him growing hot and tumescent. He bore down on her and with a final hard thrust he began to come.

Kane got up and went into the bathroom. There was a sound of running water. Kim lay naked, staring at a white wall with a white door in it at the other end of the room. Beyond the door were Dog's men, in the house and on the grounds. They were there to protect Kane. But they were also there to stop Kim from going anywhere. The two paintings seemed finally to represent all she could hope for, an imaginary flight.

Blood was everywhere, the white silk bedspread, the white rug, her torn white dress on the floor. Kane was at the sink trying to stop the flow of blood. The water was turned off and he emerged from the bathroom. He paused at her dressing table and examined the cut on his forehead, then came away to the bed.

"Look at all this blood. The maid will think I took an ax to you."

"No, just your fists," Kim said. Her left eye had begun to puff up and her body felt bruised where he had kicked her. "And your foot."

"You brought it on yourself. Besides, it's my blood."

Kane's rage was gone. They might have been a married couple who had had a spat, except for the extraordinary amount of blood.

"Mulcahy is the sort of person who has a hard time asking directions to the men's room without scattering flowers in the horseshit. But your little talk with him left even a practiced horseshit decorator like Mulcahy hard up for flowers."

Kim lay with her back to him and stared straight ahead.

"He made up for it after you left. I let him give his speech. You have to allow these people a little flag waving and righteous indignation for the Fourth of July picnic. Once it's out of their system they can think clearly. For Mulcahy it was a problem of crisis management. There's nothing they can do to me, I'm stuck in this hole. But he's up there, he could go to jail. . . ."

"Why are you telling me this?" Kim said. "Because you think it makes you look clever?"

"No," Kane said, "because it shows how naïve you were to trust a man like Mulcahy just because he's a United States senator."

She had wanted to shut him up, and in fact for a moment she succeeded. The silence had a dead quality in the room with its white walls and no windows and the cool dead air of the central air-conditioning system.

"In any case," the flat, unemotional voice resumed, "Mulcahy is out in the guest cottage. He might not be sleeping soundly, but he's grateful for the chance to think of you as my crazy mistress. You ever stop to think that you're under a delusion about who you really are?"

"You'd like that," Kim said. "But I know who I am."

"That's more than Mulcahy knows. He thinks you're Nicole. He's already doing his best to forget the other girl."

Kim had to close her eyes and clench her fists to keep from attacking Kane and trying to scratch out his eyes. But he might choke her again and she didn't want to die. She realized unhappily that she might be the kind of person who would continue to cling to life no matter how degrading or hopeless it became.

"We ended up laughing about the way I got away to Carib," Kane said.

He had told the story many times. He liked to tell it.

"Mulcahy and I had a mutual friend in the Miami office of the federal drug agency. Word came down from Washington and he advised me to leave the country. Made it easy, put some new agent on my tail didn't know his ass from his elbow. Kid followed the wrong man all the way to Key West. I always wondered what happened to that kid. Probably pumping gas somewhere."

Kim tried to shut out the voice, curled up in a pitiful, beaten position.

"My friend, now—should say our friend; Mulcahy's the one who introduced us—I know what happened to him. His name is Newton Bishop. They're talking about making him the new director. I'm going home and Newton Bishop will be up there, right at the top, just where you like your friends to be."

The satisfaction in Kane's voice was unmistakable.

"You know the first thing I'm going to do? I'll be a guest on one of those national phone-in radio shows. Ninety percent of the people who call in will be wringing their hands over the terrible treatment I suffered from the Justice Department. I don't know what it is about America. It brings these creeps out of the woodwork."

Kane paused. He laughed.

"Second thing, I'm going to find that kid who tailed the wrong man, offer him a job pushing dope. It's the least I can do. Only there's one thing Mulcahy is concerned about," he said. "After he finally got around to telling me that it's my own personal affair, he felt compelled to warn me that I wouldn't be able to go back to the United States if anybody ever found out whose daughter you are. I can't afford to have you around any longer."

The statement came quickly and indifferently. Kim had

always known it would end this way. Was he going to grab her now and strangle her, or would Jones drive her into the jungle tomorrow and make her kneel on the ground and put his gun against her head and pull the trigger?

She was terrified but she didn't move. She was sure Kane was waiting for her to run for the door, a senseless flight, and she wasn't going to give him the satisfaction.

"You're going to kill me," she said.

"Why should I kill you? I've got a job for you in Peru. It'll give you a chance to pick up Spanish and learn the value of a dollar, or rather a sol, which is the currency you'll be paid in."

She listened as Kane described the house where she would live. It was in the middle of a slum by a river that was like an open sewer. The girls who worked in the house were hard-faced Indian girls whose minimal attractiveness disappeared entirely when you got them in a light and saw the signs of premature rot. The men who came there were tough little Indians of the lower or criminal classes. In the barroom downstairs a dwarflike woman sat outside the urinal, holding her hand out to all the men who went in to take a leak. The Chinese woman who ran the house was named Madam Chew. Kim would split her earnings fifty-fifty and pay room and board. She might have as many as twenty-five or thirty customers a day and she would get used to contracting and being cured of venereal diseases. But eventually she would be of no use to Madam Chew, who would throw her out of the house, and then she would see that the dwarflike woman who slept on a mat in front of the urinal was the lucky one, because at least she had a place to stay.

"You're going to sell me to her."

"Jolly will arrange the deal and fly you there. The Madam's boys will pick you up and bring you into Lima."

"I'll be working as a prostitute."

Kane saw what she was thinking. "You won't get away. The Madam's not going to risk a good investment by letting you wander free. She'll shoot you full of heroin and all you'll be able to think of is where your next fix is coming from."

"Why are you doing this to me?" Kim said. "Why can't you let me go? I won't tell!"

"You're lying."

"What did I ever do to you? You didn't even know me!"

"Blame your father," Kane said. "He should have retired a year earlier."

He went out and locked the door.

5

KIM lay on her bed now, the white wall absorbing her vision. It offered no hope or consolation, and instinctively she thought of her father and the boys she had been friends with in school. They were proof of who she really was, no matter what Kane did to her.

Once she had come into her dad's office overlooking the village green and found him sitting with a photo of her mother on his lap. Without embarrassment he put the photo back on his desk, a little misty-eyed.

"I was just thinking what a lucky girl you are," he said. "Your mom was the best-looking, smartest person I ever met. She could run circles around every other lawyer I knew, man or woman. God, I can remember how excited she was when you took your first step. It meant a lot to her to know that she had a daughter who would follow in her footsteps after she was gone. You got your brains and your good looks from your mom."

Kim sat in his lap and slung an arm fondly around his neck. "And what did I get from you?" she said.

"I dunno," her dad said. "Do you have flat feet?"

That was her old man.

Tommy Ryan was the boy who had taken her on her first date when she was thirteen. Tommy liked to talk tough when the other boys were around, his way of treading the thin line between being the nice guy he was and being thought a wimp. He picked her up at her house and they walked into town and had hamburgers at the drugstore and then went to a movie. In the balcony of the old movie house Tommy put an arm around her and tried some good-natured moves. But shortly they were into the movie itself, an extravagent space opera that sent them out of the theater laughing and shouting enthusiastically about intergalactic warfare. After that they were best buddies. He was Ryan the Lion, and she was Mitch the Itch. Tommy even stopped talking so tough, because now he had a girlfriend.

Thinking of her dad and Tommy made her think of Archie Rice, the former plantation manager. Kim had never even seen a picture of Archie, but she had an image of him all the same: a white-haired, red-faced Englishman, proper sort, up before daybreak and out all day in the hot sun, making sure things were run just right. At five o'clock every afternoon—Kim was certain of it—Archie Rice would be in his study with a gin and tonic. And a book

Kim knew the place of every book in the study, and now she imagined herself going down along one shelf. There didn't seem to be any purpose in it; she was just letting her mind wander. Maybe she was easing the pain by remembering all the books she had read, the only hours of relief from the nightmare.

There were ten volumes of *A Thousand and One Nights,* bound in white leather with gold titles on the spines. Then two fat old books, *Through the Brazilian Wilderness* by Theodore Roosevelt, and *The Letters of T. E. Lawrence,* edited by David Garnett. Kim was fond of both Roosevelt and Lawrence; they were curiously alike—one a politician who was at heart a naturalist passionately interested in describing exotic animal and bird life, the other a soldier who was at heart an artist pleading to be free of pestering newspaper reporters after his discharge from the R.A.F.

Kim skipped past the book that came after these two fat ones. She knew the book was there but it was one she had never read before; it was easy to overlook because it was thin and inconspicuous next to Roosevelt and Lawrence.

There were two novels, *Brideshead Revisited* and *Lost Horizon.* Then—

In her imagination Kim stopped. It was as if Archie Rice had touched her shoulder and said, "Wait a minute, young lady, you missed one." She seemed to see Archie take her

hand and guide it to the thin book she had just skipped past.
She saw herself remove the book from the shelf and look at
it. The book was a guide on how to fly a plane. The title was
Here's How to Fly. Kim remembered glancing through it a
number of times over the years. But she had always rejected
the idea of escaping in a plane as an impractical illusion.

Kim lifted up, aware that her heartbeat had quickened.
She stared at the painting of the black women walking down
a country lane with bundles on their heads. She had fled
many times down that lane toward the jungle-covered
mountains in the distance. But now her eyes found the sky
above the mountains. The artist hadn't done much with the
sky, none of the cumulus clouds or specklike vultures that
were common features over the island.

It was just an empty blue. It seemed to go on forever.

Kim was ready two nights later when Jones came to her
room. She had waited two whole days in her elegant white-
walled prison, hoping to be let out, just once, before Kane
sent her to Peru.

"Kane wants to see you," Jones said.

Downstairs he brought her to the study at one end of the
old plantation house. He opened the door and then closed
it behind her.

Kane looked up from his desk and Kim thought she saw
a flicker of annoyance. Maybe he was disappointed that she
hadn't fallen apart—given up eating and bathing and simply
collapsed and vegetated in an agonized stupor. In her dressing-table mirror just now she had seen a freshly scrubbed
face whose only sign of affliction was a black eye. It was the
face of an active young woman who might have been smacked
in the eye by a tennis ball. She wore a tennis shirt and shorts
and a crimson band to hold her hair neatly back from her
high forehead.

The impression of youthful happiness would be can-
celed by the hatred in her eyes. But Kim tried now to show
no emotion. Because what she felt beyond hatred was a
knowledge that after two days she was finally in Archie Rice's
study.

The study still had an old look of a time before refriger-
ators and electric fans; Kane hadn't spoiled that. There were
an old map, a cricket bat, an African woodcarving, a hurri-

cane lamp, and all those rows of books along one side.

Kane studied her a moment. Then he said, "Jolly is flying you to Peru tomorrow morning. He's made arrangements with Madam Chew."

"When will she put me to work?" The question was direct and practical.

"That's up to her. I've told her she'll have to watch you."

"How long will it take to get there?"

"Depends on Jolly. He might sleep when he stops to refuel or he might decide to go all night. It will be two days anyway. He lands in Tingo María. It's about three hundred and forty miles northeast of Lima. The Madam's boys will be there, waiting."

"Can I bring anything?"

"You can bring whatever clothes you choose to travel in. I wouldn't wear those tennis shorts. It's damp and chilly in Lima this time of year. Wear a nice dress. It'll help you with your work and give you status with the other girls."

"Jewelry?"

He shrugged. "If you want to bring your necklace and earrings it's okay with me."

"You're generous," Kim said sarcastically.

This time she was sure of his annoyance. It wasn't that Kane would expect her to cry and carry on; he knew her better than that. But he was obviously irked by her attitude of making the best of the new life he had arranged for her.

"I want a book."

"What for?"

"To read."

"You won't have time to read."

"I only want one."

Kane gestured brusquely. "Go ahead . . . take one."

Kim went straight to the ten volumes of A *Thousand and One Nights*. She didn't see them except as a white-leather blur; all she was aware of was her thudding heart. She took down the first volume and pretended to look through it. The print swarmed before her eyes; it might as well have been the original Arabic. She returned the book and took volume two. Kane was watching her.

"What—are you going to look at every damn one?" he said.

"You said I could take a book."

It was a flat statement. She didn't plead; she held him to his word. She continued to stare stubbornly at the swarming print until Kane grew bored and looked away. Kim put the book back and went on to volume three.

Out of the corner of her eye she was aware that Kane had risen. He took a cigar from his humidor. He cut the end off with a small scissors, stuck the cigar in his mouth, and lit it with a match. Carelessly he tossed the book of matches onto his desk. He turned to the French doors and opened them. The warm air of a tropical night invaded the study. Kane stepped out onto the veranda and stood smoking his cigar. His back was to her.

Kim didn't wait to see if he intended to stay outside. She crammed volume three back into its place. With her heart thudding she went quickly down the row to the two fat old books she knew were there, Roosevelt and Lawrence. Squeezed in beside them unobtrusively was the thin red-covered book that her memory hadn't fooled her about. She snatched it out and opened it. There was a chapter: "Takeoff and Landing." She found it. With the thumb and fingers of one hand she took hold of the entire chapter and tugged it gently. The binding was old, almost rotted. The threads at the top pulled away, then held firmly midway down the spine.

Kim gave one glance over her shoulder and saw that Kane's back was still to her. She tugged harder. The chapter came away bit by bit with a breaking of frayed threads and brittle glue. She felt an urge to glance over her shoulder again but she resisted it fatalistically. The effort she was making now was evident; either Kane would see it or he wouldn't. She gave a final desperate tug and the chapter was in her hand. She stuffed it frantically into the front of her shorts and then, unable to resist the urge any longer, swung around to see if she had been observed.

Kane was standing in the French doors. He was looking straight at her but his face was as hard and expressionless as always. Behind him the floodlights cast a lunar glow over the grounds, interspersed with deep black shadows.

"I've decided not to take a book," Kim said abruptly to cover her agitation.

She was afraid he had seen what she had done and was only pretending ignorance to taunt her.

"Suit yourself." Kane shrugged.

In confusion Kim stepped to the map on the wall. "I want to see where I'm going," she said. She stood with her back to him, staring blindly at the map. It was a blurred collection of colored shapes. It meant nothing to her now except as a means to hide her face.

She waited for Kane to speak. She imagined him going calmly to the book, which she had neglected to put back, picking it up, opening it, noting with amusement the extracted chapter.

"Are you going to stare at that all night?" he said.

She turned, her face a rigid mask of deception. The thin red-covered book lay where she had left it on the edge of the bookshelf. But it was small and unnoticeable compared with the enormous space it had occupied in her mind.

"You can have Jones bring me upstairs then," she said, "unless there's anything else you want to tell me."

There was a pause. It was as if Kane had become alert to something curious. He considered her a long moment, and the look in his eyes frightened Kim.

"You better leave," he said at last, "if you know what's good for you."

Kim walked out and Jones took her up to her room and locked the door. In that moment of prolonged consideration she had been convinced that Kane had been going to kill her.

Kim had a number of times in the past considered taking the book in the study. But she hadn't done it, because even if it was possible to learn how to fly a plane from a book, she was never allowed near the airstrip. Jolly always kept the keys to the two planes and you would need a gun to get them away from him.

But now Jolly was going to bring her to the plane. If she could get him to leave her alone inside it, she might have a chance. Kim was sure she would never get the plane off the ground, and if she did she would probably crash. But what difference did that make? She had no other choice.

In her room she took out the chapter she had stuffed in her shorts. "Takeoff and Landing." She sat down and began to go through it. Crash course, she thought. I'm not sure I like the sound of that.

At first the terminology distressed her. But she forced

herself not to be buffaloed by it and to grasp the basic fact that flight was a matter of getting up enough speed so that when you pulled the wheel back there would be enough air flow under your wings to lift you. The strange terms were the names of parts and instruments that enabled you to maneuver the plane. But it was the speed that got it into the air.

There was a series of drawings that showed what to do for each step of the takeoff. Kim sat on the edge of her bed and went through the sequence of motions, imagining herself gaining speed down the runway and rising over it.

Once she was in the air she would have to turn toward South America. It was the closest large body of land and it was too big to miss. She practiced the hand-and-foot moves for a banking turn, which the book said could be scary. Kim took off and turned, took off and turned. Don't be afraid of the speed, she told herself. Use it. That's what it's for. She knew landing the plane would be the hardest part, but she only glanced at the section on landing. Just get it off the ground. Then you can worry about getting it down.

She truly didn't believe she would get that far.

Kim had been at it most of the night. She lay back and tried to sleep. But with a nightmarish persistence her brain kept noting over and over the various readings of altimeter and airspeed indicator on an instrument panel that never left her gaze.

The sound of her door being unlocked woke her. Daylight was visible at the door. "Hey, it's dark in here," a voice said. "Where are you?"

It was Jolly. She had expected Jones to bring her down to the airstrip. Jolly had never been in her room, which explained his surprise at the darkness.

Kim was on the bed.

"There you are," Jolly said. "I thought maybe you were hiding somewhere to bop me. C'mon, we got a little trip."

"I'll be right there," Kim said hastily. She had fallen asleep without hiding the pages. She was afraid Jolly would turn on the wall switch and see them. She grabbed the pages and stuck them under her pillow.

"Christ, I can't see a thing. Don't you have any windows? Where's the light? Oh here we are." He found the switch and clicked it on. "Say, this ain't bad," he said, entering the room. "I don't have a fancy rug like this, just a plain old wood floor. But wood suits me. I like to hear the sound of feet. A rug like this you can't tell if anyone is sneaking up on you."

He crossed to the bed and Kim was afraid he had seen her grab the pages, in spite of his talk about the dark. She was clutching them under the pillow. Jolly reached down as if to say, "Hand them over."

"Let's go," he said instead.

"Right now?"

"I want to get on the road."

"Can't I take a shower?"

"C'mon, c'mon."

Jolly was ready. Clean T-shirt, clean white pants, gun in a shoulder holster strapped to his side. He had an ugly sunburn at the edge of his white-blond hairline.

"I'm in a hurry. It takes a couple of days to get there and I'd just as soon get it over with. Say, what's that?"

"What?"

Jolly was looking at her closely and she was afraid. He smiled.

"You got a shiner. Makes you look like the Lone Ranger. How'd you get it? Kane smack you one?" He shook his head sympathetically. "Guy's a piece of work."

"It'll only take a few minutes to shower," she said.

"Okay," Jolly gave in, "I'll go down to the kitchen and have a cup of coffee. But ten minutes is all you get."

Kim showered with a terry-cloth towel around her head. She dried herself and put on clean tennis shorts with a clean shirt and underwear. She wanted to bring the pages with her, and the shorts were a good place to hide them. She brushed her hair back into a pony tail and put a rubber band around it. Jones brought a breakfast tray but Kim had no appetite. Besides, Jolly was already back.

He pulled out a pair of handcuffs.

"You're not going to make me wear those," she said.

"Gotta do things by the book."

Jolly clipped one handcuff to her wrist and the other to his own, and Kim's heart sank.

"My purse," she said. "Kane said I could bring my purse."

She dragged Jolly to her dressing table and got her purse. She would need the purse now more than ever.

They left the room. Jolly led her down the stairs. As they came out the front door Kim saw several black men standing around wearing dark glasses and guns. She wondered if Kane had arranged for them to see her off. Then she recognized the limousine in the driveway and knew that the president of Carib was visiting Kane.

Next to the limousine Jolly's beat-up old Pontiac looked pitiful. The hood was bleached white, the roof was a rusty orange, and the four doors were variations of the original green. One rear door was caved in and the tailfin behind it crumpled and rusted.

Jolly pushed her into the front seat; it was burning hot and there was an odor of baking vinyl. The dashboard was littered with pencils, a plastic spoon, old rags, an unopened Band-Aid. The car started with a rumble and headed for the airstrip at a squeaky crawl.

"Jesus, I wonder what Livingstone Coote wants now," Jolly said. "Black bastard is trying to move in on our operation. His men have been nosing around asking questions."

"About what?" Kim asked.

But the presence of the limousine had soured Jolly's mood. "I don't care how far away you're going," he said. "It's none of your business."

"Jones tells me all about it."

"He always did have a big mouth. One day it's going to get him in big trouble."

Jolly fell into a grumpy silence. Kim tried to humor him out of it.

"Jolly, when are you going to buy a new pair of shoes?"

"What's wrong with these?"

"Look how dirty they are. Doesn't Kane pay you enough to get new ones?"

"These are all right. I'll wear them until they fall apart."

He was driving through the jungle, one hand on the wheel, the other casually at his side, attached to her wrist by the handcuffs. Kim wanted to keep him talking. She wanted him to let down his guard.

"Why don't you and me run away together," she teased.

"I got things to do," Jolly said stiffly.

"C'mon, it would only be for a few days. Kane would never even know about it."

"He'd find out. They're waiting for you in Peru." Uptight, Jolly put an end to the discussion. "I don't want to run away with you anyway."

They took the turnoff, passing under patches of sunlight and shadow and coming out of the jungle to the airstrip. Jolly pulled up at the hangar. In a clear crescent of glass that had been cut in the grime on his windshield Kim saw the plane—small, single-engined, painted bright red, with a tricycle wheel on the nose—and she lost all facility for light conversation.

"Are we going to take right off?"

"Gassed and ready to go," Jolly said.

Jolly was being too efficient and it frightened her. Handcuffed to him, she had to get out on the same side as he did, hoping he wouldn't say, "You forgot your purse." She had stuck the purse between the seat and the door on her side.

The back of her shirt clung to her as it came away from the seat. Then Kim was out of the car and Jolly closed the door. There was a light breeze, and she looked for the windsock and saw the large tubular sleeve on its pole over the hangar, blowing toward the other end of the runway. That meant she would have to take off from that end. Kim didn't know if it was possible to take off with the wind. She only knew that the book said against the wind and like Jolly she was going to do things by the book.

The year they had moved to Foxhaven Kim had built a sleek fiberglass soap-box racer in her garage with her dad's help. She had dubbed it "Kim's Cannonball" and entered it in the annual race held in town every spring. The cars were powered only by the gravitational pull of the sloping main street. She had rolled off the wooden ramp that gave the cars initial momentum and come straight down the street with only the top of her head in a plastic helmet showing over the body of the car. She had won in her division, and afterward people had commented to her father about the killer look in her eyes. Kim wasn't afraid now to fly the plane. She was afraid she wouldn't get the chance.

She tried to make small talk again. "It would be nice to go for a swim. It's hot as hell."

"It won't be so bad upstairs."

Jolly walked her to the plane, released the handcuff from his wrist, put her into the passenger side, and left her. Kim sat in the cabin with the handcuffs in her lap and watched him making an examination of the plane. He ran his fingers along the propeller blade, climbed onto the wing strut and checked the gas tank, kicked the tires. As he went on back to the tail Kim glanced quickly to see where the rudder pedals and throttle were. Then she stared toward the jungle at the other end of the runway and thought, Just get me that far. That's all I want. Then it will be time to think about getting into the air.

The other end seemed miles away.

Jolly came around and got in beside her. "Buckle up." He flicked a switch, put the key in the ignition, opened the throttle a hair. The prop became a blur as the engine roared into life.

Kim waited as he warmed up the engine and moved some levers. She started to speak and stopped. She forced herself to count . . . eight, nine, ten.

"Oh damn, I left my purse! You've got to let me get it!"

"Tough," Jolly said. "I'm not going all the way back to the house for your purse. I told you I'm in a hurry. You should have remembered it."

"It's not at the house. It's in your car. Please, it's the only thing Kane's letting me bring. It'll only take me a second to get it."

Jolly scowled. "I'll get it. I don't want you running off and wasting any more time than you've already wasted."

He clipped the free handcuff to the steering wheel, put on the brake and got out. Kim watched him walk to his car. She locked the door. As Jolly reached the car and was leaning inside to look for her purse she switched seats and locked the door on that side, too. Her hand settled around the throttle knob and she released the brake. Slowly and steadily she pushed the throttle forward. With a brief tremble the plane began to roll down the runway.

Now the jungle at the other end was frighteningly near. She would have to travel the length of the runway and turn the plane in order to take off properly—against the wind.

6

KANE had never accepted the idea of permanent imprisonment, even in a prison as idyllic as Carib. When he fled the United States it was with the intention of one day going back. He had been forced to flee with practically nothing. All his possessions—homes, businesses, autos, yachts— were put on the auction block. His lieutenants were rolled up in the net that had been cast primarily to catch him, and his overseas suppliers were also in jail.

Kane had had to start from scratch.

He had his estate with its airstrip and its access to the sea. He had Kiki Soldano, an eager young street pusher whom Kane had taken a liking to and was willing to build up, on the understanding that Kiki was simply holding the fort until the day Kane could return. And he had Jolly.

Jolly had shown up at the estate and asked for an interview shortly after Kane arrived in Carib. The guard at the gate phoned up to the house and Kane, bored, said, "Let him through."

Jolly appeared in his study and Kane got right to the point.

"What makes you think I need you? What can you do?"

"Name it," Jolly said.

Kane was skeptical of the abilities of this weirdo with his faggot-blond crew cut and his T-shirt with a picture on the front; over the years there would be a succession of absurd emblems as the T-shirts wore out and were replaced. But gradually, in Jolly's affable, flaky presentation, the details of an interesting background emerged: a degree in chemical engineering (an old school tie about his neck would become another familiar feature, though he was tieless during this first interview), a knowledge of dynamite and plastic explosives, helicopter combat missions in Vietnam before he was booted out of the army for some unspecified reason, which he alluded to with the bitterness of a permanent grudge. Kane sat up and took an interest.

"What do you know about dope?"

"You kidding? Ask me what I don't know."

"Ever deal it?"

Jolly shrugged engagingly. "I mean, c'mon . . . deal it, cut it, sniff it, shoot it. I know it from all dimensions." He gazed out the French doors, nodding to himself, putting two and two together. It didn't have to be spelled out to him, though undoubtedly his psychic intuition would get the credit for telling him the obvious. "You got a terrific setup. It's gonna work out fine."

Only toward the end of the interview did Jolly show a less affable side. "One thing," he said, speaking with intensity, "that Indian and the big black guy . . . if I work for you, they don't tell me what to do. I run my own show."

"Nobody is going to tell you how to run it," Kane said, "as long as you run it."

Jolly had found a Peruvian connection and made it work. The two Cessna Stationair 6s in the hangar were small single-engine planes, but they had a maximum useful load of 1,666 pounds. In the old refinery he supervised a crew of black workers in converting the raw base to pure cocaine. Kiki Soldano had it picked up by plane, boat, or mules, and he paid top price. It wasn't a big operation. But it more than covered the casual payoffs that were a fact of life in Carib, and until Kane went home to America, it would do.

The section off in the jungle, comprising the airstrip and sugarcane refinery, was Jolly's private domain. He kept to himself, inhabiting a few seedy rooms upstairs over the hangar, cooking his own meals and seldom going to town. In his spare time he tossed basketballs outside the hangar, tinkered with guns and bombs in his workshop, and regularly had up to his rooms one or another of the young black boys who were as plentiful on the streets as stray dogs.

Jolly was hard to get along with, but he did a good job,

and in one unique respect he had shown himself to be indispensable.

Once in Miami Kane had had a hooker up to his hotel room. At some point during the evening the hooker took a tumble out the window, later accepted by authorities as a suicidal leap. The girl had grown smaller instantly, like a balloon that flies around a room shriveling up as the air escapes. Kane's philosophy had always been that if you didn't get what you wanted out of life you were a fool. Watching the girl fall all the way he had realized that this, too, as much as money and power, could be a part of the American dream.

Jolly had procured young girls for him before, thirteen-year-old streetwalkers, urchins with stubby fingernails and hard flat palms who slept in the rickety sidewalk stands that were used during the day by street vendors for the display of cheap merchandise. The girl Nicole was something else: a theft from the heart of the country he had fled, a proof that he was still able to take from it what he wanted.

Jolly had announced he was going to fly one of the planes up to New York "to see some old army buddies." Kane could imagine the macho freaks with whom Jolly would hold a reunion, but he took advantage of the opportunity.

"When you come back bring me a girl."

Jolly's boyish face grimaced. They were in Kane's study.

"From all the way up there? What for? I can go into town right now and get you a—"

"An American girl."

"Oh you mean *white*," Jolly said. "Like some little girl fresh off the farm from Minnesota, tight red shorts, big jigaboo pimp, been fucked by Daddy since she was in diapers and now she wants to get paid for it. Is that it?"

"No," Kane said. "I don't mean a runaway."

After Jolly left he remained at his desk, thinking of the last call he had got from Newton Bishop before fleeing America. Bishop had said, "That bastard Tom Mitchell in New York isn't going to let up. You better start packing your bags."

Kane thought of the squalid little country he had been condemned to: the flat, scorched, treeless sugarcane fields, the shanty towns, the clogged streets of the capital, the burning rubbish dumps, the incessant racket of barking dogs and steel drums, the black vultures patrolling the roads for dead dogs, dead mules, dead men, the fear to speak, the torture rooms under the palace, the secret police, and the illiterate sarcasms of calypso that were the people's only relief.

Then he thought of the job he had just sent Jolly on.

He had said to Jolly, "Tom Michell has a daughter. I want her."

"Jesus," Jolly had said. "That could be risky."

"Then kill her. Either way I want him to pay."

Three weeks later, when Kane was beginning to wonder if Jolly would disappear out of his life as casually as he had entered it, Jolly came back with the girl.

Jolly had brought the girl. Now Jolly was taking her away, but Kane hadn't seen her off. He was in his study listening to the president of Carib complain angrily about the United States. The complaint was an old one, but Kane had never heard it this early in the morning before.

"The United States is planning an aggression! I know it! What did your Senator Mulcahy say about that?"

"He doesn't see a chance of it," Kane said.

"Did he see a chance of Grenada? All those American marines to subdue a handful of Cuban construction workers."

"Different situation. There you had an overthrow of the government and a thousand American citizens whose lives were supposedly in danger as a result. There aren't that many Americans in Carib and they're not under any threat. I ought to know. I'm one of them."

"And you'll be the first the Americans will be interested in, if they do invade."

Kane laughed. "Don't think I'm not aware of it," he said.

The president stopped pacing and laughed, too—at the idea of one American "hostage" who had no desire to be rescued.

They faced each other smiling, Kane at his desk. After eight years of a mutually beneficial arrangement, they were old friends. It was a friendship based on the solid foundation of the regular payments Kane made to the president to secure his asylum in Carib. But Kane also knew that he and Livingstone Coote had an instinctive regard for each other as equals; and that he was one of the few men Coote could trust.

Coote was a tall, husky, light-skinned black man with a full beard and an easy manner. He was dressed in black: black sunglasses, black silk shirt, elegant black slacks, and loafers. He looked more like a basketball superstar than a military dictator. When he had taken power in an army mutiny ten years ago he had announced that all democratic freedoms would be fully restored to the people; most of the people who had taken him at his word, of course, were now dead.

"Mulcahy says that his colleagues in the Senate are more concerned about your human-rights record than they are about your ties with Fidel," Kane told him.

"Oh yes, I know all about it, Amnesty International making a lot of noise," Coote said. "The only political prisoners in Carib are in the pay of the CIA, and that's exactly the problem I have to put up with."

Kane shrugged; he didn't care to argue the point.

"As for Fidel, he's more trouble than he's worth. You know what he's always telling me? Be prudent. You know what that means, don't you?"

"I give up."

"It means he doesn't want to give me any more arms or money. The Russians are worse. Stingy bastards. They both want something for nothing. I'm supposed to serve their purpose, while the United States goes ahead and undermines my own government because the most I can pay a private in the People's Army is two hundred dollars a month." Coote stood before the desk, looking down at Kane, calm, serious, imposing; his cap of hair and full beard were like a black hood worn over his head. "It's not like the old days when I took over the radio station and the fort with a few World War II rifles. I need fuel, I need spare parts, I need transport, I need uniforms. Carib used to have a tourist industry and foreign investment. Now there aren't enough jobs, and the people are beginning to take their views from the Voice of America. With all the money the CIA is spreading around I can't even trust my own police."

He waved his arm disgustedly and wandered off again. Kane glanced out the French doors. Outside on the veranda

Jones was talking to three of the president's security guards. The government-owned newspaper always made a point of presenting Coote as a leader who was completely accessible and had nothing to fear from his people. It was one of those patent deceptions of a police state; the guards were always with him, and not only for protection. They were his eyes and ears, and the infamous subject of jokes told all over the island in reference to mysterious midnight disappearances.

Next to Jones the three on the veranda looked small and neat and deceptively harmless in their dark glasses and jackets, with revolvers unobtrusive in holsters at their sides. Jones had taken off his jacket in the early-morning heat; his white shirt clung damply to the rolls of fat around his waist and there was a wet spot under his left armpit where his big .45 was strapped.

Beyond the veranda, lawn sprinklers sent up glittering curtains of spray in the glare and a black workman gathered a windfall of dead brown palm leaves.

Kane watched Coote from his desk. It wasn't uncommon for the president to pay him a visit. Coote was always on the move, traveling about the island to attend ribbon cuttings or other ceremonies, or to see personally to less public business. But he didn't often show up at the estate this early in the day. Kane waited for him to come to the point.

Coote had paused at the bookshelves now, his back to Kane. He picked up a thin red-covered book that had been left lying out. He opened it and shrugged with a perplexed snort. Without turning, he held the book up carelessly.

"Here's how to fly," he said. "Makes it sound easy as walking."

"It is, if you know how."

"That's right, you fly a plane."

"Now and then," Kane said.

He waited, watching Coote's back in its black silk shirt. Coote returned the book to a proper place on the shelf. He turned and faced Kane.

"I want to get into the dope business," he said.

Kane was amused. "You already are. You must be getting at least a third of my profits."

"I mean full-scale," Coote said. He let Kane consider what he meant before elaborating. "My army at your disposal, planes, boats . . ."

"You must have lost big at the track," Kane said.

"It's the only way I can finance a military buildup. It's the only way I can make Carib strong against the aggressive intentions of the United States government."

"Jolly warned me you were thinking about something like this. He told me some of your boys were down at the refinery asking questions . . . getting a quick course in processing cocaine."

"Jolly is a difficult person," Coote said.

"They noticed that?"

"He's lucky my men didn't shoot him. He came out waving a gun and telling them to get off the property."

"I understand they got."

"Oh yes, they were quite upset, though. Jolly should be warned to stay out of the capital."

"That shouldn't be too hard for him. I'm not sure I like your gunmen coming out here without being invited."

"They did it on their own. I didn't send them."

"The hell you didn't," Kane joked. "Those guys don't unzip their flies without your permission."

Coote laughed. "You know as well as I do I'm not trying to take over your business. I need you. I can't trust my own people to run something like this."

"Look," Kane said, "I always said you should get into the business. But the scale you're talking you need some big suppliers. What Jolly has is peanuts."

Coote dismissed the problem with a wave; his smile was a sly display of white teeth in the cowl of his black hair and beard.

"I have a Bolivian colonel," he said. "He wants to bring me two hundred kilos of cocaine base next week. Can you handle it?"

"Sure I can handle it," Kane answered without hesitation; he saw why he had always liked Livingstone Coote, and he understood now what all the preliminary snooping by Coote's men had been about.

"How did you dig this colonel up?" he asked, intrigued.

"He dug himself up. He had a falling-out with the Colombians and was looking for somebody new to take his product."

Coote had stepped back to the desk. He gazed down at Kane.

"This colonel is not just talking about one deal, Wilson. He wants a permanent relationship. And he's not the only one who has contacted me recently. You'd be surprised at some of the people who come knocking at a president's door."

"Why should I be?" Kane laughed. "I did, didn't I?"

He was in a good mood—Coote's proposal couldn't have come at a better time. Mulcahy's visit had held out the promise of a return to America, and Kane had an appreciation of what it would mean for his chances of rebuilding what he had had before, if he could count the government of Carib as his major supplier.

He rose, smiling. "It looks to me like you've just bought my business."

"You're making the right decision. It will be good for both of us."

They shook hands. "Once I'm back in Miami," Kane said, "there's no limit to what I can take from you."

"In that case," Coote joked, "maybe I'll start flying the stuff in myself. I'll have to borrow that book and learn how to fly."

"What book?"

"The one I was just looking at . . . with the pages torn out."

Kane was still grasping Coote's hand. For an instant his grip tightened involuntarily, and he almost jerked Coote across the desk. He saw the white teeth of the president's grin vanish into the president's beard, and the look of startled puzzlement on his face.

"What's wrong?" Coote said.

Kane dropped the hand, moving quickly from behind his desk toward where he had seen Coote standing at the bookshelves a moment ago.

"What book? Where?"

But he had already found it. It was an old book, the dust jacket long gone. The instant it was in his hands Kane felt something wrong, the red covers collapsing together limply.

He opened the book and saw what the problem was. An entire section of pages had been torn out. He turned the book over to read the title. He seemed to know what it was going to be even before he saw it, remembering how the girl had asked if she could bring a book to Peru, how he had gone out on his veranda to smoke a cigar while she searched for one. . . . On the red spine the words of the title were arranged in a vertical column, one word at a time in black square letters, each word like a blow:

HERE'S

HOW

TO

FLY

Kane didn't believe the girl could escape in a plane by learning to fly from a book. His overreaction came from a frightening understanding of all that would be lost—the one thing Mulcahy had warned against—if she did.

He stepped past Coote and jerked open the French doors. Jones and the three security guards looked up in surprise. Kane moved on Jones angrily.

"Give me your gun!"

Jones reached for his .45 and Kane grabbed it from him, aware of the sudden agitation of the guards. He didn't stop to explain. He ran from the veranda and dashed around to the front of the house. The president's limousine was there, gleaming in the heat and sun of the early morning, with several of the ominous, stubby black cars of his security force. He jumped in one of the black cars and Jones caught up with him and managed to get in beside him. One of the guards had run out and was waving his arms and shouting. But the guard sprang aside at once to keep from being hit as Kane roared off.

Kane drove the car like a weapon. It tore along the paved road that wound through the landscaped part of the estate, past the unused swimming pool and tennis court, where groundskeepers stopped and looked up in the sunny morning. It came onto the dirt road and began to bounce up and down.

Jones, enormous in the front seat beside his boss, held on. Behind them he saw a cloud of dust boiling up and obscuring the stable. Then in front of him he saw the wooden barrier before the jungle. With alarm he gripped the dashboard. It seemed to him Kane was going to crash through the barrier. But the car screeched to a halt, Kane shouting angrily at the Indian guard, who jumped to open the gate. Kane didn't wait for it to be all the way open. He roared through.

At once the view of spacious green lawns was replaced by the close walls of trees and underbrush, and the only view was ahead, down a narrow, twisting dirt track. There were so many turns it was like a corridor through a maze, and the jungle made it impossible to see where the turns were coming. But Kane drove with cold ferocity.

He was almost at the airstrip, the car careering back and forth between the leafy walls, when all at once he overshot the turnoff. He didn't stop. The track was too narrow and he would waste more time trying to turn around in it than if he simply followed it to the end and came back. He kept on going without slowing down.

The car shot out into the clearing where the old sugar refinery stood in its barbed-wire compound. For an instant another of Dog's short solemn men faced them. Then, before the Indian had a chance to react, the car erased him from view, spinning around and shooting back out of the clearing.

Kane sped back to the turnoff. He slowed down to make the turn and then speeded up again. The road was even narrower here, two worn wheel tracks on either side of a weed divider, the walls of the jungle closing around them like a green tunnel, and at the end a vision of sunlight toward which Kane raced recklessly.

There was a bump near the end. The car flew over it, Jones leaving the seat heavily, thrusting out a hand to keep from hitting the windshield. The car entered the sunlight as if from the air, crashing down and skidding to a halt.

They were at the airstrip. At first glance nothing seemed wrong. The plane was at the far end of the runway. It had taxied there and turned to take off into the wind. Jolly was flying the girl to Peru as planned, and Kane, who did not make a fool of himself before anyone, faced the fact that he had made a fool of himself before the president of Carib, running out of the house and grabbing a gun, like a madman.

He had been tricked into it by two separate incidents—

the girl looking for a book last night, Livingstone Coote finding one this morning with missing pages in it—that had come
together in a flash of bogus revelation. The bitch couldn't
learn to fly a plane from a book, Kane thought, even as he
braked the car and rammed it into park and seized the .45
beside him and leaped out without bothering to turn the
motor off, staggering forward and staring at the plane that
was just starting back down the runway. . . . Because look,
nothing was wrong; everything was normal.

He was still in the grip of furious momentum and was
trying to sort out a confusion of impressions that on the surface seemed utterly benign: the black tar of the runway under the glaring sun, a salty sea breeze blowing the windsock
over the hangar and stirring the palm trees at the other end,
and the noise of the plane now drowning out the rumble of
the car. Then he found he wasn't looking at the airplane.
Something had caught his eye that he had been moving too
fast to see, some apparently trivial detail whose actual significance suddenly seemed to catch up with him and make
him stop as he was about to stride onto the runway for a
closer look at the plane.

Jolly's car was parked near the hangar. The door on the
passenger side was open. In the dirt before it lay a purse.

Jones had noticed the purse before Kane. He had got out
of the car and gone to it. He bent down and picked it up.
With the purse in his hand he looked like King Kong, his
size reducing all objects to smallness. He held the purse out
to Kane. "She left this," he said. He opened the purse and
peered into it with his ugly face, as if peering curiously down
the front of Fay Wray's dress. "Necklace, earrings . . . she
don't want her jewels."

Now Kane did stride onto the runway. Only seconds had
elapsed since he had jumped from the car, and the plane
was still surging toward them. For a moment the sun glaring
off the cabin window made it impossible to see who was
inside. Then all at once the plane veered—and there was
the girl, unmistakably at the controls. In the next instant Kane
discovered the reason for the sudden veer. Jolly was clinging to the wing on the other side.

Kane ran toward the plane. He didn't think the girl could
get off the ground. She would crash into the jungle at the

side of the runway with Jolly hanging on the wing. His only thought was, The bitch is going to wreck my plane.

Then the girl righted the plane and she was coming straight down the runway again and Kane was directly in her path. He raised the .45 and fired. The pistol bucked twice in his hand but the plane kept coming and he had to jump out of the way. He was still thinking, She'll never make it, she'll never get off the ground, she can't. But as the plane sped past and he turned to keep firing he saw that the fat round tires were no longer on the runway.

One moment the plane seemed to hang indecisively. The next it rose as if levitated by a huge invisible spring. Ten feet in the air Jolly let go of the wing and dropped. Immediately the plane began to roll to the left, but once more the girl managed to straighten it out. Kane kept firing . . . boom, boom, boom, boom. She's going to crash into the hangar, he thought, she'll kill herself. Then the plane cleared the hangar and was flying away and the gun was going . . . click, click.

Kane flung the gun. He came at Jolly as if to kill him with his bare hands. "You let her get away, you dumb bastard!"

Jolly was writhing on the runway. "Christ . . . Christ." He rose, doubled over in agony, clutching his knees. "She tricked me! She said she left her purse in the car! I had her handcuffed to the wheel! How was I to know she could fly!"

He had lost his eyeglasses and his face was twisted with pain. It wouldn't have taken much for Kane to shoot him right there, if he had had a loaded gun.

"What the hell do you call that?" He gestured toward the plane.

Jolly didn't look. He was squinting at the ground, searching for his glasses. He took a step and winced.

"Jesus, all I did was leave her for a second. She kept bugging me while I was warming up the engine. So I got out to get her purse. Next thing I know she's taxiing up the runway. I thought she was trying to kill herself. How the hell did she learn to fly?"

"I thought you were psychic! She learned it from a book!"

Jones had picked up the .45 and come over. He was filling the clip with bullets. He shoved the clip into the butt and stuck the gun back in his holster, while Jolly continued to protest in disbelief.

"A book! She might have learned to take off from a book! But she'll never land it! She don't even know where she's going! She'll run out of gas! You don't have to worry about—"

Kane grabbed him and shook him in a rage. "Go get her! Get the other plane and go after her! Don't come back without her!"

Standing on the front steps of the main house, Livingstone Coote was puzzled by what had happened. He stared off toward the jungle where Kane had disappeared. But the jungle offered no answers. The only thing he saw was a red plane that appeared above the green trees in the distance. Small, light, and insignificant, it circled away unsteadily toward the sea.

7

As the plane rose over the hangar Kim moved the wheel forward slightly to gain speed. Then she pulled back slowly with her handcuffed hand, the other on the throttle, and felt the nose of the plane rise. She was climbing. The plane was in the air. She couldn't believe it. She was shaking.

She had been aware of Jolly running alongside the plane. But she had blocked him out just as she had the spectators behind the bales of hay in the soap-box race, even when Jolly managed to grab hold of the wing as she made the turn into the wind.

She had been frightened when the plane began to veer with Jolly on the wing. But her biggest scare came when he dropped off and she had to turn the wheel quickly as the other wing dipped sharply.

She had barely noticed the man firing a gun at her from the runway. He had been like one of those nameless, faceless figures that hover at the edges of dreams.

It was only after she cleared the hangar that Kim realized the man had been Kane.

"Take it easy," she said, trying to stop shaking. "Don't clutch up. Just keep going. Jolly is off the wing. I hope Kane didn't hit the fuel tank. I don't think he can hit me now. I must be out of range."

She was babbling, trying to impose a sense of reality over the dreamlike fact that she was in the air, trapped in a machine that had a momentum of its own—that was moving steadily away toward the fringe of trees along the beach, moving too fast to give her time to think. She was over the palm trees and the great curve of white beach at once. There was a line of frothy surf, then only the ocean stretching away, vast and glittering. Carib was behind her.

She knew she had things to do. But she was afraid to move, afraid that the least attempt to control the plane would cause it to stall or go into a spin. The compass on the instrument panel said she was going east. There was only the Atlantic Ocean out there. Even staring blindly at the map in Kane's study she had understood that.

She thought of the old map, its heavy paper warped and bulging in a thin wooden frame. Carib lay off the coast of Guyana, the island an infinitesimal speck above the huge multicolored shape of South America. On the map it was a straight drop south to the light pink of Guyana and then on downward to the sprawling yellow of Brazil. The light pink was only an inch away.

Kim didn't know how hard or easy it was for a plane to stall and she didn't want to find out. She just wanted to keep on going, as if her only need were to get farther from Kane. But Kane was ancient history. She had to turn south.

Do it. Show him you can do it. Stick it to the bastard.

But she decided to gain some altitude first, in case she went into a stall and needed time to get out of it. She watched the long needle going round on the altimeter like a second hand as the short needle edged upward imperceptibly. In front of her was blue sky with a large cumulus cloud off to one side; it looked as if she would scrape past one fat glistening white edge of the cloud if she continued heading as she was.

Without warning the plane sank abruptly, giving her a scare. But the sensation passed. It had been like a sort of bump in the road and she guessed she had hit an air pocket.

When she looked up again she saw the cloud had moved directly into her path and she was climbing toward the center of it. Her entrance into the cloud occurred by precipitous stages that she was helpless to forestall. One moment the cloud was looming before her like an iceberg. The next, she was aware of the trailing hairlike wisps and pudgy cotton balls at the outer edge. Then, before she could do anything about it, she was surrounded by the dead white mass of cloud and moving deeper into it with each second. Kim had no heart for climbing all the way through the cloud, which from the outside had seemed to tower upward and outward enormously.

Time to turn and get and hell out, she thought.

She turned the wheel and touched the rudder pedal, and as one wing rose and the other fell the plane entered a banking turn, leaning over like a bicycle going around a corner. Instinctively she leaned the other way. Buckled into the seat and handcuffed to the wheel, she fought the urge to stare out the window at the wing dipping downward into thick cloud. She came out of the turn and discovered she was holding her breath. The compass bobbed around by degrees to the letter S.

Done. She breathed.

She was still in the cloud, but she expected to emerge momentarily. She was almost able to forget about the cloud and the scariness of flying through it and allow herself a feeling of accomplishment.

Her gaze wandered from the compass and settled on another gauge. It showed a figure of a plane head-on. She had noticed while she was climbing that the figure had been above a line representing the horizon. Now it was below the line.

She was heading down!

Trying not to panic, Kim increased her throttle and pulled back on the wheel until the figure of the plane rose above the line. But as her eye darted again to the compass she saw it was bobbing eastward and off course once more. A feeling of panic came over her. She felt blinded by the cloud. She was wandering around inside it in growing confusion with nothing to guide her except these capricious unfamiliar instruments that were like impossible video-arcade games.

She turned the wheel and touched the rudder pedal, and gunning the plane desperately, she shot out of the cloud into color and sunlight, and for one giddy instant stared at the wing that was dipping sharply toward the black flashing water below.

As she came out of the turn Kim found herself whimpering. This time she didn't need to look at the gauge to see she had lost altitude; the actual horizon was before her and the nose of the plane was below it.

Once more she pulled out of a descent and began to climb. She was still whimpering, still unhinged by her experience in the cloud. Then she gave a quick look back to one side and saw the shore of the estate. She was moving away from it, heading south. Kane, Jones, maybe Jolly, would have seen what she had done, and it gave her a savage satisfaction.

Screw you, Jack, she thought.

The climb to cruising level seemed to take forever, and Kim talked to herself all the way, keeping up a babble of urgent exhortations with silent pleas to God, fate, and whatever skills or luck had put her where she was—where she still could not believe herself to be.

"Keep on going. That's it. Just keep going. Do what you're doing. It got you off the ground. You're in the air. Oh Christ, you're actually in the air. You're leaving the bastards behind. Kane must be going crazy. He was trying to shoot you. Did you see that? Look!"

There was a spiderweb of shattered plastic around a bullet hole in the cabin window on the passenger side.

"The son of a bitch missed. What was he doing down there? How did he find out? It doesn't matter. You got the bastard. And Jolly! Hanging on the wing like that! I hope he killed himself. You got them. You got them both."

She was climbing slowly and steadily. She was afraid she would stall if she climbed too fast. The important thing was, she was moving farther and farther away.

Finally she leveled off. The sky was blue and clear. The ocean stretched before her, wrinkled and white-capped in the sun. She was heading for South America, the scrunched formless shape of Guyana as she had seen it on the map.

"One inch. Just one lousy inch."

She gave in to an impulse to clown, turning the wheel right and left as if to test her control. The wings waggled.

"Cool it, Mitchell. So you're in the air, that's the easy part. How are you going to get this thing down? Answer me that."

Soberly Kim flew on, keeping a steady backward pressure on the wheel and working to stay on course. Her other hand was on the throttle. She wanted speed right where she could call upon it in an instant. Speed was her best friend. Speed had stuck by her. She wanted to hug and kiss it.

After a while she dug into the back of her shorts for the pages she had stuffed there. She used them to go over the three rows of gauges on the instrument panel. The artificial horizon and turn-and-bank gauges told her what she could already see in the clear bright sunshine; she was flying straight and level. The vertical speed indicator was for climbing or descending, so she didn't have to worry about that either. All she had to do was keep the altimeter at two thousand feet and the air speed in the green quadrant.

She began to study how to land the plane. First you have to find a place to put it down . . . *try* to put it down, that is. You don't want to settle for just any old place. You want a nice big airport, as big as they come, with a nice long runway and a friendly control tower where maybe you can get them on the radio so they can see you don't know what the hell you're doing and can help you do it, and with ambulances just in case you ef up. Or at the very least a small airport with, say, a soft grass runway that won't hurt so much if you bounce up and down a few times. How about a cow pasture? That's all I need, a few cows scattered in my way. No thanks. I want something that hasn't got a thing on it for a hundred miles. It just might take a little time . . .

Hours later—or what seemed like hours—Kim was still out of sight of land and that inch on the map had begun to seem interminable. She should have spotted land by now. How much longer would it be?

More than once she had encountered thick white cumulus clouds like the first. But she hadn't veered away. The scary thing about flying through a cloud was the feeling that suddenly you would see a tractor-trailer truck looming at you out of the fog; you would swerve and go off the road and down a sheer embankment, your car turning over and over, bursting into flames. It was a silly feeling but she felt it each time, and each time she emerged unscathed and saw water below.

She had begun to think the world was made of water when far off she saw something that looked like land. Her only thought was cold and practical: Now the airport.

The drawings in the book were simplified and made it look easy. A cartoon pilot pushed a stick forward, a cartoon plane went down. These were fine if you were practicing on the edge of a bed. What they lacked was a sense of motion. Motion was a monster at her back. Each step, now, would be as if in desperate flight from it.

You brought the plane down to eight hundred feet and came in with the wind at your back. You pushed the wheel forward, and as the plane descended in a glide and the wheels touched down, you pulled the wheel back to drop the tail. The plane would go into a stall and you would be rolling along the ground. That's what a landing was: a stall inches off the ground. If you pulled the wheel back too soon you would hit the ground hard or maybe even crash.

The land came up, a desolate coast under a harsh sun, waves breaking against high rocks. Off to her left Kim glimpsed a fishing village, tiny, primitive, and solitary. There was the rectangle of a field adjoining it. Two goalposts at each end, like assemblages of matchsticks, told her it was a soccer field. The field was out of sight at once, motion pursuing her past it before she could appreciate its significance.

That's it, she thought. Go back. But she changed her mind. To hell with that. I want my airport.

She was passing over a dust-colored wilderness dotted with trees. The trees became numerous. It was a jungle. She wasn't discouraged. The fishing village had inspired her, a place where people actually lived, a first small outpost of the sprawling center of population she expected to sight at any moment.

The jungle didn't end. It stretched before her as far as she could see, as monotonous and unpromising as the ocean. It can't go on forever, Kim thought. This is a country, Guyana. It must have towns and cities. But the only thing she could remember about Guyana was that it was where some crazy cult leader had convinced his followers to commit mass suicide by drinking punch laced with cyanide. What Guyana truly seemed to possess instead of towns and cities was jungle.

She wondered if she should change course. But what good would that do? Any change might be for the worse, might take her farther from the airport, big or small, she had hoped for. It can't last, she told herself. Sooner or later there will be a city or a town—or maybe even a soccer field.

But she had lost her chance for a soccer field. The only variation now was an occasional flash of sunlight from a brown coil of river buried within the endless green. It came to Kim that she would run out of gas before the world ever ran out of trees. The tank was two-thirds empty and she was ready to settle for that cow pasture.

She spotted a field in the distance and decided to try for it. She didn't know which way the wind was blowing, so she would go straight in and hope for the best. She pushed the wheel forward and saw the trees come up frighteningly. The jungle was too close now for her to see the field up ahead. The treetops were passing under her very fast and she reduced speed frantically.

The field came into view. It was huge and long, acres and acres. But it was covered in tall marsh grass that made it impossible to tell what the ground was like underneath. In the middle was a small island of jungle that cut her landing room in half. Kim was out over the field and coming toward the island of jungle, as if to land beyond it, and just then, as she zoomed over it, almost touching the trees, she thought, There's nobody here! How am I going to get these handcuffs off?

In a panic she pulled back on the wheel. The nose of the plane went up abruptly. For an instant she seemed to hang suspended and totter on an invisible brink of air. Then, with a sickening sensation, Kim felt herself sliding backward, and she knew she was in a stall.

The plane went down, like a safe dropped from a window. It slammed into the ground. Then it was plowing through the tall grass toward the jungle at the other end, and the only thing she could think of was the time her dad had spun out one winter morning on a glaze of ice and an eternity had seemed to pass as the car zigzagged crazily, possessed of a will of its own, with nothing her dad could do about it except to hope and pray he and his daughter would be alive when it finally came to rest.

8

RHODES had never been outside the state of Florida before, unless you counted all the times he had been alone in a small boat out of sight of the mainland on the Gulf Stream. Being alone in a small boat on the Gulf Stream could sometimes make you feel far from home, especially when you were letting out your lines and the boat gave a small lurch and you almost went overboard. Then you thought of what it would be like, you in the water and your boat traveling steadily away and nobody in it to turn around and come back for you. Rhodes would tell himself he was the damnedest fool in all creation not to wear a life jacket. But a life jacket was too hot and uncomfortable and he never put one on.

Now he knew he was outside the state, outside the whole country of his birth, by the way these kids kept looking at him. They were cute little buggers, jet-black hair, copper-colored skin, and big brown eyes that kept glancing at him secretly, as if to take in the rarity of his red hair and white skin, his foreignness.

Joaquín was at home with them and that was the kicker. In South Florida it was easy to think of Wok as just another Hispanic with a heavy mix of Indian blood. But flying over the jungle this morning, seeing the jungle going on and on, and knowing that they were heading for some village that, incredibly, was stuck out in the middle of all these trees, Rhodes had looked at his partner at the controls and thought, The guy's a fucking Indian.

109

"What's your tribe?" he had asked.

"Makiritare," Joaquín said. "They're good people. You'll like them. They're tough farmers, hunters, and fishermen with a good sense of humor. They're really not much different from the people you grew up with. They have the same basic problems, how to get crops to grow in poor soil, how to put a little food on the table. They're not fancy but they're fun."

They had come in sight of the large-humped shapes of the lodges of the village, glimpsed in the trees on the curve of a big river, and touched down on a little field in the tiny two-seated Cessna 152 that Joaquín's old lady had bought him—a generous old dame, Rhodes liked her. At the edge of the field were all these kids and women and a few young men who had come out to see the plane, and in the middle of the group was an old man who had obviously once been sturdy but who now stood grasping the bare shoulder of one of the small boys, as one would a walking stick. "That's my uncle," Joaquín said. In bare feet, faded blue jeans, no shirt—and a New York Yankees baseball cap that Joaquín said he had given him on his last visit, bought at a spring-training game in Fort Lauderdale—the old man looked to Rhodes like an ancient Amerindian Huck Finn.

Joaquín climbed out of the plane, and all the kids and women crowded around and he shook hands with the old man and clapped him on the back, while Rhodes stood by, pretty much ignored, though he was already beginning to get those curious sideways stares from the kids, like he was a visitor from outer space. He looked at Joaquín again, as he had in the plane. Same guy he had been sitting next to in the front seat of cars, going on three years now. Made drug buys with, talked to informants with, once or twice got shot at with. Also gone hunting with. But before this it had always been on Rhodes's home ground, and it was Rhodes who knew the towns and roads, who to pop in on to find out where the game was, and what roadside joints to stop at for a drink, where he would be sure to run into old buddies who would tell him the news.

Joaquín introduced him to the uncle, who spoke a vigorous Spanish, mangled by brown crooked teeth, that Rhodes was just able to keep up with. With their backpacks and bow cases they went into the village along a worn path through the woods, Joaquín asking his uncle about the hunting and Rhodes picking up something about a jaguar that was killing cattle at the outpost of a ranch upriver. The village was almost familiar to Rhodes. There was a great irregular circle of bare earth, like a dirt main street. Situated on it were lodges with high-domed palm-thatched roofs that were like enormous shaggy caps of hair. Dogs came barking out at them, there was a smell of wood smoke, and through the trees at the edge he saw women tending scraggly mandicoa patches, while the men were off hunting and fishing. It was like a little one-street Southern town.

The uncle's lodge was a big, roomy, dirt-floor enclosure strung with hammocks that hung down like cocoons from the bamboo framework. It was shared by an extended family of kinfolk, and lunch was like a Sunday picnic, babies being nursed and dogs nosing for scraps and everybody sharing from a big pot, a sort of stew of fish and mandioca. The old man didn't stop talking. He was like the old men back home, sitting on the porches in their overalls, cans of Prince Albert at their elbows, rolling cigarettes as they swapped stories. He ran through all the local gossip and Joaquín finally got him back to the jaguar.

Was there really a jaguar? Oh yes. Hector Rosales and his son work up at that little outpost where the big ranch keeps some of its cattle. Two boys from the village went to visit them the other day. They came back and all they were talking about was this jaguar. Big, maybe three hundred pounds. It goes out killing cattle every night. Doesn't eat them, kills them just for the fun of it. You should go up there, take some dogs with you. Do you remember Hector? It doesn't matter, he'll remember you. It'll take you two days to get there with an outboard motor. That's settled then. Now tell me some good stories.

The uncle meant car-chase and gunfight stories. He thought car chases and gunfights were all that happened in what he thought of as his nephew's single-handed fight against the dread *narcotráfico*. It was a terrible business and these people should all be put in jail and left to rot for the rest of their lives. Joaquín had told him all about it. Did Rhodes have any good stories? In his imperfect Spanish

Rhodes made up a story that sounded like something he had got from the new TV series in which the two heroic drug-enforcement agents dressed like male fashion models. It gave Rhodes immediate status in the uncle's eyes and the uncle went off to take a siesta, apparently assured that the war against the dread *narcotráfic* was in good hands.

In his hammock, then, the old man rolled and smoked a fat cigarette that smelled awfully suspicious to Rhodes.

"I do believe that's an illegal substance," Rhodes said.

Joaquín grinned. White teeth, wicked grin. The savage back home, about to take a bite out of a missionary.

"Not down here it ain't, Ernie," he said.

Rhodes strapped a leather armguard onto his bare left arm. He fitted on a leather finger tab to protect the fingers of his right hand. The cute little buggers were watching him expectantly and he felt like a knight putting on his armor to go into battle. He hadn't taken the bow very seriously. But now, after all the talk about a jaguar, he figured he had some practicing to do.

Rhodes had a poor Florida farm boy's bias against bow hunters, having grown up hunting and fishing for the purpose of putting food on the table; he had encountered too many whitetail that had been gut shot and let to run off to die by inept bow hunters. But the bias had worn away and become a sort of standing joke between him and his partner, in which the good old country boy was played off against the ecology-minded sportsman.

The joke had begun on their first trip up north to the Panhandle to celebrate a drug bust, Rhodes eager to introduce Joaquín to some of the good hunting and good times he had known as a boy and young man. They had pulled into a pine wood and Joaquín had taken a hunting bow from the truck instead of a shotgun.

"Jesus," Rhodes had said, "an environmentalist."

He had remained skeptical until Joaquín picked off a running rabbit for the stew pot; then Rhodes had known deep down in his redneck's heart that he couldn't allow this exotic expertise to go unchallenged forever.

Might as well be now, he thought.

Joaquín handed him his bow. He had put some arrows

in the quiver that was attached to the handle. The broad-heads of the arrows were four-bladed, as sharp as razors, and were protected by a cover that fit over them.

"It's good up to fifty yards. But I wouldn't try for any-thing that far until you know what you're doing."

"I knew I could depend on you for those encouraging words," Rhodes said.

"C'mon, your fans are waiting."

With the kids screaming around them they walked down to the river and up along the bank to where a big tree stood overlooking a bend in the river. A rope hung from a branch over the water. On the end was tied a large bundle of marsh grass that had been fashioned into the shape of a four-legged animal. Rhodes climbed into a canoe and was pushed off by some boys. A rock was dropped over to anchor it and the canoe swung to. Standing up, he faced the bundle twenty-five yards upriver as Joaquín instructed him from the bank.

"Grip the bow loosely. If you're gripping too hard you'll twist it when you release. Draw it all the way back till the tip of your finger touches the corner of your mouth, thumb at the back of your jaw. . . . That's it."

Rhodes had an arrow in the bow and was aiming at the bundle.

"Hold it for three," Joaquín told him. "Now pull your shoulder blades together and release."

The arrow sailed out over the bundle, the aluminum shaft flashing in the sun, and landed far upriver. From behind the bend a boy swam out to retrieve it.

"Hell, I was right on it," Rhodes said.

"You have to aim about eighteen inches below the tar-get. Try another."

Rhodes kept trying, while Joaquín continued with his encouragement and advice. "Nock the arrow with the odd feather away from the bow. Three fingers on the string. Hook them deep. . . . Now all the way back."

On his fourth try Rhodes hit the bundle in the rear end. A cheer went up from the children on the bank.

"Keep on like that," Joaquín said. "You'll get the hang of it. I'm going back to the lodge for a siesta."

"See if I care. At least my fans appreciate me."

When Joaquín returned, Rhodes was drawing the bow

for a shot. He had got the basic sequence—aim, draw, hold, release, and follow through—down. The arrow hit the front part of the bundle, as it had been doing for some time now.

"Not bad," Joaquín said.

Rhodes was pleased with himself and his arm was sore. "Let's have a drink."

"Drink! You have work to do."

"I'm hitting the damn thing."

"Yeah, but that jaguar isn't going to sit around waiting for you to get ready. He'll be moving."

"I don't give a damn. If I keep this up any longer my arm will fall off."

"Good. That shows you're using muscles you haven't used in a while. C'mon, try a few moving shots. The boys are just going to bring the bundle up and let it swing down in front of you."

Two boys were already in the water, swimming the bundle over to hand it up the bank.

"The important thing is to be quick but not too quick," Joaquín said. "You always have to concentrate on making a full draw."

"Where the hell you going?" Rhodes said, seeing him walk away.

"You're right about that drink," Joaquín said. "I think I'll have one."

He was back an hour later.

It had been a frustrating hour for Rhodes, who had stopped counting the number of times he had missed. The two boys would jump in and bring the bundle back and it would swing down again and he would miss it again. But Rhodes kept at it, concentrating on getting a good lead on the fast-swinging bundle and on overcoming the tendency to let go his shot before reaching a full draw, and eventually he hit it.

He began to hit it regularly, nothing vital, a leg, the belly, a piece of it. He became more comfortable with the bow and was able to think of the target not just as a bundle of marsh grass in the shape of an animal, but as a real jaguar, leaping from a tree, in flight.

Joaquín had come up on the bank to watch. The bundle came swinging down. Rhodes let go his arrow. He saw it strike. Then, partly because it was a hot day and the river

looked enticing, and partly because he felt he owed it to the
kids who had been helping him all afternoon, but mostly
because he had seen his arrow strike at last deep into the
heart and lungs of the beast, Rhodes let out a shout and allowed himself to topple over the side of the canoe.

He went into the river with a splash.

Joaquín had a flashlight, and its beam thickened the mist
that hung over the river as he and Rhodes came down the
bank in the early-morning dark and found the dugout canoe,
a single piece hollowed out of a large tree trunk, carefully
shaped, and modernized by the addition of a decrepit twenty-
horsepower outboard motor. Rhodes got in the bow, the three
dogs jumped in, and Joaquín was about to push off, when
an old woman appeared. She handed him something and
disappeared back up the bank toward the black shapes of
the lodges. The outboard motor broke the silence of the village as Joaquín jerked it into life. Then they were puttering
up the river into the vaster silence of the jungle.

Soon it was light, and they were buzzing along in the
fresh lovely morning. In the middle of the canoe with the
dogs was their gear: two backpacks, two hammocks made of
palm-leaf fibers, two hunting bows, transported compactly
with the limbs knocked down, in cases. Joaquín had packed
spare bowstrings with good nocking-point locaters clamped
on them, and also an amazingly compact graphite fly rod that
broke down into six pieces in a fifteen-inch case. Neatly
folded on one of the backpacks was a brightly colored hand-
woven shirt, which proved that the old woman who had
handed it to him in the dark had not been a ghost.

"Is this jaguar a tall story or what?" Rhodes asked.

"I think there might be something to it," Joaquín said.
He could see that Rhodes was beginning to take the hunt
seriously.

"I shot one in my sleep last night. Son of a bitch was
made of marsh grass."

The dogs lay patiently on the floor of the canoe. They
were lean, eager dogs with pointed snouts and skinny tails
and they all had scars on their thin coats from past mishaps
with big cats or herds of peccaries. Joaquín liked the alert
way they lifted their heads whenever he pointed something

out to Rhodes—a colorful parrot, a monkey's arm extending through the foliage—and the solemn way they listened to even the most absurd comments or endearments he addressed to them.

Two afternoons later he was surveying with interest the disposition of three dead steers. Stiff and crawling with flies, they lay at separate points, as if scattered by an explosion, giving Joaquín a vivid image of how the jaguar had gone first to one, then the other, and finally the third, disemboweling each fleeing steer with a single stroke. The farthest carcass was half eaten, which suggested a serious purpose for the carnage. But an abundance of ocelot tracks around it showed that most of the eating had been done by the smaller animal, scavenging off the jaguar's kill.

Joaquín knelt and examined a print bigger and wider than the ocelot's. He saw the deep holes that had been made by the claws when the jaguar had dug in for its final spring. Cat like this had probably been hunted before and killed its share of dogs. Had learned it was easy to kill dogs and cattle. Had learned not to be afraid. It was the kind of cat who liked to get in high grass and wait for your dogs to come by, knocking them off one by one. And then it might knock you off, too, Joaquín thought.

"How long has he been hunting here?" he asked the boy who was standing with him and Rhodes.

"Two or three weeks," the boy said. "I went after him but he killed my only dog."

They walked back across a pasture to the bunkhouse of the outpost where the boy and his father worked. The bunkhouse of old unpainted boards had a tin roof patched and spotted with rust. The only other structures were a rickety horse corral and an improvised rack for hanging strips of jerked beef to dry. The dangling strips drew flies and also accounted for a permanent bracelet of vultures circling high above in the early evening. The father was heating a pot of beef and rice over a fire out back. He and his son both wore cowboy hats and boots, but they had the black caps of hair and copper-colored cheekbones of the Indians of the village. The son was about sixteen and had shone a big white-toothed grin when Joaquín gave him the new shirt his mother had made for him. They all sat on logs around the fire to eat supper.

"Tomorrow morning," Joaquín said, "we'll let the dogs go and see if they can strike a fresh trail."

"You don't have to," the boy said. "I know where the jaguar goes. There's a dry marsh upriver with a tiny island of jungle in the middle of it. I tracked him there the other day and caught him lying up in a tree."

"Did you get a shot?"

"Shot!" the father said. "You should see what this crazy kid goes hunting with." He went into the bunkhouse and came back with a beat-up single-barrel shotgun. "This piece is so old you have to say a prayer and hope it won't fall apart whenever you break it to put a shell in. The pin is no good . . . and look!" He held up two moldy shotgun shells. "That's all his ammunition!"

"Sometimes the gun doesn't go off," the boy admitted.

"What happened?"

"The cat killed my dog."

"And then," the father said, "my son had to ride like hell so that the cat wouldn't kill him."

"Like this," the son said, looking over his shoulder and making a face of comic fright.

They all laughed. The father's eyes grew especially merry when he was looking at his son.

"You could go through the jungle on foot or by horse, five or six miles, and come right out to that dry marsh," the boy said. "But with your canoe it would be quicker if you just went up upriver. I'll tell you in the morning how to get there."

The next morning they ran the dugout upriver to where the boy had said to go. Joaquín was in no hurry. The big cat hunted at night and he wanted to give it plenty of time to get back to where it lay up during the day. A jaguar that had learned to kill cattle and dogs didn't often get caught in a tree. But the field of marsh grass around the island of jungle made it feel secure. He would give Rhodes the first shot and back him up. Rhodes was busy in the bow of the canoe sharpening broadheads; the three dead steers and the boy's story had evidently inspired him.

It was late in the morning. Joaquín spotted the place and drove the canoe up onto the bank. The dogs were already standing, noses in the air, and he leashed them together. There was nothing that could make smell visible as vividly as a dog's nose. For a moment the nose of the lead dog wandered aimlessly among a confusion of animal tracks, old and new, scarring the mudbank. Then a big hand seemed to reach out and take hold of the nose and pull it with irresistible momentum toward a precise spot. As the dog reached the spot it broke into a deep full-throated baying. Joaquín looked down and saw a replica of the wide paw print he had seen yesterday afternoon. The ridges between the toes, which always dried quickly, were still wet, and he guessed the jaguar had passed less than an hour ago.

They started through the jungle, the dogs pulling him along eagerly. They hadn't gone far when he heard a small plane coming in low over the trees.

Joaquín stopped and looked up, arrested by two contradictory pieces of information. The plane seemed to be coming in for a landing. But why would a plane land out here?

He heard the drone of its engine. He saw a flicking shadow in the sunny treetops and caught glimpses of red paint. For a second the plane was visible in a patch of sky beyond, two bright-red wings, two fat black tires on struts under a bright-red fuselage. It droned away and the patch of sky was empty.

"Where'd he come from?" Rhodes said.

"Where's he going is more like it. He must be in trouble."

They continued to watch where the plane had gone, the three dogs straining on the leash. Above the trees in the distance Joaquín saw black specks spilling upward into the sky.

"Looks like it scared up some vultures."

They went on, the scent of the jaguar taking the dogs in the same direction as the plane. They came out to a corner of a huge field of marsh grass; it was half a mile long and in the middle of it, dwarfed and isolated by the expanse of tall grass around it, was an island of jungle. Beyond, sitting in the grass down at the other end, was the red plane.

The dogs were in a frenzy now. Joaquín jerked the leash and spoke angrily and the dogs stood shivering and whining in frustration. They went down along the side of the field, past the island of jungle and on toward the other end.

After heavy rains, when the surrounding creeks overflowed, the marsh would be underwater. But now the ground was dry and there was a stench of the rotted fish that had been stranded when the waters receded. The vultures would come and circle above the field and land in the trees around it and sit and stare in stupid bafflement at the smell that seemed to promise a feast, when all that was left now were the brittle, delicate fish skeletons that crackled underfoot as Joaquín and Rhodes cut across toward the plane.

The plane had stopped short of the jungle. From a distance it looked undamaged. Joaquín saw no sign of the pilot, and wondered if he was okay. He began to move with some urgency now, plowing through the belly-high grass, Rhodes behind him.

Joaquín came up to the plane. He saw the pilot slumped over the wheel. Injured, he thought. Then he saw that the pilot wasn't injured but was only working on something with intense concentration. The pilot was a woman.

"Are you all right?" he shouted.

The girl turned, startled. She was a young woman. She had a pony tail of brown hair and a face with high, slightly flattened cheekbones that curved smoothly toward a broad jawline. It had the elegant sculptured look of a fashion model's face, an impression heightened by the kinky detail of the mascara she was wearing around one eye. The girl was in white shorts and had long slender legs.

Joaquín plowed through the last of the tall grass around the plane. The door of the cabin was open. He reached out to help the girl and she lunged at him with the blade of a large screwdriver.

Joaquín stepped back. Rhodes had come up and the two men stood with the dogs, staring at the girl in the cabin. What they saw had nothing of the fashion-model aura now. It was a frightened young woman. The mascara, Joaquín saw, wasn't that at all; it was a black eye. Her wrist was handcuffed to the wheel of the plane and in her other hand she was holding the screwdriver like a weapon.

"Get away!" she shouted. "Don't come near me!"

9

Kim had been battered and dazed by her landing. The plane had slammed into the ground with a vicious impact that went through every bone of her body. Then there was the wild ride, ending with a brutal jolt. The plane had come to rest before the trees at the end of the field. It sat in the tall grass with a profound stillness and Kim collapsed against the wheel and thought, You're down, you're alive.

Around the edge of the field was a flapping of large gray wings. The wings subsided into the squat ugly-headed shapes of vultures, settling into the trees.

She was alive, she was down. But she was badly shaken and she was aware of a tremendous sense of unreality. She felt she was outside her body watching herself.

She unbuckled her seat belt and opened the cabin door, as if to climb out, and discovered she was handcuffed to the wheel. She looked in the glove compartment and was unreasonably pleased to find a screwdriver. Kim inserted the blade into one of the links that held the handcuffs together and tried to bend it. But even in a daze she saw it wouldn't work. Holding the wheel to keep it from vibrating, she struck it with the point of the blade. She managed to gouge out a thin slice and was encouraged. It might take hours, it might take days, but she was damned if she was going to let her skeleton be discovered years from now, handcuffed to the wheel of a small plane in the middle of a convention of vultures. It didn't seem to be her, though, but rather somebody else who began to hack and dig with stubborn persistence at the tiny nick in the wheel.

When the two men surprised her a part of her brain told her she was overreacting. She turned and thrust the screwdriver at a face that was leaning down into the cabin. It was a startled gesture and words came with it.

"Get away! Don't come near me!"

The man had black hair and a broad, handsome face with high cheekbones and copper-colored skin, Indian features. He was wearing faded blue jeans and a sport shirt of popular design that emphasized his broad shoulders. Over his shoulder another face appeared. It belonged to a man with red hair, a fair complexion, a rugged, plainer build, and a little less sympathy in his eyes. This one looked at her, then at the screwdriver, and pursed his lips skeptically.

There were other faces, too, three dogs with sad brown eyes who approached, poking damp noses at her bare ankles, completely unperturbed by the screwdriver.

"Are you all right?" The Indian's voice was patient, his eyes watchful.

"She looks okay to me, Wok," the red-haired one said. "But she's acting funny." He had a Southern drawl.

"Do you have any broken bones?" the other persisted.

"You think she'd be trying to stab you with a screwdriver if she did? You're asking the wrong questions. Ask her what she's doing handcuffed to the wheel."

They were talking about her as if she weren't there and Kim guessed she wasn't. She was still back in Carib, from which she couldn't believe she had escaped that morning, flying an airplane. She was still trying to get away and everyone looked like a pursuer.

"Want to know what I think?" the red-haired one said. "I think she's in a state of shock."

"What should we do?"

"We came to hunt, didn't we? Let's go on over and see if that jaguar is there."

"You mean forget about her?"

"She's not going anywhere. By the time we get back she'll be tickled to death to see us."

The two men turned away and moved off through the grass, their dogs bounding about them and suddenly filling the air with loud barks. They weren't going to leave her, Kim thought. They couldn't. She scrambled out of the cabin and was held by the handcuffs. The men were heading for the island of jungle that stood at some distance, rising like the brilliant green plumage of an exotic bird out of the huge expanse of yellow grass.

The red-haired one had used the word "shock" and Kim saw now that this must be what she was in; it explained the way she seemed to be observing herself, as if she were two people instead of one, and it explained the way she was acting toward these two men who were trying to help her.

"Don't go! I don't know what I'm doing!"

The two men stopped and looked back. The Indian silenced the dogs with a single sharp command and a yank of the leash. Kim felt she was being watched by a big audience, including the six sad brown eyes of the dogs. She thought they were waiting for something and she decided it must be a demonstration of trust.

"Here! Look! I don't want it! You can have it!"

She flung the screwdriver. It disappeared in the grass somewhere in front of the watching eyes. She looked at them.

"Please! Get me off this damn thing!"

The men turned and came back. The Indian retrieved the screwdriver from the grass. The red-haired one motioned Kim back into the plane to give them room.

The men had the quiet, serious demeanor of physicians arriving at the scene of an accident. She half expected them to start feeling her bones for signs of a fracture. Instead they both leaned forward and scrutinized the handcuffs.

Kim looked at their faces closely now. She had a sudden memory that seemed to wipe away the last seven years as if they had never happened. It was of her first summer in Foxhaven and the pleasures of going barefoot, eating ice cream cones, and lazing in the sun on the high rocks of the swimming hole outside of town. She had fallen on the rocks and banged her head and had had to go to the emergency wing of the hospital. The bang had made her very sleepy and she remembered the gentle fingers of the doctor who had examined it. Now she waited for a pronouncement from these two, as if expecting to be told she would have to be on crutches for the rest of the summer.

"Huh," the red-haired one grunted at the handcuffs.

"Don't like the looks of those. You're not going to get 'em off with that screwdriver. You got anything else in the glove compartment . . . like, say, a hacksaw?"

"Well," the Indian said, "the first thing is to get her off the wheel. We can worry about the handcuffs later."

"Move over," the red-haired one said.

Kim got out of his way. He climbed up between the seats, braced himself with his head scrunched under the low cabin, raised one foot, and brought his sneaker down hard. The sneaker bounced off the wheel. He braced himself more firmly and tried again. This time he nearly kicked her arm. He fell over backward into the seats behind him and swore.

"Shit! What are you doing in those things anyway?"

"C'mon, Ernie," the Indian said. "Let's get her off and worry about that later."

"I'm open to suggestions." The red-haired one climbed out of the cabin.

"We'll have to get the ax in camp."

"Yeah, which one of us is going to do that?"

"You got a quarter?"

The red-haired one dug into his pocket and flipped a coin. "Call it."

"Heads."

"Lucky bastard."

He left, taking the dogs with him. Kim remained in the cabin. She felt tired and depressed. It was hard for her to appreciate that she was alive. She was more aware of the fact that she had landed in the jungle. It seemed a terrible anticlimax.

The cabin was hot and there was a smell of fish in the humid sticky air. The Indian watched the red-haired one leave and after a moment came back.

"It'll take him about an hour. We've got a bit of a wait." He sat beside her in the pilot seat. "His name is Rhodes, by the way. Ernie. I'm Joaquín. Wok, for short. And you are . . ."

Kim gave her name flatly. Kim Mitchell. She hadn't been called Kim Mitchell for a long time.

The Indian nodded. It was just another name to him.

"Some landing. . . . Another few yards and you would have been in the woods. No telling what the ground is like under all this grass. Were you trying to land?"

"I started to. I changed my mind."

He accepted the answer as if it explained everything.

"Well, you look okay. . . . We'll get you off the wheel.
Those handcuffs won't be so easy. Are you running from
the law?"

The question was casual. He might have been asking if
she thought it would rain today.

"No," Kim said. She didn't go into detail.

He shrugged; it was no big deal.

"Where am I?" she asked. "Is this Guyana?"

"You're a little off. You're in Venezuela."

"Are there any towns or cities near?"

"There's an Indian village downriver. Caracas is about
five hundred miles."

"How do I get there?"

"Well, let's see. . . . There's the outpost of a cattle ranch.
You might get one of the cowboys to bring you to the main
ranch. It's a three-day ride. The owner has a small plane.
He'll be able to fly you to Caracas. He goes back and forth
all the time. You might have to pay the cowboy a little something for his trouble."

"I don't have any money "

"It doesn't matter. They're pretty good about that sort of
thing."

He went on talking, friendly, helpful. He didn't seem
curious; he was almost indifferent. Kim felt like someone
who had stopped a stranger in a city to ask directions to the
bus terminal.

"If you want you can come with us. But we're going to
be here a week. We came up from the Indian village to hunt.
We're camped on the river. If you don't mind waiting we'll
bring you back to the village with us and you can get a lift
from the supply helicopter that comes once a week."

He was being polite. Kim wasn't happy about either
choice. They both seemed long and complicated.

"Your best bet is probably the ranch," he said.

"The ranch will be fine."

She would be passed along to some cowboys who would
consider her as big of a nuisance as this man did.

"Are you an Indian?" she asked. "You look like an Indian but you don't talk like one."

"My mother was an American."

She was silent. The man went on, as if to make conversation.

"There's a big jaguar that likes to lay up in that island of jungle back there. We were going after it when we saw you coming down. You're lucky. The only people out here are those two cowboys. If they didn't see you it would just be these vultures, and somehow I don't think the vultures would be interested in—"

He stopped and looked up, hearing something. Kim heard it, too. It's nothing, she told herself. It can't be. But her face gave her away. The man looked at her.

"What is it?" he said. "What's wrong?"

"Nothing," she said. But her face wasn't so sure.

The man said, "I hear a plane."

The sound of the plane came toward them steadily out of the sky. With each rising decibel it grew in significance.

She knew it wasn't Jolly. It was just somebody flying over the jungle. Over all these trees with no place to land.

But why did her face feel this way?

The man named Joaquín got out of the cabin. Kim couldn't see the upper part of his body as he stood watching the sky. She leaned to her window and looked in the direction he was facing. High up in the distance was a flash of sunlight. It flickered out and became the precise winged shape of a small plane. It was moving far off to one side of the field.

She tried to follow it, pressing her face against the scratched plastic of the window. It's going away. It's not him. I knew it couldn't be. Then she saw the plane go into a banking turn.

"It's coming back," Joaquín said. He glanced in at her.

Kim stared straight ahead and her face felt like a mask. She could feel him watching her closely. Then his big, broad-cheekboned, copper-colored face went away, and she listened to the plane.

It passed straight overhead, high up. The sound faded and her ears strained as if to determine the precise point at which sound went out of hearing. There was a moment when it was gone and then another when it was there again.

The plane came down along the side of the field, lower than before. But Kim didn't look out to see it. She stared grimly at nothing, a pit of fear in her stomach, and thought what an insidious sound the steady puttering drone of a small airplane could be, coming and going, circling closer, like the whine of a mosquito.

When the plane came back for the last time she thought it was coming in for a landing. She heard the drone growing suddenly and implacably louder, coming straight at her. She glanced fearfully at Joaquín. But he continued to stand outside the cabin, watching.

The plane came over with a roar. Kim ducked instinctively, thinking of Jolly and his bombs. Jones had always grumbled about how Jolly was going to blow himself up in his workshop one day, "fooling around with them bombs," and now, steeling herself against the roar, she thought, He's going to drop a bomb on me and make it easy for himself.

The roar swooped over them and went away and left the air shuddering behind it. It faded and died and Kim listened for it to come back. She listened a long time. There was only the dry buzzing of insects in the heat. Once more the vultures were lowering squat bodies into the trees with a heavy flapping of wings.

Joaquín climbed in beside her. The look on his face was no longer the bland helpful look of someone giving directions to a bus station. "They were going to land. But even if they could bring her down safely they'd never be able to get up enough speed in this grass to get off the ground again."

He was facing her and there was nothing friendly or careless in his gaze; it was as hard and direct as his voice. "They were interested in this plane. It wasn't idle curiosity. Who are they?"

Kim was in the grip of panic. "Are they gone?"

"It looks that way."

"Is there anyplace they can land?"

"There's a pasture out back of that ranch outpost. That's about the closest place that's safe."

"How far is it?"

"Five or six miles through the jungle." He wasn't about to be put off; he wanted an answer to his question. "Who are they?" he repeated.

She clung to the hope that the plane was just somebody who happened to be flying over the jungle and had caught sight of her and come in for a closer look.

"Did you see them?" she asked.

"There were three men. The pilot had a preppy look, blond hair, crew cut, eyeglasses. You know him?"

Kim nodded. She was too confused to speak. Jolly had found her and it was her own fault. She had shown off by putting herself on course right in front of him and she had stuck to the course. She had known Jolly kept another plane in the hangar, but she hadn't considered the possibility of pursuit; all she had thought of was getting away. Now she saw it was obvious Kane wouldn't just let her go. He would have sent Jolly after her. The other two must be Jones and Dog. They had found her. She didn't know how—by luck or skill or cruel miracle. They had flown off, looking for a place to land. But they would be back.

"Who is he?" Joaquín said. "Is he a cop?"

"No, I told you."

"What are those handcuffs, then?"

"He was going to take me to Peru."

"What for?"

To sell me, Kim thought bitterly. She didn't want to answer questions. One question would lead to another. It was too painful, and she was desperately afraid.

"He'll find that pasture and come through the jungle. I've got to get off this plane."

"Rhodes is bringing an ax. We've got plenty of time. It'll take them hours to get through the jungle. Why are you so scared? What did you do? Kill somebody?"

She shook her head distractedly.

"What was he bringing you to Peru for? To put you in jail?"

"No. Not jail."

"Then what for? I want an answer."

He was acting as if she were a criminal, and that was what Kim felt like now. She had blamed herself years ago for allowing Jolly to catch her alone in the girls' gym, and the questions touched a raw nerve of guilt.

"You stole his plane," Joaquín said.

"It wasn't his. It belonged to the man he worked for."

"But you stole it," he kept on.

"I took it."

"You stole it."

"I didn't want his plane!" Kim cried. "It was the only

way I could get away! Look! I don't even know how to fly! I never flew a plane in my life! I did it with these!"

She grabbed up the loose book pages that had been scattered in the crash and thrust them at him.

The look of surprise on his face didn't make Kim feel any better. But at least for a moment the questions stopped.

Joaquín accepted the book pages dubiously. He needed both hands to hold them. He stared at the mess of pages and picked one out and saw it was a page from a book on how to fly a plane.

He had been curious about why the girl was handcuffed to the wheel. But he had been prepared to let the answers come out on their own, until the other plane had flown over. The other plane had reminded Joaquín how hard it was to get away from work, even all the way out here in the jungle.

She was probably a dope dealer's girlfriend, he thought. Like Nellie Ochoa, the girl who had jumped on his back the other night, beating him with her fists, screaming, "You bastard! You bastard!" Joaquín felt bad about Nellie. She was as much a victim of the drug scene as the kids whose lives were ruined by it. She was human and had a normal amount of corruptibility. It was the Nellie Ochoas who always got caught, while the guys who put heads in plastic garbage bags stayed free.

He examined another page. "Jesus," he said, "this is all you had?"

"Please," the girl said, "I don't want any questions. I just want to get to Caracas."

Lay off her, Joaquín told himself, seeing how upset she was. You come all the way down to Venezuela just to bust some dope dealer's girlfriend? What are you, some hot shot?

The question was Reuben's and it echoed in his mind. Hot shot? Hot shot? Joaquín saw a man in a white suit and dark glasses coming out of a Cuban restaurant and climbing into a white Cadillac and heading off down U.S. 1, like a phantom he was condemned to pursue for the rest of his life.

"All right, all right," he said with sudden annoyance, "no more questions."

He got out of the plane and walked off to watch for Rhodes.

10

KIM sat in the plane and stared at the wall of trees she had almost crashed into. Now that Joaquín had left her alone she missed his company. She realized she was acting distraught and mistrustful. She was having trouble regarding other people without suspicion. It was an instinctive response that had served her well in the world she had escaped from. Suspicion and mistrust had been reliable emotions in Kane's world.

After a while Joaquín glanced in and said, "Here comes our ax." He disappeared again. It took some time for Rhodes to travel the length of the field behind her. Kim knew he had finally arrived when she heard his voice.

"Who belonged to that other plane?"

"Friends of hers," Joaquín said.

"Coming to the rescue?"

"The other kind of friends. The kind you don't need any enemies to make up for."

"Cops," Rhodes said.

"She says not."

"She's lying. If they ain't cops, who are they?"

"They were going to take her to Peru. She didn't want to go. She took their plane."

They were standing outside the cabin talking about her like two surgeons discussing an anesthesized patient on an operating table, or like two professional movers wondering how best to get a heavy piece of furniture up the stairs.

"She says she never flew a plane before," Joaquín said. "She did it from a book."

"It don't strain my powers of belief any more than anything else I've heard. Where'd she come from?"

"She didn't say. She was trying to get to Guyana."

"She missed it," Rhodes said.

"She wants to go to Caracas. I figured one of the cowboys could bring her to the main ranch and she could get a plane ride from there. But now I don't know. . . . Those guys might've landed out back of the bunkhouse."

"Hell, Wok, there's your solution. Hand her over to the cops."

"It might be something else."

"If it is, I want to know what."

"She's upset. She doesn't want to talk."

"I bet she don't."

"Look, Ernie, we can't just leave her attached to the wheel. We'll take her back to camp with us and tomorrow I'll run down to the ranch and find out what it's all about."

"Why'd she have to go and pick this field?"

"It picked me!" Kim called from the cabin.

There was an abrupt silence—the piece of furniture had spoken.

"Reckon that settles that," Rhodes said. He looked in at her sourly. "Well, come on out of there then. I would hate to take your arm off."

Kim felt she had achieved a dubious recognition. She climbed out of the cabin and stood as far from the wheel as the links of the handcuffs would allow.

Rhodes leaned inside and took a chop. The blade went into the glossy black plastic of the wheel. With an effort he jiggled it out and chopped again. He began to chop steadily, sending up chips of plastic.

The ax slipped. "Watch out," he crabbed.

His back was to her. It made Kim feel shunned. Joaquín stood waiting beside her with his hands on his hips.

"I was looking forward to that jaguar," Rhodes said over his chopping. "If any more planes fly over they'll put up an international arrivals building and the son of a bitch'll be on the wall before we know it."

The ax broke through the wheel with a dull sound. Rhodes handed it back to Joaquín, handle first, as if it were a surgical knife or forceps. He leaned into the cabin and carefully disengaged the bracelet. When he turned he was holding it in the tips of his forefinger and thumb. He deposited the bracelet into Kim's hand.

"You'll have to hang on to that until you get to Caracas," he said, "or wherever the hell else you're heading."

The sun was going down and a shadow had moved out over the plane at one end of the field and the island of jungle in the middle, leaving a last corner of sunny marsh grass at the far end. It felt good after a day in the hot cramped cabin. Joaquín led the way through the heavy grass, Kim holding the silver twin of the handcuff around her wrist. They went along the side of the field past the island of jungle and entered the trees.

"Next time you'd be better off wearing long pants," Rhodes said, "unless you're planning to land on a tennis court."

The walk to camp was made mostly in silence. Getting her off the wheel had provided a semblance of familiarity. Now she was just walking with two strange men in the woods.

After a while she heard barking up ahead and they came out to a clearing on a riverbank. Kim had seen the river from the air, a trivial thread in the jungle. On the ground she saw it was big and broad and she had an immediate appreciation of how useful it would be, down here, to get you out of all these trees. The three dogs were jumping excitedly on their leash, and she noted two backpacks and two rolled hammocks as signs of a camp. Rhodes put the ax in one of the backpacks.

"I don't know about you all, but I'm going for a swim."

He stripped to his shorts and disappeared down the bank with a bar of soap. He reappeared, walking out to the end of a sandbar that extended through the shallows, dove in, and swam across.

Joaquín dug a shirt and belt out of a backpack. "Try this on. It should cover you."

Kim undressed in the trees. The shirt hung below her panties and the belt held it down. She came out to the top of the bank. The two men were swimming in their shorts, Joaquín with a long smooth stroke, Rhodes bludgeoning in the water like a paddle wheel. A dugout canoe with an outboard motor was pulled up below and she guessed it was this that would bring them to the village. The wide slow-moving surface of the river looked peaceful in the dusk.

She picked her way down the bank, walked to the end of the sandbar, and swam out. The three of them treaded water and made awkward comments about how refreshing the river felt after a hot day. Kim knew the awkwardness was mostly her fault. It was difficult for her to accept Joaquín and Rhodes for what they obviously were: two nice guys who were going to help her get home, even though she hadn't given them much incentive in the way of answers.

C'mon, she thought, give 'em a break. They're not monsters. You know that as well as you knew your father. Or Tommy Ryan. Or Archie Rice. It was Archie Rice who saved you. Archie taught you everything he knew—then he taught you how to fly a plane. Now these guys are going to save you, too.

But she was tired and depressed; she couldn't open up.

Joaquín and Rhodes reminded her of the boys she had swum with at the swimming hole her first summer in Foxhaven. It was like something she had to get back to, some state of normal girlhood where she could be herself and trust people again.

The two men got out to start supper. Kim washed herself with the soap and settled back against the sandbar in the shallows. Her right hand was clenched tightly and she realized she was still gripping the throttle, still flying the plane.

Relax, she thought. You got away. You did it.

But she didn't believe it. She was frightened about Jolly.

When she came up the bank the two men had dried off and were back in their clothes. Joaquín was placing some rocks together in a circle for a campfire. He pulled a towel from a backpack.

"I'm afraid we all have to use the same privy."

Rhodes, fitting together the pieces of a fly-fishing rod, gestured to the woods. "The great green privy," he said.

She emerged from the great green privy a while later into a smell of wood smoke and a crackling of burning branches. Joaquín was slicing potatoes and onions into a frying pan.

"Do you live in the village?" she asked him.

"No, I just come down to visit. I haven't lived there since I was a little boy. When my dad died I moved to Florida to live with my mother."

He looked very comfortable in his big shoulders. He didn't have the overdeveloped look of a muscle builder.

"Is there anything I can do to help?"

"It's all done, except for the important part. You better go check on our supper."

Rhodes was standing at the end of the sandbar casting the fly rod. Kim went down to him, thinking of the fishing trips she used to take with her father. Rhodes had the same, informal, effortless technique as her dad. She watched him stripping line easily with his free hand as he brought the rod forward, a cigarette dangling in his lips, one eye squinted against the smoke. In her old man's case it would be a pipe, stuffed with Barking Dog; when the luck was bad her old man would always say, "A barking dog never bites and neither do these fish, honey."

She walked out to Rhodes. He had caught two fish. They were gold with reddish fins and had tiny sharp teeth. The bass poppers had been left in their mouths, badly chewed up.

"What are they?"

"Dorados," Rhodes said. He had a hit and struck it. He swore and reeled in. "Look what that uppity little bugger did." The fish had bitten through the hook. "They're good eating but they do a right smart job on your hooks."

He pulled out a plastic pouch of red-and-white bass poppers, tied on another and went back to casting.

"One more, that'll give us two fillets apiece."

"Okay if I try?" Kim asked.

"You know how?"

"Sure."

Rhodes scowled reluctantly as if in anticipation of a bird's nest of fouled line. "With those handcuffs?" He didn't believe her but he handed over the rod.

Kim took the rod and lifted it in a casting motion. It was tricky using her free hand with the handcuff grasped in it. But she worked some line out, and as she brought the rod forward she used the same double-hauling maneuver Rhodes had to send the bass popper sailing straight toward the deep

water. There was a splash as a fish went for the popper and
she struck it and had one on.

"Where did you learn how to do that?" Rhodes asked,
impressed, as she reeled the fish in.

"My old man taught me. He used to take me fishing."

Kim thought of telling him about her father. But she didn't
even know if her dad was dead or alive. It seemed too much
to say.

Rhodes gutted and cleaned the fish and cut six fillets.
Joaquín rolled them in mandioca flour, and when Kim asked
again if there was anything she could do he said, "Go feed
the dogs."

In one of the backpacks she found a plastic bag contain-
ing pieces of dried beef. The dogs began to leap eagerly
when they saw her coming. They swarmed about her. She
took out a piece of beef and a dog snatched it from her hand
with a soggy slap of jaws. Kim laughed.

"Hold on, not so fast."

She backed away and began to play a game, tossing the
pieces of beef. The dogs were like shortstops making amazing acrobatic leaps for line drives, catching the pieces with
a funny slapping of their mouths.

All at once Kim stopped. She had been hearing the sound
of her laughter. It was a sign of the girl she had once been;
it had come out spontaneously and much sooner than she
had believed possible a short while ago in the river.

Christ, she thought, when was the last time you laughed
like this?

And for an answer traveled all the way back to a baseball
field in the spring.

They had supper around the campfire, Joaquín eating out
of the frying pan with his fingers, as there were only two tin
plates and two forks to go around. Kim began to feel human
with some grub in her stomach, washed down by one of the
beers kept cold in the river. Rhodes talked about the game
he had hunted and cooked as a boy. If a rabbit smelled strong
you soaked it in vinegar and water overnight to draw out the
blood and make the meat whiter. A young squirrel could be
put on a stick and roasted right over a fire, but an old one
improved if you hung it up by the neck with the skin still

on for a day. Opossum was good with sweet potatoes. . . .
Rhodes went on in his Southern drawl, a backwoods gour-
met, until Kim almost knocked over his beer can with her
handcuff.

"Sorry," she said, "these things are a real nuisance."

"Who knows, you keep wearing 'em maybe they'll become the latest fashion . . . and nobody will ask any questions."

There was a silence. Rhodes was scraping up the last of
his onions and potatoes. He spoke to his plate.

"What beats the dogshit out of me, Wok, is we didn't
even look in the plane. You didn't, did you, when I went to
get the ax?"

"No," Joaquín said.

"Why not?"

"I'm on vacation."

"That's a pisspoor excuse. There could be anything under the seats or in the tail section."

"You're right, we should have looked."

"Hell, it's our job."

"What's your job?" Kim asked.

"We're narcs," Joaquín said.

He looked at her, as if expecting a visible reaction. She
felt like hiding the handcuffs behind her back.

"I mean, shit," Rhodes said. "We know those cops are
after her."

"They're not cops," Kim said.

"But if they are," Joaquín said, "they're going to get you.
It's their job. If they don't get you here, they'll get you in
Caracas."

He was offering friendly advice. Kim had the feeling he
had made up his mind about her.

"It doesn't matter what you did. Sometimes it's a matter
of being in the wrong place at the wrong time."

Kim knew all about being in the wrong place at the wrong
time. But this man was going to tell her anyway.

"It's like the dope dealer's girlfriend. She's in it for the
fun. Guy buys her expensive clothes, pays the rent on her
apartment. It's a good deal . . . until one day he brings ten
kilos up to her place and he's cutting the stuff on her kitchen
table when we bust in."

Joaquín dug into a backpack as if to give her time to think it over. He turned back with a can of fruit.

"Dessert, anyone?"

"No thanks," Rhodes said. He rose. "We all do our own dishes," he told Kim grouchily and walked away from the fire.

Kim saw his silhouetted figure disappear down the bank and reappear on the sandbar, squatting in the posture of a man scrubbing a plate. Joaquín scooped out some sliced pears for her and she ate them with difficulty. She felt he was watching her and waiting for answers to questions he had decided not to ask. She almost wished he would ask them now instead of leaving it up to her.

He's got your number, she thought. You're the dope dealer's girlfriend. Kane's crazy white bitch. You lived on his crummy estate and he screwed you whenever he wanted. You took him for whatever you could get. But it's not the truth. So tell him. Tell him how Kane had you kidnapped. Tell him how you fought him. Tell him how you never once stopped thinking of getting away. It wasn't your fault. They won't hold it against you. They'll just sort of move away, like you're a rare disease. Go ahead and tell them.

But the words stuck in her throat. She didn't want to risk being regarded as a rare disease.

"More pears?"

"No thanks."

"Sure?"

"Yes."

"In that case, since Ernie has sworn off desserts . . ." Joaquín helped himself to the rest of the pears as if they were all he was thinking about.

The silhouetted figure came up the bank, traveled through darkness, and entered the firelight, acquiring the specific detailed features of Rhodes, still scowling. He knelt and stuffed his plate and utensils into a backpack; he rose, and for a moment Kim thought he was about to grill her anyway.

"Who gets her?"

"Oh right," Joaquín said. "What are we going to do about that?"

"You and me can't fit in one hammock. She's going to have to sleep with one of us."

Kim had the same feeling she had had earlier of being a

piece of furniture who had no say in her disposition.

"What d'you say?" Joaquín asked her.

"You don't have a choice," Rhodes put in.

"I can sleep on the ground," Kim said. "All I need is a blanket and I'll be fine."

"The mosquitoes will kill you," Joaquín said. "That's what the netting is for. And they're not all you have to worry about. The fire ants will eat the starch from your clothes."

Rhodes flipped a quarter and clapped it on the back of his hand. "Call it."

"Heads."

He looked under his cupped palm and said, "Tough luck, old buddy. I got the ax. You got the girl."

He wandered off and began to let down his mosquito netting.

"I could sleep in the canoe," Kim said, "and put a blanket over my head."

"You underestimate those mosquitoes. They'll drive you into the river. You'll duck underwater to get away from them and the minute you come up there'll be a cloud of them around your head. Take my word. . . ."

He wasn't happy. He had lost the toss.

"What the hell." He shrugged. "In the village a wife usually strings her hammock under her husband's. But if the need arises they share. It can't be too bad."

When Kim came back up the bank a while later the camp was pitch black except for the embers of the fire and a circle of light inside Rhodes's mosquito netting. Rhodes was reading a paperback book by penlight. Kim put away the toothbrush that Joaquín had lent her and he handed her a sweater and a pair of pants.

"Put these on. It gets cold at night. I've got a blanket for us, too."

He was being practical and impersonal. Kim had already worn one of his shirts in the river. She wasn't small, but on her the shirt had been like a bathrobe. She put on the sweater and pants. She had to roll up the sleeves and cuffs and cinch his belt around her waist, as tight as it would go, before she felt reasonably intact.

"Here's our blanket and here," he handed her another of his shirts, "is your pillow."

He lifted the mosquito netting for her and Kim climbed

into the hammock. She had a moment to appreciate its surprising roominess and to feel with her hand what she had barely noticed before—that it wasn't made of cloth but of strands of something, held together in a sturdy web by knotted threads. Then Joaquín climbed in beside her and she rolled against him as the hammock sagged heavily.

He hesitated as if expecting a crash. After a second he said, "It seems to be holding up okay," and settled back.

They were facing each other, stretched out in the sagging cocoon. Joaquín had become the center of gravity. It would have been natural for Kim to lay her head on his shoulder and let him put his arms around her, just for friendship and comfort. But she didn't feel natural.

"Let's see now, what's the best way to do this?" He turned on his side with his back to her. "How's that?"

"Fine," she said. She turned away from him and clung tightly to the strands to keep from weighing on his back, the shirt bunched into a ball under her head.

In the glow from Rhodes's penlight she saw the trees of the jungle in front of her. Then from across the way Rhodes called, " 'night." The glow vanished and darkness crashed around them with a noisy sonorous croaking of frogs along the river.

They lay together in the hammock and all the unasked and unanswered questions lay between them, signified by the formality of their two opposed backs. Kim stared out through the gauzy enclosure of mosquito netting at the black shapes of the trees. She had got out of Carib and she had been gotten out of the plane: two well-defined prisons. Now, presumably free, she had become as hesitant as a little girl venturing onto a frozen pond, listening for the telltale wheeze and crackle of ice that could no longer bear her weight.

She had a vision of Jolly, somewhere out in the darkness. At the ranch? At the plane? Lost in the jungle? It seemed impossible that he could ever find her. But she didn't think he would just give up and go away.

Thinking of Jolly, she decided that he would be a good starting point for what she had begun to regard as her full confession, a first risky step out onto the ice.

"Jolly dyes his hair," she said.

"Who?"

"Jolly. The man who was flying the plane. The one with the blond crew cut. It's not really blond. He dyes it."

"I see."

"He has a gun. He put it on to take me to Peru. He wears it in a shoulder holster. The other two always carry guns."

"I wouldn't worry. Nobody is walking around in the jungle at night. Anyway the dogs will let us know if anyone comes near."

Reassurance. But Kim didn't want reassurance now. She wanted questions. Ask me, she thought. Anything you want. Ask me who Jolly works for. Or how I first met him. Or why he was taking me to Peru. I'll tell you. Only I need help. You've got to pry it loose to make it easier.

But she had told him she didn't want to answer questions and Joaquín was taking her at her word.

In the absence of questions she fished for reassurance. "Sorry I loused up your hunt," she said.

"Don't be silly," Joaquín said. "I'm glad we could get you out of that plane."

Kim was still clinging to the side of the hammock. In Kane's world it didn't pay to trust anyone. That had been the ultimate effect of his cruelty. She knew that sooner or later she would have to prove to herself that the effect was temporary. So go ahead, she thought. Start with this guy. Show him you can at least trust him enough to accept the comfort of his back.

She took another step out onto the ice, letting go of the hammock's webbing and settling against Joaquín's back. Joaquín accepted her weight without comment. His back was there to be used.

" 'Night," Kim said.

After a moment, half asleep, Joaquín said, "Good night."

11

THE father and son had worked all morning repairing barbed-wire fence in a tiny pasture some distance from the bunkhouse. It was necessary to keep the fence in good condition so that cattle wouldn't wander off and get lost in the jungle. There were places where it had been knocked down or where the fence posts had been broken, and the father and son repaired them all, working up a good sweat and a good appetite, and then headed home along the old ox-cart trail.

They were almost home when they saw a plane coming out of the sky over the jungle.

The plane circled the field out back behind the bunkhouse and came in for a landing. The father and son urged their horses into a fast walk, and as they reached the field the plane was taxiing to a halt at one end. Three men got out and the father watched them come toward him and his son.

The one who had flown the plane had hair that was cut so short it stood up like the bristles on a peccary, and you could see his naked sunburned scalp under it. He wore eyeglasses, a T-shirt with a picture on the front, and a necktie around his bare neck. Of the other two, one was a big black man. The other was short, an Indian, like the father and son. But the Indians of the father and son's village had friendly smiles. This one had a fat face that squeezed his eyes almost shut and his thick lips were set in a straight unsmiling line. All the men wore guns.

"Hello, amigos," the one with the bristly hair said in

Spanish. "We had a little engine trouble and had to land in your field. I don't even know where we are."

"You're on the Hernandez ranch," the son spoke up happily. He was excited by the arrival of strangers and proud to show off his knowledge.

"This doesn't look like much of a ranch . . . that little shack."

"It's only an outpost. The main ranch is way over that way." The boy gestured toward the mountains. "My girl is the cook at the big house. It takes me two or three days just to visit her."

"I see," the bristly one said. "You get hungry, so you go to get something to eat from the cook."

The father didn't like the way the man said this, as if his son's innocent and natural visits were something dirty. He wondered why the three men were carrying guns.

"Are you hunters?" he asked.

"Hunters?" The bristly one was surprised. He spoke to the other two in English, laughing. Then in Spanish he said, "That's right. We're hunters. What is there to hunt around this place? Termites?"

"Oh no," the father's son said. "You'll find plenty of game in those woods. If you want I'll show you."

"Go get lunch ready," the father said.

His son was talking too much. The father didn't think these men were hunters. He didn't know what they were.

"You are welcome to have lunch with us," he told the bristly one as his son went off. "I'm sorry I can't help you with your plane. If it was a horse I could probably fix it."

The bristly one laughed loudly, as if the father had told a marvelous joke. The son had warmed up some beef and rice, and they all sat down on logs around the fire.

"So there are just the three of you," the bristly one said, "staying out here."

"Three of us? No, there are only my father and me," the son said.

"Who was the man we saw when we flew over that field over there?" He gestured toward the dry marsh miles away across the jungle.

"Oh that," the son said. "That must be Joaquín. He came up here from our village with another man to hunt a jaguar."

"He's just another Indian then," the bristly one said.

"That's right," the father said. "He's just another Indian."

He didn't like this man who had too many questions, nor the other two, who had none but just sat eating sullenly with their guns on, the big black man shoveling food into his mouth, the short fat Indian curling his lips in disgust, as if the rice and beef were scraps meant for a dog.

"How far is your village?"

"Two days on the river."

"And these two jaguar hunters, where are they camped?"

"Probably upriver near where you saw them." The boy was chattering away, full of information.

"Could you take us there?" the man with the bristly blond hair asked. "My friends and I have never seen a jaguar."

"Sure I can take you."

"No you can't," the father said.

"Why not? I don't mind. I'll take them this afternoon."

The father gave his son a hard look. "You have work to do. Get these plates and wash them. Bring us a can of peaches. Do as I say."

The boy got up and collected the plates from the three men. The black man pulled out a handkerchief, wiped his mouth with it bunched in a ball, and stuffed it back in his pocket. He found a book of matches and began to pick his teeth with the corner. The Indian sat as stiffly as if he were part of the log the three men were sitting on. The father felt bad about speaking sharply to his son, who was just being open and friendly. But he had begun to fear these men.

He was not a talker. But now he faced the bristly one and said, "My son cannot take you. He has work to do. We are both very busy. As you see, there are only two of us and there is a lot of work for two people. Anyway, you should set out for the main ranch as soon as possible. I can give you horses and all you have to do is follow the trail. I will also give you hammocks and cans of food. Just leave the horses and the hammocks with the foreman at the ranch. He'll fly you back here and fix your plane."

"Fix my plane!" the bristly one exclaimed, grinning. "It doesn't need to be fixed."

"I thought you said it had engine trouble and you had to land."

"No, no, you must have misunderstood me. My Spanish isn't so good."

"It seems very good to me."

"I take that as a compliment," the man said. "Now these two here, they're so stupid I don't know why I travel with them. They can't speak a word of Spanish." And as if to prove it, he began to speak English to the other two.

The father sat listening to him. He didn't understand what the man was saying but the foreign words frightened him. The man turned back to the father, laughing.

"I was telling them how you thought our plane broke down. That's not why we landed. And we didn't come for your stinking beef and rice or canned peaches. We came because we want somebody to take us to where those jaguar hunters are camped. And if you don't help us my friends are going to be very angry."

The black man and the Indian got up and came over to the father and grabbed him. "Hey, what are you doing!" the father shouted.

He was afraid for his son. He hoped his son would hear him shout and run to the corral and get a horse and ride away as fast as he could to get Joaquín and tell him what was happening.

"I don't know where those hunters are! They could be anywhere along the river. Just go there and look for yourselves!"

The black man had the father around the neck and the other one was punching him in the face. The son came running out of the bunkhouse. He had his old shotgun.

"Let go of my father! Let him go!"

The bristly haired man threw up his hands as if terrifically frightened. "Hey watch out! Don't shoot!"

The boy stood holding the shotgun on him and trembling. "You tell them to let go of my father!"

"Sure, sure, just don't pull that trigger. You could kill somebody."

As the two men released the father, the bristly one lunged and grabbed the barrel of the shotgun and swung it away. The boy pulled the trigger. But there was only the dry click of the hammer.

"Hey!" the bristly one exclaimed, surprised and happy.

"It's not even loaded!" He jerked the shotgun away from the boy. "You've got a lot of guts running out here with a shotgun that's not loaded. These guys could've killed you both."

"It's loaded," the boy said sheepishly. "But sometimes the pin doesn't work. I wasn't really going to shoot you. I just didn't want you to hurt my father."

"Sure, I understand, no problem."

The bristly one was being friendly and forgiving. The father stood, shaken and angry. But he saw now that he and his son would never be able to fight these three men.

"Look," he said, "if you want us to help you find those men we will be happy to, as soon as we finish our work."

"Forget it," the bristly one said. "We can find them ourselves. As you say, they've got to be somewhere along the river. I'm sorry we had this trouble."

"Well then," the father said, "why don't we all sit down and have some peaches."

The bristly one laughed. "Sure, why not?" Then he exclaimed, "Say, look at this!" He had broken the shotgun open and removed the shell. "It's not the pin's fault. The pin works okay. See the little dent." He showed the boy. "This shell must've been lying around for a hundred years. Have you got another?"

The boy produced his other shell apologetically. "It's my last one. It's pretty old, too. It probably won't fire either."

"Well, let's take a look," the bristly one said.

He dropped the shell into the chamber. As he closed the shotgun he swung it toward the boy and pulled the trigger. The blast tore half the boy's face off.

With a howl the father flung himself on the man. The other two grabbed him, but he fought insanely. He wanted only to kill them. They pinned his arms until he was like a helpless, writhing bundle of hatred. They dragged him to the fire and pushed his face into the soft bed of ashes. The father saw the fiery glow of the embers beneath. He felt the searing pain of the hot coals on his face. Then something hard crashed into the back of his head and the pain was gone.

"Don't come back without her!" Kane had shouted. He had grabbed Jolly and shook him. Jolly, in agony, had felt understandably abused. It wasn't his fault the girl had got away. He wasn't the one who had let her have a book on how to fly a plane. He had done all he could to stop her, hanging on to the wing like that.

The plane, rising, had created a sudden frightening distance through which Jolly dropped with horror. As he landed, his legs buckled and his knees smashed into the runway. Rolling on the tarmac in excruciating pain, Jolly had a distinct impression of his skeleton—leg bones that had been rammed up into his pelvis, kneecaps torn from their pitiful beds of muscles and tendons, and a swelling lump where his forehead had once been smooth. It was this agonized and fleshless skeletal arrangement that seemed to pick itself up and hobble tenderly in fits and starts before Kane.

Kane was just a voice to him, though a voice that could apparently exert a furious grip on the skeleton's bony arm. For Jolly had lost his eyeglasses, and without his eyeglasses Jolly might as well have been knee-deep in fog. Kane's voice kept shouting at him, and Jolly heard his own voice protesting weakly. But his real concern was finding those glasses and restoring the world to his eyes.

The toe of his jogging shoe came into contact with them, and as he seized the glasses and lifted them to his eyes, there was the plane, climbing away toward a big white cloud.

The plane entered the cloud. When it emerged it was making a shaky turn toward the south. It came out of the turn and began to climb again.

"Jesus, she's still in the air!"

Only then did he turn to the voice. He was about to say, "What the hell do you care? You were gonna get rid of her anyway." But Kane wasn't just a voice anymore. Jolly saw the look on his face.

"Okay, okay, for crissake," he said, his own face twisted with pain, "leave me alone." He doubled over, grasping his legs, and discovered two circles of blood like Japanese suns spreading on the knees of his white painter paints. "Look what the bitch did to me. Of course I'm going to get her."

Jolly didn't really think he had a chance of getting the girl. He was just trying to pacify Kane. He straightened up and attempted a step, gesturing at Jones.

"I'll need him . . . and Dog."

"How you gonna find that girl?" Jones said irritably.

"You could look over the whole Atlantic Ocean and South America and never find her."

"I'll find her, I saw where she went."

"In a tiny little plane you saw her. But do you see her now?"

"That don't matter. I know where she is better than she does."

"You're crazy," Jones said.

"Go with him," Kane ordered. "Get Dog and go with him. Take Jolly's car."

Jones glared. The deep creases slanting downward on either side of his broad flat nose looked like the chiseled grooves in an African woodcarving.

"How long we going to be gone for? A year?"

"As long as it takes," Jolly said.

He tossed his car keys to Jones and watched the big man listing ponderously away. The car started with a clanky roar and Jones took off to find Dog on his rounds, leaving Jolly alone with Kane.

Kane, having legitimized Jolly's authority, became now the beneficiary of Jolly's reassurance.

"Girl don't know what she's doing. She turned south, but she'll drift west in this wind. You know what she's gonna be flying over?"

Kane was too angry to humor hypothetical questions.

"Jungle!" Jolly exclaimed. "That's all there is down there. So what if she crashes and kills herself in the jungle? You want her even then?"

"I want the bitch back," Kane said, and then he, too, was gone, in the car he had taken from the bodyguard.

Jolly limped up to his room over the hangar. He took off his pants, peeling the soaked fabric from his bloody knees. The bleeding had stopped. He cleaned the blood off with a damp washcloth. He got a Carib beer and a packet of cocaine from his refrigerator, cracked the beer, and cut two lines, which he drew into his nostrils with a pound note.

He sat back in his jock strap with his bruised knees and hairy legs apart, gazing out the screened window over the runway, waiting for Jones and Dog. That big nigger was pissed, he thought. See, what they forget is that even though I don't see Kane every day I'm the one he always comes running to. I don't want to see Kane. He's a pain in the ass.

Jolly poured the local beer down his throat as if to toast his dismissal of Kane, the boss who had given him all he wanted: two planes in the hangar below, a workshop where he could tinker with bombs, and a basketball net. This was Jolly's own world, where Kane left him alone and allowed him to think of himself as he often did as "Numma One." It irked Jolly that Kane didn't always treat him like "Numma One," grabbing him and shouting at him in front of that big spook, for instance. So now he thought, I don't need him. He needs me. Who flies his goddamn planes? Who goes to Peru? Who went and found him a little smartass bitch when he asked me to, and look what she's done now. He better watch out. One of these days he's gonna find himself with no place to hide except his own asshole, and I won't be around to help him.

Outside there was a clanking of Jolly's car as it bumped out of the jungle on nonexistent shocks and pulled up to the runway. Jones and Dog got out. Jolly watched them coming over in the glare, their stupidity emphasized in his mind by surly expressions and the ridiculous difference in their sizes and shapes. He waited until they had reached the hangar. Without leaning forward, he called out, "Bring the car around back. I don't want her sitting there all week." It amused him to know he couldn't be seen behind the window screen but was only an invisible voice giving a command. He watched Jones going back to the car. He laughed, making a gleeful hissing through his teeth. Turkey, he thought.

The beer and coke had pulled Jolly together and he thought clearly now. The girl wasn't that far ahead. He would put himself on her course and follow after her. It didn't make much difference if he found her or not. She would crash and kill herself, anyway. But he better be ready, just in case. No use sitting around and waiting. Waiting had been the worst part of Vietnam. Jolly had always looked forward to going out to pick up grunts in the LZ, flying close over the tree-tops at the risk of enemy fire.

Jones moved the car and came back, and Jolly drank his beer as the two men waited below. In the muggy heat his apartment smelled of cockroach killer and a mildewed odor that had escaped from his refrigerator when he had opened

it. He finished the beer, crumpled the can, and belched. He
got up, put on a clean pair of white pants, and went down.

Jones and Dog were in the hangar with the other plane.
"What the hell you bozos doing, standing with your thumbs
up your ass," Jolly said. "Push this plane out."

"You push it out," Jones said.

"I'm busy."

Jolly crossed the hangar to his workshop. Every morning
a woman came to his rooms upstairs to make his bed and
take out his dirty clothes. But nobody was allowed in his
workshop. Jolly unlocked the door and pulled a string to turn
on a light bulb in the ceiling. The room was made of cinder
blocks. It was dark and cool and had the dingy, cluttered
look of a toolshed. A sack of weed killer leaning against the
wall added to the impression. The weed killer was sodium
chlorate, and when mixed with sugar it became a powerful
explosive.

On his workbench were a pile of ordinary child's building blocks, bunches of red circuit wire, and a clutter of flashlight batteries, detonators, and wristwatches. He put some
of these in a canvas bag, tossed in sticks of plastic explosive
from a crate under the bench, and got a pair of field glasses,
a hypodermic syringe, and a bottle of the drug he adminis-
tered with it from the large cabinet where he kept his guns.

Outside Jones and Dog had pushed the plane onto the
runway, one on each wing. "We going or ain't we?" Jones
said. "That bitch be in South America before we get started."

"You let me worry about her. Here," Jolly thrust the canvas bag at him, "sit in back."

"Back, hell. Dog can sit in back. He's the short one."

"You're too big. I can't see past you."

"Shit," Jones said.

Jolly let them wait in the small cramped cabin as he took
his time fueling the plane and checking it out. Finally he
got in. He was about to start the engine. "Hold on, I forgot
something."

"What is it now?" Jones said.

"Say, wait a minute," Jolly said. "Are you flying this plane
or am I?"

"Go get what you forgot," Jones grumbled.

Jolly got out and went upstairs to his rooms. When he
came back down he was wearing a necktie.

* * *

Out back of the bunkhouse now, Dog was kicking the body of the man he had just shot in the head, who lay face-down in the ashes of the fire.

"What the hell you kicking him for?" Jones said. "He don't feel a thing."

But Dog was still in the grip of the violence of their struggle with the man. Unlike Jones, in his heat-wilted seer-sucker jacket, Dog took some care with his appearance. His shiny black hair was combed sleekly back, like elegant plumage. His squat body was clothed in a tan safari jacket and tan slacks, and on his feet he wore fancy brown boots. He gave a final kick and paused as if expecting the dead man to raise his head. But the dead man didn't move.

As Dog came away he glanced at the man's son, who lay sprawled with his arms out and his face a bloody mess.

"You gonna kick him, too?" Jones said.

Dog lifted a side of his safari jacket to return his gun to its holster. He flicked a silver lighter and lit a cigarette.

"Pissed me off," he said. "Tried to bite me."

"What you expect him to do after Jolly kill his son like that? Blow you a kiss?"

Dog, a man of few words, blew smoke in reply.

"Okay, boys," Jolly said. "Let's not be catty. We got school."

He was sitting on a log. He pulled a charred stick from the fire and drew a squiggly line in the dirt.

"River," he said. "Got that?"

The two men stood looking down sullenly. Jolly made three jabs with the stick.

"This is us. Those hunters must be somewhere along the river, and the girl came down . . . about here."

"It would have been easier to find her if Dog hadn't shot that old man," Jones said. "I was trying to get him to talk."

"Dog was right. The old man was playing games. He would have got us off in the woods and lost us."

Jolly rose, and turning, pointed his stick beyond the bunkhouse.

"That dry marsh is over that way straight through the jungle. If you hurry you can reach it before dark and the girl might still be in the plane."

"Who you mean, hurry?" Jones said.

"You and Dog."

"Jolly, you're too bold. That girl be your business. You go look for her."

"Somebody has to stay here. Those hunters might show up with her."

Jones sat down on another of the logs, shaking his head in stubborn refusal. "You must think I'm stupid to come all this way because you let that bitch escape, and now you're telling me to go off into the jungle."

Dog was practical and indifferent. "What if she's not in the plane?"

"You'll have to spend the night there," Jolly said. "It'll be too dark to go looking for her. But as soon as it's light go to the river and try to find where those hunters are camped. She'll be with them, if they don't bring her here first."

"C'mon, let's go," Dog said to Jones.

Jones sat mopping his big ugly face with a handkerchief, as if he intended to spend the rest of his life sitting on the log. But at last he rose.

"Shit," he said. "This be one I owe you, Jolly."

Jolly watched him lumbering after Dog toward the jungle. Then he sat on the ground with his back against the log and his face lifted to the sun, thinking how the day had begun so simply and then become suddenly complicated and interesting.

Jolly felt himself to be charmed. Did he need any more proof than that he had found the girl? He had followed the girl's southerly course without correcting for the westward drift. But he hadn't had much faith. He had been ready to turn back when he spotted the red plane—easy to see in a field of yellow marsh grass. It was more than luck. It was a sign of destiny. Jones had wanted to drop a bomb. But Jolly had said, "What part of the bitch do you want to bring back to Kane? An arm or a leg?"

The only thing that bothered him was the man they had seen when he had swooped low over the field.

Now he drew a triangle in his mind. The imaginary lines went from where he was sitting, to the plane, to the camp of the hunters, and back to himself. Jolly thought of it as an enchanted region in which he was all-powerful. A sudden thought disturbed him and he sat forward. He picked up his stick and made a jab beside the squiggly line representing the river. The Indian village. That's the only other place they could go. He didn't want to forget that.

He settled against the log again, sunning himself, one of three motionless bodies out back of the bunkhouse, one with his face buried in a pile of ashes, another with barely any face at all. Through squinted eyes Jolly watched the vultures overhead. Wheeling round and round in a ceaseless circle, they were like a whirlpool, drawing him down, downward into the sky.

"You Numma One," Jolly said.

12

JOAQUÍN woke with the girl's head on his shoulder. Sleep and the hammock had brought them comfortably and unselfconsciously together. Above the black trees he saw a patch of dark sky with some stars in it. But the frogs and insects had grown quiet and the sky would soon begin to lighten. In a while he would get up and make a fire and go down to the river and get some water to boil for coffee. The girl was sleeping soundly with one arm flung across him. There was a pair of handcuffs on her wrist.

What the hell, he thought, she probably is mixed up in something. The cops were bringing her back to face charges and she grabbed their plane.

So why are you helping her? Because you found her. It's your tough luck. What were you going to do, leave her handcuffed to that wheel?

She says she never flew a plane before. You believe it? She tore some pages from a book. Got it up in the air. Got it down. Must have been desperate. But anybody who thought that desperation was all it took was a fool.

Joaquín thought of the time he had first gone undercover to make drug buys. There was a truck driver named Orville, a shambling, bear of a man who had taken a liking to him, had him over to supper, treated him like one of the family. Orville sold amphetamines and bennies to his fellow truck drivers to help keep them awake on long trips, and Joaquín remembered how, on the day he arrested Orville, a red-haired freckle-faced kid had come running out of the house and begun to hit him with a red plastic baseball bat—"You can't arrest my pa! Git outta here! Go on, git!"

This girl reminded him more of that wiry courageous kid than of a dope dealer's girlfriend.

Rhodes had wanted to grill her last night. So why didn't you grill her?

Because you didn't want to be lied to, he thought.

Besides, maybe she's telling the truth. She didn't act like somebody trying to con him. It was more like she didn't want to talk about it because it hurt too much.

He thought of the plane that had flown over them. It had come in too low to be shrugged off as an indifferent presence, and the look on the girl's face hadn't been a phony act. She was scared.

So what if they're not cops? It's hard to believe. But what if they're not?

Joaquín removed his arm carefully from under the girl's head and steadied the hammock as he got out. The girl lay curled up, asleep. He put on his sneakers and took his bow and crossed to the other hammock. Rhodes stirred. He flicked on his penlight and shined it at Joaquín.

"What," he said. His voice was alert and fully awake.

"I was thinking about those men."

"The cops."

"Yeah, we're going to have to check it out. She told me they're armed."

"I would be, too, if I was going after a fugitive that stole my plane." Rhodes lifted his mosquito netting and found his sneakers. He shook them out, as Joaquín had his, to make sure no little creatures were in them. He put them on, yawned, and scratched himself. "Go on."

"I thought I'd take a look, see if they're at the plane. Maybe have a talk with them."

"Good idea."

"If they're at the ranch they'll probably come through the jungle, maybe get the father or son to show them the way. But they might decide to come up along the river."

"I see, you want me to take a walk."

"You better take your bow just in case," Joaquín said. "Give me your light. I'll need it to get through the jungle. You'll have plenty of light along the river."

Rhodes handed him the penlight. "What about her? Will
she be all right?"

"The dogs will bark if anyone comes near."

The three dogs were waiting expectantly, tied to a tree
at the edge of the clearing. Joaquín patted each one as
he left.

"Sorry, boys, you'll have to stay."

He went off through the woods with the penlight showing the way. After a while he flicked it off and saw the night
was gone. The trunks of the trees and details of branches
and leaves had begun to emerge. He went on without the
light. It was easier with the whole jungle before him, even
as a charcoal blur, rather than simply what could be con-
tained in the circle of light.

He came to a fallen tree, stepped over it, cut through a
last stand of trees and came out in a corner at one end of the
dry marsh.

A mist hung over the field and everything was gray and
featureless. He could make out the island of jungle off in
the middle. The plane at the other end, half a mile away,
was impossible to see. Joaquín went along the side of the
field cautiously. He missed his dogs now, afraid of running
into the jaguar on its way back from its nightly hunt. But the
dogs would have defeated his purpose of an inconspicuous
look around.

He passed the island of jungle, a black shape dissolving into the grayness around it, and thought of the jaguar
lying stretched out on the branch of a tree, as the boy had
seen him.

The black winged shape in the tall grass at the other end
of the field came into view. He stopped and stared toward
it. In the grayness there was no color. The plane seemed
even more of a mystery to him than when he had seen it
yesterday, bright red in sunlight.

He saw no one. Either the men had come and already
left, which was unlikely, or they would come later today—
or they would never come; maybe they weren't as interested
in the girl as she thought.

And what if they were cops? What would he do then?

Turn her over, Joaquín thought.

As he cut across the field his pant legs became immediately soaked with dew. He wanted to search the plane in case he had overlooked anything yesterday. But more than that he wanted to retrieve something he already knew was there: the pages that had been torn from the flying guide. Joaquín wanted to see those pages again. He wanted to hold them in his hands and make sure they were real—read the underlined sentences and the scrawled notes in the margins.

Then he would stuff them in his pocket and bring them back to camp as proof that the girl had at least told him the truth about one thing.

He was advancing when a dark figure jumped out of the black shape of the plane and gave a shout of unmistakable threat. Joaquín stopped. The cops made it, he thought, and he realized he was disappointed.

They must have come through the jungle and spent the night in the plane, and now he was bound by professional obligation to turn the girl over to them in spite of his feeling that any girl who could learn how to fly a plane from a book deserved any number of second chances.

The dark figure came charging clumsily through the high grass, and Joaquín had a moment to consider the exchange that would occur between them, a friendly chat between equals. Yes, he knew where the girl was. What had she done? Was she a drug dealer's girlfriend? Then the man was before him, no longer a dark figure in the gray light, but a short fat Indian, waving a .38 revolver with unprofessional agitation. Joaquín threw up his hands.

"Where's the girl?" the man shouted.

"What girl?" The situation no longer seemed so simple.

"I'll kill you!" The man thrust his gun as if to fire.

"Hey, wait a minute! Don't shoot! I'm just out hunting! Look," Joaquín showed his bow, "this is all I got!"

"Throw it down!"

Joaquín tossed the bow away in alarm. He didn't think the man would hesitate to shoot him and he was sure the man wasn't a cop. The plane was quiet, and he guessed the other two men had left the Indian to guard it alone. He tried to play dumb.

"Is that your plane? I thought you might need help."

"You stinking shit! We saw you with the girl when we flew over yesterday! Where is she?"

"Oh you mean her?" Joaquín said, as if the girl were of no importance to him or anyone else, certainly nothing to argue with a gun about. "Sure I know where she is. You want me to show you?"

He saw how little his life meant to this man whose face was a contemptuous mask of slit eyes and thick lips, puffy from a bad night's sleep in a tiny cockpit. The man would rather shoot him and be done with him than listen to a story. Desperately Joaquín gestured with one raised arm toward the island of jungle at his back.

"She's over there. In that little jungle. That's where we spent the night."

"Pig's ass," the thick lips said, "them cowboys at the ranch told us you was camped on the river."

"What do those cowboys know? I'll take you to her."

The fat face considered him suspiciously. Joaquín thought of a blowfish's distended, spiky belly. The slit eyes seemed to be calculating whether to dispatch him now or later. Into them came a dim appreciation of the fact that a gunshot would be heard by the girl, if she was near.

"Go on, take me to her," the man said. "And keep your mouth shut."

He jerked his gun at Joaquín and they started off through the heavy grass.

It was a quarter of a mile to the island of jungle. Joaquín was glad for the walk, regarding it as an extension of a life that was as good as over. He dismissed the idea of making a break for it. The man would have the whole field to blast away at him in.

"Slow down," the man said. "You're walking too fast."

The mist was gone and the sky had begun to lighten. At a distance the island of jungle had been a vague, dark shape. Now, drawing near, Joaquín made out stands of bamboo around the outside, and as they came up to it and entered there were large trunks of trees surrounded by tangled undergrowth.

In the trees the light was cut off, and it was almost dark again. But Joaquín saw at once what he was looking for. The cat was stretched out on the branch of a big tree, back for the day after a night of roaming the fringe of jungle along the grazing lands.

The cat saw him, too. It lifted its head and watched the two men coming through the trees. In the dark it looked like part of the tree, but Joaquín saw how big it was and how still, as it watched them. The cat wasn't afraid, only curious. This was its domain and the two men were insignificant intruders. It would take a sudden movement or threatening gesture to frighten it.

"Where is she?" the man with the gun said. "I don't see her!"

They were almost under the tree. Joaquín stopped and faced him. He couldn't see the cat now but he felt its presence at his back, big, darkly invisible, and watchful. He stood very still and let the other man do all the talking, all the moving.

The man was like a mechanical toy gone haywire. His face jerked this way and that. There was no sign of the girl, and he began to jabber excitedly. "She ain't here! You're lying!" He shook his gun at Joaquín and shouted, "I'll kill you! I'll kill you!"

The cat let out a roar as it left the tree. Joaquín saw the look of surprise on the other man's face; he saw the gun jerk up and, as he dove, scrambling away, he heard the gun go off. Then he was fighting his way out of the dark blur of jungle, branches cutting across his face.

He came out into the early light, running. He plunged into the marsh grass, beating his way through it. There was another gunshot, and looking back, he saw the Indian emerge from the island of jungle. The cat was chasing him.

In the high grass he couldn't see the cat. He saw only the path the cat made. It was like a path made by the wind. It exited from the island of jungle and seemed to slither outward. It advanced in a swift, rippling furrow of parting grass toward the man who was trying to flee. The man glanced back. He stopped and turned, as if realizing that his short legs would never carry him through the grass as fast as wind could move. His sleek black head and stubby arm could be seen above the grass as he thrust out his gun and fired. The gun bucked. The sharp crack sent up a flurry of flapping wings all around the field. He kept firing, though he might as well have been shooting at a ghost, the gun bucking again, twice, three times, a fourth. Then, with no more warning than a flash of spotted coat, the wind, the swiftly moving furrow took shape and sprang, and the cat was on the man, dragging him down.

There were glimpses of hind claws raking spasmodically and of the large square head tearing at an inert bundle with brutal jerks and dragging the bundle through the grass. In the next moment the cat lay down and was gone.

Joaquín stopped and looked back. His run had brought him halfway to the plane at one end of the field. In a part of his mind he was still taking a long walk at the point of a gun, and he hadn't had time to get used to the idea of still being alive.

In the gray light he watched to see what the cat would do. There was no stirring of grass. He stared toward where he had last seen the Indian, a spot some distance behind him and off to one side. He glanced away and when he tried to come back to the spot he had lost it. The field was completely still.

For a second Joaquín tried to tell himself the cat was crouched in the grass, feeding. Then he thought of the three dead steers he had seen two days ago lying as if scattered by an explosion, and he knew that that wasn't it. The cat was waiting and watching, just as he was.

He took a step and felt something terrible gathering somewhere over his right shoulder. He glanced back, and it was as if he could actually see the wind spring up and take a direction. The grass was parting again and it was parting straight toward him.

Joaquín began to run. It's not fair, he thought, I've been a dead man once already this morning. The plane wasn't far, only several city blocks. If he could get to it and clamber inside before the cat caught him he would be safe. But the heavy grass was impossible to run fast in. It took hold of one of his sneakers and twisted his ankle and sent him sprawling. He scrambled up and plunged forward, bulling through the grass desperately, aware out of the corner of his vision that the cat was cutting across the field at an angle and gaining on him fast.

As he ran, he became aware that the sun was up. The shadow that had moved across the field late yesterday afternoon was now retreating, and suddenly he was running in sunshine. There were details he had missed in the gray light, dew on the long blades of grass, the concentric threads of a spider web. Something else caught his eye, too, as he passed. He turned and made a grab for it, seeing as he did how quickly the cat was closing the distance. He almost lost his balance as he yanked his bow free from the' grass it had become entangled in. Then he was running again.

That cost you your life, he thought. Three seconds to grab a bow you haven't got time to use.

The plane was near. But with a frantic look back he saw what the Indian must have seen. The cat was coming up too fast to outrace. He knew then why he had stopped to grab the bow and he knew also that he had better find time to use it. He faced the cat without seeing it. He pulled an arrow from the quiver on the handle, nocked it, drew the bow all the way back, and held it. He couldn't see the cat, only the invisible windlike presence moving toward him with incredible swiftness, shortly to take shape. The arrow flew. There was an instant when Joaquín could almost see the parting grass stop. Then it seemed to erupt into a wild, snarling, whirling ball. The arrow was in the cat's throat, and the cat was somersaulting with pain.

He threw another arrow into the spotted blur and didn't wait to see where it hit. He ran toward the plane. As he reached it he glanced back and saw the cat had straightened out and was coming at him. He scrambled onto the back of the wing and stood and nocked another arrow. The full draw seemed an elaborate slow-motion ritual. The cat was already in the air. Joaquín swung his bow and let go and the arrow struck deep into its chest. He didn't wait to see the effect of the hit. He dove over the top of the cabin and landed with his clattering bow on the other wing. He started to lunge down off the wing in order to grab the cabin door and scramble inside. Then he froze.

The cat was below him. It was thrashing furiously in the grass under the plane. It was trying to knock the arrow from its chest and blood was spattering the yellow stems.

Don't move, Joaquín thought. Stay right where you are.

It was a long time before Joaquín left the wing. He felt very patient waiting for the cat to die. The struggles subsided and ceased. By then Joaquín had begun to shake. But still he remained on the wing. Trembling quietly, he watched the sun clear the treetops and the dew dry. He felt the heat of the day begin.

13

JONES was walking down along the river in the early morning.

His seersucker jacket wrinkled and covered with leaf debris, his face, his arms, and the flesh of his belly pinched by the chilly air, every inch of exposed or insufficiently clothed skin raw and welted from mosquito bites, and his brain a hot coal, Jones lumbered forward obstinately, kept in motion by the single burning thought that somebody was going to pay for the miserable night he had spent in the jungle.

Dog had tricked him into going to the river last night. But Jones knew he couldn't shoot Dog, so he had decided it would have to be the two hunters. Then he would take that girl, he would beat her senseless, he would break every bone in the white bitch's body, before dragging her back to where Dog had spent the night comfortably in the plane.

They had got to the plane just as it was getting dark, after walking all afternoon through the jungle. The plane was empty and Jones settled disgustedly into the front seat.

"That's it, she's gone. Look at here, that Indian chopped the wheel."

The cabin was too small for his big body. There was no room to stretch his legs, and the thought of sitting in the cabin all night offered no hope of rest.

"You go on to the river," Dog said.

"I ain't going nowheres."

"The girl will get away."

"I don't care where she gets."

"Those hunters are camped on the river. It's not far. One of us has to stay here in case they come back for the plane."

Jones didn't know anything about flying. Maybe it was possible to take off in the high grass. "I'll stay and you go to the river," he said.

"You're too fat to spend the night in this little plane," Dog said.

"Fat, shit," Jones said. "I'll put a bullet in your fat face."

Jones sat in angry silence. The idea of being stuck out in the jungle was extremely offensive to him. He was spoiled by his life in Carib. Wherever he went on the island he was aware of his impact. He liked the prestige of his job and the big salary he was paid and the whores who were always glad to see him, and he would have given anything now for the luxury of a whore's skinny mattress and vigorous ministrations.

In the morning, he or Dog or both of them would have to go to the river anyway. By that time the girl might have left the camp of the two hunters and they would have to chase after her. Dog was right; she might get away.

He was right, too, about the plane being too small. Inspired by the cramped cabin, Jones began to form an exaggerated notion of how free and unconfined a night on the riverbank would be. With it came a vision of swift success. In the dark he would see a campfire; he would walk up and plug the two hunters and take the girl. There was a chance he could be back in Carib by tomorrow evening.

But still he sat. First Kane had made him go with Jolly. Then Jolly had made him go with Dog. And now Dog was telling him to go to the river. Jones was sick of being told what to do.

Dog, in the meantime, had climbed into the back of the cabin. He stretched out across the two seats with his arm under his head and plenty of room for his short legs. Indifferently, his hand groped and came up with a page torn from a book. In a dull stupid voice he read aloud:

" 'Lift is not created except with proper speed. The normal concept is to pull back on the wheel to increase back pressure but this will worsen the stall. The instinct will go away and—' " He crumpled the page into a ball. "What is this shit?"

He tossed the ball at Jones's head, flicked his lighter at a cigarette, and blew smoke.

"You better hurry," he said. "It's getting dark."

Wearily Jones climbed out of the cabin. "You lazy pig. I'm going. But not because you're saying so. I want to get away from you."

It had been the beginning of a series of accumulating afflictions. The river turned out to be farther away than it had looked from the air. Jones was overtaken by darkness and blundered through the jungle in a panic. When he finally stumbled out on the riverbank, clouds of mosquitoes came off the water and swarmed about his head and drove him back into the jungle. There he spent the night, huddled against a tree with his jacket over his head.

At first light he had risen thinking savagely of murder. The hunters would be camped either above or below him. He started downriver. If they were below he would come upon them. If they were above he would spot them on their way down to the Indian village.

One way or another Jones was going to shoot somebody.

Rhodes had left camp in the dark and gone down to the river, where some light was beginning to appear in the sky. He splashed water in his face to wake himself and wet his hair back out of his eyes. Above, in the clearing, he could see the black sagging shape of the hammock in which the girl slept, and he saw the alert figures of the three dogs, standing and staring at him on their leash, wondering where he was off to and why they hadn't been invited.

He set off. He had his bow, and there were three arrows in the quiver attached to the handle. With jungle on both banks it was like looking down a dark alley whose dingy walls towered to an unwinding ribbon of gradually lightening sky. Glancing back, he could make out the camp. But as he went on, the river entered one of its broad turns and the camp was out of view.

Rhodes continued down along the river without urgency. He didn't mind the early-morning stroll. Neither did he take it seriously. He had no anticipation of running into three men who were supposedly so interested in the girl that they would tramp all the way up from a ranch outpost miles downriver. What crime could she have committed, what unique value could she possess, that they would go through all the trouble?

Rhodes would have liked the answer to some questions last night. But now he was in no hurry. There was plenty of time for answers. The funny thing was that, in spite of her unwillingness to talk, he liked the girl. He consulted himself and decided it was because of the not so hard, but possibly more reliable, evidence of the girl's unguarded actions—such as the way she had laughed when she fed the dogs. It had not seemed the laughter of a crazy person or a criminal, which was what he had thought she was at first. His bias had begun to erode when he saw her casting a fly rod. Rhodes was a sucker for coordinated girls.

He traveled two bends in the river. The gray ribbon of sky had separated from the tops of the trees and begun to acquire some color, and walking downriver he could see the banks taking on detail.

He sat on a boulder, extracted a Camel from one of the two packs he had allowed himself to bring on the trip—an absurd discipline that would have him crawling on his hands and knees by the end of a week—lit up, sucked smoke, and broke into a murderous hacking cough that pushed the blood into his face. Damn fool habit. Showed he hadn't got away after all. He was still one of those dumb kids staying up all night in a jail cell, each one bragging how short his life was going to be. Proud of their vices and their ability to take death lightly. "Naw, I don't suspect I'll live to be much older than twenty-seven. I'll probably die in a car crash or shot by a cop. I figger I'll have had just about all the pussy I want by then." Hearing himself say this to the others but thinking all along, Jesus, boy, what a half-assed attitude. He had escaped it, he was over thirty now, but here he was with a cigarette in his lips, which proved he was still the same damn fool, pretending he didn't care how long he lived by this fatalistic clinging to the habit that had killed his old man. He remembered his last visit to the hospital, his daddy reaching out for a final shake of the hand and then prolonging the grip with sudden intensity. "Ernie, you're a good boy, I'm proud as hell of you, but for God's sake, son, you've got to cut down on the weed! It's what done me in."

Rhodes flicked the Camel toward the middle of the river. It made a small circle that expanded and disappeared with his own absence of urgency. He rose and idly raised and sighted his bow at an imaginary jaguar on the other bank. He rehearsed the proper motions: draw, hold, release. Thunk. One dead jaguar. Must remember to make a full draw, he told himself. Can't hurry your shot.

Rhodes started back.

He had gone a ways when he heard the dogs begin to bark in the camp up ahead. What's this? The girl must have gone off to use the great green privy and the dogs were making a fuss at her return. They were full of energy and resented being left tied to a tree while everyone else went off to have fun.

But why were they carrying on like that? By now they should have poked their noses at her and verified her to be the good guy who had fed them beef jerky last night. There was a note of frenzy in their clamoring.

The first gunshot was followed immediately by two more. The reports came rolling down to Rhodes, overtaking the first and shaking the air in the soft light of daybreak.

Rhodes was suddenly afraid for the girl's safety. It seemed a betrayal of his basic philosophy, which favored the plainest, most obvious interpretation of the facts. If you were wearing a pair of handcuffs you had done something wrong.

Yet Rhodes was running—all for a young woman's laughter.

Suddenly in Kim's dream there was a barking dog.

It had been like one of those dreams in which you search endlessly for a way out of a dark house with a growing sense of anxiety, only in this case it wasn't a house but a jungle and she was flying over it in a plane, looking for a place to land. The plane had finally run out of gas and gone into a tailspin, but just as it was about to crash it had become a bicycle. Kim was pedaling through the rolling farm country outside the town of Foxhaven and a dog was barking.

The dog was herding cows across the road and through a gate. The cows were going into a barn for the night. The hour reminded Kim that she was late for her paper route.

"Better hurry, hon," the farmer said.

"Okay," Kim said, "I'll be back."

"Be home for supper."

"I will."

"Don't be late."

"I'll be home. I'll be home."

The promise seemed an especially significant one for her to give and for the farmer to receive, and in her dream now Kim saw herself pedaling along the streets of the town. She tossed a newspaper at a house and it hit the front porch and immediately there was the same dog again. It came running out at her and Kim was frightened. She tried to swerve away but the dog rushed at her, barking ferociously and baring its teeth in an ugly snarl. With a scream she fell off her bike, and then she woke.

She was lying alone in a hammock and it was daylight. Jones was standing over her with a gun. Kim stared at him a moment as if he were a part of her dream. But she saw the gun was real. The three dogs, tied to a tree, were all barking loudly.

Jones reached down and grabbed her by the wrist, his big face angry. She twisted away and the hammock came to her aid, turning over and spilling her out. She scrambled up, and for an instant they faced each other, separated by the hammock. Jones was caught off balance, big and clumsy. As he lunged to grab her, Kim jumped back, and he stumbled over the hammock and fell.

She hesitated a second. She still wasn't fully awake. With a desperate glance she took in the camp. There were the ashes and charred pieces of wood of a campfire, two backpacks beside it, three dogs straining and barking on a leash. Across the clearing was another hammock. Empty. In her half-awake state the camp had the funny look of one of those puzzle pictures in which you're supposed to find which detail is wrong. It was the two men. They were gone. For one illogical moment Kim thought they had abandoned her. But they wouldn't have left without their gear or the dogs. They were going to bring her downriver to the village. They had got her off the wheel with an ax.

On the ground Jones was struggling to rise, his fat cheeks stunned and flabby with exertion. Darting around him Kim ran to the backpacks by the pile of ashes. The small ax would

be in one of them. She grabbed a backpack. Her fingers fumbled with the buckle. She got it open, threw back the flap,
and dug into it, flinging out shirts, underwear, a razor, soap,
deodorant, a paperback book. There was no ax. She turned
and grabbed the other pack. But Jones had finally made it to
his feet. He came toward her heavily. Kim was trying to un-
buckle the pack but he grabbed her. She swung at him with
her free arm and the handcuff dangling from her wrist cut
across his face. Jones let out a cry, and she tore away from
him and ran.

In her bare feet Kim ran toward the dogs at the edge of
the jungle. She wasn't thinking of the dogs. She was thinking of escape. The only weapon was the ax in the other
backpack and she couldn't get to it. If she could flee into the
jungle, somehow elude and hide from Jones, find the two
men, wherever they had gone . . . and why, why, why had
they disappeared, and oh God, I hope they're still alive,
please make them still alive. . . .

The dogs were simply part of the blur before her eyes.
Then, as she was about to flee past them, they seemed to
shape themselves out of the blur and become the noisy agitated animals that they were. She gave a quick glance back.
Jones had recovered from his pain and surprise and was
coming for her. Kim dove at the tree that held the dogs. The
leash was tied in a simple bowknot. She jerked the end and
it came undone, and the straining dogs did the rest.

In an instant Jones was surrounded, as the three dogs
came barking and snarling at him savagely. His huge body
was immobilized and under attack, his arms in his seersucker jacket upraised, one foot kicking to fend off the dogs.
The dogs were lean, tough fighters. They weren't scared of
this man. He was just another treed animal to them, and as
they closed about him growling and snapping, Kim turned
and ran to the backpacks.

She grabbed the second pack. She opened it, and snatched
out the ax. It took only seconds but in those seconds there
were two loud gunshots, and she knew Jones was shooting
the dogs. She tore off the leather cover on the ax head. Turning, she saw two dogs lying on the ground. The third had
Jones by the leg and Jones was pointing his gun at it. He
pulled the trigger and the dog fell away with a painful yelp.

Kim ran at Jones, raising the ax to hit him on the back of the head. But the last dog was gone and he turned. As she brought the ax down it grazed the side of his head. Suddenly blood was spouting from the dangling upper part of one ear and the ax handle was running red and slippery with it. Jones grabbed the handle and yanked it from her grasp and flung the ax away and came after her, howling, a look of savagery in his eyes.

"You bitch! I'll kill you!"

Kim darted around him and Jones lunged. She was almost out of his reach and not looking where she was going, when she stumbled over the dog he had just shot, one of the three lying about them, dead or dying on the ground. In that instant Jones achieved a sort of big man's clumsy quickness. His hand went out and caught her sweater, and he held on.

Kim fought. Her struggles took place in a world shaped and governed by the size and strength of Jones; each move or act by Jones became, as long as it lasted, the center of her fury and the focal point of her life. She proceeded from one to another in a confused blur: his grip on her sweater, the crushing impact of his body as, stumbling forward, he fell on top of her, the violent clout he gave her with his gun, and finally, as he jerked her to her feet, the embrace of his huge arms in which she continued to struggle as if in a straitjacket.

Blood was spattered on his seersucker jacket, so much blood from a little dangling piece of flesh.

"I'll kill you!" Jones cried. "I don't care what Jolly say! Jolly be damed!"

Kim lunged fiercely, as if to goad him into the act. But Jones was bluffing. He wrestled her to the edge of the riverbank. The sleeves of the sweater and the cuffs of the pants, which she had put on last night, had become unrolled. She squirmed out of his arms and sprang away. The sweater stretched and grew taut in his grip.

Jones dragged her down the bank and out onto the sandbar. He grabbed her by the hair and pushed her head underwater. Kim struggled but Jones held her under with deranged fury. It seemed he had decided to drown her. He jerked her head up and held it over the water.

"You want more! You want more!"

He shoved her under again before she could catch her breath. Kim tried to get her head up but it wobbled helplessly as if in a vise. She began to black out. Then the enormous weight went away.

Kim lifted her head, choking and gasping for air. Jones was sitting on her back at the edge of the sandbar. He had lost interest in her and was applying his handkerchief fretfully to his ear.

"You going to come back with me now? I got to bring you to Jolly and I don't want any trouble. I didn't even want to come on this trip, and look what it cost me!"

He soaked the handkerchief and squeezed out blood and water.

"You be lucky if this ear don't fall off before I get home. Because if it do, you don't know what meanness is till you see how mean I can be. You just better pray it stay on till I can find a doctor to sew it on."

Jones gave her head a rough slap. "Where are those two men who got you out of that plane?" he said. "They probably run off. They ain't stupid. I'll shoot them if I can. Jolly and Dog already kill two cowboys who tried to get smart. Nobody want to help you, if they know what's good for them."

He sat trying to stanch the blood.

After a while he said, "Now I'm going to get up. We got a long walk to that ranch where Jolly is and first we got to go to the plane to get Dog. So don't try anything because if you do, I'll beat you, I'll kick you, I'll break every bone in your white bitch's body."

Jones lifted his rear end off her and stood up. He gestured with the gun. "Let's go. Jolly didn't give me the key to the handcuffs, so I got to hang on to—"

There was a shout. Kim didn't hear the words. She heard the noise, a sharp bark of command. She looked up and saw Rhodes. He was standing down along the bank, facing them with his bow drawn and an arrow aimed at Jones. Rhodes shouted again and Kim realized he was telling Jones to drop his gun.

"Watch out!" she tried to shout.

But the words came weakly. And they were already too late.

Jones had raised his gun without warning and fired. The roar of the gun washed around Kim and shook the air, like something trying to push her underwater again. She was still collapsed on the bank, gasping. She saw Jones give a little stagger backward and heard a painful grunt, forced from deep inside, as if somebody as big and heavy as he had just sat on him. Jones clapped a hand to his shoulder and the bloody handkerchief fell to the sandbar. Sticking out between his fingers was the shaft of an arrow with yellow feathers.

Everything began to go fast. She saw Jones charge into the shallows and heard the roar of his gun as he fired again at Rhodes. In the same instant another arrow thunked into the sandbar, missing Jones completely. Kim was aware that the two men were both still standing, facing each other, one with his gun, the other with his bow.

An arrow was drawn back and ready to fly. She hadn't seen Rhodes put it there and now she didn't see the arrow leave the bow. She only saw Rhodes suddenly go into a crouch and fling the bow, an act incredible, absurd, the roar of the gun washing around her once more as she saw Jones swat the bow aside with his big paw as if it were a harmless mosquito.

Then, as the roar died Jones seemed to pause out of curiosity. On the back of his seersucker jacket a red spot appeared. In the middle of it was the broadhead of an arrow. Jones looked down at the other end of it protruding from his breastbone. Taking a step backward, he grasped the aluminum shaft as if to steady himself. He raised his gun and Rhodes, frozen for an instant in a crouch, dove for the trees.

Jones pulled the trigger and there was a click. He staggered, as if at an enormous and deafening sound. Bewildered, he stood a moment, and with a wistful look his gaze wandered to himself. He took stock of the situation. There was the one stick in his shoulder and the disappointing news of the other in his breastbone. He was standing in a river and holding a gun whose chamber was empty.

Jones turned away. He wanted nothing more to do with the man on the bank. Somberly he made his way back to the sandbar. He had lost interest in Kim, too, and gave her only a bitter look of reproof as his mouth filled with blood and he sank to his knees and rolled over on his side.

* * *

Kim picked herself up unsteadily. Her wet hair hung about her face, her arms and hands were out of sight in the long wet sleeves of Joaquín's sweater, and his unrolled pants hampered her bare feet. She stood like an urchin in borrowed rags caught in a rainstorm. Rhodes came sloshing through the shallows toward her.

"Watch out!" he shouted.

She looked around in alarm, thinking of Jolly and Dog. But it was Jones he meant.

Jones lay on his side with his back to her. One hip rose like a mountain and sloped toward his shoes at the water's edge. He looked like a slumbering sunbather except for the curiously emblematic broadhead that was protruding from the back of his jacket in a circle of blood.

Rhodes dropped his bow, which he had retrieved from the shallows, and grabbed the gun still clutched in Jones's hand. He threw Jones over and began to tear at his clothes, pulling the pockets of his jacket and pants inside out, scattering loose coins, a wallet. He jerked the clip from the butt of the gun, looking for bullets even where he knew he wouldn't find them. The gun was useless. He glanced up and down the bank, as if expecting imminent attack. There was no one. He came to Kim, the empty gun in his hand, a deadly serious look on his face.

"Is there anyone else? Where are the others?"

"They're not here. One's at the plane. Another's at the ranch. They're waiting for him."

"Christ!" Rhodes was in the grip of emergency. He grabbed her by the arm. "Are you alive?"

Kim nodded lightheadedly. She made a show of performing some simple moves to prove it. She got a hand out of one sleeve and used it to pull back a soggy lump of wool from the other. "I've swallowed half the river." She took a step and was dizzy. The pant legs unbalanced her and she stumbled against Rhodes. "I think I'm going to be sick."

He helped her up the bank, sat her down, and anchored her to the spot with a firm shake.

"Stay here. I've got to find Wok."

Then he was gone.

Kim pulled the wet sweater over her head. She lay in a

stupor, primarily aware of sunlight and air. The air was a gift. The sun warmed her bones. It was amazing how noisy, with croaking frogs and strange calls, the jungle could be at night and how silent it was in the day.

Jones was lying on the sandbar below. Kim imagined him rolling over, struggling to his feet. But a voice inside her said not to worry, Jones was dead and would never close the distance that separated them where they both lay on a sunny riverbank in the middle of a jungle.

She heard voices above her then. They were the voices of the two men who had got her off the plane. Yesterday, last night, she had seen them through the eyes of Nicole, two strange faces in a world of strange faces. But when she had woken this morning with Jones standing over her she had had an instant knowledge of them as real people with real names, as old friends, grown-up versions of the boys she had known as a girl, her only chance of getting back to where she had come from.

The voices came from a region somewhere above in the sunlight and air, discussing events. It was like listening to news bulletins of a third world war. Two men were dead. A jaguar was dead. Bits and pieces of war news filtered down from far away.

"I don't know what the hell he wanted," Rhodes said. "He didn't give me a chance to ask. He damn near drowned her and I still don't know what it's all about. But I can tell you one thing, I ain't looking forward to going through his billfold, 'cause the fact that he was a brutal son of a bitch don't prove one way or the other which side of the law he was on."

There was a note of frustrated grievance, ending in a final exasperated observation—"And it don't particularly do wonders for my disposition that another one is still alive somewhere."

Jolly, she thought. His name is Jolly. He's the one to be afraid of.

"Is she okay?" Joaquín asked.

"Yeah," Kim heard herself say. Her own voice sounded as if it, too, were coming from somewhere above. She opened her eyes and saw the two men looking down at her. She sat up groggily. "I'm okay."

Joaquín knelt and gripped her shoulder. "Sure?"

She nodded.

"Good," he said shortly. He wasn't offering sympathy; his face was grim and harried.

Rhodes had walked off, as if to control his exasperation. Kim started to get up but the hand on her shoulder kept her firmly in place.

"Sit. We're making coffee."

"I'm fine. Let me help."

"No." There was nothing friendly about it. "Do as I say."

She obeyed. The two men rolled the hammocks and packed the backpacks, brought the gear down, and loaded the canoe. Their activity seemed to have the purpose of helping them to compose themselves. Kim sat with a tin cup of coffee that Joaquín had put in her hands. In front of her Jones lay on his back with his mouth open, his inside-out pockets like deflated white balloons.

The men were done. They returned to where she was sitting. Uneasily she glanced up and saw them watching her closely. Some things had been left unsaid and she was going to be asked to say them.

"Who is he?" Rhodes said. He jerked his thumb at the dead body on the sandbar.

"His name is Jones," she said.

"What's his profession?"

Kim thought of the first time she had ever laid eyes on Jones, when she had come out of the swimming-pool cabana where Kane had raped and left her, and found Jones waiting for her—the routine of her new life had begun with Jones.

"Look," Rhodes said, his voice shaking, "I killed him because he was trying to kill me. Now I want to know why, and don't just tell me he was going to take you to Peru and you didn't want to go."

"He was my prison guard," she said. "He went wherever I went and kept me from getting away."

Joaquín's gaze was no softer than Rhodes's. Kim attempted a short painless version of her life; it was the least she owed them.

"I was kidnapped when I was thirteen," she said.

Their looks were an alert, watchful question. Kidnapped?

"I was held prisoner. It was to get back at my father. My father was a criminal prosecutor." She saw it all happening again—Jolly landing at the little airstrip that seemed cut off from the rest of the world, driving her up to the main house, walking her across the lawn to a man at a table by the swimming pool whose dark glasses were just another part of the cruel hard mask of his face.

"The man who had me kidnapped kept me for seven years. Then he decided to sell me to a house in Peru." Without bitterness, in a plain statement of clarification, she said, "A whorehouse."

"Kept you?" Rhodes wasn't being unkind—asking skeptical questions, she saw, was a professional reflex with him.

"Kept me. Used me. I was his crazy mistress is what he told people. But he did what he wanted with me."

The two men were facing her with quiet astonishment and concern. Old friends. Grown-up boys. She was able to meet Joaquín's gaze now without guilt.

"I'm not the dope dealer's girlfriend."

"I believe you," he said.

She wanted to tell them everything then. But most of all she wanted to tell them this—"I never stopped trying to get away."

"And this one," Rhodes gestured toward Jones, "was sent to bring you back."

"Him and the other two. Dog is the name of the one who was at the plane. The one who's waiting for them at the ranch is named Jolly."

"He's got a mighty long wait," Rhodes said.

Kim noticed how kind his cold blue eyes could be when he had made up his mind to like you. She watched him descend to the sandbar almost cheerfully and pick up Jones's wallet, as if finally convinced it held no terrible surprises.

"I tried to tell you last night," she told Joaquín. "It seemed too much to say."

"Don't worry," he said. "We'll get you home, wherever you're going."

"It's Connecticut, where my dad lives."

"It'll take us two days to get to the village. Then we'll jam into my little plane. You'll be home before you know it."

"What about Jolly?"

"I'll notify the police. The father and son at that little ranch will have to put up with him until then."

"They're dead," Kim said.

"No," he said.

She saw his dismay. "Jones said they killed them. That's the kind of people they are. I didn't know I was bringing them with me. I just thought I was running away. They killed the father and son, they killed the dogs, and they would have killed you, too, if they had had the chance."

Rhodes came back, cackling gleefully as he searched through the contents of the wallet. "Jones was a man who liked to play both sides of the street. Here's a card for a girlie joint and another for a fundamentalist religious sect. One rubber contraceptive. That would be for the girlie joint. One five-pound note. Hey, Wok, look at this. Just goes to show, a Florida redneck can go through life and never hear of a hot little country like Carib and suddenly it's all he hears about."

Kim saw Joaquín stop and stare at Rhodes in confusion. He turned to her. "Carib? Is that where you're from?"

The look on his face went beyond his dismay at the father and son's death, and of all his looks that she had seen so far—helpful stranger giving directions to bus station, nice guy offering a lecture along with a can of pears—she understood it the least. It made her feel like a ghost risen from the grave.

"This guy who kidnapped you," Joaquín said, "what nationality is he? What does he do? What's his name?"

Kim felt obliged to take each question in turn. "He's an American. He's a dope dealer. His name is Kane."

14

JOAQUÍN was watching the girl now. Tom Mitchell's daughter.

He saw a young woman, smashing girl. Lovely brown hair, cut in bangs across her forehead. Tomboy look. Beautiful tomboy. Cheekbones that flattened outward smoothly, giving her eyes a catlike slant. Eyes made it all work. Intelligent, frank. She had opened up, wasn't acting morose and suspicious, like yesterday.

They were motoring downriver, the girl sitting in the middle of the dugout canoe with the backpacks and the rolled hammocks. Black eye had begun to fade. She had a nice bruise on one cheekbone where Jones had given her a clout. She wore it like a warrior and there was no sense of a bruised personality beneath it. Joaquín thought of his mother, tough old broad with a facility for picking up the pieces. That was her philosophy, that getting through life was a matter of learning how to pick up the pieces. There were those who never had any pieces to pick up, who always played it safe. His mother wasn't like that. She had gone through a messy divorce from her first husband but hadn't retired to her room to gorge herself on chocolates, like a poor little rich girl. She had set off on one of her long-distance solo flights and crashed in the jungle.

What this girl had gone through wasn't just a messy divorce. But her attitude seemed to be the same. She had told them, "I never stopped trying to get away." She had flown a plane. She was going to pick up the pieces.

Joaquín thought of a young girl who had been kidnapped and held prisoner for seven years on a West Indies island, and he thought of a kid who was hot stuff, just out of agent school, sitting in a car outside a Cuban restaurant in Miami eight years ago, waiting for a man in a white suit and dark glasses to come out and drive away in a white Cadillac.

He had been the boy with the limitless future, a big, friendly, outgoing jock, smart enough to get by in school without busting his balls, who had got the bright idea that it would be exciting to be a drug-enforcement agent for a while. In case he ever wanted to go into politics.

Instead he had followed a man in a white suit, in a white car, and the limits of his future had grown suddenly as narrow and inexorable as the two lanes of U.S. 1. Key Largo . . . Seven Mile Bridge . . . Stock Island . . . all the way to Key West.

After that, no matter how good he had become at what he did, no matter how many busts he made or risks he took or how much coke he kept off the streets, it was always the same; he was still chasing a phantom in a white suit.

Joaquín looked at the girl now and felt admiration and awe. She was his twin. They had both been stuck in time by Kane. He had wanted to tell her at once and then he had caught himself. He was the one who had loosed Kane on the world. It wasn't an admission he cared to make to this girl, and Rhodes had understood as much, no words necessary.

So instead they talked what amounted to shop. They were almost matter-of-fact about it. Sure they had heard of Kane. Hadn't everybody? What did he do, holed up in Carib?

He smuggled dope, what else?

How did she know?

Kim laughed. She had eyes and ears, didn't she? And what she hadn't picked up on her own, watching and listening, she had gotten from Jones.

"Jones had a big mouth. You'd ask him a question and he'd refuse to answer and two minutes later he'd be telling you the whole story."

She told them how Jolly would sometimes be gone a week at a time in one of the planes and how, when he got back, he would meet visitors at the main gate and bring them down to the old sugarcane refinery to transact business. Jones re-

ferred to the visitors disparagingly as "mules," and it was
Jones who eventually gave her the details—how Jolly brought
back cocaine base from Peru and oversaw the conversion of
the base into pure cocaine, how the mules were sent by a
dope dealer in Miami named Kiki Soldano.

Joaquín caught the look that Rhodes gave him across the
length of the canoe. It was a look that called to mind a phrase
Rhodes sometimes used—"like stubbing your toe on an alligator."

On his own face he felt a silly grin. He was thinking of
Kiki's nephew Jerry, whom he had sat on recently, sticking
a gun in his face. Jerry cutting coke in his kitchen. Jerry
driving out to Gulfstream Park while his girl did favors for
him in the front seat of his car. Jerry going around town to
all those pay phones. Returning the calls he got on his answering machine.

Waiting to hear from Numma One.

This was an admission that Joaquín felt able to make. It
was a present for Kim. Something that would get a laugh—
or suggest to her that maybe their paths had been meant to
cross. He sprang it on her, like a good joke.

"Ever hear of a guy called Numma One?"

And saw the joke fall flat.

The look in her eyes was frightened. It gave a glimpse
of the paranoia that was your natural defense if you had lived
for seven years in a world made up of men who worked for
Kane.

"That's what Jolly calls himself," she said. "Do you
know him?"

"Not really," he said hastily to reassure her. "We've just
been listening in on his long-distance telephone calls."

The canoe motored on.

He watched her.

Saw the nice shape her breasts gave to her tennis shirt.

Saw the unpretentious way she put together lunch, digging into a backpack and coming up with a can of sardines
and a box of crackers, finding an onion and a knife to slice
it with, hauling in the mesh bag that kept the beers cold in
the water. She cracked open three beers and handed two
out, and they all drank and sighed contentedly, munching
on sardines, onions, and crackers.

"They have a calypso song about Kane on the island," she said. "It has a verse for every word that rhymes with his name—pain, quatrain, cocaine. But the word that suits him best is *insane*. Kane isn't happy in Carib."

Joaquín thought of the powerful man he had once been assigned to tail, his important friends, his rumored Cabinet post, his skill with the media—all that ambition confined to a country the size of Carib.

"It beats doing time in the United States," he said.

"Except Kane is counting on going home soon. He thinks the charges against him will be dropped."

"What does he do for fun in Carib?"

"He goes to the track two or three times a week. Jones always went with him. Nobody gets near the estate who isn't allowed. There's a big wall in front and a jungle out back and short little Indians who took orders from Dog guarding the place. Kane will have to find two new men."

"No other hobbies?" Rhodes said.

Joaquín saw at once that he was sorry he had asked.

"No," Kim said, "I was his only other hobby. I was Kane's sickness." She was quick. "Hey, don't worry. I'm okay. I've got to tell somebody. I'd rather have it be you guys."

So she told them about her elegant white-walled white-rugged prison cell with no windows and two native scenes on the walls, about the green prison outside that, with its spacious lawns and fringe of jungle, its activities—swimming pool, tennis court, beach, like a vacation resort, if you didn't notice the numerous replicas of Dog patrolling the grounds—and about the town of Raleigh, where if you succeeded in escaping to it you were returned at once by a police chief who didn't want to become involved in "domestic squabbles."

"The whole country was my prison. If I had gotten away to the capital, somebody, the police or the army, would have brought me back to Kane and I would have paid for it."

She stared at the jungle as it passed and Joaquín saw her staring at the white walls.

"Kane's basic attitude is contempt," she said. "It's only when I think of what he did to me . . . the first time, out by his swimming pool where Jolly first brought me to him . . ."

She grew quiet. The canoe ran on steadily. The freshness of the morning had given way to a soggy heat. Blinding glare came off the river and the trees loomed over them like a dead presence. Up ahead there was a familiar rushing sound and Joaquín cut the motor, lifted the prop out of water, and drew a paddle from the bottom of the canoe.

"Rapids."

Rhodes took a paddle, too, and as the canoe rounded a bend the rapids were before them. Joaquín felt the steady pull of the river drawing them on, then the first firm clutch, like putting your foot on a ledge of snow that was giving way, and all at once they were in the middle of a snowy avalanche of leaping white water. They rode down it, he and Rhodes paddling hard. A large rock at the end was coming up. They slipped past it, bumping and scraping against the side, and were into still water.

"That was great!" Kim said. "Are there any more of those?"

"Two more farther down," he said.

They were all grinning. The canoe had achieved a state of profound gravity in its own colorful reflection. Kim settled back.

"I'm done with Kane. There's only one other thing, since confession is good for the soul. Before I left I bashed him with a plastic hair dryer. You should have seen the bastard bleed."

Joaquín felt as if he were bearing a rare jewel before him in the palm of his hand. He showed the jewel off to the jungle. Look at this, you bums. Flies a plane. Knows how to use a hair dryer. Survives without breakage.

Of the three skills, survival without breakage was the one he didn't believe.

"Correct me if I'm wrong, buddy," Rhodes was saying. "It was just a week ago we were listening to him tell us all about your ancestors. How they were such mean mothers, going around doing a number on all the other Indians. Cooking babies and smoking arms and legs. Ever give you the feeling that bad odors follow us around? That it don't matter where we go or what we do. Bad odors just won't leave us alone?"

"I've noticed that about you."

They were standing on the bank, watching Kim swim

across the river. She had seemed a little awkward with them when she had come out of the trees a moment ago, wearing Joaquín's shirt and belt in place of a bathing suit. It was as if she thought she had done too much talking, told them too much, and had begun to wonder what they really thought of her.

She had smiled hesitantly. "You coming?"

"Soon as we put up the hammocks," Joaquín had told her. "You go ahead."

So Kim had gone down the bank and dove in.

On the other side a huge rock wall rose in craggy stages to a great ledge of overhanging rock, draped in vegetation. The river was broad and still, almost pondlike, deepened by the rush of water from the second stretch of rapids that they had just come down. Rhodes and he had camped here on the way up and there was already a ring of smoke-blackened stones waiting for them.

Rhodes stuck a Camel in his mouth.

"We shoulda gone after the bastard. I could see you thinking about it."

"I didn't want to risk it. We'd have to wait until dark, or he might see us coming. We'll get the cops down here. There's a shortwave radio at the mission."

"Hell of a vacation so far. Big black guy trying to blow my head off."

"I would have gone for it if it wasn't for Kim. Wait until dark, catch him in his hammock. But I want to get her home."

"You're right." Rhodes paused with a match under his unlighted cigarette, lifted his face toward Kim, who had reached the other side and was splashing around under the high wall. "Get her home. It's going to be hard enough on her."

"I'd like to get Kane, too. But there's no way to get Kane."

"Might put a crimp in his style, though, if we could nail his flunky, get the cops out here fast. That, and her getting away . . ."

Struck a match, lowered his face to his cupped hands, shook the match out. Sucked and blew.

"Numma One," Rhodes said. "If that don't beat all."

"It sure does."

"Like stubbing your toe on an alligator."

* * *

They came out on the bank stripped to their shorts. On the other side Kim had climbed out and begun to make her way up the face of the rock wall along a rising ledge. Her wet hair was pulled back and the wet shirt clung to her body. The sun had begun to go down behind the wall, glinting through the underbrush at the top, casting a shadow toward where he and Rhodes stood, still in sunlight on the opposite bank.

Kim arrived at a point just below the overhanging ledge. Joaquín started to shout, "Be careful!" But she didn't give him a chance. She made a long dive and entered the water smoothly.

"What d'you expect," Rhodes said. "She learned to fly a plane from a book. She's not about to be put off by a little height."

They swam out to her.

"You should try that dive!" Kim cried.

"Go ahead," Joaquín said. "Lead the way."

He followed her up along the tricky ledges of wet rocks and slippery vegetation. At the top he stood beside her. Across the river their camp was in shadow now and the trees above were a sunny green ocean stretching away to the mountains in the distance.

"It looks terrific," she said, "unless you're flying over it, searching for a place to land."

Below, Rhodes was splashing back and forth with his burly, inelegant stroke.

"There was an old marble quarry that was used as a swimming hole outside the town where I lived. It had big rock walls like this. We'd go out on our bikes and lie around on the rocks and do crazy stuff . . . jumping in sitting on a guy's shoulders, all the way down, ten or fifteen feet. Great way to break your neck."

Joaquín thought of the sort of regular guy she must have been, horsing around with the boys at the marble quarry.

"Where was that?"

"Connecticut. Foxhaven. Little town, two blocks of stores, village green with a statue of a Union soldier, big old elm trees along the streets, a church with a tall white steeple. I only lived there about a year, but everybody in town knew who I was. I made the baseball team at school. It was a big deal. People wrote letters to the local paper about me. Little kids asked for my autograph. I was famous."

"What position?"

"Pitcher. I had a terrific fastball." She was boasting playfully. "What's the village like that we're going to? Were you really born there?"

"I was. It's still pretty primitive. No electricity or indoor plumbing. No real schooling except for the priest at the mission station."

"How old were you when you left?"

"About five."

"Do you remember anything?"

"I think I do. Maybe it's just seeing things now and hearing stories and thinking I remember. It was like growing up in one big family. We all ate and slept together. When my mom left I had plenty of mothers to look after me."

"Why did she leave?"

"It wasn't her world. It's a hard life. You have to be born into it."

"I stopped thinking of my own town a long time ago," Kim said. "But I thought of it today, coming downriver. Remembering things."

"Like?"

"Like riding my bike in the summertime, going along the streets under all the trees with my baseball glove slung on the handlebar, or how the town looked after a snowfall with ridges of white in the rain gutters and on the limbs of trees. It would be nice if I could go back to it just the way it was, as if nothing had happened, same town, same girl."

There was nothing he could say that would make it so.

"I'm not so hot with people, in case you haven't noticed," she said.

"I hadn't."

"I was Kane's crazy white bitch. Even the maid never smiled at me. I became an expert on the sound of feet. I could tell who was coming into a room just by the sound of their feet."

Joaquín felt like putting his arms around her and telling her she was a super girl. But he wasn't sure how she would take it, after what she had been through. They were standing slightly stooped under the big overhang of rock, so the gesture would have been difficult anyway.

He saw Rhodes getting out of the river and trudging into the woods to change into his dry clothes.

"Well, who's first?"

She smiled. "I led the way up, you can lead the way down."

Joaquín dove. He went into the water, and the force of his dive yanked his shorts off. He came to the surface struggling foolishly to hike them up, and saw Kim coming down with her knees drawn up in a cannonball. She hit the water with a splash, grinning like a young girl, the girl she had been seven years ago.

He went underwater and found her swimming on the bottom. She didn't look like a young girl now. She was an exotic long-legged creature, her hair streaming, a silver bracelet on her wrist. Joaquín took hold of the handcuff and drew her to him and kissed her, a corny move, like one of the boys at the quarry might have pulled—his way of trying to give her back the years she had lost, so she could go back to where she had started from and begin again.

They swam back to shore. And for fisherman Rhodes, who was laying down an elegant line in front of him, emerged from the water very formally and separated to opposite sides of the great green privy.

"The takeoff? Oh that was a cinch. I didn't know what I was doing. Other than that it was just like driving 'Kim's Cannonball.' "

"Kim's what?"

"That was the name of the soap-box racer I drove as a girl."

"I see. And that got you off the ground."

"It must have. I can't figure out what else I did. Oh there was one thing that was pretty funny. . . . As I was coming down the runway I kept telling myself, 'Don't pull back too far, you've got to get some speed up.' I knew I would never clear the hangar if I didn't have enough speed. All at once this strange man came running out, shooting a gun at me. So I said, 'Well, I guess it's time.' So I pulled back on the wheel and up I went."

"Who was the strange man?"

"It was Kane!"

"Where was Jolly?"

"Jolly? Where else? He was hanging on the wing."

They were laughing. They were having the celebration they hadn't had last night. It was like celebrating the success of an old friend, her first solo flight; they had adjourned to the local bar to get pleasantly sloshed and let her crow.

"I was flying a plane in my sleep all last night," she said.

"And I'll probably be running from jaguars tonight," Joaquín said.

He was running now. He saw himself plowing desperately through the marsh grass. He felt it pulling at his legs, trying to drag him down, and as he glanced back, the swath of parting grass was coming toward him, and he knew, as he always would in one part of his mind, that he was never going to make it.

He had waited a long time for the jaguar to die. Then he had climbed down off the wing and knelt beside the big cat and studied the claws, the teeth, the handsome coat, in which the bent and broken shafts of three arrows stuck out. He had gone looking for Dog, plowing back through the grass, taking his time, like a naturalist on a field trip, motivated by scientific curiosity. The mess that was Dog was a rare specimen. But as he was admiring it there had been a sound of gunfire far off—Jones shooting the dogs—and he knew his casual field trip had been a terrible mistake.

"The worst part," Kim said, "was when I came down. It was like a roller-coaster ride. I was barreling through this tall grass and I could see the trees coming up and just as I thought I was going to crash into them the plane stopped, and I looked out and all around me were these vultures, sitting and looking at me like a welcoming committee. It wasn't exactly what I expected. I had sort of been hoping for a brass band."

They were sharing a cup of rum. She borrowed it and took a sip and put it back in his hands. She leaned against him fondly, young girl on a camping trip, flirting with the goofy kid who had stolen an underwater kiss. Joaquín felt the pleasant weight and shape of her breast. He didn't sense desperation so much as eagerness. She wanted to be happy.

She wanted to show she hadn't forgotten how to trust people, or even how to just have a good time. She was talking, telling them how she was finally ready to believe she had escaped, how she hadn't been able to yesterday, how she guessed she needed to fight Jones to find out that she wasn't going to let anyone take her back, no matter what, even though the roots of her hair "still hurt like hell" from the way Jones had dragged her down to the river. She hoped Kane, back in Carib, was nursing an ulcer "as big as Mount Everest," and she wondered if Joaquín would let her take the controls for a while when they flew to Caracas "just to prove that it wasn't all luck."

She was looking forward to all the things she had to do—going back to school, catching up, maybe going to law school and becoming a lawyer like her dad—getting dangerously ahead of herself until, with a foolish look she stopped.

"Jesus, that rum must be getting to me."

So she came back to the present, the river, and wasn't it terrific, she didn't even mind the heat and the mosquitoes, and weren't those rapids amazing and wasn't she lucky to have found two such great guys to help her remember what human beings were really like so that she didn't make a complete ass of herself when she got back to . . . "the real world."

Rhodes went away and came back and fed some branches into the fire. He announced he was going to bed. No, no, he had to stay for a nightcap. The bottle was almost empty. Solemnly Rhodes shook the last drops into his cup. Standing before the fire, he told a story about how he had once been on a camping trip with a young lady and they had been together in a sleeping bag on the ground when a bear had appeared in the dark and begun to chow down on their food supplies.

"What did you do?" Kim asked.

"We were both very careful," Rhodes said.

He drained his cup and went off to put down his mosquito netting, leaving Joaquín alone with her. They got busy, cleaning up after supper, brushing teeth, getting the hammock ready. Practical things that had nothing to do with Rhodes's funny story.

* * *

In the hammock they were suddenly kissing, as if they had both been thinking of nothing else. The rum helped them overcome their hesitation and the hammock did the rest, folding them together in its sturdy, sagging network of palm fibers.

"I've been waiting to do this all night," she said.

"Me too."

"You can't just kiss a girl underwater and swim off."

"I ran out of breath. Then I didn't want to disturb Rhodes. He was catching our dinner."

In the dark Rhodes's mosquito netting was ghostly and quiet in the trees across the way. He had flicked off his penlight and said good night shortly after they had come up from the river.

After a while Kim said, "Mm, I like that."

"So do I. But how do I get this off?"

The hammock had pulled her on top of him, and he was working at her sweater. There was a moment of awkwardness and Joaquín wasn't sure if it was him or her. He had been thinking all day of a man in a white suit and dark glasses whom he had let get away, and of how, for eight years, he had regarded the event solely as a personal disaster, affecting no one but himself. So maybe it's you, he thought.

She seemed shy, but mostly he sensed the same young girl's desire to be happy, normal, and loving, and all he wanted was to help her.

Kim straddled him; it was finally the most natural position allowed by the hammock. Sitting up, she was a dark figure against the white netting, lost in the baggy woolen sweater he was helping to pull over her head. He got the sweater off and lifted her shirt. Her breasts flopped out from under the tight-fitting fabric and he got the shirt over her head, and immediately forgot about everything else, except the sweet taste of her nipples. The only awkwardness now was caused by their eagerness. Kim was going after the buttons on his shirt and they were both attacking each other gleefully.

"I want you," she said.

"Not as much as I want you."

Joaquín had hooked his thumbs into the waist of her shorts and was attempting to pull the shorts down over her buttocks and past her knees, and all at once the hammock tipped. He caught them as it was about to spill them out. He rolled back, restoring the hammock's center of gravity. They began to laugh, their faces close together. They were trying to be quiet so as not to wake Rhodes, but the effort only made them sillier.

"There must be some way of doing this," he said.

"Why don't we just get out of the hammock," Kim said; she was pressing her face against his neck to stifle her laughter.

"That's too simple. Why didn't I think of that?"

They climbed out of the hammock and undressed hastily. They climbed back in, bringing their clothes rather than leave them outside for little creatures to crawl into. Then they were lying together and Joaquín felt her whole length, lovely shoulders and long legs, against him.

"What's that you're doing?" Kim asked.

"You like it?"

"You bet. Don't stop. Please don't stop."

They were whispering excitedly to each other, hugging, kissing, fondling, like mischievous children. After a while Kim sat back and took hold of his erection inquisitively; he felt the delicious pressure of her palm.

"What's this?" she said.

"I dunno," he laughed.

She seemed shy again. There was a hesitation, not so much reluctance as the sort of pause one might take before making a long dive.

Soberly she said, "How are we going to do this without falling out of the hammock?"

"I think the trick," Joaquín said, borrowing an idea from Rhodes, "is to be very careful."

He sensed a frank appeal and he reached out gently to guide her. With a stately shyness she raised her hips and Joaquín saw himself disappear into the dark patch of hair between her thighs as she lowered herself slowly; then they were welded, as tightly as two people can be.

Kim lay with her knees drawn up on either side of him, her arms around him, her head on his shoulder. She was clinging to him, as if for safety. Joaquín didn't think it was entirely because of the unstable hammock. He understood

it as a request; she just wanted to be held. So he held her
and recognized the wetness of tears on his shoulder.

She kissed him then, fondly, as if to tell him she was
okay. The hammock began to move in a little rocking motion
caused by her knees. The rocking went on for some time
and all the while they were whispering eagerly to each other.

Joaquín felt the pleasant weight of her buttocks, the
brushing touch of her nipples as she lifted up to kiss him,
then he felt a sudden heat, ovenlike, creating a sense of urgency for both of them. Their whispers quickened along with
the rocking. Kim gripped him with her thighs and he pulled
her hard down onto him. The weld became intense, prolonged and final. Then it relaxed and the hammock was still.

After a moment Joaquín grew aware of the croaking of
frogs and the faint, eerie sound of the rapids a short distance
above, and through the gauzy netting he saw the flickering
black shapes of bats darting and skimming over the river.
Kim lay, a quiet untroubled burden in his arms.

"I sure am glad you tied this hammock tight to those
trees," she said.

"I think I'll ask to be their sales rep in the States. It's a
testament to native handicrafts."

"That's what my old man used to say about the hamburgers at our local drugstore."

The croaking frogs and whispering rush of the rapids made
the silence of the jungle palpable. The bats flickered.

"You're the first person I ever made love with," Kim said.

"I feel lucky as hell."

"So do I. I was scared."

"No need to be," Joaquín said.

He had a moment to consider the lameness of the statement before she spoke.

"Oh yes there was," she said. "Yes there was."

Then, as if afraid she might have hurt his feelings, she
reached up and clapped his cheek—two sleepy little slaps,
as if they had been friends and lovers all their lives.

"Good old Wok," she said. "My dear old Wok."

Joaquín held her now as if to tell her how much finding
her meant to him. Maybe it's in your genes, he thought;
maybe you just inherited your old man's weakness for girls

who crash-land planes in the jungle. But there was something else, something harder to say, and his arms weren't enough for that.

"Listen, you know what you said this morning about the father and son who were killed, that you were just trying to get away; you didn't know what you were bringing with you. It wasn't your fault, of course. But you were right, you never know who might be hurt by something you do . . . or don't do."

Kim was listening to him with her head on his shoulder. They had pulled a blanket over themselves and were hugging each other tightly under it for warmth. Joaquín realized he was afraid to say what he had to; he didn't want to spoil what they had.

"You were kidnapped seven years ago," he said. "That was one year after I became a narc."

He was silent a moment, as if the one year told it all.

"Drug agents aren't exactly shy, retiring types; they have this peculiarity of liking to work narcotics cases and most of them are pretty ambitious."

"What about Rhodes?" Kim asked.

"He's sharp as a tack. Don't let that cracker accent fool you. Whenever we're talking to a suspect he's the one who gets to play the bad cop."

"I've noticed."

"Got only two vices that I know of. One is Camels."

"What's the other?"

"Twinkies. General store in the town where he grew up carried Twinkies and he got hooked on them in his youth. Rhodes always puts on a suit and tie to go on a stakeout and he carries two attaché cases. One is filled with extra ammunition, the other is filled with Camels and Twinkies."

He was glad to talk about Rhodes. But now he thought, Quit stalling; either tell her or drop it.

"So I had all these guys looking at me like I'm the new kid on the block, which I was, and my supervisor, who was more of a politician than a cop, assigned me to tail a big dealer. The biggest of the big."

Kim lifted up and faced him intently in the dark, and Joaquín felt something, felt it in her whole body, bare arms and legs: a profound pause.

"The dealer was about to be indicted. He found some-body who looked like him and they switched places and—"

She put her hand gently over his mouth, almost a gesture of forgiveness. Joaquín looked at her. The meaning of the gesture was unmistakable.

Kim lay her head back on his shoulder. "I know," she said. "You followed the wrong man."

"How did you know?"

"It was one of Kane's favorite stories. He liked to brag about his friend in the drug agency who tipped him off and then put a young kid on his tail."

"I was the young kid."

"If it hadn't been you it would have been somebody else. So in a way I'm glad it was you. It gives us something in common. We were both burned by Kane."

"Did Kane ever say who his friend was?"

"Newton Bishop," Kim said.

She spoke the name as if it had no consequence, but for Joaquín the name seemed to resonate about them in the dark, like an echo of disaster.

"Bishop was my supervisor," he said. "They're talking about making him the new director."

"Don't worry," she said. "I'm going to get him for you. I'm going to get him for both of us."

After a while, shivering and whispering in the cold, they got out of the hammock, struggled with their clothes, clam-bered back in, and pulled the blanket around them.

"Hold me," Kim said. "Keep me warm."

The croaking of the frogs had subsided and there was only the peaceful sound of the rapids.

"It's not like flying a plane," she said. "You can do that from a book. It's like walking out across a frozen pond. I keep listening for the ice to crack. Somewhere in the middle the ice is very thin. I've been listening all day."

"Yes?"

"It hasn't cracked yet," she said.

15

JOLLY woke and lay in the hammock and knew it was another morning. Glints of sunlight came through cracks between the old boards; the chill of the night had been replaced by a hint of mugginess under the mosquito netting. He had spent two nights in the bunkhouse since sending Jones and Dog off after the girl. It had been amusing to watch them go, knowing they would be forced to stay in the jungle while he at least had the comfort of this smelly hammock. But the quiet emptiness of the bunkhouse reminded him that Jones and Dog hadn't come back yet, and Jolly was worried.

If the girl wasn't still in the plane they would have gone looking for the camp of those two hunters. That shouldn't have been hard to find. Christ, a river only had two banks and all you had to do was walk up and down it.

Soon he would have to take one of the horses from the corral and go hunting for the girl himself. He never should have sent Jones and Dog. It was his impulse to push them around that had made him do it, and he blamed himself scornfully now.

Asshole, he thought. For a man who was extremely sensitive to personal affronts Jolly suffered considerable abuse from some merciless part of his brain.

When he had come out of the bunkhouse yesterday morning the sky was black with vultures, circling low overhead, drawn by the dead bodies of the father and son. Some had landed at a safe distance and were hopping forward nervously. At his appearance they lifted off. Jolly dragged the bodies into the underbrush, and soon the vultures were back, swarming over the bodies like maggots. They lifted off again when he crossed the yard to go to his plane, but settled at once, and he got a good look at them—ugly bald heads, big fretted wings, and sharp, greedily tearing beaks—through the field glasses he had brought with him.

Jolly had spent most of yesterday sunning himself on a wing of the plane. Bored, he got one of the building blocks from his canvas bag. A pattern of red circuit wire was already stapled on it. Soldered to one end were a flashlight battery and one of the crappy wristwatches that he bought by the dozen from street vendors in Carib. Idly he attached a detonator to the other end and made a package of several sticks of plastic explosive bound together with masking tape. Shit, he thought, I might have to use a bomb after all. On his way back to the bunkhouse at dusk he had paused to look down at the horribly flattened remains of the father and son, and that had been the end of another day.

Climbing out of the hammock now, Jolly consulted two tangible measures of elapsed time, tilting his nose toward his armpit and rubbing the side of his face. He hated when the black whiskers began to show. A full black beard went well with a blond crew cut; it had a deliberate effect, especially if you wore a clean T-shirt and clean white painter pants. But it took weeks to grow a beard, and by that time his crew cut would darken at the roots.

With water from a big metal drum outside, Jolly made a pot of coffee. He sat on a log by the fire and watched the early-morning sky. The map he had drawn in the dirt was still there. It showed the dry marsh where the girl had come down, the camp of the hunters on the river, and this shitty ranch where he was stuck waiting. He picked up his stick and drew lines between the three points. He drew them over and over, as if to create a triangular prison from which no one could escape. But his eye kept straying to the mark he had made for the Indian village—far downriver, definitely outside the triangle. Impatiently he erased the map with his shoe.

Jolly had always been able to dismiss the girl. But now he thought of how she had tricked him into going for her purse, how she had wrecked his knees, still bruised by his fall from the wing. He couldn't let the girl get away.

At noon he went to his plane and got the field glasses and stood on the wing and scanned the edge of jungle. He kept trying to will Jones and Dog to emerge from the jungle with the girl. But the jungle offered nothing.

Without thinking, Jolly tried the sky.

Something caught his eye. He didn't know what it was at first. Specks. Far off, in the direction of that dry marsh. It's a fire, he thought. That's exactly what it was, cinders swarming upward in a hot draft of air caused by an inferno. Tiny cinders swarming . . . But who the hell started a fire?

Jolly lowered the glasses to ask himself the question. Then slowly he raised them again. Fire, hell. That's no fire. He knew what the specks were now.

Vultures. A shitload.

Three men had come after her. Two were dead.

That left the third. Numma One. Joaquín had the voice on tape. He could go home and put the cassette in his Sony Walkman and go jogging to it. Hear the imitation of a stoned grunt surrounded by VCs in the jungle. Hear the lecture on the Carib Indians. Hear the voice make its leap across the Intracoastal Waterway: "By the way, any fuckface who shouldn't be listening, this is for you . . ."

He thought of the voice and of the preppy, blond-haired man he had seen flying over the dry marsh. He put them together. They were one, and it was necessary to take the product of this combination seriously.

"You think Jolly will run?" he asked Kim.

They were motoring downriver. Her wet, just-washed hair was pulled back, and her scrubbed face was raised to a sun that hadn't yet cleared the trees. Sort of face that made the fading smudge of gray under one eye and the red welt on one cheekbone look like beauty marks. Girl who flew planes, wielded a mean hair dryer, and who listened for the scary wheeze of ice on frozen ponds. Same one who had tumbled out of the hammock that morning while Rhodes was whipping up pancakes for breakfast, who had pulled off her shirt and shorts at the river's edge, given Joaquín one quick mischievous grin over her shoulder and dove in before he could catch her, grab hold, and hang on.

"No," she said, "Jolly is stubborn. He won't run."

Joaquín thought of the mother who had put a new hand-woven shirt in his hands the other morning. He thought of the son laughing about his narrow escape from the jaguar and the look of concern and love and pride in the father's eyes when he had reprimanded the boy for being foolhardy, and he wondered how he was going to tell the mother that her husband and son were dead, that three strange men had dropped out of the sky and killed them for no reason she would ever understand.

"Good," he said. "I don't want Jolly to get away."

They planed along, the sun flickering like an old-time movie between the tall trees. A howler monkey stuck his head out and screamed at them. Joaquín screamed back, showing off his ability to imitate the wild cry.

"I used to eat them when I was a kid. It was Sunday dinner for us. My dad would take me hunting. Just like a father taking his son duck hunting in the States. The only difference was he used a blowgun instead of a shotgun."

He remembered watching his father fashion one of the long six-foot blowguns that the men of the village hunted with. It took two months to make a good one and his father would ream the bore until it was as smooth as a fine shotgun's. Then there would be the collecting of vines for the making of curare and the singing of hunting songs as the darts were treated with the poison.

He would follow his father through the jungle, looking for movement high in the trees, and he remembered the distinctive way his father would raise the blowgun to his mouth and rear back and throw himself forward to shoot the dart. The end result would be a dead monkey, tossed ignominiously on the fire.

Sunday dinner.

In the afternoon a ghastly white blanket of clouds settled over the jungle. It seemed to cut off the air, trapping the muggy heat and turning the river into an endless ordeal. Far off there was a flash of lightning.

"Are we going to overtake that?" Rhodes asked. "Or is it going to overtake us?"

"Either way, if it hits us we'll be swamped."

Joaquín turned in and cut the motor, and they drifted up

onto a flat mudbank. They got out and unloaded the canoe. With a heave he and Rhodes lifted and carried it to a group of jagged, slate-colored boulders on the bank. They lowered it carefully, propped upside down across the boulders for a roof. Kim helped them lug the backpacks and hammocks up, then the three of them hunkered under the canoe and waited for the storm.

The clouds moved into the sky like dirty gray icebergs. The tops of the trees across the river darkened strangely. The air became tense and electric, and suddenly under the canoe it was very dark.

Kim had become quiet. The scrubbed eagerness had left her face and she looked tired and withdrawn. The clouds seemed to have gotten to her.

"This should make the last stretch of rapids fun," Joaquín said.

She managed a smile. "I've just begun to realize I'm going home and I'm not sure I'm up for it. I feel like some monster that's being brought back to civilization."

"Like *King Kong?*"

"I was thinking more of *The Creature from the Black Lagoon.*"

A bolt of lightning shot straight into the ground like a spear, paling the darkened tops of the trees. Over a splitting boom of thunder Rhodes shouted, *"The Thing!"* Two fat raindrops plopped onto the hollowed log over their heads, and all at once the sky opened up.

In an instant the river was at their feet, and they huddled together as the jungle revealed itself fitfully behind a roaring white sheet. They waited out the storm in a contest of nostalgic recollection—*The Beast from 20,000 Fathoms, The Blob, The Fly, Rodan, Them*—all the tacky celluloid fakes.

The rain stopped. They dragged the canoe down the muddy bank and set off again. On the swollen river a litter of torn branches and leaves was being swept along, and soon the jungle was steaming and drying on both sides like an enormous hothouse.

There were the rapids. The canoe was bounced from one end of the tossing white blanket to the other and thrown out into the calm of another dusk, not far from another ring of smoke-blackened stones.

Swim. Supper. Joaquín chilling in the river a bottle of

Meursault, which he described as Comtefalon's finest, vintage '81, recommended by a wine-loving lawyer acquaintance who went by the unlawyerly name of Lawless.

But the white burgundy didn't do for them what the rum had the night before. Joaquín saw it in her face. It was a double realization. She was going home. Something terrible had happened to her.

"I pitched a game the day I was kidnapped," Kim told him. "It was the last game of the season. We had gone undefeated up until then, so it was a pretty big game."

They were lying in the hammock and Joaquín thought of the sort of splendid day it must have been—the anticipation of getting out of school for the summer, the students collecting autographs in their yearbooks, the girls eager to see what the boys they had crushes on would write. By the ball field there had probably been one of those drinking fountains with a tricky handle that you had to turn just right to keep water from shooting up your nose.

"Did you win?"

"Just barely. By one run. Then I went off to the showers," she said. "I thought it was just chance at first. It wasn't until later that I realized Kane had sent Jolly on purpose."

Joaquín held her and tried to comfort her.

"I never got to go to the prom or get drunk on beer or try pot. I never went for a driver's license. I never got a car for graduation. I didn't get to lose my virginity with a boy I liked."

He felt her fingernails digging into his sides as she buried her face against his shoulder.

"Oh God . . . I just heard the ice crack."

Her father was Tom Mitchell, the prosecutor who had brought Kane down. He had retired and moved to Foxhaven, Connecticut, where he kept a small office over the main street. Kim would drop by every day after school and do her homework while her dad finished up work. She remembered everything about the office—rolltop desk, electric typewriter streaked with Wite·Out, a copying machine, and an incomplete set of *Corpus Juris Secundum*, missing the letter *E*.

"He used to tell clients he could handle any problem as

long as it didn't begin with *E*," she said.

Her father liked to play catch with her, getting up from the dinner table every night complaining humorously about his enslavement to the national pastime. He had a terrific memory for facts and figures.

"But I could always beat him at baseball statistics."

Joaquín thought of Tom Mitchell as a man who had been forced to go on living as two people, the one going through the motions of daily life, the other staring at an enormous vacancy. He tried to change the subject.

"Who had the highest single-season batting average?"

"Hugh Duffy. He hit .438 in 1894. Ty Cobb had the highest lifetime average, .367." She nudged him. "C'mon, you can do better than that. What's the most home runs that 'Home Run' Baker ever hit in one season?"

"I give up."

"Only twelve. But he hit them when they counted. Who threw the pitch that Babe Ruth hit his sixtieth home run off? Tom Zachary. Washington Senators, 1927. Pack it in. My dad used to say, 'Betcha a hundred dollars you can't stump her.'"

So they had got back to her father anyway.

"I thought of calling him from Caracas. But it wouldn't be any good. He'd probably think I was a crank. Even if he didn't, I'd have to hang up the phone sooner or later, and there's too much to say."

"I agree. The phone is no good."

"I want to go up and tell him myself. I don't want any newspapers or television or government officials. I just want it to be us."

"I'm sure it can be arranged."

"I'm scared. It's been so long. He thinks I'm dead. He's had seven years to get used to the idea. I don't want to hurt him."

She seemed to understand that hurting her father was unavoidable. She lowered her expectations.

"I just hope he's alive."

The croaking of the frogs filled the silence.

"My father smoked a pipe," Kim said. "The name of the pipe tobacco was Barking Dog. On the can were the words 'Barking Dog never Bites.' So that's how I'll know if he's in his office."

"How?"

"Because he doesn't have an air conditioner, and in the summer with the window open you can smell Barking Dog all the way down the street."

She seemed to drift into sleep. Then, as a sort of sleepy afterthought she said, "I'll go up the stairs and knock on his door and go in and say, 'It's me.' And if he doesn't remember me I guess I'll just have to hit him with some baseball statistics."

16

OVER the noise of the outboard motor, Joaquín heard a helicopter. It came skimming over a green-forested mountain and on over the jungle, the hard chopping of its rotor swelling toward them. He knew it must be the supply helicopter that visited the village once a week.

As it reached the river it hovered overhead, long enough for him to try some sign language, jabbing a finger at the helicopter and then pointing to himself, to indicate that it should wait for them. The pilot, a Pancho Villa lookalike, round face, droopy mustache, waved from his bubble; whether he understood the signal wasn't clear; then the helicopter swooped away ahead of them. Joaquín goosed the motor, and the canoe went planing swiftly downriver.

It wouldn't be impossible for all three of them to jam into his little two-seater. But they had the two backpacks, and it would be easier if Rhodes hopped a ride with the chopper, since it was here.

In Caracas they would land at Carlota airport in the middle of the city and go to the American Embassy. He wanted to make Kim's return to the real world as painless as possible. Moral support, he thought. And one practical connection: Fisher, the ambassador, a sandy-haired career diplomat with his courteous low-key sociability and a bad complexion that, oddly, made you like him even more. But moral support and practical connection aside, he wasn't about to let Kim get away, on the theory that super girls who dropped out of the sky in red planes didn't come along that often.

The helicopter was out of sight. The canoe sped on, its wake sweeping out behind, glittering in the sun.

They passed a group of fishermen from the village, gathered in dugout canoes in a backwater of the river, some standing with long poles to stir up the water, others holding nets to catch the frightened fish. They passed the mission station; there was no sign of the priest who dispensed medicines with a scrupulous awareness of the thin line he had to walk between helping the Indians and interfering with what was left of their culture.

Far ahead now he glimpsed the tops of the trees behind which the helicopter would have settled onto the cleared field of the airstrip. The sky above the trees remained empty, and he guessed his signal had been understood.

"When we get to the field you hop out and tell the pilot to wait!" he shouted to Kim. "We'll go on to the village!"

"Does the pilot speak English!"

"No!"

"Then how am I supposed to tell him not to go?"

"Just grab him and point to the ground and don't let him get away!"

Joaquín thought of his progress toward the village as something that was inevitably diminishing the last moments of an old woman's happiness. And there is nothing you can tell her that will make it any easier, he thought. Except that you didn't forget to give her son the shirt.

He would be glad when the duty was over.

"I'll get one of the men to run us back up!"

They reached the cleared field. The helicopter sat in the middle, its big rotor still, its tapered tail pointing toward the river, and the bubble of its cockpit facing away. The usual crowd of Indians was gone, having evidently picked up the mail and supplies and brought them back to the village or to the mission station. Beyond, through the trees, Joaquín could make out the high palm-thatched roofs of the lodges, half a mile farther on.

Slowing abruptly, he came in alongside the bank. Rhodes and he held the canoe steady as Kim climbed out. The bank rose gradually and then steeply, cutting the helicopter off from view.

"Might as well take the backpacks," Joaquín said.

They each handed out a backpack. "Need a hand?" Rhodes asked. But she was already lugging one of the packs up the slope, and he said, "What a stupid question."

Kim left the backpack at the top and came down for the other.

"I don't know how long we'll be," Joaquín said. "I have to tell that old woman about her husband and son."

He saw the pained look in her eyes. "If I hadn't gotten away," she said, "they'd still be alive."

She took hold of the other pack and lugged it up the slope and turned and gave a short nod of self-acceptance.

"I used to blame myself for what happened to me. It was my own fault for going into that locker room alone. I never should have let Jolly get me. I should have fought harder to get away. But I knew there was nothing I could have done. I know it now, anyway."

Kim shouldered the pack in a practical motion and scowled at her dirty shorts. "I need a change of clothes." Then she smiled and raised a clenched fist triumphantly, the handcuff dangling from her wrist. "And I can't wait to get out of these."

She started across the field. Joaquín thought she called, "See you!" But he couldn't be sure over the noise of the outboard as he sped up again.

He glanced back and saw Kim walking toward the helicopter with the backpack on her shoulder. Then she was out of sight and they were speeding on toward the village.

Before they knew it they were past the tree on the bank where Rhodes had practiced with his bow. Rhodes's head turned quickly as it caught his eye, going by: the rope hanging from the limb, the bundle of marsh grass on the ground beneath it.

"There goes my jaguar."

The sun was high in the sky. Sunlight came off the river in a silent, blinding explosion. The canoe seemed to enter the explosion and penetrate to the heart of the silence, so that Joaquín was suddenly aware of it. Ordinarily the sound of the outboard motor would have brought children.

He pulled in and cut the motor and the silence was complete.

"Where's my fan club?" Rhodes said.

"Doesn't show much faith in your hunting ability."

Each took a rolled hammock and a bow case and went up the bank. A path was worn through the long grass and they walked along it single-file.

Joaquín came to the edge of the great irregular circle of bare earth on which the lodges of the village were situated. There were no women working, no children playing. The large, high-domed lodges had an otherworldly quality, like huge monoliths. They were the color of earth, the caplike roofs of palm leaves browned by the sun.

The path had ended and Rhodes joined him and they both stood, each with his hammock and bow.

"Where is everyone?"

"They must be on their way back through the woods." But it was unlikely that the whole village had emptied out to see the helicopter. "I've got to find my uncle. I'll need his help to break the news to the old woman."

They started across the circle. The curve of the river had put his uncle's lodge above them now, toward the airstrip.

Joaquín stuck his head in the first lodge. A cooking fire was smoking with a pot over it. But no one was tending it. The hammocks strung from the sturdy bamboo poles were limp, the perfect curves of their undersides unmarred by the elbows or knees of sleeping figures. He took a step inside to confirm his impression. He shrugged. "Nobody home." Rhodes was gazing up under the high dome of the ceiling, examining the palm-leaf thatching with interest. Joaquín listened for the shrieks of happy children, the babble of gossiping women. In the silence he heard the rustling of a small bird or a beetle in the dry brown palm leaves. He almost thought he could hear the seeping of the smoke through the charred logs of the fire.

As they came back out, a dog appeared from somewhere on the other side and charged across the circle of bare earth, barking at them, filling the silence with its angry noise and calling up the absurd notion of a solitary dog defending a deserted village. They waited for it. The dog recognized Joaquín. It approached them, friendly and eager, and Joaquín patted its head.

"I'll bet this fellow knows where everyone is."

"Those must've been men from the village that we passed upriver," Rhodes said. "Looked to me like they were fishing."

"That's what they were doing. They use those long poles to scare the fish off the bottom and then they catch them in nets."

They neared his uncle's lodge. It stood on the edge of the woods that separated the village and the airstrip. Joaquín looked into the trees for any women or children who might be on their way back from the helicopter. He glimpsed men running. But they weren't coming toward the village, they were going away from it toward the airstrip, and they were armed with bows. He thought absurdly of stories his uncle had told him about squabbles that would break out between villages in the old days. One village would try to rip off another village's planting grounds and there would be a war and then a peace, celebrated by festivities in which the men would get drunk on hallucinogenic snuff and the headmen of the rival villages would exchange blows in a friendly joust.

From the entrance of his uncle's lodge Joaquín saw a boy look out and wave to him urgently. He went to the boy. There were women and children gathered together inside and as he entered they pushed forward anxiously, all talking at once.

"A gun!" the boy tried to tell him.

"What gun? Where?"

"A gun! The man has a gun!"

The women were crowding around him. Joaquín turned and shoved away from them. In Rhodes's face he saw his own understanding of the terrible mistake they had made. The boy was running after him, pointing toward the airstrip, his tiny voice shouting.

"A gun!"

Joaquín ran.

To Kim, coming up the bank, the cleared field looked deserted. The helicopter sat in the middle of it, facing away from her, and she saw no sign of the pilot. At one end was a shedlike structure of poles and palm fronds that protected Joaquín's plane from tropical sun and rainstorms.

The field was bright and hot in the sun and the jungle around it was dark with shade under the tall trees. Shouldering one of the backpacks, she cut through the heavy grass at the edge of the field, scaring up some butterflies that went winking away like green and white and yellow confetti. She felt happy and tough, one of three great guys who had made it downriver and were on their way to Caracas.

Figure it this way, she thought. You were in an auto accident. It put you in a coma for seven years. You just woke up. No more tubes in your arms or up your nose. You're out of the hospital. Or maybe you were carried off by a tornado. That would make Kane the Wicked Witch. But even in a joke it was hard for Kim to think of the two men in the dugout canoe as scarecrows or tin woodmen or cowardly lions. And your old man isn't whatever the aunt's name was back in Kansas. He's just your father and you're going to see him. Got it, Mitchell? You're actually going to see him. Soon.

The pilot lay on his stomach across the two front seats. He was reaching under the far seat to pick up something that had dropped on the floor of the bubble. His boots with crepe-rubber soles stuck out at her; dirt had accumulated in the wrinkles and on one heel were the smoothed and hardened remains of a piece of chewing gum.

"Hi," Kim called. "I'm glad you haven't left. We have somebody who needs a ride."

The pilot, with his head down, didn't answer. He probably wasn't keen about having his rear end spoken to in a foreign language. She decided to wait for him to sit up. But the pilot didn't move.

Kim climbed into the bubble, thinking she might be able to help him find whatever he was looking for. She touched him on the shoulder. "Hey, can I help?" The black hair at the back of his head was matted and soggy with a substance that looked as thick as oil. His face was blown away and flies swarmed up from the blood that was dripping from it.

When she turned she saw Jolly. In the time she had spent talking to a dead man he had come running from the shed and was almost up to her. He was in his T-shirt and floppy white pants, a necktie was around his bare neck, and something was clutched in his hand.

Kim jumped out of the helicopter and ran. The village

wasn't close but she thought if she could get into the trees she might be able to elude him. She shouted for help. But the trees seemed to close off the sound of her voice. So finally she just ran as fast as she could.

Jolly was smaller than Jones, but he was also quicker. He caught up with her as she reached the woods. She darted around the trunk of a fallen tree, too fast to see where she was going. She tripped over a tangle of vines that had been pulled up by the trunk. She felt the stab of a needle. Whirling, jerking away from it, and trying to rise, Kim saw a hypodermic syringe dangling from one leg of her shorts. Jolly grabbed her ankle. She swung at him with her free handcuff. She was sure she could get away from him. But as she struggled to her feet, a wave of nausea staggered her. Oh God, she thought, he got me with the needle. Then, with a suddenness that she remembered from long ago, the necktie was around her throat.

She fought like a demon, clawing at the necktie, flailing out at Jolly. But in a moment she was at the helicopter and Jolly was wrestling her into it, and she realized her stubborn battle was a drunk's illusion. Jolly clipped on her free wrist the handcuff that dangled from the other. Her effort to stop him produced only a feeble lurch. She could barely hold her head up. The helicopter broke into a loud chugging, and looking down, Kim saw they were suddenly in the air.

The needle hadn't knocked her out. But it made everything a blur, nightmarish and unreal.

Below her, seen through the transparent bubble, was the field. Two men were running across it. She knew the helicopter must be hovering, because the field didn't go away. The shadow of the helicopter lingered on it like a permanent feature. She saw the men run past the body of the pilot and go on to the end of the field and disappear into, what was that, a house? But it wasn't a house. It was the shed where Joaquín kept his plane, and with what remained of consciousness Kim thought, They're going to get the plane. They're going to come after me. They won't let Jolly get away.

A sudden shift of the bubble threw her forward. Her face was pressed against the hard transparency. Directly below her, as if the abrupt change in direction had been made for her specific instruction, the two men were pushing a small airplane from the shed. The helicopter hung there an instant, shaking. In the next instant the plane and the men pushing it were gone in an explosion of black smoke and flashing flame.

Then the helicopter spun around, sailing and rising away, and Kim sank into a darkness filled with cries of grief and rage.

17

Kim came to, waking from one darkness into another. She was lying on a hard stone floor. It was all she knew and even this was a guess. In the dark it was impossible to be sure. She lay very still, feeling the hard surface under her. She wasn't ready to investigate the darkness.

Hesitantly she started with herself. A mental list was made. She was wearing her tennis shirt, shorts, and sneakers. Her head ached. A taste of nausea lingered in her sinuses. She felt lightheaded when she sat up and she tried not to be sick. The darkness pressed around her and she hugged her knees, as if for protection. The handcuffs were fastened to one wrist.

Jolly had grabbed her and stuck a needle in her. Had he brought her back to Kane's estate, or was she in some cell in the police station used for torture or solitary confinement? Or had Jolly brought her to Peru, as he had intended, and was she in the whorehouse? Madam Chew's. That must be it. Jolly had landed outside of Lima and she had been dumped in a car and transported to the house by the Madam's men.

But there were no smells of incense or perfume or of anything associated with human commercial activity, only the cold stone odor of the floor and a faint odor of decay, as when a small animal dies inside the walls of a house and its smell lingers. It stirred the faint nausea in her throat. Kim held her arm to her nose and smelled the warm neutral odor of her flesh. This, at least, was human.

She listened. The silence was as deep as the darkness.

She scratched an itch on her leg and heard the soft scraping of her fingernails. The darkness was an intimidation to speech. She faced it and opened her mouth to speak. But the only sound that came was a groan of anguish.

The groan brought vision, too, as clear and vivid as if it were actual. An image flashed in her mind, the bright-or-ange explosion of flame springing upward from the ground, obliterating everything, the plane, the two men beside it. Kim covered her face. "Oh God . . ." Her voice fell flat and dead in the darkness and was no consolation.

She stayed this way a long time, trying to blot out the vision. Finally she got on her hands and knees. Carefully she felt her way along the floor. At once she was lost. The darkness gave her nothing to go by. She kept reaching out in front of her, exploring the flat slab of the floor and inching forward. She came to a wall that seemed to be made of cin-der blocks. Unsteadily she stood up. The rough texture of the blocks was unvarying as the smooth floor. She edged along the wall squeamishly, not knowing what she might encounter. The odor of decay wasn't reassuring. She came to a corner. But what was a corner in a room where she couldn't see? Kim felt a dizzying sense of disorientation. She had to force herself to go on. She went along the other wall. It was cinder blocks, too.

Her bare leg came in contact with a cold, hard, damp, smooth surface. She groped down and her hand touched water. She withdrew it and found a familiar object. Kim lifted it and let it go. It fell with a wooden bang. A toilet seat, something definite among the unvarying surfaces of floor and walls.

She reached for the handle and pushed it. The water swirled sluggishly around the bowl and gurgled downward into pipes that sounded rusted and old. The toilet continued to hiss loudly, the metal handle trembling as the bowl filled with water. Then it was still.

Kim went along the wall, searching for a light switch. She came to another corner, then a door. It was a heavy metal door and it was locked. There was no light switch beside it.

She took a chance then. In the dark she judged where the toilet was and crossed straight to it without going back along the wall. Kim found it and sat down beside it and felt a small victory. The toilet was the center of her universe. She could move out from it and come back to it and it would always be there, exactly where it was now. In this way she could begin to acquire a sort of blind man's sense of the space she was in.

But in the dark she saw a jungle and a river winding through it and two men, one casting a fly rod with the same strength and grace as her old man, the other swimming deep underwater, reaching for the handcuff dangling from her wrist.

Trying to hold her head up made her sick. She lay down and seemed to sink into the hard floor, too broken to care about what the dark hid, wanting only to blot out the river.

When she woke it was because a light had come on. She was lying by the toilet. Kim sat up and saw the room was as bare and celllike as it had felt. The cinder-block walls were illuminated by a weak light bulb in the middle of the ceiling. There was the sound of a bolt being shot open on the other side of the door. She thought of Peru, her new life. But Jolly's old dirty jogging shoes, tied with frayed broken laces, walked in.

The rest of Jolly was immaculate, blond crew cut, clean T-shirt that showed off his biceps, freshly laundered white pants. Shaved, Jolly's face was almost boyish. But the dead look in his eyes didn't match his phony grin.

"Hey, little girl, I brought you something to eat!"

His cheerful tone suggested a treat. A candy bar. An apple. Squinting painfully, Kim saw a plate of greasy plantains with a skimpy portion of rice.

"Sorry," Jolly said, shrugging. "I tried to get that old bitch in the kitchen to stick in a few pieces of pork. You know what she said? 'That crazy girl be better off in a lunatic asylum.' The truth is, she wants to save all the leftovers for herself and her do-nothing husband."

Kim had no appetite. She put the plate aside.

"I thought I was in Peru," she said dully.

"Hell no, you're back home. I was going to bring you upstairs to your old room. But Kane said no way, down in the basement is where you go."

She had always known there was a basement, where the cook's husband would occasionally disappear to fetch a bottle of wine, a piece of lawn furniture, a hurricane lamp.

"Kane is sore as hell," Jolly said. "He didn't even wait for me to come up to the house yesterday when he saw me coming in. He jumped in his jeep and got his ass down to the airstrip. He wasn't so mad about you crashing his plane. It was Jones and Dog being dead that really got to him. What did you do to those two?"

Kim didn't answer. But it was okay with Jolly. He went on talking as if he and she had shared a great adventure.

"You know how I knew about it? Two jackets! I saw these vultures way off in the distance, so I hopped in my plane and flew to where they were. About all that was left of Jones was his seersucker jacket. Then I fly to that dry marsh and come in low and all that's left of Dog is his safari jacket. So I said, 'Shit, man, you better get to that Indian village fast.' "

Jolly was eager to show how clever he had been.

"I circled far away from the river and came back way ahead of you. They got a sort of mission at the village with this dumb priest. I landed out back and gave him a story and he put me up for the night. I had two lucky breaks. A helicopter and you. Both at the same time."

"You killed the pilot," Kim said. "You killed those two men."

"Hey, whose fault is that? They shoulda stayed out of it. It was none of their business." Jolly's tone became defensive and cranky. "You want to see what you done to me?"

He pulled up his pant legs and she saw two large ugly scabs, one on each kneecap. They seemed to confirm the fury of her drugged struggle. Then she remembered how Jolly had fallen from the wing of the plane. He displayed the scabs now as unforgivable injuries. In Jolly's world two men blown up by a bomb were fair payment for his two battered knees.

"What the hell," he said obligingly, "I don't hold it against you. In the end you did me a big favor. You know what I didn't like about those two guys?"

Kim thought he meant Joaquín and Rhodes. Then she realized it was Jones and Dog. Jolly had never gotten along with either of them.

"They thought they were important because they were around Kane all the time and saw him every day. Christ, if

I wanted to I could see him, too. But that's just it! I don't want to see him! He's a pain in the ass. What do I want to see Kane for?"

Kim had a vision of the long, lonely hours that Jolly spent talking to himself in just this way, tossing a basketball out by the hangar. In the privacy of Jolly's fantasy he was the real mastermind. Smiling, winking, he confided to her the true state of affairs.

"I'm the one who runs things around here anyway. I'm Numma One. Numma One G.I. Kane just don't know it."

"Are you going to leave the light on?" Kim said as he turned to go.

"Sorry, boss's orders."

"I thought you were the boss."

Jolly looked offended. "Hey, sometimes you gotta let the other guy think he's giving the orders."

"Please," she said.

He shook his head in annoyance. Her last remark had soured him.

"You're lucky," he said. "It's only a little darkness. Figure it this way, the worst that can happen is he'll kill you."

The door closed. The bolt was shot. Kim's eyes, accustomed at last to the weak bulb, searched her cell urgently and saw only the rough, porous cinder-block walls. Then the cell was gone and it was dark again.

In the dark she saw the river, two men in a dugout canoe. Jolly was wrong, she thought. The worst had already happened.

18

"MORNING, Jerry."

At the table with his lawyer, Jerry scowled—probably still thinking of the way Joaquín had knocked him down and stuck a gun in his face the first time they met.

"Ernie will be with us in a minute. Can I order anything up for anybody? Breakfast?"

The lawyer said, "We had breakfast upstairs. I put it on the room." He had a bush of kinky black hair, a beak nose, an olive complexion, and a large overbite that gave his smile a pained, apologetic air.

"Good, no problem," Joaquín said. "I hope it was a big one."

He sat down at the table and saw that his affability was lost on Jerry, who turned away and gazed out to the balcony. The southerly view took in the Intracoastal Waterway, Port Everglades, the glittering ocean beyond, and an immaculate blue sky. It was another morning.

There had been a morning in Caracas, after the day it had taken for them to get out of the jungle, using the priest's shortwave radio to summon a plane. And a morning after that, boarding a passenger jet to fly back to Miami, followed by an afternoon in which he and Rhodes had driven up to Fort Lauderdale to arrange this meeting, going to work on Jerry's lawyer to convince him that it would be wise for Jerry to consider pleading guilty and making a deal.

This was the third morning, the beginning of what Joaquín thought of as the fourth day of his new life.

The room was nice. It had been a condition of Jerry's

213

that the meeting be held at the most expensive hotel in town,
and Joaquín had obliged. Anything to please Jerry. It was a
lot classier than the agency office on the top floor of the federal courthouse downtown. The office was like a cave, its
only windows facing inside, looking out on a walkway corridor and a concrete balustrade, and the main room was
dreary: a dozen metal desks, usually empty, bare walls with
no maps or pictures, boxes of files stacked on the floor, and
in one corner—where the press conferences were held after
drug busts to display evidence for reporters and TV cam-
eras—a pile of duffel bags.

No, definitely wouldn't suit Jerry.

"I've been meaning to apologize for the way I jumped
on you," Joaquín said now.

"Don't bother." Jerry stuck a piece of chewing gum in
his mouth.

"You scared the shit out of me when I saw you going for
your gun."

"Hey, I didn't know you was a cop. I thought you was
some scumbag trying to rip me off. You think I woulda gone
for my piece if I had known?"

"Then I did both of us a favor, didn't I, Jerry?" Joaquín
strove to establish some level of mutual concern. "I saved
myself from getting blown away and I saved you from killing a federal agent."

The look on Jerry's face told Joaquín not to do him any
favors.

Rhodes came in. He nodded curtly to Jerry and the lawyer, pulled a chair away from the table, and sat with his legs
propped on one of the beds. He tossed a file folder onto it,
extracted a cigarette from a crumpled pack with his lips. Lit
up, scowling impatiently.

After an uncomfortable silence the lawyer began hesitantly. "I, uh, talked to my client yesterday after meeting
with you gentlemen and I relayed to him the possibility that
you might make a strong recommendation for leniency if he
agreed to cooperate with your investigation. I feel con-
strained to point out that initially my client was rather vigorously disinclined to go along with the suggestion."

"I told him no fucking way, is what I told him," Jerry
said.

"However," the lawyer said, "after giving the matter some consideration my client has decided it might be a good idea."

"You understand, Jerry," Joaquín said, "we can't make any promises. All we can do is ask the court to go easy."

"You mean so I don't have to do time."

"There's no way you can get out of doing time. It's a question of how much time. You'll have to tell us what you know."

"So go ahead," Jerry said with a shrug. "Ask."

Joaquín wasn't encouraged; he had heard the offer to go ahead and ask before, and knew it was a stone wall.

"What about your Uncle Kiki?"

"I don't have an Uncle Kiki. I have an Uncle Henry. That's what I always call him. Enrique. Son of a bitch pisses me off. Got a big house in Miami. Never invites me to the pool."

"How did he pay for his big house, Jerry?"

"He owns a string of businesses."

"What sort of businesses?"

"Christ, now you got me. I think he's got a car wash, a liquor store . . . Tell you the truth, I ain't sure what he's got. Why don't you ask him?"

"I mean his real business. What you were doing for him."

"You mean dealing? Hey, man, you got it all wrong. That was my show. It was a big mistake, first-time offense. My uncle didn't have nothing to do with it."

"How often do you see him?"

"Once, twice a year. At the most. Just 'cause the guy's my uncle don't mean he gotta be nice to me. He and my father never got along. See, my father was for Castro and Kiki couldn't stand Castro; that's why he come to Florida."

"Who's Kiki?" Rhodes asked. He had started a mustache in the jungle and in the last few days it had matured; it made him look like the accountant he had never become, except for his eyes.

"Kiki," Jerry said. "My Uncle Kiki. I thought that's who we're talking about."

"Oh," Rhodes said, "I thought we were talking about your Uncle Henry." He didn't glance around at the group; he inhaled his cigarette and made a backhand wave. "Listen, what are we doing with this turkey?"

The lawyer showed his overbite apologetically. "I can't

make my client tell you what he says he doesn't know."

"You ever see *Henry* socially?" Rhodes asked Jerry.

"You mean at a party, something like that? I told you, he don't even invite me to the pool."

"Never take you out to a restaurant?"

Jerry shook his head and made a face. "Nah."

"Never put his arm around you, show how much he likes his young punk of a nephew?"

"Hey, what is this?" Jerry said.

From the file folder on the bed Rhodes took out a photograph. He tossed it on the table. It was a photo of Kiki Soldano sitting with a group of men in a restaurant. Kiki's arm was around his nephew and big grins were on their faces.

"You left this lying around your apartment," Rhodes said.

"That don't prove nothing," Jerry said. But the appearance of the photo seemed to cause a quiver in the excess flesh of his chubby face.

"This is a waste of time," Rhodes said. "I say let's see him in court."

"It's up to Jerry," Joaquín said. He addressed the comment to the lawyer as if in sympathy with the lawyer's pained smile. "Maybe you and he should talk it over again. We can't make a recommendation for leniency if he doesn't level with us. It all depends on the quality of the information he gives us and what he's willing to testify to. Don't you understand, Jerry? We're trying to do you a favor."

"Some favor!" Jerry protested. "My life ain't worth shit if I squeal on my uncle!"

"You're our star witness, Jerry. We don't want to lose you. Nobody'll even know you're talking to us until you get up in court."

"What about after?"

"We'll put you in a safe house. Change your name. No one will ever be able to find you." Joaquín bore down, calm, reasonable, sympathetic, even his threats expressed in a tone of serious concern for Jerry's welfare. "Because, Jerry, you should realize we got you in your girlfriend's apartment with all that coke and your girlfriend is going to tell the jury that you brought it up there and cut it on her kitchen table, and how many other times you did it and who you sold it to and for how much. . . ."

"That bitch," Jerry shook his head. "I tried to get a hold of her after I made bail."

"We're keeping her under wraps," Rhodes said.

"Look," Joaquín said, "we're not asking you to make a formal statement or sign anything now. All we want is some idea of what we're going to get as our part of the deal."

"I gotta talk to my lawyer."

"We'll give you three minutes," Rhodes said.

"You can have as long as you like," Joaquín said.

Jerry was nervous. He took the chewing gum from his mouth and stuck it in the black plastic ashtray between them.

"Crissake," he said, "I gotta think."

"Where those ten kilos come from, Jerry?"

It was the first question of the afternoon. Joaquín asked it amiably. They were all at the table, including Rhodes. It had taken Jerry most of the morning to make up his mind, agonizing over the decision, trying to clarify the deal he was going to get, backing out emphatically several times before finally agreeing to talk. He was jaunty now; he had had two rum and Cokes with lunch.

"Carib," he said. "Ever hear of it?"

"Sure," Joaquín said.

He and Rhodes had gone out for lunch to give Jerry additional time to feel unpressured. Jerry and his lawyer had ordered up from room service, and the room's original neatness had been modified by a clutter of dishes and utensils and the visible remains of leftovers that had been moved from the table to the mirrored dresser.

The blue sky beyond the balcony had turned white, and Joaquín, who had just come in from the sweltering heat, felt the sweat on the back of his shirt drying coldly in the air-conditioned room.

"Lot of guys never heard of it," Jerry said.

"We've heard of it," Rhodes said.

"Who was your supplier?"

"Guy named Kane, used to be a big wheel. Skipped the country long time ago. I was just a kid. Him and Kiki were good friends."

"You handled everything with Kane."

Jerry shook his head. "He's too big for that. Has some

asshole named Jolly runs the whole show for him."

Joaquín sat very still. He didn't want Jerry to see they were going exactly where he wanted. Jerry would lie and evade if he thought he could get away with it. But he was at a disadvantage now, thinking it was Kiki they were interested in. He would talk freely about Kane and Jolly, just to show off and prove he was leveling with them.

So far Jerry was doing fine.

"Don't ask me if it's his first name or last," he said. "Jolly is all the mules ever called him. I never even talked to him."

"How did you do business, then?"

"Hey, that was the whole thing! I didn't have to talk to him. It was all done on my answering machine."

Jerry spread his hands expansively and Joaquín saw he was about to enter a boastful phase. Whatever Jerry said now it would pay to act impressed.

"Jolly would call me whenever he had something ready, so I would know when to send the mules. Then he would call me again to let me know the stuff was on its way. All I had to do was get the message."

"How long was this going on?"

"Long time, seven, eight years, since Kane left the country. I just come down a few months ago to run it for Kiki."

"So you sort of inherited Jolly. He was a voice on your answering machine."

"You got it," Jerry said. "He don't even use his own name. Always calls himself 'Numma One.' Like he's the boss, you know."

"Numma One," Joaquín said.

"I told you the guy was an asshole."

"You're conducting millions of dollars' worth of business a year with this guy," Rhodes said, "you never even spoke to him, never met him?"

"All I know is what the mules told me. What do they know? They fly to Carib and go out to Kane's estate. Jolly meets them at the gate. They give him the money, he gives them the stuff. That's it. He's a creep, that's all they ever said."

Jerry was lost, trying to put together what little he knew about Jolly.

"Got a good connection in Peru. Bunch of black guys on

the estate to do the work for him. Delivers a terrific product, you gotta hand him that. There's no way you can touch Kane anyway, where he is. He's paying the whole government off to protect his ass."

"What does Jolly know about you?" Joaquín said.

He hoped the strain in his voice now wasn't obvious. He didn't want to undermine Jerry's fragile capacity for honesty.

"About me?" Jerry said, puzzled. "He don't even know I exist."

"He know what you look like? Ever see a picture of you?"

"What would he see a picture of me for? Look, all he knows is, I'm Kiki's nephew. What else would the mules tell him? There were guys before me, and if Kiki has anything to say about it, there'll be guys after me. You wanna know what I was to Jolly?"

"What?"

"An answering machine. A fucking answering machine. I got the message."

Joaquín glanced at Rhodes and their eyes met. Rhodes got up from the table and went out. A bewildered, worried look came into Jerry's face; it was beginning to occur to him that he might have given away something important. Something he could have used to bargain with.

Joaquín reassured him, "We're coming along fine, Jerry. Most of this is just routine. Now I want to know about the mules you ran. Names, what they looked like, how many there were, anything you can tell me . . ."

Joaquín lay in the dark, surrounded by the air-conditioned air of a luxury hotel room. With the drapes pulled back from the balcony's glass door he could make out the outlines of the room, black silhouettes of table, dresser, and TV. He could turn on the TV but he didn't want to wake Rhodes, who was snoring softly in the other bed. The TV wouldn't help anyway. It would only emphasize his inability to act.

He could go up to the revolving restaurant at the top of the hotel and have a drink at the bar. It would go round and round, showing him all of Fort Lauderdale at night, and that, too, would demonstrate that he wasn't going anywhere, just yet.

He had questioned Jerry all day, and there would be another day of questioning tomorrow. But asking questions hadn't made him tired enough to sleep. He hadn't really slept in four days.

Quietly Joaquín got up and went to the dresser and found his portable tape recorder. He was in his boxer shorts. Bare-chested and in his bare feet he stepped onto the balcony and slid the door closed behind him. There was a smell of salt air and he felt the warm night against the cooled surface of his skin. In the dark he saw the lights of yachts moored in the slips below or moving along the Intracoastal, and he made out a battleship at anchor in the port beyond. Sitting in a balcony chair with his tape recorder in his lap, he put in a cassette and pushed the play button.

There was the beep of an answering machine. A voice said, "Hey, man, this is Lucho. When you gonna call? You don't love me no more?" Then the clunk of a receiver being hung up.

Joaquín pushed the fast-forward button. Stopped. Listened. Heard another short message. "Call me, man. Lemme know what's going down." Clunk.

He spun the tape ahead. Stopped. Listened.

The voice wasn't just a voice now. It came with a face—blond-haired preppy, big eyeglasses—and with a history of deeds. It was like a piece of bad news. It reminded him that he had failed to take the owner of this pathetic, sappy voice seriously.

"Numma One here. Roger, Numma One. Go ahead. Got a little problem, amigo. I'm up to my ass in dead grunts. I need somebody to take 'em off my hands . . ."

Joaquín spun the tape ahead carefully now. A short sprint forward, a quick stop. He was looking for something specific, something he remembered that hadn't been clear when he had first heard it weeks ago.

"—bet you never knew that the word *cannibal* comes from *Carib*."

This was it. It was somewhere in the middle of Jolly's lecture on the Carib Indians.

"—good guys were Arawaks. The bad guys were Caribs. Don't ask me why, the Caribs were real shits. They sort of wandered up from South America, going from one island to another, doing a number on the poor old Arawaks. Kill and eat the men. Take the women as slaves, do what they want with them . . ."

It was getting close. It was right here.

"Remind me of a guy I know, got exactly the same mentality. Just like a real Carib."

Joaquín cut the voice off. He thought, Remind me of a guy I know.

The black ocean stretched away toward a black sky. Far out, the lights of a tanker appeared to be moving with meteoric speed against the darkness.

Time to be a Carib, Joaquín thought. Time to be like your ancestors.

He had promised the two young men from the village that he would teach them how to fly. They had built a shed to protect his plane from sun and rain, and they had run to push the plane out, knowing he would want to go after the man who had killed the helicopter pilot.

Joaquín thought of the thunderous boom and the hot blast of air that had knocked Rhodes and him back into the trees as they had come onto the field. When they had gotten to their feet the plane was burning. It had looked like an enormous crumpled bug, collapsed on its side, one wing torn off, and there had been something else, an odd, shrill, piercing sound that was like a curious continuation of the explosion. When Rhodes and he had approached the wreckage they had found one of the boys still alive, though not for long. It was the boy who was making the terrible sound.

In the helicopter Jolly had dropped down out back of the mission station, and a moment later his plane had risen above the trees. Joaquín had watched it until it was gone and the sky had become an empty, silent accusation.

On the balcony now he sat very still. He felt as if his arms were bound by wires that held him powerless.

He thought of what Rhodes had said that evening, after Jerry and his lawyer had departed. Rhodes had been trying to cheer him up. He had said, "Hell, we might even be able to get Kane."

Joaquín had spoken suddenly. "To hell with Kane. It's Kim we want. I don't care about Kane."

And it came to him that the man in the white suit and

dark glasses had been exorcised at last. He was no longer chasing a phantom.

Rhodes was off. Somewhere in the hot hazy afternoon outside the glass door to the balcony. Doing things that had to be done.

That means it's just me, Jerry, and the tape recorder, Joaquín thought. The lawyer, sitting with his hands pressed together as in prayer under his beak nose, seemed to have tuned his client out. He and Jerry had made short work of another room-service lunch. Then Joaquín had put the tape recorder before them and pushed the play-record button.

"Don't let this bother you, Jerry."

But Jerry had had two run and Cokes again. Before long he was telling his life story, and Joaquín was listening.

Watching. Listening. Trying for something more than the tape recorder.

He saw a cocky kid proud of his street smarts. Proud of the job he had done for his uncle. Jerry was eager to sell himself as a Horatio Alger hero. He had started at the bottom. Pushed drugs on the street in New York. By bus, plane, or train, run drugs up from Florida to other states. Brought drugs into the country from Bolivia.

"But face it," Jerry said, "there ain't no future in being a mule."

His reward had come. Jerry was like any young upwardly mobile executive being put in charge of a big account. Carib was a prize and he was on his way to the top. "Working my ass off twelve hours a day," he complained, running the mules, taking care of them if they got busted, cutting the stuff, deciding who to sell it to, keeping everyone happy, and making sure his uncle didn't take any heat. "If there was any heat I'm the guy who took it."

He also did what he called "special requests."

"What sort of special requests?" Joaquín asked.

Jerry shrugged. "Guy thought he was a big shot tried to undercut our kilo price. I chopped his ass off with a meat cleaver."

But mostly what Jerry did was wait to hear from Numma One.

"How often did he call?"

"Depended. Sometimes he wouldn't call for weeks . . . meant he was in Peru picking up some new stuff."

"But eventually he would call."

"Oh sure, and then I didn't have enough mules to keep up with him."

"How would he feel now if you paid him a visit?"

"You mean right now? For business?"

"Say you decided to take a walk before the trial. Would he mind if you showed up?"

"I think it's a good idea," Jerry said. "You gonna let me?"

"As a matter of fact, Jerry, we're going to recommend a little vacation. But just up the road to North Palm Beach. We got a nice bungalow where we want you to stay until the trial."

"I dunno," Jerry said. "What's my uncle gonna think?"

"He's going to think you skipped out to keep from testifying against him. He's going to love you, Jerry."

"Love, shit," Jerry said gloomily.

He seemed depressed at the thought of the betrayal he was committing. Joaquín leaned forward to put it in perspective.

"Jerry . . . remember what happened to your predecessor when it got out he was just thinking of making a deal? You want some kid to find your head washed up in a plastic garbage bag on Miami Beach?"

Jerry's lawyer lifted his beak nose and nodded his head of bushy hair. "Gentleman has a point," he said.

"It's for your own good," Joaquín urged, "and it's all on us, swimming pool, TV, refrigerator, bar, and two agents to go out for you, get you whatever you want."

"Yeah," Jerry said, "just so long as they both don't go out at the same time."

"Good boy," Joaquín said. "Now you got the picture."

At the end of the day, after putting Jerry in the care of the two agents, he came back to the room and lay on his made bed with the tape recorder in his hands. He rewound the tape and played it. He listened to Jerry's voice like an actor who builds a character from the bottom up, trying to absorb Jerry through his pores. Outside the sun was going down.

Joaquín slept at last.

He woke as the light came on. It was night, the darkness visible and complete beyond the balcony. Somewhere Jerry's voice was still answering questions. Rhodes came over, reached down, and picked up the tape recorder that had fallen beside the bed. Joaquín sat up groggily.

"Jerry put me to sleep," he said.

Not fully awake, he could almost believe that Rhodes with his new mustache was a stranger and that the voice blabbing on the tape recorder was his own—"time I had to sit on Kiki's head to keep it from being blown off—"

Rhodes turned Jerry off. On the night table he placed two passports, a photo. He was back. He had done the things he had had to do.

19

THE Carib *Guardian* was Kane's only company now, where before in the mornings there had always been Jones, coming out to tell him he had taken care of a piece of business or to give him the real news of the country as opposed to what you got in the *Guardian*.

There was a news photo of the president cutting a ribbon at yet another public-works project, half the money for which had predictably disappeared into various official pockets; and a photo of the island's number-one cricket hero. The photos were of equal size, suggesting to Kane that the cricket hero had better beware; nobody upstaged Livingstone Coote for long in Carib, and the hero was liable to find himself in a room under the presidential palace with electrodes attached to his testicles and a cattle prod up his rectum—later to be dumped at the side of a road for the *Guardian* to lament his end as the tragic result of alcoholic poisoning.

Kane, breakfasting on the veranda outside his study, was the one man in the country whom Coote had no reason to fear.

A small plane rose above the jungle at the limits of the estate. Jolly. Going off again. He hadn't wanted to go; he had protested that there were too many things for him to do, meaning that now that Jones and Dog were gone he intended to take their place. Kane had listened to Jolly's song and dance—too many things to do, base to pick up in Peru, new plane to buy to replace the old one, and what about the girl, what did Kane want done with her—listened to it all, and then told him: Go.

The plane circled overhead and puttered away, and there was only the sunny silence of the landscaped grounds, the jungle, and the glittering edge of sea beyond.

When Jolly had returned two days ago Kane had jumped in his jeep and raced down to the airstrip. Seeing the girl's unconscious body in the back of the plane, he had felt a tremendous relief. For three days Kane had lived with the bad news that if the girl got away he would never be able to go home to America.

She was locked in a room in the basement now; it had a toilet that had been put in for use by workmen who came to the house to do odd jobs, a forgotten convenience in a forgotten room.

Last night Kane had gone down to the basement and shot back the heavy bolt of the door and entered the small, airless workman's bathroom. The girl was sitting beside a grimy toilet. On the back of the toilet was a roll of paper. Beside her on the floor was a cracked enamel plate with a film of grease.

The girl raised a hand against the light. When she saw who it was she seemed to gather herself against the wall, an instinctively defensive move. But there was nothing cringing about it and the look on her face made no plea; it was coldly hateful. She was waiting for him to attack her. But Kane didn't like to be boxed in by other people's expectations.

"You shouldn't have done that," he said. "All you did was make a lot of trouble for yourself. I hear two men helped you. Jolly says they're dead. That's what you got for them."

He saw pain behind the hatred. His instinct was to treat her as indifferently as if he had never doubted she would be brought back.

"The plane is gone. Stuck out in the jungle. Maybe the monkeys will get some use from it. Jones and Dog are dead. Did those two men kill them? Or did you? Jolly said you're not talking."

She said nothing. She wasn't going to give him the satisfaction.

"It doesn't matter," Kane said. "They're dead."

He thought he better leave. If he stayed he would kill her.

"Do you want the light on?" he asked.

The girl looked up. The look on her face didn't change, her voice was hard-edged with defiance. But no mistake, it was a statement of desire.

"Yes," she said.

Kane studied her, thinking what his rage could accomplish, if he let it. He turned away and went out and closed the door.

Then he switched off the light.

Kane was out at his swimming pool, his life on hold—nothing to do but wait for Livingstone Coote's Bolivian colonel to show with those two hundred kilos. The expanse of lawn was empty except for a solitary egret that stood, white and long-legged, far off at the edge of the jungle. From the house he saw one of Dog's army of relatives appear and come toward him, an unpleasant reminder that he would have to get somebody soon to replace Dog. It was Dog who had ensured that nothing went wrong—that no strangers got through the main gate without being frisked, that the borders of the estate were reliably patrolled, that the floodlights came on at sunset. Without Dog the others would still be back in their village in the hills or squatting over displays of native crafts on the sidewalks of the capital. This one was cut, as they all were, from the same short, stocky mold as his late benefactor. He approached hesitantly and stopped before Kane.

"A man is down at the gate to see you, Mr. Kane. He says he works for Mr. Soldano."

"What does he want?"

"He didn't say."

"Didn't you ask?"

The fat face stared at him stupidly.

Kane assumed it was one of Kiki's mules. No reason to see him, except, now that he was here and had made the trip for nothing, might as well send word back about the two hundred kilos, make Kiki's day.

"Tell him to come up."

The house blocked the front of the estate from view and he wouldn't see the gate swing open to let the mule's rental car through. He dove in and swam three laps. He was drying himself when he saw Dog's relative emerge from the path that came around past the guest cottage and point a young man toward the swimming pool. Even at a distance the man didn't look like the sort of seedy functionary reduced to carrying dope. Probably hadn't been frisked either, something Jones or Dog or Jolly had always done, but which the guard at the gate wouldn't think of. Kane felt a chilly finger of fear, realizing how vulnerable and undefended he was, standing in wet trunks with only his poolside cabana for protection. He saw coming toward him across his lawn the personification of whatever hit man might have been sent to settle an old score. It showed how spoiled he had become with Jones around that he hadn't had to think of such things in years.

The egret lifted off, rising slowly and interminably, a lazy white spear. The man stopped at the edge of the border of flagstones.

"Mr. Kane?"

"You ever been here before?"

"No, sir."

"They're not supposed to let anyone in that they don't know."

The man had an Indian face, primitive with broad cheekbones and dark skin, a hard face, good looks not even softened by a showy Latin pompadour, sort of build that even in his tailored suit looked dangerous. His voice and eyes were as level and watchful as Kane's. The flagstones separating them seemed an isolated island in the middle of the spacious manicured grounds.

"I did what Kiki said . . . rented a car at the airport, drove across the island. I had to get directions in that little town down the road. Stopped at the gate and the guard called up . . ."

"Usually Jolly meets the mules at the gate."

"Yeah, I was surprised, guy didn't even frisk me. I almost offered to do it for him, only some people get sore you tell 'em how to do their job. Somebody should talk to him. You gotta have your eyes open all the time. I once had to sit on Kiki's head to keep it from being blown off. We were going down Flagler Boulevard one night and I saw something coming. They blew every window out brand-new Lincoln, but Kiki's head stayed on."

"That what you do for Kiki," Kane said, "sit on his head?"

"Only that one time. Now your place here . . . you got

this big wall, broken bottles along the top, only what good are bottles if a guy can walk right through the gate? I could pull a piece right now, ice you, jump in my car . . ."

"You wouldn't get off the island alive," Kane said.

"That's what Kiki told me. Said you own the whole country—police, army, even the president. But it's your lucky day, Mr. Kane"—a hand disappeared under the custom-tailored jacket and for a second Kane imagined himself falling back into his swimming pool with bullet holes pockmarking his naked torso—"the only thing I'm carrying is this."

It was an American passport. Kane resumed rubbing the back of his neck with his towel, as if he had expected nothing more. Received the passport, opened it, one hand. Noted that the photo inside was of the young man before him. The name of the bearer was Jerónimo Soldano.

"You a relation of Kiki's?"

"You got me, Mr. Kane. Kiki is my uncle."

The young man raised his hands, under arrest. Then a grin. White, even teeth in a dark-skinned face. The hit man was gone, in his place a cocky, likable Cuban who looked like his uncle, as Kane remembered Kiki from years back.

"Most people just call me Jerry."

There was another photograph, a candid snapshot tucked into the passport for unofficial identification. It showed Kiki Soldano sitting in a festive group at a restaurant table with his arm around this same young man. Kane glanced at it, stuck it back in the passport.

"Kiki's getting fat. He was a skinny kid when I knew him. Now he looks like Al Capone."

"It's all that easy living," Jerry said. "I try to get him to join my health club. It's a big craze. They got treadmills. They got bikes. They got machines for every muscle in the body . . . triceps, biceps . . . all except one. Unfortunately that's the only muscle Kiki is interested in. For that, the only machine any good is eighteen-year-old blondes."

"That sounds like Kiki."

"Better believe it. 'Don't give me any of that fitness crap,' Kiki tells me. 'Just give me the girls.' "

"You remind me of him," Kane said.

"A lot of people say that. It must be in the blood. Remember those Cubans come over in the boats when Castro was getting rid of all his crooks and loonies? They all ended up at Kiki's door claiming to be his nephew. I'm his real nephew. I been with him since I was a kid. I've run stuff for him, serviced his stash . . . I do special requests."

"What sort of special requests?"

"You name it," Jerry said. "Some guy thought he was a big shot tried to undercut our kilo price. Kiki said, 'Go teach the son of a bitch a lesson he won't forget.' "

"Yes?" Kane said, wondering what the unforgettable lesson was.

"I chopped his ass off with a meat clever." Jerry shrugged as if at a regrettable duty. "Then I had to lie low 'cause the guy's friends were looking all over town to chop my ass off. Comes in handy."

Kane laughed.

"Well, if you're down here to pick up stuff I got nothing for you. Jolly had to leave early this morning."

"What, he go to Peru?"

"No, the States." Kane thought he saw something more than idle curiosity in Jerry's face. "It's what Kiki might call a special request."

"I get it," Jerry nodded, receiving his passport back casually, no big deal. "Tell you the truth, Mr. Kane, I didn't really come down to pick anything up. I'm sort of on a permanent vacation. I got busted."

Kane looked at him, watching through his dark glasses. He took the trouble to note that Kiki's nephew was the sort of sharp young hood he would like to have working for him.

"The feds caught me fooling with ten kilos on my girlfriend's kitchen table," Jerry said. "My lawyer said I might be able to wiggle out of it. But the bitch is gonna testify against me. So I decided I better take a walk. It was either that or do time. The bastards wanted me to make a deal—I tell 'em what I know about Kiki, they go easy on me. I pretended to go along, told 'em what they wanted to hear. It won't do 'em any good. The trial is in four weeks but I ain't gonna be there."

"I'll bet Kiki was glad to get rid of you."

"You can say that again. Gave me a big kiss, stuffed a bundle of money in my pocket. 'Don't worry about me, kid, I'll be all right.' "

Kane had stretched out on a pool lounge. Jerry hesitated, seeming to take it as a sign that his visit was over. He slapped his passport against the palm of his hand.

"So anyway, Mr. Kane, I was wondering what there is to do in Carib."

"I hope you like cockroaches, trade winds, and tropical heat," Kane said.

He made Jerry pull over a chair, and as Jerry sat facing him respectfully, Kane gave him a rundown of tourist attractions—nightclubs featuring female impersonators who enticed unwary males into dancing with them for the amusement of the other patrons; boats to take him out to coral reefs on the windward side for snorkeling or scuba diving; thirteen-year-old hookers if he was interested; and in the one big hotel a gambling casino where the blackjack dealers would steal his shirt unless he was the world's greatest card counter.

"The hell you want to waste your time for," Kane said. "You'll go stir crazy by the end of a week."

"As a matter of fact, Mr. Kane, you're right. I don't know how long I'm gonna be stuck here. Could be forever. Scuba diving won't do it. I gotta be doing something. I was hoping you could put me to work."

"Like special requests?"

"Wash your car, I could even fly stuff in for you. I used to make trips to Bolivia for Kiki in my own plane."

Kane wasn't just thinking of the loss of Jones and Dog or of the two hundred kilos due in any day, which he could use help with in Jolly's absence. He was thinking of when he would be back in Miami and would need somebody to run interference with Livingstone Coote. Somebody more normal than Jolly. He wanted Jolly off in the jungle where on hot glaring afternoons you would sometimes see a cloud of smoke and hear a muffled boom—Jolly and his hobby.

"You go to Kiki behind my back," he warned, "you know what happens."

"Yeah," Jerry said, "I do a high jump over all those broken bottles, end up singing soprano for the rest of my life."

His black servant tiptoed around the table by the pool with a plate of ham sandwiches and cold bottles of beer: a wiry old man who heard no evil, saw no evil, and spoke none, except to grumble whenever his afternoon nap was disturbed.

"I lost two men last week," Kane said. "One looked after me and the other ran these Indian boys who guard the estate."

"They quit?"

"They were killed."

He watched for a reaction. Jerry was unmoved.

"It was outside the country. Nobody on the island is gunning for me. But I don't want some narc grabbing me and smuggling me out in a mailbag."

Jerry understood.

"Guy I had kept people away, drove me around. He made payoffs to the police chief in Raleigh, the president, everyone. Stay in the guest cottage. You can swim, go to the beach, play tennis. Just as long as you're around when I need you."

"What about the Indian boys? Who handles them?"

"They're good at taking orders but they won't take them from any of the blacks on the island, and they don't like Jolly. Jolly has been playing the boss for two days and they're already complaining."

"I never met Jolly."

"You'll get a chance."

"He was just a voice on my answering machine," Jerry said. "Some of the mules would talk about him, say things."

"Jolly is good at what he does but he rubs people the wrong way. I'm going to need somebody to really run things around here soon. Right now there's not much to do, couple hundred kilos coming in from Bolivia tomorrow or the next day. This afternoon all I'm interested in is getting a ride to the track from somebody I can trust to sit on my head, if he has to."

"I'll need a piece," Jerry said.

"Jolly keeps an arsenal in his workshop. Go on, take a swim, we'll go down pick one out for you."

He watched Jerry get up from the table in his black skin-tight bathing suit, go to the end of the pool, dive in—and do three lengths underwater before he came up swimming with his broad shoulders as if he had miles to go.

Then they were bumping along the jungle road, Jerry at the wheel of Kane's jeep in a *guayabera* shirt, new slacks, and deck shoes that he had got from his bag in the guest cottage.

At the old sugar plant, half a dozen black workers were idle in the high-ceilinged dimness, waiting for Jolly's return. Kane took his new man past drums of ether, shelves of refining chemicals, and two stained, encrusted vats, to a window at the other end that looked out on a junkyard of discarded and rusted drums. Jerry going on about Bolivia, how the inflation was so high you had to carry bundles of money to buy a pack of cigarettes, how the latest craze was smoking something called *bazooka*.

But as for himself, "I don't like drugs and they don't do much for me." Which in Kane's opinion put him another step ahead of Jolly.

"Where'd you learn to fly?" he asked.

"I was driving along one day, passed a little airfield and there was a sign—'Flying Lessons.' So I pulled into a motel across the road and stayed a week. When I got back Kiki said, 'Where the hell you been? We thought somebody cut loose on you.' I was learning to fly."

They went on to the airstrip. In the glaring sun the runway lay silent and deserted. At one end the two-story hangar looked as untenanted as a condemned building. At the other, palm fronds rattled quietly in a salty breeze. Jerry pushed back the hangar door and the sense of abandonment was complete.

"No planes."

"Jolly's off in one. The other was lost a week ago."

"Along with your old bodyguard."

"Something like that." Kane gestured conversationally at the hangar's emptiness. "Jolly gets pissed off if even I take one of the planes up."

The workshop was closed by a heavy metal door. It didn't budge when he tried the handle, evidently secured by a dead bolt inside.

"We'll see if there's a key upstairs," Kane said, though he seemed to recall that Jolly was always pulling from his baggy white pants a fat bunch of keys that never left his possession.

The lock to Jolly's apartment had the cheap flimsy quality typical of the island. It broke after several hard jolts. Inside, it was like a seedy unused motel room. The dead air smelled of cockroach powder and saltwater mildew. The tin wastebasket with a rust-spotted painting of a Caribbean sunset was empty, the pitiful bed lumpy and unslept in.

There was a clutter of junk in the drawer of a table by the window. There were T-shirts with faded emblems in Jolly's dresser drawer and extra pairs of white pants in his closet and ratty paperback editions of *Seth Speaks* and *The Unknown Reality* on Jolly's night table. But no key.

"The dumb bastard ran off with the keys. You'll have to wait for your piece."

"The mules said he was kind of weird," Jerry remarked.

Kane was angry. He returned to the table, where he had seen something in the drawer: a pocket memo book. He took it out and looked through it. Jolly's handwriting was large and scrawly and possessed a tortured angularity hinting at some peculiar standard of perfection. The names and numbers were scrunched together in a pattern that only Jolly could easily untangle. But at last Kane found what he was after: 51, the country code for Peru. He faced Jerry and held up the tiny book.

"Any objections to running stuff?"

"I've done it all my life."

"What about girls?"

"No problem."

"Hang on to that." Kane made a toss.

Jerry's hand went up as if snatching a fly out of the air. Then he paused, and Kane saw pass between them an understanding of the violation that was being committed, his new man facing him across the length of Jolly's smelly apartment with all of Jolly's contacts and connections in his hand.

Jerry deposited the tiny book into the pocket of his *guayabera* shirt. "Whatever you ask me to run," he said, "I'll run."

20

THE Bolivian colonel arrived noisily overhead the next morning while Kane was in his study talking, mostly listening, to a used-aircraft broker named Rawlings. Jerry had become acquainted with Rawlings the night before at the Yacht Club bar. The Yacht Club wasn't as fancy as it sounded, a collection of splintery docks, a one-room clubhouse. But its prodigious circular bar was a favorite spot for cutting the shady deals that were an honored custom in Carib.

Rawlings looked like he would fit in with the crowd. His red hair and red mustache might have been clownish in a bank clerk. But he had a mean, stringy, muscular build like a garage mechanic who hot-wired cars, and cold, sarcastic blue eyes. Kane wondered if he had done time.

"They oughta close that bar down once in a while. Twenty-four hours is asking for all kinds of unlooked-for hell." His southern drawl seemed soured more than usual by a hangover. "There was a fight after Jerry left. Two black guys jumped on a white boy and near beat the shit out of him. His buddies had to come to the rescue and promise to settle up for the turtles."

Rawlings patted the pocket of his white short-sleeved shirt and found the wallet he was looking for. Stubby and black, with a torn inner lining, it was stuffed with business and credit cards; they spilled onto the desk as he searched through them. He swept up the cards and handed one to Kane.

It was a plain, dog-eared rectangle. The back had been used as scratch paper for several telephone numbers. Kane glanced at the formal designation on the front.

EARL RAWLINGS
Used Aircraft Broker
Kingston, Jamaica

"Mind if I smoke?" Rawlings said.

He plucked a cigarette from a squashed pack, stuck it in his mouth, and began to flick at it with a lighter. He drew in smoke with an audible sucking of air, blew it out in a long stream. He gestured at the business card with his cigarette.

"Kingston is my home base. I try to hit these islands every few months."

Then he gazed out the French doors to the veranda and the swimming pool beyond and rubbed the top of his head vigorously, as if to clear his brain.

"Way it happened . . . these two turtle fishermen come in and there's this big white guy sitting at the bar. He looks out the window and sees two turtles on the dock, musta gone fifty pounds apiece . . . gets up, goes out, picks these two turtles up and tosses 'em back in the water. I have a sneaking suspicion he was trying to make some sort of ecological statement. But when you get right down to it he was just your basic, damn-fool drunk."

"What can you get me?" Kane said.

Rawlings received his card back. "I'm assuming you mean airplanes."

"That's what you do."

"It's what my business card says. But it's just sort of a sideline . . . keeps me in the air, if you know what I mean; don't have to answer so many questions, flying in and out of one country or another. I thought Jerry told you."

"He told me you sold airplanes."

"I do," Rawlings said, "if I can get hold of one that'll make it worth the effort. I got a mechanic in Kingston don't cost me much 'cause he's unlicensed labor. As a mechanic he leaves something to be desired. But he's a whiz at forging the releases for components and making all the repair tags look official. Then we both cross our fingers and hope to hell the son of a bitch don't fall apart until we're out of the country. As my daddy used to say, anybody who's fool enough to go up in the air oughta carry a parachute."

The statement was made flatly, without humor. Rawlings sucked at his cigarette, waved it.

"But every once in a while I come across something decent, and I think I got just what Jerry said you're looking for. Piper Saratoga. Four years old. Seats six to seven passengers. Maximum load sixteen hundred pounds. . . . Sound about right?"

"How do I know it won't fall apart, too?" Kane said.

"I'll bring her right to your airstrip, and you can see for yourself."

"It can't be registered in my name."

"No problem. Easiest way is for me to buy the plane and lease it to you. I'll need cash up front. Sixty-five thou, plus five percent for the insurance. Call it sixty-eight we got a deal."

"You can stay in the guest cottage with Jerry until it's delivered."

Kane saw Rawlings hesitate. Then Rawlings shrugged.

"I'll have to wire the money to Kingston. I must look awful dumb, Mr. Kane, if you think I would run off with your money. I had a long talk with Jerry. He said you were looking for people."

"You get me that plane," Kane said, "we'll talk about it."

"Fair enough," Rawlings said; the look in his eyes told Kane not to be fooled by the early-morning hangover, the country-boy palaver, or the fly-by-night operation, into thinking he couldn't do as he said.

"What have you been moving," Kane asked, "in and out of one country or another?"

Rawlings gestured easily. "Booze, drugs, cigarettes, girls. . ."

"Girls?"

"I used to hit every whorehouse in South America, fix these girls up, sell 'em as aristocracy. Wasn't hard persuading the girls. A few of the smart ones ended up married to the guys I sold 'em to. They made out better than—"

He was interrupted by the colonel's conspicuous arrival. There had been the rumble of an approaching plane and now the plane came booming low over the house, shaking the French doors in their frame. Rawlings, as if used to loud incoming noises, showed no surprise, nor even curiosity.

Kane got up and went out on his veranda into the soggy heat of the day. The plane had circled and was making an approach over the fringe of jungle along the ocean. It dipped below the trees and was down.

Rawlings had come ou. and was standing at his shoulder. "Is that one of yours, Mr. Kane?"

"No, it's a Bolivian army plane. We've got work to do." He glanced curiously at Rawlings. "These Indian boys don't like to take orders from just anybody. You think they'll take them from you?"

"Only way to find out is for me to give 'em an order."

"Well," Kane said, "since you're going to be around, you might as well try."

Rawlings struck him as useful. He didn't quite trust him not to run off with his money, but Rawlings wasn't going to pull anything with Jerry keeping an eye on him in the guest cottage.

"You ever do time?" he asked him.

"I did seven years for armed robbery."

"I've done eight," Kane said. "In Carib."

"All due respect, Mr. Kane," Rawlings said, not a smile in his cold blue eyes, "I would say you done your time in a country-club prison."

The Colonel was waiting for them at the airstrip. He came across the tarmac from the chubby silver body of his twin-engine plane in the blinding sunlight and ovenlike heat, and seized Kane's hand and flung a brotherly arm around him as Kane got out of the jeep and met him halfway.

"Mr. Wilson Kane? My good fren! We are going to do a lot of business! Make a lot of money! Become rich!"

He hugged Kane to him and clapped his shoulder warmly, and Kane, as interested as the colonel in a long, happy relationship, embraced him with equal sincerity, but not so much noise.

"Rich!" the colonel shouted. "We will die rich!"

He was a burly Indian with a broad, lizardlike face, but he had left his primitive village far behind. He looked almost dapper in a green beret with a military insignia on the front, and he spoke his broken English without embarrassment, a man of the world. He glanced with concern at Jerry and Rawlings, the only other men who had stepped from the jeep.

"Where is the president? President Livingstone Coote. I thought he would come to meet me. But he is a busy man. Is a hard job being a president. I admire very much what Livingstone Coote is trying to do for his people. You and I will handle everything." The colonel recovered gracefully from his disappointment at the absence of an official welcoming committee and turned toward the plane, shouting in Spanish now. "Hey c'mon, you lazy bastards! Are you going to sit on your asses all day? Let's go, before I get tired of you and decide to shoot you!"

The shouts brought to the open door of the cargo hold a ragged crew of young Indians dressed in old work clothes who looked like a hastily organized peasant militia, all armed with revolvers and all hatless except for one, who wore a brown derby. They had the same lizardlike face as the colonel. But these were scrawny young lizards.

"My soldiers!" the colonel told Kane proudly. "In the Bolivian army I am only a colonel. But in my own army I am the general. These are all privates. I am teaching them to speak English. I am teaching them how to say 'asshole,' 'motherfuck,' 'son of a bitch,' all the useful phrases. Okay, let's go, you snotnoses!"

The boys piled out and began to unload the crates of cocaine base. The colonel didn't stop talking throughout the unloading, and Kane let him go on. After the first few crates, Jerry went over and opened one, took out a plastic bag of raw base, examined it, tested it, and nodded approvingly to Kane.

"Of course it's good!" the colonel exclaimed. "Is *más puro* than pure cocaine. Because now you have to add the acid, too, to refine it even more."

The truck appeared from the sugar refinery, men clinging to the high sides as it came bouncing and swaying out of the jungle and pulled onto the runway. Kane suggested to the colonel that they go up to the house for a swim, but the colonel didn't know how to swim.

"I am afraid I would drown in your swimming pool. When I become a rich man, then I will pay a pretty woman to teach me."

Kane suspected the colonel was nervous about getting too far away from his private army. He sent Jerry up to the house to bring the money down and told the workmen to wait before loading the crates.

"How about a beer?" he said. "You won't drown in that."

"Hokay," the colonel said, "I'll hab a beer."

Rawlings brought a beer down from Jolly's apartment over the hangar, and the colonel stood drinking it with his shirt off in the hot sun, his upper torso showing preliminary signs of flab.

"I love America!" the colonel cried expansively. "Is my favorite country! The American government tells the Bolivian government it must stop the *narcotraficantes,* else it will not get any more American foreign aid. So the Bolivian government sends me to the mountains to destroy the coca leaf. We build fires. You should see the fires we build! Soon comes a helicopter with a visitor from the American Embassy in La Paz. He looks at the big smoke we are making with our fires and goes home happy. Into the fires we throw everything— broken boards from falling-down shacks, old tires, dead dogs, garbage, whatever we can find—everything except the coca leaf. That I keep for myself."

The Indian boys had retreated from the blistering sun and lay sprawled indolently in the cargo hold, which was empty now, the crates stacked and waiting beside the plane. The boy in the derby was eating coca leaves from a small cloth bag, picking them out and chewing them one by one impassively. The colonel's voice rose with feeling.

"America is making me a rich man! If I become rich enough, maybe I will take over the government and become the new president of my country! I owe it all to America!"

The jeep was back. Jerry had a suitcase. The colonel opened it and saw the neat bundles of money packed inside. He closed the suitcase.

"Don't you want to count it?" Kane asked.

"I trust you, my good fren. If the money is not all here I will fly over your house and drop a bomb on it."

Everyone laughed. The colonel's joke was a great success.

The workmen loaded the crates on the truck. The truck drove off. The colonel threw his arms once more about Kane and climbed back in his plane; and the plane took off with an abrupt lack of fanfare.

Four days later, the crates of refined cocaine were sped out in Carib army launches to a freighter idling off the coast. The freighter's destination was Galveston, Texas, where an obliging Customs inspector would know the crates by a special mark and put them aside for one of Kiki Soldano's lieutenants to collect; and as Kane watched the last launch depart from his dock he was moved to think about America along the same grateful lines as the colonel. America with its international airports. Its thousands of miles of boarderline. Its great harbors. America with its black junkies and fashionable druggies, its Senator Mulcahys and Newton Bishops, its crooked cops and judges, and its banks so conveniently forgetful of currency-reporting requirements.

This was the country Kane was going home to.

That afternoon the same relative of Dog's who had brought Jerry to him the other day and who was now taking orders from Rawlings, came running up to the house from the main gate. He handed Kane a telegram as if extending a piece of raw meat through the bars of a lion's cage. The telegram said:

ARRIVING TOMORROW NOON. NUMMA ONE.

There were a lot of these dinky little airports out in the middle of nowhere in South Florida—no Customs, no tower, a shack for an administration building, a row of small planes parked by the runway, blistering in the sun—and Jolly had found one and landed.

He had given himself a week; he didn't want to be away any longer.

"Howdy," the red-haired, freckle-faced man behind the desk said as Jolly entered. "That you I just saw rolling by? You can park her next to those other planes. Be three dollars a day."

"You the man in charge?" Jolly said.

"Just me and everybody else in here."

The only other people were the candid snapshots of weekend pilots littering the walls. On the desk were a radio transmitter, an anemometer, and a soiled card with ten commandments. Jolly read, THOU SHALT MAINTAIN THY AIR-

SPEED LEST THE EARTH RISE UP AND SMITE THEE.

"How long you fixing to stay?" the man asked.

"A while."

"That's a good answer."

Jolly saw that no amount of rudeness would cure this Florida cracker's affability.

"I need a car," he said.

"Well, we don't have a Hertz or a Avis. But there's the airport car. . . . I keep it around as a special service. Ten dollars a day and the rate goes up if another pilot flies in and wants to use it. Supply and demand, as the feller says. Tank is near empty and the gas is your responsibility." The man peered forward as Jolly opened his wallet to pay him some money in advance. "If you don't mind I'd like that in ones. The local radio station is running a contest . . . has to do with the serial numbers on one-dollar bills. I been collecting 'em. I got forty-seven one-dollar bills right here in the cash box."

"Now you got sixty-two," Jolly said.

He was massaging the back of his neck, stiff from the long flight.

"Something wrong?" the man said, coming out from behind his desk with a look of concern. "Here, let me help you there." He grabbed Jolly's head and gave it a hard twist.

"Stop it."

The man laughed. "Naw, don't worry, I won't charge you any extra." He handed Jolly a business card that identified him as a chiropractic clinician.

"Don't ever do that again," Jolly said.

The airport car was an old jalopy on one drooping fender of which was a sticker that said: HE WHO DIES WITH THE MOST TOYS WINS. In this vehicle Jolly set off on his quest.

He drove north and then west, past mangrove swamps, seas of saw grass, and stands of cypress and slash pine. He stopped in little towns and ate in drugstores, but never got so far away from the airport that he couldn't get back by dark. He slept in his plane and washed and shaved every morning in the bathroom in the administration shack. He didn't want to check into any motel where a desk clerk might remember him.

On the fifth day he saw a girl of about thirteen in a

schoolyard playground. She was alone except for two small boys she was pushing on swings. He watched her a long time. Cute, blond hair, playing nicely with the boys.

All-American, he thought.

At noon the girl went away with the boys through a woods by the playground. Jolly drove into town and had a bacon, lettuce, and tomato sandwich on toast for lunch. In the afternoon he returned to the playground and the girl was there again, baby-sitting the two boys.

The next day Jolly went shopping. In one town, with the air of a henpecked husband buying clothes for a fat wife, he bought a chemise. In another, a woman's blond wig. Then he sent a telegram to Kane, which amounted to a prediction of success.

It gave him a sense of power to know he was able to satisfy Kane's secret itch. Kane was losing his little smartass bitch and he wanted another to take her place. Jolly would bring him the kind he liked, all-American.

When he grabbed the girl in the woods the next morning the two boys stared at him with fright. They were little kids and would describe for the police a big blond woman in a straw beach hat, wearing sunglasses and a plastic sun protector over her nose.

Jolly drove back to the dinky airport, watching his rearview mirror, careful not to go over fifty-five. He turned off onto the country road that wound along under a canopy of trees. As he neared the airport he saw a state police car out front. Frightened, he drove on past and kept going. The girl was in the trunk of the car, unconscious; he had stuck a needle in her. He wondered if he should dump her at the side of the road.

After a moment common sense prevailed. The cops couldn't be after him so soon; they would still be hearing about the big blond woman. Jolly turned the car around and went back to the airport. The police car was gone. He got out and entered the administration shack.

"How y'all this morning!" The red-haired, freckle-faced man looked up cheerfully. He was having a cup of coffee and a slice of Key lime pie for breakfast.

"You been having some trouble?" Jolly asked.

"Trouble? Not that I know of."

"What was that cop car doing?"

"Oh him . . . that was my cousin Dewey. He brought me a piece of pie that his mama made . . . my Aunt Pearl, a great old gal. Lots of folks from out of state think you can use just any old limes. But that ain't so. You need the limes from the Keys, if you want a real genuine honest-to-goodness Key lime p—"

"I come to pay my bill," Jolly said.

"Oh sure!" the man exclaimed. "I'll get it ready for you in a jiffy." He put the half-eaten slice of pie aside, wiped crumbs from his mouth with a handkerchief, and got to work on the bill.

On the novelty card of ten commandments Jolly read: THOU SHALT RESPECT THY HEALTH FOR HE THAT USETH DRUGS SHALL SURELY ANOINT HIMSELF FOR ETERNAL REST.

"Let's see now, you give me a deposit when you come in. That was fifteen dollars. You been here six days. That's eighteen dollars parking fee and sixty dollars for the car, minus the deposit, plus the gas you asked me to put in your plane, comes to—"

Jolly had stepped behind the man, as if to watch over his shoulder. From his pants he drew his gun with a silencer screwed on the muzzle and shot the man in the back of the head. The man's head thumped forward on his desk and knocked over his Styrofoam cup of coffee.

That's for the neck rub, Jolly thought.

21

THE meals were always the same, cold plantains, a bit of cold rice. There was no way to tell breakfast from lunch or dinner, or of knowing for sure how many times a day she was fed. The darkness would be there, pressed against her face, like a suffocating blanket. Then, as if in a dream, the light would come on. Her eyes would flinch and she would turn away. She would hardly have time to see the bare floor, bare walls, the light bulb whose weak glow was enough to blind her. The door would be unbolted, a plate of food put before her, the empty plate taken away. The bringer of food would depart; the light would go off and the darkness would be there again.

Jolly had only come three times. After that it was one of Dog's Indian boys who brought the food. By then the darkness had begun to get to Kim. Her great strength—what had saved her in the past—had been her sure knowledge of who she was. But this profound absence of light made her doubt her own existence. She would have to construct a sense of herself out of it. She decided a definite sequence of time would help.

With her free handcuff she scratched a mark on the floor beside her. She made some arbitrary decisions. This is night, she thought. The meal I just ate was supper. I am being fed two meals a day. Kane doesn't want to be overly generous. But he doesn't want me to look too emaciated for Madam Chew either. Then, as was fitting for nighttime, she slept.

She woke when the light came on. Before her was the

mark she had made: Night, supper. She was almost eager to be rid of the Indian now. She handed him her empty plate and took the full one. The Indian went out and the light went off. With the handcuff she made another scratch. Then she sat back, satisfied, and ate the cold plantains and rice.

Morning, she thought. Breakfast.

When she had collected four marks her calendar was a fact. Before, the pain she had felt at the death of Joaquín and Rhodes had seemed to be all around her constantly. Now there was a past to which she could at least pretend to consign it and even forget it for a while. And there was a future in which she could imagine a day when the darkness might actually end.

She found herself looking forward to going to Peru. Once she was out of this cell, into the light, there would be a chance of escape. She had gotten away from Kane and she could get away from Madam Chew. She would have to pretend to like her work and keep an eye open. Only let it come soon, she thought, before this darkness drives me crazy.

She thought of the girls she would work with, hardened youngsters who had been doomed to the life, whose mothers had themselves been whores, whose fathers had raped or beaten them. She would learn from them, follow their example. Pressing up against men to entice them. Taking them to a foul-smelling room with a lice-ridden mattress. Making sure to get the money first—she felt certain this would be a major point for Madam Chew. She tried to be cold and practical about it. But finally her only solace was to think of the strong arms that had held her protectively in a hammock in the jungle.

I was just trying to get away, she thought. I didn't know what I was bringing with me.

What she had loved most about Joaquín was that he had seen who she was. That she was Kim Mitchell. That what had happened to her could have happened to anybody. But that who she was was special.

Along with her calendar came a daily regimen. It began with breakfast. She called it bacon and eggs and drew the meal out as if savoring it. Breakfast was followed by a pep talk, the purpose of which was to persuade her to go through with the rest of the regimen. You've got to do it. You can't just sit on your butt. Get up and get started with it. At last she would push herself to her feet and begin a period of exercise. There were push-ups and sit-ups and jumping jacks, performed a minimum number of times. This was a warm-up for the big event of the day: jogging in place. She imagined a distance of four or five miles and kept at it as long as she could, working up a good sweat. Done, she gave herself a chance to cool off. Then it was time for school. She would try to remember everything she had learned from all the books she had read in Archie Rice's study. She would think: *Every body continues in its state of rest, or of uniform motion in a right line, unless it is compelled to change that state by forces impressed upon it.* Or: *Champollion is the name of the man who discovered how to decipher hieroglyphics. He realized they weren't just pictures; they were letters. He was helped by the discovery of the Rosetta stone, which had a column of Greek next to a column of hieroglyphics.*

But usually at some point she would stop and be unable to go on. What good was it? The darkness would never end. She would sink to the floor and lie in a stupor of despair. This became as permanent a part of her regimen as any of the others, and it was just as valuable, for it helped to pass the time, to get her to another scratch mark on the floor.

She had made fourteen scratch marks now and the light came on yet again.

The Indian entered. The exchange of plates was made. The Indian left, and as the light went out Kim scraped another mark. It represented the end of the seventh full day since the beginning of her calendar. She sat back against the wall and ate the cold plantains and rice.

Night, she thought. Supper.

Outside, the grounds of the estate would be bathed in the cold white glare of the floodlights. The tropical night would be all around but it would be a sweet darkness, not the impenetrable, suffocating blackness of her cell.

She finished her meal and set the plate aside. She had gotten through another day. She had stuck to her regimen, complete with morning and afternoon exercise periods divided by the long period of helpless discouragement and despair. She said her prayers. They were not formal prayers. They were simple pleas for help and expressions of grief for her father and the two men who had died for her. Then she lay down with her head on her arm and closed her eyes. The exercises had the benefit of making her tired, and sleep would enable her to get through the next twelve hours.

She had begun to fall asleep when the light came on.

The door was unbolted and a man came in. On the edge of sleep, Kim had difficulty lifting her head and opening her eyes. It took a moment for her to recognize the man, struggling with the visual evidence that he wasn't an Indian and that there wasn't a plate of food in his hand.

"Get up," Kane said.

She averted her face and raised her hand against the light. She heard herself ask a question.

"Where am I going?"

He didn't answer. He was wearing sunglasses, a fact that in her groggy state she had difficulty understanding.

She grasped the toilet seat and got to her feet unsteadily. Kane came forward and held out his hand. She extended the dangling handcuff and stood like an obedient child as he unlocked it and clasped it on her free wrist. She felt a submissiveness that was almost like gratitude. Kane was a savior who had come to bring her out into the normal darkness of the night. It was all she wanted. She was going to Peru.

He took her by the arm and led her out. His grip had the intensity of controlled rage. He closed the door and switched off the light. The basement was dark but it was a darkness in which she could make out shapes—the edge of a wall, a mountainous jumble of stored furniture, a banister—outlined by some distant source of light.

Kane brought her up a flight of stairs. As he opened the door at the top she saw that a basic assumption of her calendar had been false. The kitchen was filled with sunlight.

"What time is it?"

The question was a statement of dazed surprise. It required no answer, even if Kane had been willing to give one. She knew the look and feel of the house in the late morning. The sun was bright on the lawn out back but the bougainvillaea outside the windows was still in shadow, a hummingbird darting and hovering over the blossoms. The cook would be at the marketplace in town, haggling over the fish of the day. The butler would be washing Kane's limousine or polishing Kane's shoes or hiding from work. The churning of a washing machine in the laundry room off the kitchen told her the whereabouts of the maid.

They went through the pantry, crossed the red-tiled dining room, and came out through the French doors onto the veranda. The sunlight made her turn away and stumble in Kane's grip, squint-eyed as a mole. He jerked her up and propelled her around the side of the house. The jeep was out front. He pushed her into the front seat and got behind the wheel.

The driveway made a wide circle away from the house and around behind it toward the jungle at the back. She remembered the estate as something in a dream, the deserted swimming pool and tennis court, the whispering lawn sprinklers. As they came onto the dirt road and bumped along past the horse stable, a cloud of dust obscured the house and grounds from view. After the perpetual chill of the basement the heat of the day warmed her bones. But it didn't make sunlight real. Sunlight was a trick.

At the jungle an Indian swung the barrier aside as if Kane and she were ghosts and the jeep a phantom vehicle. The narrow twisting track brought them out to the airstrip by the ocean.

Kane pulled up beside the runway and turned off the motor. The runway was empty; there was no small plane waiting to take her to Peru. The hangar was open and she saw that it, too, was empty; the plane was gone and it occurred to her that Jolly's disappearance was due to an actual departure, not just an apparent lack of interest in bringing her meals.

In front of the hangar two men stood facing each other in tightly coiled attitudes, one with a basketball in his hands, the other crouched with his arms outstretched. They paused as the jeep came up. The one with the ball glanced at it; then, as the other relaxed his guard, he made a sudden move, scooting around him and making a shot. The ball went through the basket. His opponent caught it and they switched positions, continuing their game of one-on-one.

"Who are those men?"

The question was as involuntary as her dazed question

about the time. Kane surprised her by answering it.

"They work for me."

"I've never seen them before."

"They're new."

"Where did they come from? Where's Jolly?" She was staring at the two men.

"Why?" Kane said. "Did you think you were going to put me out of business?"

She didn't hear him at first. Then she shook her head in confusion.

"I don't know what you mean."

"By killing Jones and Dog."

"I didn't kill them."

"Your friends did, the poor bastards who tried to help you."

The man with the ball was darting, spinning, dribbling quickly back and forth. The other man lunged to cut him off. They suddenly seemed to rush away from her and become very small, as if seen through the reverse end of a telescope. She looked down at her wrists, handcuffed together in her lap.

"I would have killed them if I had had the chance."

Kane got out of the jeep and looked in at her. "But I have two new men. And the plane you stole will be replaced. So you really didn't get away with anything—not yourself, or my plane, or my men."

He walked away to the hangar. The two men stopped their game and faced him. One had unruly red hair and a red mustache. The other's black hair was sculpted and shiny. Neither of them glanced toward her.

Kim stared at the men, her heart pounding.

Joaquín and Rhodes were dead. She had seen them blown up by Jolly's bomb. To imagine she was seeing them now was an aberration. She had had their faces before her in the dark. She had brought the faces with her into the sunlight and in an act of desperation had put them on two strangers. They had already become unfamiliar.

Kane gestured and the two men glanced at her without recognition or interest. It was plain they were what Kane had said they were, two men he had hired to replace Jones and Dog. In a moment she would see their faces clearly.

The face behind the red mustache would become that of a bloated weasel. The dark handsome features of the other would coarsen into ugliness.

The sun was a heavy hand on her head. It was pushing her face into a black smothering pool. Her head went down into darkness.

When she came to, the man with the red mustache was standing beside her in the open door of the jeep. He was lifting her head and holding a bottle. On the label was a gold Indian and the word CARIB.

"Sorry, it's just a beer. But as my daddy used to say, if you're aiming to pitch a long drunk and a gallon jug ain't handy, beer will have to do."

He held the bottle to her lips and Kim drank. She stopped and looked at him. The man looked back at her with a curious intentness.

"Name's Rawlings," he said. "Doing a job for Mr. Kane. I understand you'll be taking a trip shortly."

The mustache belonged to Rawlings. The kind, incisive eyes behind the sober expression were Rhodes's.

"I thought you were dead," she said.

"It's news to me. Be careful. For all I know Kane might be the world's greatest lip reader. No displays of emotion, please. Save them for later . . . if we're lucky enough to have a later."

"Kane's not looking at us. He's talking to Joaquín."

"That's not Joaquín. That's Jerry. I'm Rawlings. Funny, some folks have this strange quality that encourages others to call them by their last names. I can't put my finger on it. But whatever it is I must have it. Kane calls that fellow Jerry and he calls me Rawlings. Doesn't seem quite fair. But listen," Rhodes was serious. "I haven't got the faintest idea what state your brain is in and it's the only reason I'm here; the beer is just an excuse. So far as I know you might be so drugged or confused that you don't fully appreciate the situation. The important thing to get through your head is that whatever happens you don't know me and you don't know Jerry. Not by so much as the raising of an eyebrow. Understand?"

She heard the strain in his voice. She nodded imperceptibly. "Yes."

"Good. That's the message. Here," Rhodes put the bottle

in her hand carefully as if unsure whether she had the strength to grasp it. "Hang on to this. We don't want to strain Kane's generosity. If you spill it he might not allow you another."

She took the bottle in both hands. He squeezed her grip on it in a parting gesture.

"When you're done with it I'd like the bottle back . . . so I can shove it up his ass."

Kim watched him walking back to the hangar. She felt her face begin to break, and she bit her lip to hold it together. She drank the beer and rubbed the cold bottle against her forehead and cheeks. No displays of emotion, please.

She closed her eyes and saw a bright ball of flame so vivid it made her wince. She opened them and her vision traveled through the colorless, unconvincing glare to three men standing together in the pale shade of an empty hangar, oddly united by the fact that each held in his hand a bottle of beer.

Jerry was the one with shiny black hair and a colorful shirt. Rawlings was rough and plain. She didn't know them. She had never seen them in her life. Understand? Everything about Kane, his brusque gestures, his hard gaze, and the sound of his voice, a voice used to being obeyed, said he was the boss. But standing between the other two in his dark glasses, he looked suddenly to Kim like a blind man.

The three men were waiting for something. The beers became a way of measuring time, like her scratches on the floor. Jerry finished his first. With cocky self-assurance he tossed the bottle through the air as if it were as unbreakable as a basketball. It landed with a glassy clink in a large cardboard box of old rags and used oil cans. Moments later, hinting at some delicate streak of propriety at odds with his scruffy demeanor, Rawlings made a purposeful trek to the box and deposited his bottle gently. Bored, he began to practice a golf swing, clutching an imaginary wood and sending an imaginary ball soaring out over the palm trees at the other end of the runway. Jerry, with equal boredom, tossed the basketball idly from one hand to the other.

After a while Kane strode to the box and dropped his empty bottle in with abrupt indifference. The act seemed to release his impatience. He stalked onto the runway and

looked up at the sky and glanced at his watch. Rawlings asked
if he could bring him a chair. Without waiting for an answer,
he went upstairs to Jolly's apartment and came down with a
chair and three more beers.

Kane sat, a lone king on a wooden folding chair. His two
servants behind him began to talk about drug smuggling.
The beer, the hot sun, made Kim sleepy. Her head nodded
forward and she was back in her cell in the basement.

It was night after all.

22

"KIKI's always talking about quality control, like he's chairman of the board of some big corporation, you know, wants to get written up in *Business Week*. Means for big customers you cut it with benzocaine or procaine, if you got it; if you don't, any old shit will do."

They were standing in the hangar behind the man sitting in the folding chair. The back of the man's head was to them, and Joaquín thought how easy it would be to bring something hard crashing down on it that would take care of the man for good. But why should he do that? The man was going to give Kim to him and let him fly away with her. He was even supplying the plane.

They had known they would need a plane; it was the only way they could get out of Carib—invent Rawlings, dealer in secondhand aircraft, who would bring one in. Then Kane had made it unnecessary, which was scary. Because nine times out of ten you could bet something would go wrong and you were happy to be wired for sound, knowing help might get to you in time. Joaquín wasn't used to the luxury of having everything handed to him on a silver platter.

Kane had wandered out from the house last night while he and Rhodes were playing tennis, and when darkness had forced them off the court he had given Joaquín a job.

"Jolly is coming back tomorrow. You're going to Peru. Call Madam Chew in Lima. Tell her you're bringing a girl."

"What girl?"

"A whore."

In the dark their faces had been invisible to each other.
All around them had been a quiet buzzing of insects, and
Joaquín had thought, Whore. That's it, Kane, she's a whore.
Just give her to me and I'll kiss you.

"Where's the girl?"

"She'll be here," Kane said, cutting off any questions.
"Madam Chew will send somebody to pick her up in Tingo
María. Call Jolly's connection, too, see if he has anything to
give you, so you don't come back empty-handed."

"Jolly won't be happy."

"That's his problem. Jolly doesn't run things around here,
even though he likes to think so."

And just then the floodlights around the grounds had come
on. It had been like a final warning to Kane, revealing the
two men before him. But Kane had seen only what he wanted
to see.

Kiki Soldano's nephew Jerry. And an ex-con named
Rawlings.

It had taken two fake passports and a doctored photo.
They had caught Kane just when he needed men and was
testing his new partnership with the president of Carib. But
the real Jerry's answering machine was being listened to by
somebody else now and the message Joaquín had left on it
yesterday at Kane's order would take care of those two
hundred kilos on the way to Galveston, maybe even give
Livingstone Coote second thoughts, after the Carib freighter
captain began to talk.

Kim had passed out in the jeep by the runway. To Jerry
she was just another commodity to move.

"Trouble with lactose it tastes sweet. Spoils, you gotta
move it quick. You run outta lactose you take what you get,
aspirin, bicarbonate of soda." He was tired of playing Jerry,
tired of sounding like a punk hustling his way to the top of
the dope business, making all those phone calls, cutting all
that flake on his girlfriend's kitchen table. Saying, "That's
when Kiki gets on your ass, all the bullshit about quality
control, he's got you running around to every supermarket
in town, grabbing table salt off the shelves. So maybe he'll
make *Business Week* after all. He's got the right attitude."

There was the sound of a small plane, and the man in
the chair in front of them sat forward. They listened to the

plane, a sound high up in the brightness, moving over the estate. In a moment, out over the ocean, it would be swallowed up by an immensity of distance and sky. The plane began to circle overhead.

Kane rose and went outside, and Joaquín gave Rhodes a single look. Jolly had achieved an odd status in his mind, like some freaky rock star with an orange hairdo, dressed in Salvation Army rags. It didn't seem impossible that Jolly viewed himself in just such a way, sitting upstairs in his little apartment with jungle all around, dreaming that he was the talk of the town.

Or you could think of him as a rare force that moved with the whim of a tornado and left dead bodies in its wake—a father and his son, a helicopter pilot, two boys who had wanted to learn how to fly.

Don't think about Jolly, he told himself. Think about the plane he's bringing back. Think of you and Kim flying away in it. That's all you have to think about.

He didn't know where Jolly had been. He assumed Jolly was alone.

Kim woke to the noise of the plane as it came in for a landing. She sat up and saw it glide in over the trees and touch down, and she recognized it as Jolly's other plane.

Kane had got up and come out of the hangar. He stood facing the plane as it taxied forward, his two new men waiting by the empty folding chair behind him. When do I get to hug and kiss them, she thought. But the sleep had done her good and she could see clearly now that Joaquín and Rhodes were there, not as a miracle but as a practical solution that was still in doubt.

Later, she thought. If we're lucky enough to have a later.

Kane stood at the end of an invisible leash, watching the plane approach. As it drew near he seemed to leap forward. He strode toward the plane as if to walk into it and took a stand in front of it. The plane stopped and its engine was cut off, and in the sudden stillness Kane continued to face it rigidly, looking for something. Jolly was in the cabin. Across a gulf of heat and glare Kim saw him grin at Kane and raise a thumb.

Abruptly Kane lost interest in Jolly. He turned away and came over to the jeep. He opened the door and grabbed Kim by the arm. She resisted instinctively and he jerked her out. She stumbled and scraped her knee on the coral rubble at the side of the runway, and Kane hauled her roughly to her feet.

"You're going to Peru," he said.

Kim glanced quickly toward the two men in the hangar. All she could think was: Jolly is the pilot, Jolly flies the planes. But the two men looked on indifferently. They didn't know her. She wasn't supposed to know them.

Kane dragged her onto the runway and stopped before the plane. Jolly had climbed out. He was wearing his gun in his shoulder holster. He turned and waved jauntily to Kane.

"What did I tell you!" he called. "A week!"

Kim had a moment to consider the accuracy of her calendar. She had lived through one week of post-Jolly time. Jolly's T-shirt and white pants showed a week's grubbiness.

"Christ, I'll be glad to get out of these! I've been sleeping every night in the plane. I didn't even have a place to take a shower. But I told you I could do it in a week."

She had another moment to ask herself, Do what in a week?

Jolly turned to the plane and Kim saw he wasn't alone. There was movement in the back of the cabin. It was like a shadow, or like the first tremor of a disaster, something you barely noticed but that afterward survivors would recall as the unmistakable beginning.

A hand reached out and grasped the side of the cabin door. A sneakered foot appeared, dangling limply. A bare leg, a scraped knee.

Jolly helped the girl climb out. Her head was down and she was rubbing her eyes with the back of her hand.

"You awake?" he said.

The question filtered through her daze. The girl nodded.

Jolly caught her as she swayed. "It's a long trip. But we made it. Want to go for a swim? It's a possibility. But you have to ask the right man."

He brought her forward. He presented her to Kane almost proudly.

"Say hello, little girl."

She was twelve or thirteen. She had blond hair pulled back in a pony tail from a cute face. She wore a tennis shirt, shorts, and sneakers. She didn't seem to understand Jolly.

Her gaze strayed past Kim toward the hangar. Then it came back to Kane—the right man. She stared at him in fright. All her questions were silent but they were written on her face, and Kim knew them by heart. Who are you? What am I doing here? Where is my father?

"She's not awake yet," Jolly said, as if to excuse her absence of speech. "But she's a good kid."

Kane looked at the girl, but by no flicker of expression behind the dark lenses of his sunglasses did he acknowledge that she existed. Kim felt his grip tighten on her arm and she had a sudden sense of the permanence of his rage. Kane was a monster. But he was a monster caged, as much a prisoner on Carib as the girl before him. Kane allowed her to stare at the girl only a moment.

"That's you," he said. "That used to be you."

Then he jerked her into motion again. He led her around to the other side of the plane, Kim casting one glance back at the girl, the girl staring helplessly after her. He opened the cabin door and pushed her in. As he closed the door it came to Kim what he had meant.

She had been looking into her past and the girl had been looking into her future, and they were both Nicole.

Alone in the cramped, stuffy cabin, Kim felt completely removed. She saw Kane go back around the plane to Jolly and the girl. She saw the two men coming out of the hangar toward them. But it was happening in another world. It had nothing to do with her.

The two men came up to Kane. They were strangers again, one with his square red mustache and lean rugged build, the other big-shouldered and casual in a tropical shirt. Neither of them glanced toward her. Neither of them seemed ready to do anything. And now, as they came up and stood with the others in front of the plane, she noticed a frightening fact. Neither of them wore a gun.

Jolly was the pilot. Jolly flew the planes. And Jolly had a gun.

She looked at the gun in its shoulder holster against his side. There was a dark circle of sweat on his T-shirt under the holster. Jolly wasn't a big man but he had the arms of a man who did push-ups every day. She saw a change come over his face as he became aware of the two men. It was like the defense mechanism of a primitive form of sea life, all animation retreating from his features with a spasmodic jerk, leaving only a blank, wary exterior.

Kane introduced the two men.

"This is Jerry Soldano. He's Kiki's nephew. Earl Rawlings. He's getting another plane for us. They're working for me."

Jolly's face jerked from one to the other. The two men gazed at him without interest, as if he were applying for a job that was already taken. No one offered to shake hands.

"Working for you?"

"They're replacing Jones and Dog."

"You hired these guys while I was gone?"

"I couldn't wait. We had things to do."

"What things?"

"We're expanding the operation," Kane told him. "The president of Carib wants to get into the business."

Jolly stared at him in disbelief, too agitated to speak. He began to rub the back of his neck, searching the ground distractedly. "Why the hell didn't you tell me?"

"I wanted to see how good his connection was. It was good. We sent two hundred kilos off to Galveston yesterday."

"Coote will steal your whole business," Jolly protested.

"No he won't. He'll need me even more once I'm back in the States, and Jerry will be here to keep an eye on him."

"What d'you mean, keep an eye on him!"

"Jerry will get along better with Coote's people," Kane said bluntly. "He's going to fly the girl to Peru now. You need a rest. He'll pick up some base and bring it back, and you'll be able to get started on it with your boys."

"You let him call my connection?" Jolly's squawk came thinly and without resonance to Kim in the closed cabin, absorbed by the heat and sunlight. "You had no right! You know what it cost me to get in tight with those people?"

Jolly seemed to go into a dance of ultimate outrage. Watching him from the removed world of the cabin was like observing a curious specimen. His motions became awkward and jerky. His hand kept shooting to the back of his neck. His head turned rigidly on a bare neck that was stiff and insectlike.

"Christ, that's my connection! I got calluses on my lips

from kissing Peruvian ass. I made it work and I gave it to you! A fucking gift! And now you're taking it from me!"

"Nobody is taking your connection," Kane said impatiently. "I want you here to check out the new plane when it comes."

"To hell with the new plane!"

Jolly went on ranting. Kane was unmoved. The girl began to vomit, the aftereffect of the drug Jolly had knocked her out with. The man with the red mustache steadied her gently as she spattered the tarmac. He took her aside and she crumpled to the ground, and he waited beside her as Jolly continued to argue.

Kim thought of all Jolly's silly talk about being "Numma One." Occasionally he would be more specific—"Numma One G.I." A piece of bogus native flattery he had picked up in Vietnam and elevated to the status of supreme compliment. Jolly was taking a tremendous fall. But he wasn't the type to beg. When he saw Kane wasn't going to budge he made a gesture of disgust.

"Fuck it! It's not my problem, mon. You're the one who gives the orders."

He stood shaking his head with profound exasperation. It was impossible for Jolly to believe the injury that was being done to him.

"Shit, I need a shave. I need a shower. I sure as hell don't need a trip to Peru."

He walked away. He stopped and turned and faced the new man, Kiki Soldano's nephew. He leaned back with his hands in his pockets and a tight smile on his face, as if considering the new man cleverly.

"You forgot something didn't you? Christ, am I gonna have to teach you everything?"

His hand came out of his pocket and he made a toss to Kiki's nephew. This resulted in the only move the nephew had bothered to make so far, his hand darting upward to catch an object. It was the plane's ignition key.

"You don't get off the ground without that, pal," Jolly said.

He ambled away as if pleased with his parting shot. But Kim saw the boiled-red color of his neck.

23

JOLLY pulled a bunch of keys from his floppy pants and found the one that would lift the heavy vertical bolt of his workshop door. An enormous amount of energy went into his effort to appear unconcerned. But he felt that the back of his neck was under scrutiny, and this made all his moves seem like unconnected events with great spaces between them, deserts that took an eternity to cross, from the unbolting of the door to the turning of the handle, to a final shrug of indifference for the benefit of onlookers as he entered the workshop.

At last he was inside and the door was closed. In the pitch dark he doubled over and grabbed his head as if to tear it off.

What was Kane trying to do to him?

He had gone away a week ago in a jubilant mood. He had come back to find two new men working for Kane and his jubilation seemed an impossible emotion from another era. He tried to put it in a favorable light. But the violation was too clear. They had taken his connection. It showed a complete contempt for him.

Jolly thought of all he had been through in the last week, the discomfort, the shitty food, and his fear at the sight of the state police car that morning. He dug his fingers into his scalp in an agony of rage. There was no room in his body for such rage; bones, muscles, tendons, all felt the strain.

He groped above him and pulled the string of the light bulb overhead. The dim light gave him no ideas; it only provided a badly lit view of the clutter on his workbench. He stared numbly. Jolly's stubborn faith that the true center of Kane's universe was his own little apartment over the hangar in the jungle had been violated, and now he felt as scattered and unconnected as the parts and tools before him.

Think, for crissake!

He placed his hands on his workbench and closed his eyes and tried to sort through his confusion. Kiki Soldano's nephew was outside now, refueling the plane. He would get in the plane and fly to Peru. He had called Jolly's connection, which meant he must have broken into his apartment upstairs and taken his pocket memo book.

The drug smugglers in Tingo María had nothing to fear. They controlled the army, the police, and the revolutionaries; if anybody came in that they didn't trust they would kill him. It showed how insignificant Jolly really was that the nephew could replace him so easily. His connection would have said, "Sure, come along. We'll be ready for you."

Thinking of this, seeing how it had been, was more than Jolly could bear. The cabinet in his workshop held a variety of weapons, cartridge belts, and ammunition boxes, which he had collected over the years. He also kept an Uzi automatic rifle hidden behind his refrigerator upstairs in case some overzealous narcs ever made an appearance on the airstrip, and it was this piece, which could fire thirty-two bullets with one pull of the trigger, that Jolly thought of now as he imagined going up to his apartment, throwing open the window, and letting loose on the men below, Kane included.

In his rage Jolly allowed the old vanity to reassert itself. What did he need Kane for? He could kill him along with the other two. Go up to the house, take the money in Kane's safe—hundreds of thousands of dollars—come back down, and fly away. But Kane was the major fixture in Jolly's universe.

Rage had got a grip on the back of his neck and he couldn't think clearly. With his hand he began to knead the muscles, twisting his neck slowly, trying to work the rage loose. The answer was simple and he would find it in the specific nature of the problem. The problem wasn't Kane. It was the nephew. Jolly didn't care if the nephew flew away; he didn't want him to come back, was what it came down to.

See, Jolly thought. You got it. Didn't I tell you it was simple? You got the problem, you got the answer.

Slowly, slowly, back and forth, his fingers digging into the back of his neck.

With his eyes closed he imagined himself dissolving into the dimness around him. He left the rage somewhere outside him and came back into himself and opened his eyes and the answer was before him, separate and distinct in the clutter on his workbench: an ordinary child's building block, on which, in a moment of boredom, just to keep his fingers busy, he had already stapled a circuit wire in a pattern he had outlined with a ballpoint pen. The wires at one end had been soldered to a flashlight battery and a wristwatch dial with the plastic face and the hour hand removed.

Just don't let the fucker come back, he thought.

The use of building blocks was Jolly's special touch. It was another proof of his ability to improvise. He reached for the device and at the same time took several sticks of plastic explosive from the crate under his bench. He began to move purposefully now, aware of the plane being refueled outside. He let his hands do the work—taping the sticks together, attaching a detonator to the circuit—while his mind skipped ahead to that point in time when Kane would begin to wonder why the nephew hadn't come back. Jolly would call Peru and find out the nephew had never shown; he would have the satisfaction of being able to speculate for Kane's benefit that the nephew had probably run off with the money and the plane. It was so funny he was having a hard time keeping from laughing.

"Christ, I'm gonna break up. Compose yourself, asshole. You got things to do."

In the weak light he found a discarded carton for an electric drill with an ad pasted on it showing various accessories in colored squares. Removing his shoulder holster, he pulled off his T-shirt and put it in the box for padding. It wasn't enough. He took off his pants and jogging shoes and threw his Jockey shorts and woolen socks into the carton. He put on his pants again and slung his shoulder holster around his neck. Carefully he lay the bomb in among his discarded clothes. He sealed the carton with tape so tightly that even if someone discovered it and tried to open it, it would explode. Then he pulled the light cord and returned himself to darkness.

In the dark he tried to smile. His lips were still tense with anger. C'mon, dummy, give it some teeth.

He had wound the wristwatch and set it a full hour before it would make the crucial connection. An hour would give the plane plenty of time to be on its way and out of sight. Even if Kane heard the explosion it would come back to him innocently, like distant thunder.

Outside Kiki's nephew had lifted the hose from the squat red gas pump and was unscrewing the gas cap in a wing of the plane. Jolly raised a hand in a friendly wave as he crossed the hangar. The electric-drill carton was under his arm.

Upstairs the lock on his door was broken and his pocket memo book was gone, as he had expected. The actual evidence caused his face to tighten again. He stood looking out at the nephew below, cursing silently.

". . . dirty fucking bastard lousy stinking dirty fucking . . ."

When he came back down he had a rolled aerial map and a sweater. Kane was talking with the other man at the side of the runway and the girl was slumped on the ground behind them. Jolly sauntered to the plane.

"Hot!" he exclaimed amiably, as if to justify his bare torso. *"Mucho calor,* huh?"

The nephew glanced at him indifferently and Jolly saw his Cuban's oily black hair and loud shirt and the ease with which he fed gas with his big hand. He was glad for the indifference. The carton under his arm made him feel conspicuous. It was only a few feet to the cabin door on the other side of the plane. He could always offer the lame excuse that he wanted to say good-bye to the girl inside the cabin. But he preferred to be told to go.

His grin felt like the plastic teeth of a Halloween mask.

"Say, hope you didn't get the wrong idea. I was pissed off but Kane is right. I gotta be around to check out that new plane. Anyway, no hard feelings."

He held out his hand. The nephew let it hang a moment. Then he reached over and shook Jolly's hand. Jolly patted the wing of the plane.

"She'll take you where you want . . . long as you know where you're going. Ever make a trip like this?"

"I used to fly to Bolivia for Kiki."

"Oh, well in that case you're a pro. Nobody can tell you anything. But I thought maybe you might want to use my aerial map. I've marked the places where I land to refuel. They know me and they know this plane. They won't give you any trouble. Of course, you'll have to come across with a little *mordida*. But hell, you're a Cuban. You know all about that." He laughed to make a joke of it. He thrust the map at him, "You want to hang on to it?"

The nephew was busy. He nodded toward the cabin.

"You can put it in there. Thanks."

Thank *you*, Jolly thought. He walked around to the cabin as if in no hurry. The sun and warm air were like a blessing on his bare skin. Oh yes, he thought, yes, yes.

He opened the door on the pilot's side and stuck his head in. "So, you finally got out of that dark basement!"

Jolly had always been primarily aware of the girl in terms of his own grandiose conception of the role he had played, an angel in white who appeared at crucial turning points in her life. But the girl looked at him uncertainly, as if she had been thinking of something else and had forgotten who he was.

"Looks like I won't be flying you to Peru. This new guy is gonna do it. I've got some things. He told me to put them in here. There's a sweater for you. It gets cold in Lima, you'll need it."

Jolly leaned into the cabin and put the carton on the backseat. Then he came out and grinned in at her. He stood gabbing idiotically, out of a magician's urgent need to divert the audience's attention.

"Well, little girl, it's been nice knowing you. We've been through a lot together. I want you to know, whatever you think, I never did anything against you personally. I was just doing what I was paid to do."

He was laying it on thick.

"I hope everything turns out okay for you. Who knows, maybe one of these days if I ever get to Lima I'll look you up and buy you a pisco sour."

The girl seemed to come out of her daze, as if dimly remembering him after all. His face came into focus for her and she studied him.

"I hope I do see you again, Jolly," she said.

Jolly, eager to disarm, was himself disarmed. He patted the girl on the shoulder.

"Can't shake your hand because of those handcuffs. But you take care of yourself."

He closed the door and left her in the cabin. Walking back around the plane, he was profoundly moved by the fact that he carried nothing under his arm.

"I put the map in back," he told the nephew. "You won't need it right away."

The nephew nodded and went on feeding gas into the wing. Jolly was in a manic mood. It was hard for him to stop talking.

"That's a rebel stronghold you're flying into. That's where the Shining Path guerrillas hang out. Those bastards don't like anybody. They hate the Americans, they hate the Russians. They sit around and recite sayings. 'The Great Break has come. The Rebellion is justified.' Then they go out and shoot someone."

The nephew stared back at him, his face miragelike behind the fumes of gas that rose in the heat.

"You should see some of the shit they use. They got slings made of llama hair for tossing sticks of dynamite. They make bombs out of old tin cans. They make mortars out of fishing-line guns. I'm not trying to scare you. They're on the side of the dope smugglers. They're the ones who keep the army out. Only before you go . . ." Jolly's voice began to tremble; he felt his neck growing hot and the heat rising to his face, and he tried to keep the tremor out of his voice. "Before you go I'd like my little book. The one you stole from me. The one with all my contacts in it, that you stole from my table upstairs while I was gone."

He saw a sudden narrowing of eyes as it finally dawned on the nephew what all the palaver had been leading up to. The nephew considered Jolly a moment. Then with his free hand he drew the tiny book from his shirt pocket and handed it over.

"I didn't steal it," he said. "Kane gave it to me."

"He's the boss. That's his privilege. But I'm glad to get

it back, just in case one of those rebels takes a shot at you."

Jolly made his grin as broad and foolish as he dared. He wanted the nephew to take the grin with him. He wanted the grin to be the last memory of the nephew's life.

The gas pump clunked off and there was a glistening overspill onto the wing. Jolly dove for the hose in a parody of helpfulness.

"Here, let me get that for you."

When he came back the nephew was inside the cabin with the girl. Jolly watched him buckle up. There was a short chop and the propeller became a blur as the engine coughed into life. Jolly stood nose to nose with the plane and let the noise engulf him. One step and he would lose his head. But he continued to stand as if to show himself invincible to all the noise in the world.

In the cabin Kiki's nephew looked up at him. Jolly gave a tight smile and raised his palm and moved his fingers in a tiny wave. Then he stepped back.

The wing swung past his face and he watched the plane taxi away. The electric-drill carton was hidden in the backseat under a pile consisting of the sweater, the chemise, and the blond wig.

24

As the plane taxied away, Kim looked straight ahead. She felt a need to prolong the act of not knowing the man beside her while Kane was watching close behind. She wanted to reach out and touch Wok, to tell him about darkness that never ended, that pressed against her face like a huge hand, that made her doubt who she was. Darkness that became finally like an actual absence of air, the fundamental atmosphere of a hostile universe in which it was a struggle just to stand and do some exercises. Darkness that broke her, deprived her of the ability to feel anything except the pain of knowing he was dead. She wanted to collapse against him and let him hold her in his arms. But his hands were busy and her own hands were handcuffed together and Kane was a definite presence at their back.

"I thought you were dead," she said at last. The jungle at the other end of the runway was coming up. "Jolly put a bomb on your plane. I saw the explosion."

"It wasn't us," Joaquín said. He wasn't Kiki's nephew anymore and his face was suddenly drawn. "It was two boys from the village." He delivered the news flatly. "They ran to get the plane. They were taking care of it for me."

He braked the plane to check something, she wasn't sure what, then throttled back and was moving forward again.

"I've been looking forward to meeting Jolly. I was interested in seeing what he was like in person. We've been waiting for him to bring this plane back."

Kim began to shake. In the dark cell the idea of being

brought to Peru had come to seem merciful. She hadn't cared what happened to her as long as she could end her days in a lighted room. The plane reached the end of the runway and Joaquín turned into the wind.

"Here," he said, "I'll get those handcuffs."

"No," a defeated whisper. "Just keep going . . . please."

She could see the three men and the girl down at the other end. Joaquín made some final adjustment and opened the throttle slowly. The plane began to roll forward and he opened it all the way.

Kim felt the plane surge forward. In front of the hangar she saw Jolly raise a hand in farewell, his breasts white under the blistery red color of his neck. At the side of the runway Kane was standing beside Rhodes. But it was the girl sitting on the grass behind them who claimed Kim's attention now.

As the plane surged down the runway, the girl looked up and Kim saw her face. Then the plane lifted off, and instantly the girl was below them, her head lowered, a small blond figure in white shirt, shorts, and sneakers. The plane cleared the hangar, Jolly out front, bare arm upraised with his shoulder holster slung over it. Then the world of the runway and hangar was completely behind them and gone. . . . Forever, Kim thought.

The plane went into a banking turn and behind her, off to the right, she glimpsed the jungle, the sugar plant in its isolated compound, the immaculate white beach. Then they straightened out and were climbing away over the ocean.

"Where are we going?"

"Caracas. Rhodes will meet us. He'll give Kane some excuse and drive to the airport and use his own passport, without the mustache, in case Kane gets suspicious and tries to stop a man named Rawlings from leaving the country."

Kim knew she was free. But she didn't feel free.

"We had Jerry waiting for us back home," Joaquín said. "He was the perfect cover. If Kane had tried to check up on me he would have been told just what we wanted—that Jerry has fled the country to keep from going to jail. That's the word being put out on the street anyhow. The real Jerry is in an efficiency cottage in North Palm Beach, getting ready to testify against his Uncle Kiki."

The plane was still climbing.

"I thought you were dead," Kim said.

"We didn't know where you were. We didn't even know if you were alive. We wanted Kane to do all the work . . . tell us in his own sweet time."

"I was in the basement, locked up in the dark. One of Dog's boys brought me food. I think it was twice a day. I scratched a calendar on the floor. It gave me something to do. There wasn't any light."

"You've been there more than a week."

"When you're in the dark that long you begin to wonder if you exist. You have to invent things to prove it. I invented the calendar."

"We're going to Caracas," Joaquín said. "It's a short flight."

They would land in Caracas and go to the American Embassy and in a day or two she would see her father. But she felt pursued. It was as if the perpetual darkness were closing in behind her. Only it wasn't the darkness. It was the face of that girl, the face of her own past.

Joaquín leveled off. Dully Kim watched his hands doing things.

"I think we can get rid of these now." He reached over and unlocked the handcuffs. "Kane didn't forget to give me the key."

She took off the handcuffs and sat clutching them. Joaquín made a stab at lightness.

"You've been wearing those so long you've become attached to them."

"Kane won," she said.

"No he didn't. You got away."

"But he beat me anyway. He showed me what I used to be. And he showed that girl what she was going to become—a crazy white bitch in handcuffs, so happy to get out of the dark that she was looking forward to becoming a whore."

Soundlessly Kim began to cry. The sky, the scratched plastic of the windshield, the array of dials on the instrument panel, blurred before her eyes. She bent over and covered her face, shaking. Joaquín's hand was on her back.

"Kim," he said.

"Don't worry," she said. "I'm not cracking up at this late date. It's that girl. . . ."

"We never imagined Jolly would get off the plane with a girl."

"If there was something we could do . . ."

"We don't have a choice."

"If you had only had a gun."

"Kane was going to get me one but Jolly's workshop was locked. I'm glad I didn't have a gun. It was better that way."

His voice was hard, matter-of-fact. The girl was a bad accident he had heard about on the news, a statistic that had nothing to do with them.

"We'll notify the authorities as soon as we get to Caracas. She must have been reported missing by now. They'll already have a search going."

"Kane will kill her," Kim said. "Just as he would have killed me. He'll say he never heard of her and nobody in Carib will ask questions."

"Maybe Rhodes can get her out."

"And if he can't?"

"There's nothing we can do."

Joaquín flew on without looking at her. She saw he didn't want to talk about it.

"It's our own damn fault," he said. "We never even thought of Jolly. We didn't ask ourselves where he was going or what he was doing. We were just thinking about you."

The plane droned on.

"Kane made it easy for us. I walked through that gate and handed him a phony picture and he didn't even give it a second look. We caught him at the right moment; he needed men. We thought we were going to have to stick a gun under his nose. But he did that for us, too. . . . Put you on a plane and told me to fly away with you."

"If we had a gun," Kim said, "maybe we could . . ."

"Look," Joaquín rounded on her, "some things can't be helped. I lost you once already. . . ."

Kim stared at him. She saw how drawn his face was. The mask he had put on to fool Kane had slipped. He looked like a man who hadn't slept in days. She gave in then out of an understanding of what he had been through and a sharp memory of the darkness she had been freed from.

The plane flew on, Venezuela in front of them, Carib behind. Kim rubbed the mark that had been left by the handcuff on her wrist, a deep-purplish band like a permanent scar. The silence began to seem as long as the distance they were traveling into.

"I don't even have a gun," Joaquín said at last.

She looked up. His eyes were on the empty blue sky ahead. It seemed they could keep on going forever.

Rhodes wasn't happy. There were a lot of places he would rather be than this little airstrip in the middle of a jungle on an island that was beginning to seem increasingly difficult to escape. He stood with Kane and Jolly and watched the plane climbing away and he knew, unhappily, that it was Rawlings who was being left behind.

He was going to be stuck with Rawlings for a while and the role no longer seemed adequate. Rawlings was now supposed to be making excuses to go into town, so he could shave this godawful growth on his upper lip and board a passenger jet, using another man's passport, and skip the country with sixty-eight thousand dollars that Kane had entrusted him with to wire to Kingston—a sneaky move, but not one entirely incompatible with the modus operandi of a chap who had done eight years in Raiford prison for armed robbery.

But a young girl was sitting alone behind them at the side of the runway.

When Jolly had helped the girl out of the plane it had seemed to Rhodes a dumb trick of fate that both he and Joaquín were unarmed. At first they had assumed they wouldn't be allowed through the gate with a gun, and in fact Rawlings had been frisked by Jerry, all for show. Then, the way things were going—so nicely and smoothly that they hadn't wanted to press their luck—there had been no urgent need to get one. Rhodes had considered making a grab for Jolly's gun. Jolly possessed a personal radar that made him hard to approach and his gun was buckled securely in its holster. But the real discouragement was the look on Joaquín's face. It said, Don't try anything, stick to the plan; and Rhodes had lost his nerve for solitary heroics.

Wok had come to save Kim. It was his only reason for being here.

The plane was almost out of sight now. A glint of sunlight flared on the silver body and died into a dark speck. The dark speck was gone so instantaneously it might have been a dust mote in the eye.

Kane turned. "Get the girl and bring her up to the house," he told Jolly.

Jolly ignored him. He was squinting with alert interest toward the sound of the plane fading insignificantly in the distance. Rhodes had a moment to contemplate Jolly; blond crew cut darkening at the roots, flabby breasts in spite of his muscular arms, suggesting an addiction to sweets, and a private little grin, as if he were keeping a very funny joke to himself. He noted the silencer screwed onto the .38 automatic in Jolly's shoulder holster and he wondered what, in the week that Jolly had been away, had required an absence of noise.

Jolly finally decided to notice Kane. He shrugged indifferently toward Rhodes.

"Let him bring her up," he said. "He's a big boy, ain't he?"

"What?" Kane said.

"I'm done with little girls. Old 'Red' can handle it from now on."

Jolly was trying to be cool, but he seemed in the grip of an irrepressible gaiety, and that in itself was a curiosity. Because half an hour ago Rhodes could have sworn that Jolly was coming apart, like some overwrought machine that begins to spit out nuts, bolts, springs, sprocket wheels, and a black cloud of smoke, before the final self-destructive explosion. Red-necked and grim, barely able to hold himself together, Jolly had taken refuge in his workshop, and wonder of wonders, he had emerged ten minutes later a changed man, bobbing his head, grinning from ear to ear, as full of bogus brotherly love as a door-to-door Bible salesman.

"You can do that, can't you, Red?" he said now to Rhodes. "I mean, hell, I brought her all the way from the state of Florida. You can at least get her up to the house. The car's right there. You don't have to steal it." Jolly started away. "I'm going to take a shower. You need me," he called back to Kane without turning, "you know where to find me." He walked on. After a moment his voice came again. "I got a feeling you're gonna need me."

Kane watched him go and seemed to conclude it was the wrong time to argue with Jolly. He jerked his head at Rhodes and gave an order—"Get her."

From beyond the grave Rhodes heard a plea, "Son, you've got to cut down on the weed," and he promised his daddy, if he ever got out of this alive, he would give up cigarettes for good. Jolly had done him a favor walking away like that and leaving Rawlings in charge of the girl. For Dog's Indian boys were already a little in awe of Rawlings, who might easily drive off the estate tonight with the girl in the trunk of Kane's limousine. Rhodes didn't want to think what Kane might do to the girl before that.

The drugged look had left the girl's eyes and she drew back as Rhodes went to her and reached down to help her up.

"Where are you taking me?"

"Up to the house."

"What's he going to do?"

"I don't know."

"He's going to kill me."

"No," Rhodes said, "he won't kill you. Look, I'm going to try to help you. You've got to trust me. You'll have to do what he says."

"I'm scared," the girl said. "I was taking the boys to the playground. We were going through the woods. Then *he* grabbed me."

She glanced toward Jolly, who was heading for the hangar. It was a relief for her to be telling a friendly listener what had happened to her.

"He was wearing a dress and a woman's wig. I hope the boys got home all right. Did he kill them? Do you know if he killed them? Oh God, I hope not—they're just little kids."

"I don't think he killed them. That's why he wore the dress . . . so they wouldn't be able to describe him to the police."

Kane was at his jeep. "What's going on? Let's go!"

"We have to go," Rhodes said.

The girl rose and he led her to the jeep and got in back beside her. There was a last glimpse of Jolly disappearing up the stairs to his apartment. Then Kane started the jeep and swung around, putting the hangar behind and the jungle before them.

Rhodes's father was never far from his mind and now he felt the old man's presence more than ever. My solemn word, he thought, I'll ne'er touch another one.

Lying loose behind the backseat, within easy reach of his hand, was a jack handle. Such a nice, fine, truly inspiring instrument; he hadn't asked for the jack handle, yet there it was, as if his daddy, watching over him from above, had put it there to assist him in his hour of need. If he did a proper job with it Kane might lie out in the jungle all night before anybody thought to look for him.

Rhodes let his arm hang over the back of the seat and his fingers curl around the jack handle.

The jeep was bumping along toward where the dirt road entered the jungle. Kane's sudden jamming on of the brakes was so unexpected that Rhodes had to grab the girl to keep her from being thrown from the seat.

What now? Rhodes thought. Why is he stopping?

He glanced at the girl. Okay? She nodded. Then he saw Kane staring in the direction of the ocean toward something that had apparently caught his eye. Inside Rhodes a voice cried out, No! What are you doing? Don't come back! I'll take care of Kane!

Kane had turned off the motor. Rhodes got out of the jeep with him and they stood together. He heard Rawlings speak. "What's this? Old Jerry forget his toothbrush?" Kane scowled at the sky. The dark speck had become a glint of silver again.

Rhodes hadn't been happy about being left with the girl. But the jack handle had seemed the only solution, and now he felt like a man in a dinghy that already held two people. Two drowning swimmers were struggling toward them; if they tried to climb aboard all four of them would drown.

Rhodes was a scared little boy clinging to his father's coat sleeve. Daddy, for God's sake, tell them to turn around! Tell them you and me already took care of it! Tell them Caracas is the other way!

But his father had taken the rest of the day off to go hunting or fishing. The plane was circling overhead and coming in for a landing.

The plane landed and taxied past them and turned and came back. It stopped by the jeep at the side of the runway.

The snarl of the engine continued a moment, then the propeller jerked to a halt and silence washed over them in the sunlight.

Joaquín unbuckled his seat belt and climbed out. He raised a hand to Kane, half wave, half shrug. He was still the young dope smuggler who had flown away twenty minutes ago, Kiki Soldano's nephew and Kane's new bodyguard, Jerry.

Rhodes watched and waited.

"I need a piece!" Jerry called, laughing. It was a joke to him; an amusing status symbol of his trade. "The piece you promised me. I shoulda got one before I left."

He came over to Kane. He didn't even look at Rhodes or the girl.

"Now that Jolly's back we can get in his workshop, right? Some guys don't take you seriously unless you carry a piece."

"Go tell Jolly," Kane said.

"Okay."

"He'll let you in and you can pick one out. If he gives you an argument take the key and go in yourself."

"What's wrong? I thought everything was cool with Jolly. He gave me his aerial map . . ." Jerry hesitated. "If he's still sore maybe you better wait and see if he gets the picture. He might not like me telling him what to do."

"Go on," Kane jerked his head. "I'm not going to wait all day."

Jerry turned and walked away, and Rhodes stood waiting with Kane. They watched Jerry going toward the hangar, and he became aware of Jolly, an agitated figure framed in the window upstairs.

Jolly had poked his head out when the plane had come in for a landing, and now, as he saw Jerry approaching, he began to shout. His voice was indistinct. But to Rhodes, at the other end of the runway, the sound of his anger was unmistakable.

What the hell you doing back! You should be on your way to Peru!

Jolly's bare arm gestured toward the plane. He was telling Jerry to get on it and go at once. But Jerry wasn't listening. He reached the hangar and stopped under the window. The word "gun" was called up as an explanation. It failed to pacify Jolly.

Gun . . . came back . . . lousy gun!

The words traveled the length of the runway, blurred and torn apart. Jolly's exaggerated response didn't surprise Rhodes; he had come to expect exaggerated responses from Jolly. Watching him throw a fit in the miniature stage of his window was like watching a primitive Punch and Judy show. Jolly was a crude hand puppet who clubbed old women to death and made children laugh.

Crissake! Take mine!

Jolly vanished from the window. He came back. His gun in the shoulder holster was dropped into Jerry's upraised hands below. The bare arm gestured again.

Go on! Get outta here! Go to Peru!

Rhodes stared. There was something unreal about such a display of emotion, even for a man like Jolly. He tried to grasp it but it slipped away, leaving only an image of Jolly's private little grin: his secret joke.

What's going on? Rhodes thought.

Jerry came away from the hangar. He seemed to walk a tightrope between Jolly, who was still staring at him wildly from his window, and Kane, who was waiting for him impatiently by the jeep. He returned to Kane and paused, as if he had all the time in the world.

"Can you beat it?" he said. "First Jolly was pissed off 'cause he didn't want me to go. Now he can't wait to get rid of me."

Jerry checked to see if the gun was loaded. Unscrewed the silencer. "Don't need this." Put the gun in the holster. Buckled the holster in place under his armpit. He drew the gun as if to test his draw, and Rhodes watched him.

"I hope I don't have to use this," Jerry said. "I'd hate to run into anyone stupid enough to think I wouldn't."

He was Jerry the dope smuggler, going off on a job for his boss, looking forward to the trip, and then he was someone else, a much more serious young man who was pointing a gun very definitely at Kane.

"If I do I'll blow his head off," he said. "So do exactly as I say."

Kane didn't grasp the transformation at once. Rhodes saw a startled pause. He couldn't see Kane's eyes behind his dark glasses, but he knew the eyes were focused on the gun, and he saw Kane's face harden with a realization that the gun wasn't a joke.

"What the hell is this?" Kane said.

"She's going with me," Joaquín said.

Rhodes helped the girl out of the jeep.

"Put her back," Kane ordered.

Rhodes shook his head. "Sorry, Mr. Kane. The man is right. She's going with him."

"As a matter of fact," Joaquín said, "you're going with us, too."

"Go to hell," Kane said.

Joaquín thrust out his arm. The barrel of the gun was almost touching the bridge of Kane's nose.

"Try me," he said. "The choice is yours."

"Better do as he says, Mr. Kane. He's a mighty touchy human being." Rhodes put into his mild drawl all the sweet reasonableness of a backwoods politician courting votes. But the jack handle was now in his hand.

"Has Kiki put you up to this? What does he want?"

Joaquín said nothing and Kane understood at last.

"You're not Kiki's nephew. You must be narcs. What kind of money do you make?" He wasn't pleading; he spoke with the assurance of a man who had never made an offer that had been refused. "I can give you enough to live like kings for the rest of your lives in any country of your choice. I'll send Jolly up to the house for it right now."

"We're old friends," Joaquín told him. "I once waited for you outside a restaurant in Miami and you sent somebody else out in your place."

Kane stared at him. Behind the dark glasses Rhodes saw a stunned loss of confidence.

"I followed the wrong man," Joaquín said. "It's taken me eight years to find the right one."

Kim had climbed out of the plane and faced them. She looked away from Kane and found the girl and then came back to Kane again and fixed him with a serene, unembittered look. Her face was pale and tired, a strand of hair had escaped, and her shirt and shorts were dirty after weeks of wear. There was something new and Rhodes saw what it was. The handcuffs were no longer on her wrists. She was clutching them in her fist, and the fist was raised toward Kane.

Kane saw them, too. He let out a hoarse cry. "Jolly!" His voice sounded puny and ineffectual. "JOLLY!"

Then Jolly began to shoot at them from his window.

Rhodes reacted instinctively, grabbing the girl and bringing her with him as he dove behind the jeep. He found himself lying on top of her in the dirt. The air was torn by gunfire, raking viciously as if in pursuit, and with a quick look out he saw it was Joaquín who was being pursued.

Kane had broken away and Joaquín was fleeing. Rhodes glimpsed the track of bullets—a spitting up of broken tarmac, a puff of dirt at the side of the runway, a blowout of a rear tire—that went after Joaquín and sent him diving for cover. In the same instant, Kim, who had also run and dove, was there, too, and they were all pinned down behind the jeep and Rhodes had forgotten completely about Kane.

He hadn't had time to think. Now his thoughts caught up with what his legs had grasped at once—Jolly was shooting at them from his window. But I saw him give his gun to Jerry, Rhodes thought, even as he understood that Jolly was not the trusting sort to go to bed at night with only one weapon to protect him from unexpected visitors. The vicious jackhammering bursts gave a picture of the automatic rifle jerking in Jolly's hands. The bullets splattering all around them kept Rhodes and the girl firmly in place, faces as close to dirt as faces could get.

When the firing suddenly stopped it took a moment to realize it wasn't going to begin again. There was the whine of a ricochet off a fender, like a mosquito drilling into his ear. But instead of being overtaken by more thunder, the whine traveled away into an absence of sound that Rhodes needed several seconds to recognize as actual silence.

In the next instant there was the clattering roar of the plane starting up. A new sort of confusion began then, Joaquín scrambling over Rhodes, pushing him out of the way, firing at the plane. But Kane was already inside it and the plane was moving away fast.

What happened then didn't seem to go with anything that had gone before. Jolly was leaning out his window recklessly, making an easy target of himself. He was shouting. Over the noise of the plane Rhodes couldn't hear what. It didn't sound like language. It was more like a raw bellow of horror. The bellow reddened Jolly's face and distended his neck and became all there was to know about Jolly, a man standing in a window, completely defined by a wail of ultimate dismay. Abruptly Jolly disappeared and the window was empty.

The plane had made a turn at the other end, and as it surged down the runway for a takeoff, Jolly came running out of the hangar. On the ground, his arm over the girl, Rhodes watched with a sense of dreamlike absurdity, no way to comprehend what was happening now—this lone unarmed man running with his arms out toward a plane that was coming straight at him.

The plane didn't stop. There was a moment when Jolly seemed to see that they would meet and he flung his arms open, as if to embrace it. Then he appeared to spring upward magically out of its way and sail over the plane as if with the power of flight. His body hit the runway behind it like a heavy sack.

The plane was lifting away and Rhodes felt an urgent concern for their chances of eluding capture on an island where the army and police would be looking for them, as soon as Kane landed. They were all standing now, even the girl, staring after the plane. It was rising toward the roof of the hangar. In a second it would clear the roof and then there would be no obstacle except blue sky.

When the plane exploded it seemed a trick of the eye, occurring in two stages. There was a flash of light in the cockpit that might have been something utterly harmless, like a flashbulb going off, and for one second the wings continued to fly on, intact and unharmed. Then they, too, were gone in an eruption of smoke and fire.

The explosion shook the air and the ground. It flattened Rhodes and the others behind the jeep with a hot blast of wind. It broke the windshield and rained down glass, and created a flaming ball out of the plane, which slammed into the apartment over the hangar and plowed deep into the kitchen that Rhodes had visited twice for the purpose of fetching beers from Jolly's refrigerator, and once there it quickly set the apartment on fire.

The hangar continued to burn for some time, and soon a collection of short, stocky Indians began to appear. They stood and looked on bewilderedly. There was no one alive to dispute the story that Rawlings gave. But Jolly, at least, was intact.

Jolly's blond head lay in a bright pool of blood. His pale eyes gazed without distress at a blinding tropical sun.

25

IN loving memory in loving memory in loving memory . . .

The gravestones went on. Tom Mitchell knew them by heart. At the entrance, where the rusted wrought-iron gate was always open in the stone wall around the cemetery, were several generations of Bunkers, nine stones in a row, each sharing the same inscription . . . IN LOVING MEMORY. Way down at the other end was a cluster of Studwells, then, as the road circled back along the other side of the hill, you came across some Oldfields. There were solitary stones as well: a Mather, a Hobby. The dates went as far back as the early 1800s, with antique names like Rufus and Pruella and Jabez and Aurora, and some of the stones were so worn and smoothed with age it was impossible to make out the words, no matter how long you stood there and tried.

Mitchell went up the road under big elm trees with little rows of gravestones closely clustered on the uphill side and scattered stones on the lower slope. One or two of the gravestones were loose and would totter precariously whenever children climbed on them, and one of the grave plots had recently sunk, making a precise rectangular depression with a covering of startlingly green grass. There were tiny American flags and fresh flowers placed at a few of the graves.

One stone troubled him by what the dates told about the three family members underneath: a father and mother had outlived by many years their son, who had died at age seven. Another amused him by its statement of the exact age of the deceased: 67 YEARS 3 MONTHS AND 7 DAYS. Mitchell wondered if it would be practical to measure a man's life span in milliseconds.

The information on the stone he came to now, leaving the path and crossing the grass between rows of skinny round-topped stones, bleached white and speckled with age, was not nearly so complete. There was a name and a birth year. KIMBERLY MITCHELL, BORN 1964.

After a number of years Kim had been presumed dead. In a way Mitchell hoped she was, for he could imagine no existence following her abduction that would not have been a nightmare. The brutal, frightening death that he was sure she had suffered would at least have been over with quickly. They would have been long seconds, long minutes, as she struggled. But minutes and seconds ended, no matter how eternal they might have seemed.

Mitchell no longer thought of the struggle that a girl like his daughter would certainly have put up. He was not a morbid man. Finally he had accepted the fact she was dead and gone and would never come back, and he had picked up the pieces of his optimistic nature and put them back together again in a sort of graceful facsimile of his former self that was almost indistinguishable from the original. Occasionally his friends would notice a sad look in his eyes, but Mitchell was always quick to override it with cheerful small talk.

He had continued his law practice, the wills and real estate transactions, and he had a girlfriend now. Annie was a wonderful woman with two children in college. She had moved to town from New York after her divorce. She was an artist, and painted pictures of old barns and stone walls, which she sold through her agent in the city. Mitchell had met her at an exhibit of her paintings that she had put on at the library, and after going back to the exhibit every day he had finally got up the courage to ask for a date. He had been embarrassed by the fact that he was in his early fifties while she was still a young woman in her late thirties. But they had a lot in common and they both loved the small-town life and surrounding countryside. Sometimes they talked of marriage, even of children, though she was now over forty. Mitchell owed a lot to Annie. She had come into his life at just the right time to help him reassemble himself.

He hadn't visited the cemetery in a while. But today he had felt like coming. He woke that morning to find a chill in the air, though it was still August. The chill wore off and it had become a splendid day, pleasantly warm without being muggy. It was the sort of first hint of fall that always moved him. The hot days would drag on with unsurprising similarity. Then you would wake one morning wishing perhaps you had put an extra blanket on the night before. No matter how many days of summer followed, the summer would never fully recover. The days would become crisp, the trees would flame with color, and one morning there would be a coat of ice over the dog's water dish that would crackle apart if you touched it.

Mitchell had put in a few hours at his office and walked up the main street around noon to the cemetery on the hill at the edge of town. The summer day with its hint of fall reminded him of his daughter and made him happy. He stood before the stone with her name engraved on it. He didn't mourn for what she might have been.

Not what she might have been, he thought. It was what she *was*. That's the important thing. What she *was*. For a while she lived and was as special as this lovely day. . . .

He was looking down at the stone when a car came through the gate and drove slowly up the road. It stopped a short distance away and two men and a young woman got out.

Mitchell glanced at them and then away, assuming they were looking for a gravestone. The men were in sport jackets and sport shirts. The woman wore a pink-and-white striped dress, attractive and summery. They looked like young city people. They had come out to the country for the day and were visiting the grave of a relative.

Mitchell looked back down at his daughter's name. He had some stray thoughts about meeting Annie for tennis that afternoon and taking her to a movie that night. Then he noticed that the two men and the woman were still standing by the car at the side of the road behind him. He thought they must be lost and in need of directions but didn't want to intrude on his solitude. The young woman was staring at him hesitantly as if they were separated by a big hole in the ground instead of twenty feet of lawn. To let her know she wasn't intruding, Mitchell raised a hand and called out, "Morning!" It was like a magic word; the big hole closed up and the woman took a step.

As she crossed to him he put on a folksy manner. "I guess I should say, 'Noon.' It's past twelve. I'll have to wait the rest of the day and all night before I can say 'Morning' again."

She came up to him and smiled uncertainly. He saw a pretty young woman, indistinguishable at first glance from pretty young women everywhere. Her long brown hair was pulled back with a pink scarf over her head.

"Are you looking for anyone in particular?" he said. "I know just about every name here."

"I was looking for you," the girl said. "We stopped at your office and you weren't there and somebody said they had seen you walking up this way."

"You've caught me red-handed, young lady. I'm guilty of leaving my office early. It was such a beautiful day I couldn't resist taking a walk." He glanced at the two men by the car. They looked away unobtrusively. "I was just going to have lunch," Mitchell said. "But if you want, you and your friends can come on back to town and we'll sit down and talk over whatever is on your mind." He assumed it was a legal problem.

The girl didn't answer. She was looking at the memorial stone at his feet. She still seemed uncomfortable at having come upon him in a private moment.

"It's my daughter," he said matter-of-factly.

"I know," the girl said.

Mitchell was surprised. "Did you know her?"

The girl stared at him strangely. He had the feeling she was about to say something urgent. Instead, when she spoke after a moment it was with her same uncertainty.

"I think I knew her very well. She was crazy about baseball."

"How did you know that?" Mitchell said, pleased.

"I'll bet if you asked her who were the only two players to win the triple crown twice she would be able to tell you."

"I think even I remember that one. Rogers Hornsby and Ted Williams. Right?"

"On the money," the girl said.

Mitchell laughed. "I used to say that to her."

He looked at the girl curiously. He drew back and tilted his head. "Am I supposed to know you? Were you one of Kim's classmates? I thought I've kept track of just about everyone. But it's been a long time."

The look on the girl's face stopped him. It didn't go with his stance of foolish puzzlement. He looked at her closely now and saw not just prettiness. He saw how her hair was cut in tomboyish bangs across her forehead. He saw her high Irish cheekbones and slightly slanted cat's eyes, and the eyes themselves were glistening with tears.

Mitchell felt embarrassed. He was imagining things. The girl must be a classmate and the tears were simply a reflection of the wetness that had come to his own eyes from talking about his daughter.

"My daughter used to be a walking encyclopedia of baseball statistics," he said. "I've grown pretty rusty myself. I have a hard enough time remembering the questions, let alone the answers. Let's see now, there was one . . ." He came up with a question. "Who made the only unassisted triple play in World Series history?"

"Bill Wambsganss," the girl said. "Cleveland Indians, 1920."

He tried another. "What city had two triple-crown winners in the same year?"

"Philadelphia, 1933. Chuck Klein of the Athletics and Jimmie Foxx of the Phillies."

A quietness came over Mitchell and he stared at the girl almost in dismay.

"Who are you?" he said quietly.

Kim didn't answer at once. She was thinking of a game she and her father had used to play. Her father would grab her in a bear hug and say, "Who is this little girl? Who is this little girl I have in my arms?"

Kim would laugh. "Me!" she would squeal. "It's me!"

"Who's me?"

"Kim!"

"That's not enough! I want it all! Cough it up!"

And her whole name would finally be divulged. "Kim Mitchell!"

So now she faced her father and took a deep breath and answered his question. It was the first step in a long three-part journey.

"Me," she said. "It's me."

The two men at the car turned away. It didn't seem right to stare at a father and a daughter hugging each other in a graveyard. The hug was intense and wordless and it didn't end. It seemed to achieve a sort of permanence, like the old stones around them, and there was enough pain in it as well as joy to make staring impolite.